VINCE FLYNN

ENEMY AT THE GATES

**SIMON &
SCHUSTER**

London · New York · Sydney · Toronto · New Delhi

First published in the United States by Emily Bestler Books / Atria Books,
an imprint of Simon & Schuster, Inc., 2021

First published in Great Britain by Simon & Schuster UK Ltd, 2021
This paperback edition published by Simon & Schuster UK Ltd, 2022

1 3 5 7 9 10 8 6 4 2

Simon & Schuster UK Ltd
1st Floor
222 Gray's Inn Road
London WC1X 8HB

Simon & Schuster Australia, Sydney
Simon & Schuster India, New Delhi

www.simonandschuster.co.uk
www.simonandschuster.com.au
www.simonandschuster.co.in

A CIP catalogue record for this book is available from the British Library

Paperback ISBN: 978-1-3985-0046-4
Export Paperback ISBN: 978-1-3985-1445-4
eBook ISBN: 978-1-3985-0045-7
Audio ISBN: 978-1-3985-0716-6

Printed and bound in Great Britain by CPI Group (UK) Ltd, Croydon, CR0 4YY

ACKNOWLEDGMENTS

It's hard to believe that this is my seventh contribution to the Rapp-verse. The older I get, the faster time seems to flow.

What *has* stayed consistent, though, is the amazing team that makes the continuation of Vince's legacy possible. I've said so much about them that I've decided (for the sake of glorious variety) to just create a simple list in utterly random order.

My undying gratitude to Emily Bestler, Kim Mills, Sloan Harris, Lara Jones, Celia Taylor Mobley, David Brown, Ryan Steck, Elaine Mills, Rod Gregg, and Simon Lipskar.

You make it possible and, more important, fun.

ENEMY AT THE GATES

PROLOGUE

L UCKY.

Many years ago, Dr. David Chism had pledged to never take his good fortune for granted. That at least once per day, he would give thanks to whatever cosmic force had taken him under its wing.

He rolled down the window of his embarrassingly luxurious Toyota Land Cruiser, stuck his hand out into the seventy-three-degree air, and gave the world a thumbs-up. There was no reaction from the emerald mountains, terraced farmland, or red dirt road, but they knew. They knew that he understood the gifts he'd been given.

Based on his bland suburban upbringing, the fact that he was even in this place was a minor miracle. His parents were both accountants and had absolutely loved everything about that profession and lifestyle. The interminable columns of numbers and teetering tax forms. The complex machinations of the upper middle class. Their elaborate strategies for not only keeping up with the Joneses, but one day *becoming* the Joneses.

Despite all that, they'd been—and still were—solid, conventional parents. If only he'd been a solid, conventional child, everything would have gone smoothly.

It wasn't for lack of trying on his part. Chism had still been in grade school when he first noticed how their brows furrowed when he brought up his fascination with science. It had started with evolutionary biology and endless hours speculating about the creatures natural selection would give rise to on other planets. Then it was physics and the mysteries of gravity. And, finally, it was everything. *Why does this rock look different than that rock, Mom? Hey, Dad. What makes my Frisbee stay in the air? Ms. Davidson—if Superman can fly at almost the speed of light and hold his breath for one minute, could he make it to the sun?*

By the time he entered junior high, he'd learned to hide those interests. To feign enthusiasm for bank entries and for joining the family business after graduating from an economical local university. From there it would be a McMansion, two point five children, and a country club membership. All the things sane people aspired to.

In secret, though, he'd continued to pursue his passion. Increasingly advanced books borrowed from the library were hidden under a bunch of comics in his closet. Subscriptions to scientific journals were paid for from his allowance and addressed to the house of a friend. Eventually, his obsession with virology had relegated all other fields to little more than passing interests. It was that discipline he dove into every night after doing a calculatedly unspectacular job on his homework.

Some of the things he read, though, he disagreed with. Most of the problems weren't with a lack of accuracy per se, but more with a lack of imagination. Finally, a particularly glaring omission relating to how viruses defend themselves drove him crazy enough to write a lengthy complaint to a journal he'd subscribed to.

To his great surprise, it was published. Then it started getting a lot of attention. Finally, a reporter managed to see through the carelessly created pseudonym he'd used and tracked him down.

Chism grinned and shook his head in the confines of the car. In retrospect, using Elmer Fudd and putting his real return address on the envelope was the smartest move he'd ever made.

After that, everything had been a whirlwind: explaining to his stunned parents why there was someone at the door wanting to talk to their fourteen-year-old son about immunology. Entry into Stanford a few months later. Medical degree. PhD. The immediate appointment as the head of a research project that demanded political and fundraising skills that were well beyond him. A scientific community full of geriatric bastards who pushed back against his revolutionary ideas. Finally, burnout at twenty-three and the beginning of his less than productive drugs, booze, and women phase.

After his second overdose, he'd awoken in the hospital determined to get his life together. It hadn't been difficult to find an NGO that would take a scientist of his reputation who was willing to go to whatever shithole or hot spot they could dream up. And that had ushered in his somewhat more productive infectious disease, war, and poverty phase. It had been a huge rush and he'd loved the remote locations, the chaos, the danger. Most of all, though, he'd loved the feeling of moving away from pure theory and helping flesh-and-blood people.

It was likely he'd still be out there somewhere if it hadn't been for a chance meeting with the infamous Nicholas Ward. Or maybe it hadn't been chance. He'd never gotten a reliable bead on that.

Chism slowed as he crested the mountaintop, looking out across the stunning valley below. The intensity of the forest against the sky. The geometric blocks denoting agriculture. The craggy cliffs and clouds building on the horizon. What really captured his imagination, though, was a distant cluster of buildings to the east. They were another example of the ridiculous serendipity that tended to cling to him even when he was screwing up.

The facility was state of the art in the truest sense—benefiting from unlimited funds provided by one of the few people in the world smarter than he was. It served as a regular hospital to the rural communities around it, but also as a research facility developing a new approach to fighting viral infections. The potential contribution to mankind was incredible, with the possibility that a single vaccine could wipe out the entire coronavirus category. If he could make it work, COVID, SARS, YARS, and even the common cold would become a thing of the past.

The location was a little more remote and unstable than he would have liked, but there were no workable alternatives. In its early stages, the vaccine had potential side effects that the local population was immune to. No one was sure why—probably a coronavirus epidemic that predated recorded history—but it didn't really matter. Relocating to Uganda and recruiting volunteers here had pushed his research forward a good five years.

Chism navigated down the mountain while scanning the dense trees that lined the road. Despite numerous expeditions into the backcountry, he'd never managed to spot a gorilla. Duikers, a potentially new species of butterfly, and endless red-tailed monkeys, yes. But still not so much as a glimpse of the crown jewel of Uganda's wildlife.

Not that he was worried. One day, they'd make an appearance at the edge of the forest, all lined up and in perfect morning light. Just like one day he'd find a supermodel with a thing for geeky scientists broken down by the side of the road. That was just the way his life went.

When Chism pulled up to the front of the facility's research wing, Mukisa Odongo was waiting for him out front. The former Ugandan army doctor was a rock in every way. At fifty, his six-foot-five frame was still intimidatingly solid, and his eyes had a way of ferreting out any employee not giving one hundred percent. Despite the fact that the man was yet another gift from God, Chism was a little afraid of him. In theory, this was his operation, but everybody knew Odongo ran it. Probably to the benefit of all those involved, frankly.

"What's up, Muki?" Chism said as he climbed out of the Land Cruiser. "It's a gorgeous day, our last trials went even better than expected, and the birds are singing. Why do you always look so un-happy?"

"We're hearing rumors of guerrilla activity in the area."

"Finally! I've got my backpack in the car. Let's give ourselves a couple days off and go check 'em out."

"Not *gorilla* activity, David. *Guerrilla* activity. Terrorists."

Chism froze. "Auma? No way. He never comes this far east."

"Gideon comes and goes as he pleases."

Gideon Auma was a psychopath who had a category all to himself. He'd spent years building his clandestine army from a small, twisted cult into a force capable of wreaking havoc on the local population. He burned villages, kidnapped children, and generally raped, tortured, and mutilated his way across the region.

Terrorist activity had been a consideration in the placement of this hospital, prompting them to locate it as far east as the terrain would allow. Auma preferred to stick close to the dense forests around the Congolese border, crossing back and forth in a conscious effort to use the animosity between the DRC and Uganda to prevent any kind of coordinated action.

"Are we talking credible rumors or just the normal gossip?"

"That's what I'm trying to determine," Odongo said. "Right now, we're doing an additional backup of the computer systems and categorizing all critical research items for potential emergency removal. We'll have trucks here on standby tomorrow."

"You think that's necessary?"

"Probably not. The truth is that we've treated a number of Auma's people in the time we've been here. Combat wounds, disease, drug overdoses . . . Our continued operations benefit him more than an attack on us."

"We treat his people? Why didn't I know that?"

"It's not your business, David. You don't understand my country. In Uganda, peace is a delicate balancing act. Taking sides isn't wise."

"Even against the devil?"

The African ran a hand thoughtfully across his cleanly shaven head. "Yes, my friend. Even against the devil."

The stark white hallway was empty, as were most of the rooms it serviced. Apparently, everyone who could walk under their own power had decided to bug out back to their villages.

Worrying. When he'd used the word *gossip* with Odongo, it hadn't been meant in an entirely pejorative way. In Africa, you ignored the local chitchat at your own risk.

When Chism entered the main lab, it felt almost abandoned. Precaution was starting to look a lot like evacuation. How serious was this? You could never tell with Odongo. He'd face a nuclear war with the same disapproving frown as he aimed at the mold taking hold on the cafeteria ceiling.

"Seems quiet," he said as he came through the glass door.

Jing Liu spun, nearly dropping the box she was holding. "You're here! Have you heard? Gideon Auma is close."

At thirty-three, she was one year his senior but looked much younger. He'd raided her from a research facility in Wuhan and she'd proven to be worth her weight in gold. If only he could decipher her accent.

"What?"

"Gideon Auma! He's here."

"My understanding is that there are some rumors about him being in the area. That's all. We're just being careful."

A man appeared from a door at the back dragging a handcart. "It's about time you got here. Did you stop on top of the mountain again?"

Matteo Ricci was a brilliant virologist from Milan who had been coaxed out of retirement by ridiculous amounts of money. In contrast to Liu's, whose appearance could be described as slightly startled minimalism, Ricci had a great tan, amazing hair, and could still genuinely rock the ass-hugging slacks he favored. Today, a cigarette hung from his lips, putting a finishing touch on his aging-pop-star vibe. Apparently, he'd decided that the proximity of Gideon Auma trumped any rules against smoking in the lab.

"What are we doing?" Chism said, ignoring the comment about his tardiness.

"Odongo gave us a list," Ricci responded in his lightly accented, grammatically rigid English. "Procedures for what needs to go and when. They've prioritized getting noncritical personnel and stable patients out of here, but it sounds like we're going to be moving equipment and live samples tomorrow when the trucks arrive."

Chism laced his fingers thoughtfully atop his head. Were they overreacting here? The reasonably healthy patients and nonessential employees, sure. No point in taking chances. But a lot of the other stuff wasn't all that easy to transport and there's no reason someone like Auma would want it. It wasn't like there was a big market in the jungle for incubators and test tubes.

Having said that, if Mukisa Odongo had spoken that was it. The momentum of his edicts was irresistible. Like a hurricane, they just swept you along whether you liked it or not.

Odongo stood well back from the window, staring into the dimly lit parking area. The rain was coming down even harder now, creating a haze of heavy droplets and swirling fog.

The helicopters should have been there hours ago, but one of the bureaucratic glitches so common in Kampala had caused a delay. And now it was too late. All aircraft was grounded due to the weather and forecasts suggested that they would stay that way until just before dawn.

Chism and his team should have been long gone, but instead they were going through the mundane exercise of packing and categorizing research materials in preparation for them to be moved to a more secure location. It was an effort that would likely prove pointless beyond keeping them occupied.

Odongo's grandfather had taught him that the darkness hid evil spirits intent on making the living suffer. And those superstitions, so easy to laugh off as his education had advanced, now manifested themselves. His informants in the surrounding villages were reporting the appearance of people who could only have been sent by Gideon Auma. They were sticking to the forest for now but taking positions along the main road that led there. Cutting off escape and isolating the facility from anyone who could offer assistance.

This was his mistake. His fault. He should have ordered an evacuation the moment the rumors started. But he'd prioritized the continuity of Chism's work, concerned about the setbacks an evacuation could cause.

A flash of light became visible through the window, likely a few hundred meters distant. The strobe effect was accompanied by the unmistakable sound of automatic rifle fire.

It had begun.

Odongo used the laptop on his desk to activate the facility's alarms and strode purposefully from his office. The few staff members remaining were volunteers and all understood their roles perfectly. He felt great pride in seeing them work—removing IVs, stabilizing wounds, moving critical patients from beds to more maneuverable stretchers. They would carry them into the rain and scatter, trying to keep them alive as they were transferred to nearby villages that he prayed Auma would ignore.

Everything seemed to come into a sharp focus. The traditional pattern of the floor tiles. The scent of the rain filtered through the building. The efficient movements of the people who had been courageous enough to stay. It was incredible that a world with so much darkness could also have so much light.

He spotted Chism rushing up the corridor, having abandoned the busywork he'd been assigned in the lab.

"What's going on, Mukisa? What's the alarm mean?"

"Auma's here."

The fear on the young scientist's face was clearly visible but didn't rise to the level of panic. He wasn't as pampered as the others. The boy had lived through hard times. Some self-inflicted, but hard nonetheless. While he'd never experienced anything like Gideon Auma's army, it wouldn't be completely unimaginable to him. The other two, though, would have no context for what was coming. He prayed they would be spared.

"We need to get the rest of the patients out of here, Mukisa. They—"

"It's all taken care of, David. What's important now is that we make sure you're safe to carry on your work."

He put a hand on Chism's shoulder, leading him back down the hallway toward the lab.

Matteo Ricci and Jing Liu were standing by the boxes they'd packed, looking a little stunned. Odongo motioned through the glass for them to follow and they obeyed. Their questions were rendered unintelligible by their accents mixing with the wail of the alarm, prompting Odongo to put a finger to his lips. They fell silent and allowed themselves to be led to the eastern side of the facility.

Chism finally spoke up when they entered a small room filled with cleaning supplies. "I don't mean to question you, Mukisa, but what are we doing here? There's no way out. Not even a window."

By way of answer, Odongo moved a bucket and mop from the back of the space, feeling around for a hidden handle and opening a hatch.

"What's this?" Chism said.

"Get in."

"What?"

"No one but me knows about this place and Auma's people won't be able to find it. Wait overnight. The weather's scheduled to clear in the morning and help will come. Auma won't risk a confrontation. He'll leave before they arrive."

"What about you?" Chism said, looking down at the shadowy hole.

"I have other things to attend to."

"What are you talking about? There's plenty of room. I'm not going down there if you—"

"You are going down there," Odongo corrected. "Like I said earlier. This isn't your country, David. You take care of your business and I'll take care of mine."

They locked eyes for a moment, but then Chism looked away. The other two were already descending the ladder.

"Will we see each other again?" Chism asked.

"Of course. But I hope not too soon."

Odongo was shoved from behind but didn't stumble. The two guerrillas ushering him toward the front of the building were both in their early teens and lacked the weight to move him. What they did possess, though, was the thoughtless sadism that was unique to child soldiers.

The facility's main doors loomed ahead, and he passed through them into the rain. The group waiting was as ragtag as he expected— clothed in everything from surplus combat gear to jeans and sandals. All, of course, carried the cheap AK-47s favored by terrorists the world over. A few also wielded machetes.

He counted twenty-five people in total. Nineteen of Auma's guerrillas, four captured hospital workers, and two unconscious patients lying in stretchers that were slowly sinking into the mud. Everyone was soaked to the bone and most were starting to shiver.

It was a good sign. When Auma sent his troops on one of his infamous genocidal raids, they were generally high on a drug locally known as ajali. Under its influence, they felt no fear, no pain, no doubt, and certainly no cold. The dull messianic glow around Auma became blinding and they would do anything for him: Run until their hearts exploded. Kill their own families. Fight until well beyond the time their brains should have told them they were dead.

Not tonight, though. Tonight's raid wasn't about wanton violence, theft, or the acquisition of new disciples. Auma wanted something else.

The crowd in front of him parted and the man himself appeared. His form was hidden by a hooded rain poncho, but his eyes shone in the security lights.

"Gideon," Odongo said by way of greeting.

"Mukisa."

Odongo never spoke of the fact that he'd known Auma at university. Before the man's psychoses had reached such a pitched level. Before he'd left to pursue his career as God's avenging angel.

Auma looked over at his six hostages, absorbing the terror and despair in the faces of the ones capable of understanding what was happening.

"I was going to torture them in front of the director of this hospital. But now that I know it's you, there's no point, is there? What would you care? Your heart has always been empty. You live only by your calculations."

Auma motioned toward the hostages and a few of his men fired on full automatic. They threw their arms instinctively in front of their faces as they were mowed down. The screams that were their last act in this world went unheard—drowned out by the guns and rain.

"See?" Auma said, pointing at Odongo. "Not even a flinch. You've already forgotten them, haven't you? You've already sifted through how their deaths affect your position. Scenarios. Strategies. Tactics. You can't comprehend anything beyond that, can you? The smell of their fear. The warmth of their blood on the ground. The sorrow of their families."

"I'm not one of your disciples, Gideon. Your oratory bores me as much now as it did when we were children. What do you want?"

The cult leader's expression was still in shadow, but his eyes sharpened. "David Chism."

"He's gone."

"Do you remember me as being stupid?"

"No. I remember you as being insane."

Auma's followers continued to look at him with the expected awe but, in a few of them, that awe was marred by confusion. It was unlikely that they'd ever heard anyone speak to their messiah as an equal. As a human being like the other seven billion on the planet.

Well, perhaps not like the other seven billion. But also, not a celestial creature in danger of sprouting wings and ascending into heaven.

"Give him to me and I'll make this easy on you, Mukisa. You have my word as God's representative on earth."

Odongo just smiled at that. He remembered the school-age Auma in terms somewhat less grand.

But in one thing he was right. Quick would be better.

Odongo reached for the knife hidden down the back of his pants. The one that Auma's children had sloppily missed.

He charged and, as expected, the sound of gunfire erupted from behind. The impacts of the rounds in his back produced no pain but had the unintended consequence of propelling him forward. Auma jerked unnaturally and Odongo would have laughed if he'd had the time. The man's untrained troops had panicked and shot him.

His blade penetrated the rain hood, getting tangled in the material before it could reach Auma's throat. More gunfire, more disorienting flashes. More impacts.

Odongo's body had gone numb by the time it landed unceremoniously in the mud. He could no longer breathe, but he wasn't sure if it was because his mouth had sunk into the wet earth or because his lungs had been destroyed by the gunfire.

Not that it mattered anymore. He'd done what he could.

Gideon Auma scooted away from the knife in Mukisa Odongo's lifeless fingers. He looked down at his own arm and saw the blood streaming from where a bullet had grazed him. The pain was sharp—that of a trivial wound and not the deep ache of a mortal one.

Someone lifted him to his feet and he found himself able to stand without difficulty. A further examination of the wound would have to wait. Concern over the flesh-and-blood shell that contained his spirit would be unseemly under the adoring gaze of his disciples.

"Bullets can't harm me," he shouted through the beat of the rain and wail of the alarm reverberating through the hospital doors.

His men broke from their stunned silence and cheered as he took a machete from one of them, wielding it with his uninjured arm. Auma didn't recognize the boy who had shot him, but he recognized the panic in his eyes. He recognized the power of it and how it turned the rest against him. They shouted demands for the blood of the boy who only moments ago had been their comrade.

He swung the blade into the boy's arm in roughly the same place he himself had been wounded.

"Pick him up!" he shouted when his victim's knees buckled.

Two men obeyed and Auma continued his work with the machete. It was poorly maintained, making the effort greater than it should have been. Eventually, though, he was rewarded with a severed arm lying in the mud.

"An eye for an eye, a tooth for a tooth. And an arm for an arm."

This time he spoke quietly enough that only those closest to him would hear. But his words would be repeated to the others. And not only the ones who had accompanied him on this raid. To ones who had been left at the encampment. It would become part of his legend. Part of his canon.

"Find the white man!"

Auma's fighters averted their eyes as he strode through the hallway. They'd found nothing, but there was no way that Chism had escaped. The facility was surrounded. Every road and path was being watched. Every village where he could take refuge had been infiltrated. He was there. Of that, Auma was certain. God had whispered it in his ear.

But time was running out. Dawn was bearing down on them and the rain was starting to abate. With the sunrise would come the Ugandan authorities.

"Burn it," he told his second-in-command—a nineteen-year-old who had proved eminently loyal in the seven years since Auma had captured him. "Start at the back. We'll drive him to us like an animal."

Auma turned and started for the front of the building. It was hard to imagine what this would mean for his movement. Chism's benefactor would pay virtually anything to get him back. And with that money, he could buy the weapons necessary to take Uganda. After that, Congo and beyond. The ranks of his disciples would grow from a few hundred men huddled in the forest to millions living out in the open in cities and rural areas. Paying tribute to him. Spreading his message throughout the continent and the world.

The Word of God. The Word of Gideon Auma.

"Smoke! I smell smoke."

David Chism tried to find a more comfortable position on the hard floor but there was none. Odongo had done his customary impeccable job of camouflaging the safe room but hadn't given much thought to creature comforts. Basically, a six-foot cube with no furniture or lights.

"Can you smell it?" Liu repeated in the darkness. "The smoke?"

"I don't smell anything," Ricci said.

"It's because of your cigarettes," she responded in a harsh whisper. "Your nose doesn't work now!"

"Shhh!" Chism said. "I think it's just your imagination, Jing. This is a really stressful . . ."

His voice faltered when he realized that she was right.

A moment later, a second alarm joined the one that had been wailing relentlessly since before Odongo had sequestered them in that hole. The pitch of it was familiar from the regular fire drills he'd insisted on.

"They're going to burn us to death!" she said.

Shit.

"All right," Chism said. "You two stay put. I'm going to go have a look."

No one spoke as he climbed the ladder, felt around for the latch, and then opened the hatch a crack. Odongo had replaced the bucket and mop, and Chism let them slide slowly back before crawling out.

The door leading into the cafeteria was open a couple of inches—left that way by the brief search they'd heard earlier. He peered out at the lines of empty tables. Smoke was just barely visible, creating a haze that hung beneath a sprinkler system that must have been disabled.

Not ideal.

Chism stood and returned to the hatch, pulling it fully open. "Come up. We've got to get out of here."

By the time they slipped into the cafeteria, the main lights were out and the smoke was thick enough to burn his eyes. From now on, they'd be navigating by the red glow of emergency illumination.

A quick peek into the hallway confirmed that it was empty and that the fire was at the back of the facility.

"What?" Ricci said. "What do you see?"

"Too much," Chism responded.

"What does that mean?"

He pulled back and pressed himself against the wall, looking into the tearing eyes of his two companions.

"There's no reason for Auma to come all this way to attack a hospital. And he set the back on fire. The front looks clear."

"What are you saying?"

"That the only thing of value in this place is us. He makes his money stealing, drug dealing, and kidnapping locals. I figure he's going for the big score."

"What are we going to do?"

"There aren't many choices," Chism admitted. "I figure he set the fire to try to flush us into the parking lot."

"Where he's waiting," Ricci said.

"Yeah."

"Maybe we should go," Liu said. "He will ask for money. Mr. Ward will pay and he will let us go."

"No," Matteo Ricci said with surprising firmness. "You're the only thing here that's valuable, David. I will die a horrible death. And, as a woman, Jing's will be . . . unimaginable."

"Agreed," Chism said. "So that leaves only one option. We go through the fire and out the back. They won't expect it and they won't be waiting for us there."

"We'll be burned to death," Liu said.

"Nah. We'll be fine."

"How can you say that?"

"Because I'm super lucky."

1

CIA director Irene Kennedy stepped into the president's outer office and paused to take in her surroundings. The changes had continued in earnest since the last time she was there. The décor and artwork were even more modern and now the carpet had been replaced with a wood floor that bounced sound around the room.

The desk of the president's secretary—a barely controlled disaster over the last two administrations—was now the picture of minimalist, high-tech efficiency. As was the woman sitting behind it.

The fact that so much effort was being put into something as trivial as redecorating suggested a return to what passed for normalcy in Washington. Six months ago, a terrorist group had managed to take down the entire US power grid and keep it down for more than a month. The consequences had been dire, with hundreds of thousands of Americans dead of cold, violence, and lack of medical care. Countless devastating fires caused by exploding electrical substations, sagging power lines, and desperate people trying to stay warm had raged throughout the country. And, finally, the world's economy had collapsed in reaction to its most powerful engine being taken off-line.

The effects would reverberate for years, but the worst was over. Power had been restored to all but a few rural outposts in the Northwest, critical manufacturing and agriculture were fully back online, and areas wiped out by fires were being rebuilt. After months of world governments being too focused on the crises in front of them to create new ones, moves were once again being made on the geopolitical chessboard. Moves that it was her job to neutralize.

"Dr. Kennedy?" the president's secretary said, glancing up from her monitor. "You can go in. He's expecting you."

She entered an Oval Office that was all but unrecognizable. The wallpaper was gone, as were the traditional pleated curtains. Furniture had been updated to something that leaned toward midcentury modern, and artwork had slipped into the abstract. Only the Resolute Desk and flags remained.

The man walking toward her seemed to fit perfectly with the environment he'd created. At forty-four, Anthony Cook was one of the youngest presidents in US history. He'd managed to rise from the turmoil created by the suicide of his party's front-runner, crushing the more conventional replacement candidates endorsed by the establishment. The American people had been fed up with business as usual for a long time and that, combined with the hardship brought about by the electrical grid failure, had sent them on a search for someone different.

Anthony Cook, for better or worse, was it.

"Irene," he said, taking her hand. "It's good to see you."

She wasn't sure that was entirely true. Her relationship with his predecessor had been one of mutual respect and occasionally even warmth. Cook seemed to be incapable of either. He was a ruthless man, though one with an admittedly impressive grasp of history and America's challenges going forward. A born politician who had spent his life immersed in that world but who still managed to portray himself as an outsider. A common man who had infiltrated the political elite and was now positioned to transform it.

None of this was necessarily bad. Politics was theater and a fair amount of melodrama was necessary to get people to the polls. But what was behind the persona Cook had created? Where was he going? What did he want? Due to his understandable focus since he took office on putting America back on track, they hadn't interacted enough for Kennedy to get a true measure of the man.

He pointed her toward a conversation area, and she made note of his broad shoulders, narrow waist, and full head of hair. In his years as a political strategist, he'd been very different—a scrawny intellectual with fiery charisma, a gift for picking winners, and an icy, realpolitik view of the average American.

By the time he'd thrown his own hat into the ring, though, he'd reinvented himself. *President* Cook was good looking, physically imposing, and impeccably dressed. He oozed concern for every one of the three hundred and thirty million people under his care. He was the man with the answers. The man who would lead America into a future so bright it was blinding.

"I'm not sure you know our guest, Irene."

From behind, the man sitting on one of the sofas looked very much like everyone else in Washington—blue suit, nice posture, expensive haircut with a little gray at the temples. But when he put down his coffee cup and stood, he proved to be much more than one of the political operatives that infested the beltway.

As the world's first trillionaire, Nicholas Ward needed little introduction. He was a genius in every sense of the word who had stepped back from controlling his business empire to run a massive foundation that he'd charged with nothing less ambitious than solving the problems of humanity. Health care, renewable energy, employment, violence, poverty—if something had plagued society since the dawn of time, Ward figured he could fix it in the next twenty years.

A bit optimistic in her estimation, but he was a hard man to dismiss. Impossible, really.

"You look good, Nick. Africa seems to agree with you."

"Don't be fooled. It's all biting insects and sunburn."

She leaned in and he kissed her on the cheek.

"I take it you *do* know each other," the president said, failing to hide a hint of irritation that Kennedy found a bit worrying. She hadn't been told what this meeting was about or that the most powerful private citizen in the world would be in attendance. Had it been an attempt at a subtle power play that had now backfired?

Not yet sure how to navigate the environment that Cook had created, she was grateful when Ward answered.

"Irene and I are in the same business—we both want to keep people safe and healthy. That's landed us at a few of the same conferences and participating on the same panels." He flashed the everyman smile that he was known for. "I figure the fact that she hasn't had me killed yet makes us friends."

Fairly close friends, in fact. Their relationship had been cemented by a recent bioterrorism event that she'd had no choice but to bring him in on. The long days, long nights, and logistical nightmares they'd faced had given her a healthy respect and personal affection for the man. He was one of the most impressive people she had ever met and seemed to honestly have the good of mankind at heart. The fact that some of his views were a bit naïve was more than overcome by his enthusiasm and almost supernatural competence.

"I heard what happened in Uganda, but the details that have reached my desk are still sketchy. We have limited resources in that area and I'm not sure the local government's fully on top of things."

"I can guarantee you they're not. That's why I'm here."

"Why don't you give us the rundown on what you know," the president said, reasserting his dominance by pointing everyone to a seat and then taking one himself.

"Our facility was attacked by Gideon Auma's forces. The hospital director managed to evacuate most of the people before it happened, but the ones who stayed—including him—were killed. The exception may be David Chism and his two research assistants. They were there at the outset of the attack, but now they've disappeared."

"My understanding is that the facility burned," Kennedy said. "It seems likely that they were inside."

"That was our assumption, but our people are going through the rubble and haven't found any bodies."

"Are you sure that Auma doesn't have them?" Kennedy said. "I wouldn't be surprised if you got a call pretty soon asking for ransom. In fact, it seems to be the most likely reason he'd attack a facility that has nothing he needs and that's well outside his normal operating theater."

"It's possible," Ward admitted. "But we have people on the ground telling us that there's significant guerrilla activity in the forest to the east of the facility. As though they're searching for something."

"Irene?" the president prompted.

She leaned back and instinctively reached for a cup of tea that wasn't there. Another reminder that the Alexander administration was gone.

"I understand the importance of David Chism, Nick. Believe me I do. But the chances that he's still alive seem low to me. More likely he was hiding in the building when it started to burn. Maybe even in a safe room designed specifically for this kind of event. My guess is that a more thorough search of the ruins will turn up his body and the bodies of his team."

"But are you sure?"

"No," she admitted.

"What if they escaped into the jungle?"

"That's a big 'what if,'" the president said.

"But with what's on the line, it seems like one worth pursuing."

The two men locked eyes for a moment, but it was hard to know exactly what passed between them. The fact that they had crossed swords years ago when Cook was the governor of California was well known.

"When you say this is worth pursuing, I assume you mean by me?" Cook said a bit coldly.

"The Ugandan government has some rescue workers on-site, but they're already starting to pull out. And they say they don't want to bring in troops to search for my people because they're concerned that the Congolese will see it as a provocation. In truth, though, it's more likely that they're not prepared to engage Auma right now for political reasons."

"And they're making the assumption that Chism's dead," Cook said, standing. "Which is almost certainly correct." He offered his hand. "Thanks for bringing this to our attention, Nicholas. Irene and I will talk about it and let you know what we come up with."

To his credit, the wealthiest man in history took being dismissed gracefully, shaking hands with the president, and nodding in Kennedy's direction before leaving the Oval Office.

"Thoughts?" Cook said, taking a seat again.

"Setting David Chism aside for a moment, Gideon Auma is the leader of a terrorist organization that's allied with Islamic extrem—"

"But he's a regional threat," Cook interrupted, once again displaying his grasp of international issues. "And he's only a Muslim when it's convenient to him. He uses Christianity, animism, and anything else he can come up with just as easily. The truth is that he's a messianic cult leader who's never going to stir up any trouble outside of Uganda and the DRC."

Stir up any trouble was a disturbingly trivial assessment of the situation on the ground. The level of brutality Gideon Auma had unleashed on that part of Africa would shock even a hardened ISIS operative. The human suffering was hard to ignore, though Cook had a gift for that when the cameras weren't on him.

"Regional threats have a way of expanding in unpredictable ways, Mr. President. It's a lesson we've learned over and over."

He frowned and folded his arms across his chest. "I'm not convinced. And as far as Chism goes, you and I both know he's dead. Scientists don't just run through flaming buildings and then turn into Rambo in the African jungle."

"But if he's not? Based on what I know about his work, it would be hard to overstate his importance—both to America and to mankind in general. Another concern I have is that if he *is* alive and Auma captures him, Nick will pay whatever it takes to get him back. With a few hundred million dollars in his pocket, Auma could expand his influence."

"Next steps?"

"Send Mitch Rapp to Uganda. Let him make a recommendation from the ground."

"No. Not Rapp."

"Why not?"

"He's too valuable an asset and we both know this is a waste of time." He stood again and it was Kennedy's turn to be dismissed. "Keep my people posted of any developments and in the meantime, I'll give this some thought. Until you hear from me, though, we're staying out of it."

"Yes, sir."

He started back to his desk as she crossed the office toward the door. Her hand had barely touched the knob when he spoke again.

"And on the subject of Mitch Rapp. I'd like to meet him."

"I'll let him know, sir."

"But what are the chances that Chism is alive? Ten percent? Less?"

Anthony Cook's wife, Catherine, saw everything in terms of numbers. It was a bias that had served her well during her time as one of the world's most successful hedge fund managers. And it had been even more helpful during his rise through the political swamp. Simply put, he wouldn't be sitting in the White House residence without her icy calculations.

"Can't be much more than that," Cook agreed.

She took a seat on a sofa across from him and looked up, staring at a blank white section of the ceiling to collect her thoughts. She was still extremely attractive at forty-two, with long dark hair pulled back, an athletic build maintained with the same diligence as his own, and a pale, unlined face. Their union had produced two sons—one with significant potential and one completely useless—but the bond between them had never really been sexual. In fact, he wouldn't bet his life on the fact that she was even attracted to men. It didn't matter, though. Their goals were perfectly aligned, and neither was interested in anything that didn't relate to the achievement of those goals.

"I've quietly sold all our stock relating to Nick's health care companies and reinvested the money in competitors who'll benefit from Chism's death. Valuations are already starting to move based on the rumors coming out of Uganda. We've made millions since the markets opened and stand to make tens of millions more. And so do a lot of other people. I don't think a lot of tears will be shed around the world if Nicholas Ward takes a hit."

What she said was an understatement of truly grand proportions. Ward was looking to transform health care worldwide, and Chism's vaccine research was one of the cornerstones of that effort. Combined with Ward's work in medical artificial intelligence and his ideas about decentralizing and democratizing the medical industry, they had the status quo under serious threat. Further, wealth creation seemed to be becoming an increasingly zero-sum game. Every time Ward won, there was some billionaire or corporation that lost. Virtually no one could keep up with him and the few who could, he hired.

"But all that hinges on him really being dead," Cook pointed out.

She nodded. "There's opportunity here for us. The question is do we want to exploit it. So far, we've been fairly conservative in our actions. But we're only three and a half years from the next election. At some point, we're going to have to move forward."

"Explain."

"First, there's no question that we need to send a team to Uganda to try to find Chism. We know how Ward feels about us but to date he hasn't gotten too deeply involved in politics. We don't need him rethinking that and staking out a position against your administration. I think we both agree there's no chance of turning him into an ally, but if we do him this favor, we might be able to neutralize him as an enemy."

"So, we try to get Chism back?" the president said.

"I didn't say that."

He thought for a moment. "So, we just put on a show."

"It's a bit of a tightrope walk but I imagine a doable one. Make enough of an effort to impress Ward but not so much that we have any chance of succeeding. And make sure that the right people know they owe us for that failure."

"So, we send in an inadequate force with the excuse that we prioritized stealth and didn't want to create an incident with the Ugandan government. Maybe we even lose a few of them. That'd make our commitment look even greater. Ward would have a hard time complaining about the failure of a rescue mission that ended up with American soldiers in body bags."

"Agreed," Catherine said.

"What about Kennedy? She'll see through it."

"She'll object to not being in the loop and privately criticize the details of the operation, but that's all. She doesn't believe Chism is alive any more than we do, and she knows her job is hanging on by a thread."

"Maybe it's time to cut that thread. Keeping her on has played well up to this point, but she's dangerous. You'd have to be an idiot to think she didn't have something to do with Christine Barnett's suicide. And if she'd do it to her, she'll do it to me."

Christine Barnett had been his party's leader before her sudden and very unexpected death. While he owed his presidency to the fact that she was now rotting away in her mausoleum, the path she'd taken there was well beyond suspicious.

"There's no evidence of that at all, Tony."

"Come on. There's no way that arrogant bitch offed herself. She thought she was the second coming of Jesus. Kennedy found the skeletons in her closet and quietly did away with her before she could get her hands on the Oval Office. The problem is that we've got a few skeletons, too, and in order to keep hold of the White House we're going to be collecting more. I don't want to spend my life looking over my shoulder for Irene Kennedy."

"I agree that she was probably involved in Christine's death and that she has to go. But I don't see this as a pressing issue. Kennedy still has a lot of support on both sides of the aisle and the longer she stays, the less political it will look when we put her out to pasture."

"What about Mitch Rapp?"

"Obviously, he has the potential to be a powerful tool. And he's a simpler creature than Kennedy. He wears his motivations on his sleeve—love of country, loyalty to his comrades. He still sees America as a shining tower on a hill. Those kinds of delusions are easily manipulated."

"You're underestimating him, Cathy."

"Not at all. I'm just thinking out loud. In any event, I'm anxious to be introduced. If nothing else, it'll be interesting to look into the eyes of a man like him."

2

"BEYOND the laser, the system uses downrange drones to measure wind, humidity, temperature variations, and such. They do all the work and then signal the rifle. We kept the trigger, though. For you old-school guys."

Mitch Rapp frowned and glanced at the man in his peripheral vision. A soldier on loan to DARPA, he looked impossibly young. The kind of kid who would just stare blankly if anyone mentioned a fax machine or that phones were once attached to walls. The world seemed to be transforming into a place where anyone over eighteen had one foot in the nursing home.

"Just pull it and put the crosshairs on the target, sir."

Rapp did as he was told. The sniper rifle's trigger had a game controller feel to it, moving no more than a millimeter before offering a click that he supposed some people considered satisfying. But that was all. No crack of a round leaving the barrel. No recoil or stench of gunpowder. The weapon just sat there.

"I'd be better if I could actually shoot something," Rapp said as he maintained the crosshairs on a target three thousand meters to the north. The only movement was the slight jiggle every time his heart beat.

"The system's waiting for the moment when your aim comes together with all the environmental factors, sir. It's about patience."

Not Rapp's long suit, but it was something he'd been working on. The last six months had been about catching up with a life that had gotten out of control. He'd hired a physical therapist who'd taken one look at his X-rays and saw her kids' college tuition paid for. Which turned out to be money well spent because in less than half a year, she had his aches and pains down to a dull roar. Even better, he now had some data to assess his physical condition and create a realistic strategy for improving it. He'd never perform like he had when he was thirty, but with the right training plan, he wouldn't be that far off.

And so here he was, familiarizing himself with new technologies that he'd managed to ignore over the last few years. To what end, he wasn't entirely sure. He'd never met the new president, and the rest of Washington was fully focused on deflecting blame for the grid attack. It was something that Rapp would never understand. At some point, wouldn't it be easier to just do a competent job than to spend all your time covering your ass?

The kick came from nowhere, accompanied by the muted crack of the round leaving the rifle's silencer. The baby-faced sergeant peered through his spotting scope and smiled smugly. "Hit."

Rapp stood and dusted himself off, scanning the men standing around him. Scott Coleman, Joe Maslick, and Bruno McGraw first, but then letting his gaze fall on Charlie Wicker. The incredibly gifted sniper had been part of his core team for years.

"Wick, you're fired."

"Shiiiit," the diminutive Wyoming native said, drawing out the word for a full two seconds. "What happens if there's sand blowing around? Or it's raining? Or if someone shoots down one of those fancy drones? Hell, what happens if the target's moving? They do that some-times, you know."

Rapp turned his attention to the man guiding them through all this technology.

"It's not perfect," he admitted. "But in the right conditions, it can turn an average sniper into . . . Well, into Charlie Wicker."

"All right," Rapp conceded. "You're rehired. But you're on notice."

Wick grinned and raised his middle finger.

"What's next?" Coleman said. "Are there jet packs?"

"Jet packs? Um, no."

"You guys have been promising me a jet pack since I got into this business. When are you going to deliver?"

"We can get them in the air, but the range is crap, sir. The more fuel you put in them, the heavier they get. It's physics, you know?"

"What about those night vision eye drops?" Bruno McGraw said. "You've been saying they're six months out for years now."

"Those actually work," the sergeant said. "But they make every-thing green and kind of hazy. So, you can see at night but only about ten feet before you can't tell a human from a signpost. It's coming, though."

"Let me guess. Six months?"

"You said it, not me. Until then, let me show you something else you might be interested in."

They trailed him up a dirt track toward an old cabin on a ridge. The sun was starting to get low on the horizon, bringing temperatures back down into the seventies and signaling the winding down of a day that had started before dawn. An interesting day, though. The march of technology had turned into a sprint and Rapp knew that sticking his head in the sand wasn't an option. In a world where some dumbass who'd never picked up a rifle could take you out from three thousand yards, it was evolve or die.

The wood and asphalt-shingle structure looked like it was in the process of collapse, with no glass in the windows and no door in the frame. It contained a single room with a table in the middle and seven high-tech mannequins sitting or standing around it.

"I think you're going to like this," the DARPA man said, tapping what looked like an aerosol paint can centered on the table. "It's basically a Taser grenade. Let's say you want to clear a room with an unknown number of combatants. What do you do? Not many options. Probably your best bet is to throw in a flashbang and roll through the door hoping the enemy is sufficiently disoriented."

"How does it work?" Rapp asked.

"Push the red button and in three seconds, twelve heat-seeking cables shoot out." He snapped his fingers. "Everyone goes down just like that."

"Bullshit," Coleman said. "You've got enough power in that little can to take down twelve full-grown men?"

"We've refined the waveform. Less energy, more impact. But you don't have to take my word for it. These dummies are heated to body temperature and have sensors in them that'll give us electrical discharge numbers."

"I'm not an engineer," Rapp said. "I'm not going to bet my life and the lives of my team on a computer printout."

"Sir, we—"

"So, this is a fully functional prototype?"

"Yes, sir. It's—"

Rapp reached over and pushed the button. After a pause of less than half a second, the young sergeant sprinted through the empty door frame. His guys all just looked around, silently daring each other to move.

"I still can't feel my lips," Joe Maslick said, bringing a beer to them. "Do you think that's permanent?"

Everyone just shrugged.

Rapp finished off his own beer and then glanced around the crowded bar for their waitress.

"So, what now?" Coleman said. "Power's on and the world's getting back to its normal fucked-up self. We're tan, rested, and tech savvy. The calls for contracts are rolling in again."

"You should take them," Rapp said.

"That's it? That's your advice? 'You should take them'?"

"Look, I have no relationship with the new president and I might never have one. Hell, I'm not even sure I want to."

"What's Dr. Kennedy think about him?" McGraw asked.

"Last I talked to her, she didn't know what to make of him yet."

"So, what's *your* plan?" Coleman asked.

"I'm headed to South Africa. Claudia and Anna are already there."

"I mean on a more philosophical level. Do you find yourself surfing for country clubs?"

"Not yet."

"Then join us. Full time. SEAL Demolition and Salvage's newest recruit."

"I don't remember that working out so well last time."

"No more celebrity protection, I promise. None of us are starving and that gives us the luxury to pick and choose. And we recently went to a fully democratic model. Everyone votes on whether to take a contract and it has to be unanimous. So, only interesting stuff that pays obscene amounts of money."

Rapp shook his head, still searching for their waitress. "Look, I'll always back you guys up if you need it. You know that. But right now, I've got a chance to back away for a while. And I'm going to take it." He stood. "Anyone else need another drink?"

A couple of hands went up and he headed for the bar. The people behind it were just as overworked as his waitress, so he found a stool and settled in. For the first time in years, he had time to wait.

ISIS and al-Qaeda were on the ropes and increasingly turning inward. The Russians were still up to no good but had chosen Facebook as their primary battlefield. The Chinese were a significant threat, but despite a little naval posturing, that threat was largely economic.

Finally, the world was moving away from oil, causing the Middle East to slowly lose its strategic importance.

And America? It was being taken over by corrupt politicians, a mainstream media bent on whipping up divisions, and an Internet full of crazies.

And while all those threats were very real and as dangerous as anything he'd ever faced, they weren't the kind he was equipped to resolve.

His phone rang and he looked down at the caller information—or more precisely, lack thereof. Irene Kennedy. Impeccable timing as usual. Sometimes he wondered if she had the ability to read his mind.

"Yeah," he said, picking up.

"How's the training going?"

"Good."

"Find any interesting new toys?"

"Maybe. Or maybe it'd be better to leave them for the next generation."

"You sound a bit dejected."

Rapp caught the bartender's eye, tapping his empty beer bottle before holding up three fingers.

"Dejected? Maybe. Or maybe relieved. It's been a long road and now I may have reached the end of it. Alive."

"It's a brave new world. There's no question of that. But you've always kept step."

"This time I'm not sure I want to."

"In that case, I have some bad news."

"What?"

"President Cook wants to meet you."

"Why?"

"I don't know. It's possible that it has something to do with what happened in Uganda. Have you been following that?"

"No."

"That's okay. More likely he just wants to size you up. See if you're someone his administration can use."

"Use," Rapp repeated, knowing that Kennedy always chose her words carefully. "Can I take it that he hasn't grown on you?"

"I never said that."

"Word is that you're letting Mike handle him."

Mike Nash was a former operator who had become Kennedy's right-hand man. A good-looking, endlessly likable Marine, he had a gift for dealing with the assholes on Capitol Hill. Rapp and he had been friends for years and, in fact, lived only a few houses from each other in a private subdivision west of DC.

"Like you, I'm trying to regain a little of my life. The lull we're coming to the end of has reminded me how much I've given up."

He was a bit jealous. The truth was that he'd never really had much of a life. Getting one back had to be easier than acquiring one for the first time.

"Fine. I'll be back tomorrow. Then I have a couple days before I leave for Cape Town. If he can fit a meeting into that window, I'll make it work. If not, he'll have to wait until I get back."

"Which will be when?"

"I don't know," he said as the bartender returned with his beers. "Maybe never."

3

GREEN.

It was the word that had overtaken *lucky* to describe David Chism's world.

He knew that his takeaway from all this should be terror. Or despair. Or rage. But it wasn't. It was the color that surrounded him, pressed against him, closed in around him.

He crouched among the ferns and mossy vines, listening intently for a few moments. Nothing. Just the rustle of leaves and the calls of a few birds. Visibility was no more than ten feet and all he could smell was jungle rot and a hint of smoke from what he assumed were the smoldering remains of his life's work.

Nature's sensory deprivation chamber.

Finding no reason not to continue downslope, he stood and did so carefully. He'd never traveled through anything this dense before, but it wasn't completely foreign. Mukisa Odongo had taught him a great deal about the terrain on their expeditions to find novel insect species and those still-elusive mountain gorillas. And now Odongo was dead.

For some reason Chism was absolutely certain of that. He could feel his absence.

What the hell was going on in this world? His friend Vicky Schaefer had recently been murdered in Yemen, where she was trying to control a deadly new coronavirus. And her team—a mirror of his own—hadn't fared any better. All any of them wanted to do was help people.

Now his research facility was a pile of ashes. His people and patients were either scattered or dead. His active experiments were destroyed.

How the fuck could this be happening? It was like a big green nightmare he couldn't wake up from.

Chism arrived at the stream he was looking for and lay down next to it, using his filthy shirt to filter water into a plastic bottle he'd found. The night of their escape had been hard as hell, but with the rain, drinking water hadn't been an issue. Cold and the terrain had been their biggest enemies. Last night—their second in the forest—hadn't been so uncomfortable, but now thirst and hunger were starting to become an issue.

"Doctor Cheesmee!"

He froze at the sound of the shout, trying to pinpoint its direction and distance.

"Daveed Cheesmee! We help you! We Ugandan army!"

He seriously doubted it. There had been no aircraft in the area and based on his lengthy political conversations with Odongo, the Ugandan government was wary of sending troops to this region. Much more likely, the shout was a siren song from one of Gideon Auma's men.

Chism had tried to convince himself that Auma's goal was to steal everything that wasn't nailed down and exchange it for narcotics, weapons, and whatever else it was that kept his death cult operating. Now, though, it was impossible to deny that his men were in search of something bigger. If Chism let himself fall into their hands, they could ransom him back to Nick Ward. And that'd be real money.

When the voice called out again it sounded more distant, so Chism began working his way back up the slope. It took well over an hour, but he finally reached a wall of dirt and rock near the top of one of the mountains that stretched endlessly in every direction. To the west he could see what was left of the hospital—a black smear at the edge of the red dirt road that passed in front of it.

He eased along the steep slope, entering a bank of morning fog that significantly reduced visibility. The ground turned slick, and he tested every foot placement before committing. Just because he could no longer see what was to his left didn't mean it wasn't there. One misstep and he'd find himself cartwheeling hundreds of feet before getting hung up in the trees below.

Calling his destination a cave would be an exaggeration. It was more a deep impression covered with woven branches to camouflage the entrance. He rustled them in the coded rhythm that Jing Liu had insisted on and then passed into the gloom.

The space was tight—maybe ten feet square. The sloping dirt walls were still clinging to the moisture from two nights ago, creating a misty humidity that tasted like mold and earth. Fortunately, the heat wasn't bad. Uganda's weather could be counted on to hover somewhere between the high seventies during the day and mid-sixties at night.

Liu was sitting near the south wall, knees pulled to her chest, staring through the thick air at nothing. She didn't seem to notice him crossing her field of vision and kneeling next to Matteo Ricci. While Chism's luck had held during their unlikely escape from the hospital, the Italian had been less fortunate. His right pants leg had caught fire and had melted to his thigh. The wound was painful, but not as painful as being forced to acknowledge how much polyester had been present in his stylish slacks. The inevitable infection, though, was going to be a serious problem.

"Were you able to call for help?" Ricci said, sounding even weaker than when Chism had left a few hours before.

"I wasn't able to get signal. But maybe a little later."

It was a lie, of course. The cell tower that serviced the area had been part of the facility Auma's people had burned.

"Water?"

"That I managed to get. But you're going to have to hang on for a few more hours. It's got to sit in the sun for a while to disinfect. I have no idea what's in that stream. Maybe—"

"We have to get out of here," Liu blurted. "We cannot sleep another night in a hole."

Chism let out a long breath and turned toward her.

"We've talked about this, Jing. There are people out there trying to capture us."

"But they say they from the Ugandan army. They trying to help us."

"No, they're not," Chism said firmly. "They're Auma's men. And wherever they want to take us, I guarantee it's going to be a hell of a lot worse than where we are now."

"Then what?" Ricci said, pushing himself to his elbows in the thatch he was lying on. "We can't stay here forever."

"Look, there are things we can eat in the forest. We have access to water. The weather forecast was for clear skies after the storm we had the night of the attack. We're okay here for a while. And Nick will send people to help us."

"He thinks we dead," Liu said. "No one coming."

"That's not true. When Auma doesn't contact him for ransom and our bodies don't turn up, Nick will have to start working under the assumption we're alive. He didn't make a trillion dollars by just giving up when things turn ugly."

4

RAPP walked through his gate and used a remote control to close it behind him. The structure inside was designed to be half house, half bunker but was starting to feel mostly like the latter with Claudia and Anna gone. Surprisingly, a couple of weeks of freezer food and silence was all it had taken to make the concrete walls start to close in.

It was only 10 a.m., but temperatures were already pushing into the mid-eighties as he started up a road scattered with houses and empty lots. He knew the owners of each one—all old friends who could handle a weapon. Some a little long in the tooth, but still loyal and better than nothing if the shit ever hit the fan.

Creating a neighborhood full of shooters had been his brother's idea and it was he who had provided the incentive—buying up the entire subdivision and selling off the lots for a dollar to the right people.

The plan had been to create an oasis where Rapp could let his guard drop a bit. And it had worked. At least for a while.

Rapp was unaccustomed to wearing a suit and was already starting to sweat through it when he approached a barn on the right. It had originally been designated as a shooting range and gym but had been commandeered by the burgeoning agricultural operation dreamed up by Scott Coleman and his seven-year-old accomplice, Anna Gould. A sizable plot had been fenced off that spring and was now alive with various experimental crops. A group of sheep, led by the formidable Snowball, was testing the barrier for weakness and eyeing up the new grazing potential.

Rapp had resisted the shift to farming but was now glad he'd lost that particular battle. Coleman was at his happiest when he was screwing with plants and livestock. Except maybe for when he was perched on top of the tractor he'd had airbrushed with ghost flames and skulls.

Even better, it gave some of Rapp's retired neighbors a reason to get out of bed in the morning—particularly when Coleman was out on an op. And, selfishly, it made the subdivision even more self-sufficient. Something that would have come in handy if he hadn't been able to get America's lights back on.

Rapp finally turned into a yard strewn with toys and sports equipment. Mike Nash appeared in the front door of the house a moment later holding a couple of go-cups and a file folder.

"That's an upgrade!" he said, nodding in Rapp's direction. "Claudia finally shit-canned that suit you got at Kmart, huh?"

It hadn't actually been Kmart, but there was no point in splitting hairs. And that was exactly what she'd done—with an appropriate ceremony and exaggerated expression of disgust. He tended to own precisely two suits: one winter, one summer. And while that number hadn't changed, the quality of the merchandise definitely had.

"Maggie told me we have to take the kidmobile," Nash said, offering Rapp one of the cups before heading toward a minivan parked in front of the garage. Rapp climbed in the other side, sweeping a baseball mitt from the seat before settling in.

"You ready for this, Mitch?"

Rapp looked out the window, catching his reflection in it. His beard had grown back in and his shoulder-length hair was neatly combed for the occasion. Most striking, though, was the strange pallor to his skin. The lack of Middle Eastern operations over the last six months had kept him out of the desert sun and Claudia was quite the sunscreen Nazi. She'd become convinced that it wouldn't be a bullet that killed him. It'd be skin cancer.

"I guess."

"Don't sound so excited. How are Claudia and Anna doing in Cape Town?"

"Good."

"Are you going to go see them?"

"Yeah. Tonight."

"Gonna stay for a while?"

"Don't know." A lie, but for now a convenient one.

"Man. You are a riveting conversationalist this morning."

Rapp leaned back in the seat and glanced over at his old friend. "Tell me about him."

"The president? Not that much to say that hasn't been said before. He's smart and focused as hell. After six months in office, though, he's frustrated with the process. As a former governor who had a lot of support from local government, he's finding it hard to wrap his arms around Washington. He wants to get things done but you know how it is. Ten roadblocks for every three feet of asphalt."

"What about his wife?"

"Ah, you're not as out of the loop as you pretend to be," Nash said. "Excellent question. She's even smarter than he is but doesn't have his touch with the common man. Her element is more a private jet full of Harvard PhDs. It's a weakness she's conscious of and working on, though. We'll see how it goes. What I can tell you is that she's a full fifty percent of that team. To the point that it's a mistake to think of the president as one person. It's more like Anthony Cook is the right brain and Catherine's the left."

Rapp nodded but didn't otherwise respond.

"Irene doesn't like them. Did she tell you that? She thinks they come off as a little ambitious," Nash said.

"Ambitious with their agenda for the country or with accumulating power?"

"That's a hard question to answer. You know better than I do that there's a fair amount of overlap between those two things."

"Try."

"This I can tell you: Anthony Cook feels like he's the first president of the new era. He understands the shifts in the geopolitical landscape, in technology, and in culture. And while he's informed by history, he tends not to look back too much. His eyes are locked on what's next. He wants to knock two hundred and fifty years of dust off the country and put us firmly back into a leadership position."

"They all do at first," Rapp said. "But he'll end up like the rest. Flailing around, putting out fires, and collecting donations. Then he'll be gone."

"Always the cynic. But yeah. Probably. I hope not, though. The way I see it, this country's in worse shape than it's been in since the Civil War. We're bankrupting ourselves. We're turning on each other. We're choosing leaders who are only interested in staying in office and don't even pretend to govern anymore. We're losing our focus on terrorism while Islamic radicals still have the ability to bloody us. The Chinese are on their way to dominating us economically and the Russians are getting way further than they should trolling us on the Internet . . ." His voice faded for a moment. "Take it from a guy who spends half his life inside the beltway, man. We need some real leadership in this country. And we need it now."

———

"Mitch!" Anthony Cook said, striding across the disorientingly modern Oval Office. "It's a real honor to meet you."

His overbearing grip caused his biceps to strain against a shirt that seemed to have been tailored for that exact purpose. Every time Rapp saw a picture of Cook, he seemed to have swollen a little more. Unlike the previous president, though, he wasn't a former athlete. If Rapp had to guess, his impressive physique came as much from a syringe as from a gym.

"You've always put yourself at the center of the storm for this country," he said, releasing Rapp's hand and slapping Nash on the shoulder. "You both have. Now, grab a seat."

They took opposite sides of a sofa and the president dropped into the chair across from them. "I have a lot of faults, but ingratitude isn't one of them. So, let me start by thanking you for my job, Mitch. If you hadn't gotten the power back on, I'd be governing four million square miles of dead bodies and scavengers. The reason this country still exists is because of you. Period."

Rapp nodded respectfully, trying to hide his discomfort. He'd spent his life pursuing anonymity and being gushed over by the president of the United States was pretty much the opposite. If it had been up to him, he'd have given the FBI credit for saving the grid and faded comfortably back into the woodwork.

"Sorry," Cook said, demonstrating his famous ability to read people. "I'm embarrassing you. I know. But it had to be said and now I'm done. I promise."

"Yes, sir," Rapp said simply. Out of the corner of his eye he could see Nash grinning at his discomfort.

"Obviously, we're still mopping up the mess," Cook continued. "But I think we as Americans—including me—learned a lot about ourselves during that crisis. And not all of it was positive. What do you think?"

"I'm not sure I'm qualified to offer an opinion, sir. My area of expertise is pretty narrow."

Cook laughed out loud at that. "Beautifully put. But still, you must have an opinion. If not as an expert, as a citizen."

Rapp let out a long breath. "I think your analysis is fair. A terrorist attack like that should have pulled the country together but it seemed like it pushed us further apart. Obviously, you had to expect that it would *eventually* turn into an every-man-for-himself scenario. That's just the way survival goes. What surprised me was that people started turning on each other before their freezers even melted. And it wasn't even about anything real. Political differences and conspiracy theories, mostly."

Cook nodded. "It was a Pearl Harbor moment and we showed that we're a very different country than we were in 1941. I suppose some of that's inevitable but still we need to get some of that magic back before it's too late."

"Yes, sir."

Rapp could see why Kennedy was unsure about the man. Like all politicians, he was slick, but unlike his predecessor, Cook didn't let that façade slip in private meetings. He was as much the politician in the Oval Office as he was on the campaign trail. And while the imagery of lost magic played well on TV, it wouldn't impress a woman who preferred to work in specifics.

"Unfortunately, that's easier said than done," Cook continued, examining Rapp from across the coffee table. "And that's one of the reasons I wanted to meet you. You're an anomaly in the government. A person who actually seems to be able to get things done. That makes you worth your weight in gold. To me. To the country. Even to the world."

Now he was laying it on a bit thick. What Rapp had said earlier about having a narrow skill set was true. It was something he himself had recognized a long time ago but that still tricked others. In a way, killing terrorists was easy. The problem was about as straightforward as problems got and the solution was simple and permanent. The search for America's mojo, on the other hand, wasn't necessarily improved by a guy with a Glock.

"So, the question is this," the president continued. "Are you still in? I know that transitions in administrations aren't easy for someone in your position, but can I count on you like President Alexander did?"

It was a question that Rapp had been unsuccessfully working on for a while.

"If you have a problem and I'm the right man for the job, sir."

A hedge for sure, but not one that was too obvious.

"That's what I wanted to hear," Cook said before turning toward Nash. "And now I know that Mike's anxious to get on with my intelligence briefing. Do you want to sit in?"

"Thank you, sir, but I'm getting on a plane tonight and I haven't even started packing."

"I understand." The president stood and held a hand out. "I'll look forward to the next time. Enjoy your trip."

Rapp started down the hallway thinking that his meeting had gone pretty well. No specific demands, loyalty pledges, or over-the-top power plays. Maybe Cook really had just wanted to meet and thank him for getting the lights back on.

"Mr. Rapp! Can I buy you a cup of coffee?"

The voice behind him was immediately recognizable from television and he turned reluctantly toward Catherine Cook. A warm smile was framed by hair worn a little looser than it had been during her stint as the First Lady of California. Her tailor had the same form-fitting aesthetic as her husband's and the effect was to highlight what an attractive woman she was. No one disputed her brains and determination, but good looks could open doors, too.

"Sure," he said, knowing he had no other option. "Thank you, ma'am."

She led him back to her office and offered him a seat in front of her desk. "Black?"

"That'd be fine."

She handed him a steaming cup and then scooted a chair into a position that put them face-to-face. "It's a pleasure to meet you. I hope Tony didn't make you blush. He's a bit of a fanboy."

"No, ma'am."

She flashed that smile again and Rapp remembered what Nash had told him earlier about how she was trying to improve her interpersonal skills. It seemed to be working.

"It must be strange to be the guy every man wants to be. The secret agent who saves the world from the forces of evil. Gun in one hand, beautiful woman in the other."

Rapp laughed. "I don't remember the beautiful women. I do remember eating bugs, bullet wounds, and a couple bouts of malaria."

"Once you put a romantic image in someone's head, it's hard to get it out."

"I suppose."

"I assume he asked you if you were on board to help us like you did Josh?"

"Yes, ma'am."

"And what was your answer?"

"That I'd do what I can."

Her smile was a little more subdued this time. "So vague and mysterious. Maybe politics was your true calling?"

"I don't think so."

She warmed her hands with her coffee cup in a way that reminded him of Irene Kennedy. The clarity of her eyes and the wheels spinning behind them wasn't too far off, either.

"You know how dangerous the world is, Mitch. And I'm guessing you've noticed that those dangers are becoming more complicated. Closer to home."

"I'm not sure what you mean," he said, though he was pretty sure he did.

"Take the Russian power grid, for instance. You used it against them to get President Utkin to give up the name of their agent here."

In truth, it had been Kennedy, not him. The United States had good penetration into the Russian system, and she'd put Moscow in the dark before threatening to take down the rest of the country if Utkin didn't give her what she wanted.

"Irene did."

"And thank God it worked, right? But it won't work again. They've already completely overhauled their cybersecurity and hardened their physical infrastructure. On the other hand, do you know what Tony's managed to accomplish by way of securing our own grid? Basically nothing. He's run headlong into a maze of bureaucracy, local politics, and congresspeople who won't lift a finger unless we offer them political favors."

"Doesn't surprise me."

"No, I suppose you've been around long enough that it wouldn't." She took a sip of her coffee. "And the Chinese are no different. Even with their huge population, they can turn on a dime if they have to. Then you have the multinational corporations who don't answer to anyone but their boards. And the growing number of billionaires who are all but above the law."

Rapp nodded, thinking that this was just another example of what he had been thinking about—problems that he couldn't solve and wanted nothing to do with.

"The world used to be pretty much the same century after century, Mitch. And despite the fact that the earth is constantly moving beneath our feet, we need to figure out how to pull this country together. To put it back on top and position it to stay there."

"I don't envy you," Rapp said honestly. "But this is all way above my pay grade. I deal with external physical threats. That's it."

"What if that's not where the danger's coming from? What if it's coming from inside?"

"I don't know."

She nodded thoughtfully. "Good answer. Because it's not an easy question. Could you do me a favor, though, and put it in the back of your mind? Where do you think this country needs to go? How are we going to get there? And what role would you like to have in that? Because in Tony's administration your pay grade can be whatever you want it to be."

5

LIEUTENANT Jeremiah Grant wasn't sure if his current situation was best described as a shit show or a clusterfuck. But it was one of those for sure. In fact, he'd never been so sure of anything in his life.

It had all started out so well. He could still feel his initial elation at being put in command of this operation. *Naïve* wasn't a word he'd generally use to describe himself but, like *clusterfuck,* it fit perfectly. Of that, he was also dead certain.

Dead. Another word that would likely come in handy soon.

In his defense, being told that the president of the United States had personally requested his involvement in a critical mission was something he'd fantasized about since his G.I. Joe days. Virtually overnight, he found himself transferred to the big leagues. The leader of the free world had entrusted him with protecting God, country, and apple pie. One day, he might even find himself getting a medal hung around his neck in the Oval Office. He could almost picture the adoring faces of his friends and family as they watched.

The delusions of grandeur had faded quickly, though, leaving him with nothing but hard, ugly reality. While he had distinguished himself to some extent in both Iraq and Afghanistan, why would the new commander in chief have any idea who he was? And why would anyone pick an infantryman who had spent his combat career in the desert for this operation?

The pickup that Grant was riding in hit a particularly deep rut, nearly bouncing him from its rusty bed. Once stabilized, he went back to scanning the deep green of the surrounding mountains. There were probably more trees over one hundred square yards in Uganda than in the entire country of Afghanistan. He had virtually no experience fighting in this kind of terrain. He didn't even have experience living in it. Arizona born and bred.

Grant turned his attention to the men sitting around him and wondered if they shared his background. Because he honestly didn't know. He'd never fought with any of them and questions were very much discouraged. This wasn't the Middle East. This was secret agent shit.

One thing was obvious: they were all around the same age and outfitted in a mix of eco-touristy, off-the-shelf outdoor gear that would briefly—very briefly in his estimation—fool a local into thinking they were there to snap photos. What wasn't obvious is that all had M17 pistols hidden beneath their shirts and HK MP7s in their packs. In case things got ugly. Which he'd bet his meager life savings was exactly what was going to happen.

In the end, the situation was crazy and stupid, but not overly complicated. Four days ago, some egghead scientists may or may not have fled into the jungle when they'd been attacked by a psycho who thought he was God. The psycho in question had men—and children, apparently—searching for them, likely in hopes of securing a fat ransom. The Ugandan government didn't want to get involved because they were afraid of psycho-guy as well as not wanting to piss off the Congolese. And the Americans couldn't roll in a force of a few hundred men from Africa Command for political reasons that he didn't fully understand.

Like the situation, the mission was also equal parts crazy, stupid, and straightforward. Starting from a burned-out hospital, he would lead his eight men into the jungle, dodge an unknown number of armed cult members, and find these scientists who, after four days, were almost sure to be dead. Further, he was to do this with no outside support and intel that could be summed up as "it's two white guys and a Chinese chick. You can't miss them."

Piece of cake.

As he scanned the faces of his men, Grant felt his cynicism grow. He'd given money to the president's campaign and his wife had actually volunteered to help get the vote out. Did that have something to do with him being there? Did the men around him have similar stories? Because this was clearly the purview of a SEAL team or Delta or some of those crazy recon Marines. Men who had trained together, who specialized in these kinds of ops, and who had experience in this kind of terrain.

Did the White House figure he was so blinded by the radiance of Anthony Cook that he wanted to get his ass shot off? If so, they needed to think again. He'd supported Cook because the entire US political system needed an enema and he was the best bet at making that happen. The man wasn't the second coming, though. Just a politician who was maybe a little more competent and less sleazy than the others.

Or maybe not.

The vehicle began to slow, and Grant looked over the cab at the remains of something that only a few days ago had been a research facility funded by none other than Nicholas Ward. It wasn't much more than a burned-out ruin now, but the forest behind it was barely even singed. Based on the information he had, the fire had been set in a rainstorm that kept it from spreading. It seemed likely that Chism had been inside at the time and, as far as Grant was concerned, his barbecued corpse probably still was.

They stopped in what appeared to have been the parking lot and everyone climbed out.

"This is the place," their local guide said, raising his index finger toward the jungle to the east. "They would have had to escape to the—"

"Don't point," Grant said, assuming they were being watched. "Now get your gear together. I want to be out of here in ten minutes."

He looked around him at basically nothing. There was no reason for any of the facility's employees to return. There was nothing left that would interest looters. And the Ugandan responders had pronounced the debris free of bodies days ago. Gideon Auma's men were still in the area, though, taking the long-shot bet that the scientists were alive and out there somewhere.

His men had donned their packs and were similarly examining the tangled forest that they were about to wade into. Grant motioned them to the other side of the lot, away from their guide.

"Are we good?" he said when they formed around him.

All looked at each other, waiting for someone to say something. Finally, a man to Grant's right spoke up.

"What the hell are we doing here?"

"I don't think I understand the question . . ." He almost said "soldier" but managed to catch himself. This clandestine bullshit wasn't his thing.

The man—his man—pointed to the tree line. "There could be a battleship twenty feet away in there and we'd walk right by it. Do you have some kind of intel that we don't know about? Because, if so, I'd like to hear it. I'd like to hear that our plan isn't to wander around a hundred square miles of jungle hoping to bump into three scientists everyone knows are dead."

"We've all received the same briefing," Grant said.

"Then we are officially the most expendable sons of bitches on the planet."

"Were you ordered to take this mission?" Grant said.

"No. I—"

"Then stow it."

They fell silent for a few seconds, likely all lost in the same thoughts. Finally, another of his men nodded toward their guide. "What do we know about him?"

This one wasn't as fiery as the other. His tone was calm, and he had eyes that seemed to take in everything they passed over. Grant had a good intuition for men, and this was one who could be counted on. He'd remember that if—when—this thing blew up in their faces.

"Not much."

"He looks like he'd slit his own mother's throat for eight bucks."

Grant had come to roughly the same conclusion. He assumed that the intelligence side of this op—if that was indeed the correct word to use—had discovered that reputable tour companies tended not to operate in the same areas that Gideon Auma did. And that had left them scraping the bottom of the barrel for an asshole who probably spent more time guiding poaching expeditions than photographic ones.

"We'll let him take point," Grant said. "That way we can keep an eye on him."

That didn't seem to make anyone feel better.

"I have something else to say," his thoughtful man said. "Permission to speak freely?"

"Go ahead."

"Being expendable doesn't bother me. I knew I was expendable the day I walked into the recruiting office. But this is different. I feel like we've been set up to fail and now we're being led to slaughter. Nicholas Ward got his panties wadded up about losing his people and he promised some politician a bunch of campaign donations if he sent a rescue mission. And that politician said 'Sure, why not? We'll send a few dumbasses to Africa to put on a show. And when they're all dead, you can send over a check.'"

"Your point?" Grant said.

His man thought about the question for a moment, either not registering that it was rhetorical or choosing to ignore the fact.

"If I'm gonna die out here, I don't want to die a chump. When I go down, I at least want you assholes to know I did it with my eyes open."

The rest of the men grumbled in agreement. Grant remained silent for a long time, finally speaking at a level that wasn't much more than a whisper.

"What I say next doesn't ever get repeated. Does everyone understand? This goes to your grave."

Nods all around.

"We're going to wander around in the woods for a few days. We've got no choice in that. But I'm refocusing the primary objective of our mission."

"To what?" one of them asked.

"To us surviving. And if in the process we trip over David Chism alive, then great."

"And if we don't?" someone asked.

"Then fuck him."

6

RAPP kept to the speed limit, reacquainting himself with driving on the left as he wound through idyllic vineyards and farmland. Distant mountains were draped with clouds, but overhead the sky was a deep, unbroken blue. His window was down, and sixty-degree air was swirling around the vehicle Claudia had dropped off for him at the airport. With it came an unfamiliar sensation of peace that bordered on relief.

Unfamiliar, but not hard to understand. More and more, the United States felt like it was collapsing into some kind of internal Cold War. Views that only a few years ago would have been considered tinfoil-hat territory were now being discussed by straight-faced mainstream newscasters. Extremists on both sides of the political spectrum were flailing around breaking things with no apparent goals in mind other than to harm each other. And all the while, politicians did what they'd been doing for a thousand years—trying to figure out how to use it all to cling to power.

Being in Africa felt vastly different. Not that the entire continent wasn't hopelessly screwed up—it most definitely was. But it wasn't his problem. His problems were thousands of miles away. Far enough that if he didn't squint, they just disappeared.

The road turned to dirt and began to roll. When he reached the top of the first rise, he spotted the gray roof of the home he was looking for. His home.

A ten-foot stucco wall topped with broken glass ringed the property and the trees had been cut back almost to a neighboring farmer's vines, leaving an open perimeter with an unobstructed view. Beyond that, the scene probably hadn't changed much in the last century or so. A heavier gate. A few subtle cameras. More beneath the surface, but probably not enough. If they were going to start spending a significant amount of time there, security upgrades would have to become a priority.

The gate rolled back, revealing a pristine Cape Dutch house and two Rhodesian ridgebacks coming at his vehicle like heat-seeking missiles. He pulled in next to the armored SUV that Claudia so despised while the dogs barked uncontrollably and attacked his windows. He'd spent his entire life trying to not be remembered and it appeared to be working with them. Probably best to wait for a rescue.

The front door opened, and Claudia appeared wearing an apron and with one hand hidden behind her back. For a moment he held out hope that it was because she was holding the pistol he'd given her. When she waved, though, it turned out to be a wooden soup spoon.

His rescue came in the form of a seven-year-old girl with a missing upper incisor. Anna slipped around her mother and ran toward him waving her hands over her head.

"Friend! Friend!"

The dogs, seeing the object of their devotion coming across the grass, immediately ran to her. With the coast relatively clear, Rapp stepped out of the vehicle and grabbed his duffle from the back.

"We didn't think you were ever going to get here! It's been, like, hours!" Anna said as he crouched to give her a hug. The dogs eyed him suspiciously. They seemed to be waiting for her attention to waver long enough to turn him into a chew toy.

"My flight got delayed for a couple hours in London," he explained, lifting her in one arm and his bag in the other.

The dogs escorted them across the grass to Claudia, who threw her arms around both of them and pressed her lips to his.

"It's so good to have you home," she said when she pulled back. "Now come in and get something to eat. And don't worry. It's all on your training diet."

"How's school?" Rapp asked Anna as Claudia led them toward the kitchen.

"I already have a lot of friends. Including my best friend Ahmale. She's awesome. And she doesn't live very far from here. But it's not like in Virginia because people have big farms and yards and stuff. But still she's, like, a neighbor."

"Are you learning anything?"

"What? In school? Sure. Lots of stuff."

"Speaking of which," Claudia said in the French she tended to use with her daughter. "Is your homework done?"

"No," Anna responded in English, continuing the battle of wills between the two. "But I couldn't do it. I had to save Mitch from the dogs."

"Thanks for that," Rapp said sincerely.

"Well, he's safe now and you know the rule. Homework first, play later."

He put her down and she scurried off, glancing back as she did. "I'm going to hurry. Then I have a surprise!"

Rapp gave her the thumbs-up.

The century-old house's kitchen was quite a bit more austere than the one in the States, but Claudia had made the best of it. He wandered to a pot steaming on the stove and peeked under the lid.

"Shrimp bisque," she said. "But I substituted whole milk for the cream."

He ladled some out and took it to an old farm table by the open windows. Claudia brought him a plate piled with grilled vegetables and ringed with carpaccio before sitting.

"It's really good, thanks," he said through a mouthful.

"How'd shutting down the house go?"

"No problems."

"The animals?"

"Scott's got it under control."

"And you remembered that face sunscreen I wanted for Anna?"

"Three tubes in my bag."

She smiled. "I like the new Mitch Rapp. So calm. So efficient. So free of oozing wounds."

"I'm growing," he said, tearing off a piece of bread and using it to sop up a little olive oil.

"I think you are. And I think we could be really happy here if you're willing to give it a chance."

"I said I would, Claudia. And I meant it."

In fact, his meeting with the president—and even more so his wife—had made him mean it even more. He'd thought about his conversation with Catherine Cook for much of the thirty-hour trip there and come to a couple of conclusions: First, he probably was capable of evolving to meet the new threats facing America and the world. That realization was overshadowed by his second epiphany, though. That he wasn't sure he wanted to.

"But how do you feel about it?"

"Better than I thought."

She leaned back against the wall to examine him.

"What?"

"You're taking this too well."

"I thought that's what you wanted?"

When she spoke again, it was in French, the language she returned to when she needed to get across something nuanced. "I admire what you've done, Mitch. Everyone does. But it has to come to an end eventually. Maybe the change in administrations is fate giving you a reprieve."

"I feel like we've had this conversation before," Rapp responded in the same language.

"It's true. We have. But you weren't ready for it. Now, I'm wondering if you are."

"I'm not interested in getting myself into something I don't understand and don't know how to get out of. It's a little early to know how it's all going to play out, though. Maybe I never fire another gun again in my life."

"Or maybe you do."

He just shrugged.

"I'm not really asking you to change, Mitch. I like you the way you are. I just think it might be time to start turning down the volume a little bit. There must be some happy medium between what you do now and going into business making scented candles. We—"

"Done!" Anna shouted as she bounded through the door.

"With all of it?" her mother asked skeptically.

"One hundred percent. I left it on your desk so you can look at it."

"Excellent," Rapp said, anxious to escape this conversation. "Now what's my surprise?"

"Huh? Oh yeah! Your new bike came."

"Really? It's here? At the house?"

His idea of returning to the world of triathlons hadn't lasted long. Running those kinds of distances was too hard on the knees and the ocean that surrounded this part of Africa was full of great whites. The Cape Epic, on the other hand, was a four-hundred-and-fifty-mile mountain bike race through some of the most rugged terrain the continent had to offer. Perfect for someone who was still motivated but had a little wear and tear.

The competition was done by two-man teams and if he was going to get fast enough again to attract a local pro to partner with, his fifteen-year-old bike wouldn't cut it. And neither would his lily-white legs. There was a lot of work to be done, but he was strangely excited about it.

Anna grabbed his hand. "Come on! It's in the shed. But that's not the best part of the surprise. It's not even a surprise, really. You knew you were getting that. The surprise is that I got one, too! And it's pink. Yours is yucky green."

He let her drag him back through the front door and into the territory of the dogs still patiently waiting to tear him apart.

"And you don't need to find anyone to do that race you want to do anymore. I can go with you."

"Four hundred and fifty miles might be a little long for your first time at bat. And then there are the lions. And tigers. And bears."

"There are no bears here! Just lots of big antelope things. We call them bok. Besides, I've been practicing and I'm super fast. And it's only got two wheels, but I can ride it."

"On only two wheels?" he said as they walked through the cool air. "Prove it."

7

DAVID Chism suddenly realized he was holding his breath but still couldn't get his lungs going again. He was crouched in the cavelike depression that seemed to be transforming into his permanent home. The fronds and other foliage he'd placed in front of the opening were carefully maintained, replaced whenever they began to lose the emerald color of the rest of the forest.

He leaned in a little farther, peering through a tiny gap between them and into the bright sunlight beyond. The men that he'd heard talking came into view a few seconds later, walking along the steep slope about fifteen feet below. As expected, they were definitely not Ugandan army. One was wearing what could pass as fatigues, though they looked like they were about to rot off his body. The other was clad in jeans and a T-shirt silk-screened with a flaking Van Halen logo. His only nod to military chic was the assault rifle slung casually over his shoulder.

Neither was calling his name anymore. Those creepy, heavily accented wails had gone silent a couple of days ago. Whether that was due to strategy, hoarseness, or just boredom, he wasn't sure. What he was sure of, though, was that Auma hadn't given up his search and that there was still no sign of a cavalry charging to the rescue.

He followed the two men's movements obsessively, one hand on the living screen in front of him and knees sunk into the soft dirt. If they turned toward him to investigate the improbable wall of foliage, the plan was simple. He'd wait until they got within five feet, burst from cover, and charge. The slope was steep enough that if he could knock them over with enough force, they'd go careening down it without getting off a shot. Maybe a few shouts before they dropped over the forty-foot cliff into the jagged rocks below, but those would likely be absorbed by the forest before reaching the ears of their comrades.

What could possibly go wrong?

He managed to get some air into his lungs after they passed by but didn't get the rhythm of his breathing back until they were completely out of sight. Still lucky. For now, anyway.

The situation had changed significantly since their first night in what they'd dubbed the rat hole. Liu had stepped up beyond his wildest dreams. It turned out she hadn't grown up the privileged child of wealthy Beijing academics like he'd always assumed. Instead, she'd spent much of her youth living in a remote farmhouse, surviving on what her family could grow or raise. Once she'd accepted their new reality, her old survival skills had kicked in and she was quickly becoming his own personal ninety-seven-pound Rambo.

Thanks to her nocturnal expeditions, the ground was now largely covered with fronds and there was a well-camouflaged latrine about twenty yards to the east. Another—thankfully as yet unused—emergency latrine had been dug inside the cave in case their shaky water purification protocols failed them.

Finally, she'd fashioned a mobile cistern out of branches and a sheet of plastic he'd found, allowing them to collect water from the occasional rains and reducing the number of times he needed to make the dangerous journey to the river. Food was completely fruit based but provided them with enough calories to keep them from starving.

All in all, they could probably just outwait Auma's men if it hadn't been for one very big glitch: Matteo Ricci. The inevitable infection from his burns had set in and Chism was powerless to stop it. Antibiotics were the only thing that could help, and they were in short supply in the Ugandan jungle.

When he was dead sure the two men were gone, he glanced back at Liu, who was crouched with a jagged rock in her hand.

"We're safe," he whispered.

She dropped the rock and retreated to her homemade cistern. After wetting a piece of cloth, she crawled to Ricci and pressed it against his forehead. He was lying at the back of the cave, slipping in and out of consciousness. One day soon, he'd drift away and never come back.

The Italian reacted weakly to the cloth touching his forehead so Chism crawled over. "How are you feeling, Matteo?"

"Nothing a nice Barolo couldn't fix."

Like Liu, he'd turned out to be a lot tougher than Chism expected. His sense of humor had turned dark for sure, but it persisted.

"We only have the Cabernet," Chism responded, but Ricci was already out again.

"Not good," Liu said simply.

He nodded, staring down at Ricci's stubbled, sweat-streaked face. "Could you walk out of here by yourself, Jing?"

"What?"

"It's pretty much impossible to get lost. If you follow the setting sun you can't help but hit the road."

"I don't understand."

"Look, we know what's going on here. Those guys spent days shouting *my* name, not yours. They want to kidnap me and ransom me to Nick. If I give myself up, there's no reason for them to stay here. They'll go back to the rock they crawled out from under. When they do, you go for help and get Matteo to a hospital."

Ricci's head lolled toward them and his hollow eyes opened. "That's the stupidest idea I have ever heard, David."

"What? Why?"

"You're just going to hand yourself over to one of the most sadistic psychopaths in the world?"

"It's not like I'm excited about it, Matteo. But why would they kill me? I'm the golden goose, right?"

"They'll kill you because they're pumped full of drugs and ecstatic visions."

"Maybe," Chism said. "But . . ." He found it impossible to finish his thought, so Ricci did it for him.

"But I won't last the weekend?"

"Probably not."

The Italian waved a hand dismissively. "I don't mean to sound overly noble, but who am I? A sixty-year-old, chain-smoking scientist of moderately above average abilities. My wife is dead and neither of my children have spoken to me in years. But you, David . . . You're a man who can change the world. And as for Jing. There are many things that can happen to a lone woman between here and the road."

8

IT'S not as nice as mine."

Rapp glanced over at Anna, who was sitting on an old crate looking unimpressed. The outbuilding they were in probably hadn't been used in a half century, but with almost two thousand feet of floor space, it looked like he was finally going to get the gym he'd been denied in Virginia. Kind of a long-term plan as the roof was barely intact, the foundation appeared to be sinking, and there was no glass in any of the window frames. But with a lot of work, the potential was there. Like it was for the man standing at the center of it.

"I think those streamers you have coming out of the handlebars might compromise aerodynamics."

"I don't even know what that means. Ahmale—my new best friend, you know—has ones just like them. They're awesome."

Rapp pulled a set of carbon fiber wheels from a box and began installing a tire. The mountain bike had been custom built for him, but his new road bike was off the shelf and needed upgrades before it was ready to ride.

"Maybe I'll get a set, then. Do you know how much they weigh?"

Anna shook her head disapprovingly, threw a leg over her new bike, and pedaled off. The dogs joined her just outside the bay doors, ignoring him as they fell in behind. He took that as a sign of progress in their relationship.

There was a group of local racers that did a training ride every Tuesday and he was interested in checking out the level of talent. A few months ago, he'd had some testing done at the human performance lab at Old Dominion University and the news wasn't entirely bad. His battle with Yemeni Acute Respiratory Syndrome didn't seem to have done any permanent damage and his ability to consume oxygen had declined only about ten percent from his triathlon years. He figured he could knock that back to six or seven percent with the right training and let his increased capacity to suffer carry the rest.

On the downside, his ability to produce power on a bike had gone to shit from disuse and he had a lot of upper-body muscle that wasn't going to do him any favors on climbs. With sufficient time—something he appeared to now have—and sufficient determination—something he'd never lacked—all were surmountable problems.

So now it was just a matter of finding a good local coach and maybe getting a little cortisone in his knee. After that, he could start down the path of answering the question of how fast he could get.

Unfortunately, that path also led to a more complicated question. Would it be enough? Home. Family. Racing. Building out the gym. Cocktails with the neighbors. And then there was the long view. If he was setting a course to actually survive into old age, what then? Knee replacements? Prostate problems? Breaking the thumbs of Anna's first boyfriend for bringing her home past curfew? Fuck. Golf?

Too much reflection for one day, he decided. Introspection was a skill he was going to have to work up to. Rain was forecasted for the afternoon and he wanted to get in a quick workout before it rolled in. Then maybe a piece of the pie Claudia had cooling in the kitchen.

A very small piece.

His phone rang and he reached out a greasy hand to check the identity of the caller. After a quick wipe of his fingers on his shop apron, he picked up.

"Hello, Irene."

"How's Africa?"

"Sixty degrees and sunny. For the next few hours anyway."

"And the ladies?"

"All good."

"I'm happy to hear it. What about you?"

"Living the dream."

"Should I believe that? Probably not. Now tell me. What did you think of the president?"

Rapp considered the question for a moment. "I think Mike has him pegged. Smart, ambitious, charismatic. And he likes the chair."

"I understand that you had an opportunity to meet Catherine, too."

"Yeah."

"And?"

"My general impression is that she's not a woman to be fucked with."

"Agreed. Perhaps even less so than her husband. If I had to guess, I'd say that she's positioning herself to follow in his footsteps. She'll only be fifty if he serves two terms."

"Wouldn't surprise me."

"So, do you see yourself as having a part in their administration?"

"I don't know. I couldn't shake the feeling that this is all about them and not the country. To some extent, they're all like that, though. Are the Cooks worse? Or was I just used to Josh Alexander? I was pretty young when I first met him."

"And now you're older and wiser."

"Or just more cynical. But the country needs someone to lead it out of the ditch it's run itself into. And that's going to take some power. Maybe Anthony Cook is the right man for the job."

"Or precisely the wrong one," Kennedy countered. "Power's like a drug. In the right dose, it saves lives. Too much, though, and it becomes deadly."

"I guess the next three and a half years will tell."

"You sound a bit disconnected for a man who was standing in the Oval Office a couple of days ago."

"I'm trying."

"My understanding from Mike is that they were both quite impressed by you."

"They're impressed by what they think I can do for them."

"And what is that exactly?"

"Am I being interrogated? Because that's what it feels like. What about you, Irene? I've known you half my life and it's pretty clear you don't like or trust them. Are you staying?"

"I don't know. At some point a decision is going to be forced on me, but it hasn't happened yet."

"Well, here's something I'm sure of. When you go, I go. But for now, I'm happy to sit on the sidelines. If the Cooks blow up, I don't want it to be in my face."

"You want it to be in mine."

He laughed. "If those are my two choices, then yeah."

"It sounds like you have some time on your hands. And if that's the case, maybe you'd have a few minutes to talk to a friend of mine."

"About what?"

"He has a problem you might be able to help him with."

Rapp looked at the bike he was working on. He wanted to say no, but it wasn't going to happen. Like Scott Coleman, she'd always been there for him. Even when she should have run away screaming.

"Sure. When?"

"If he was at your house in a half an hour, would that work?"

Again, he laughed. "I hate being predictable."

"You are never that," she said and then disconnected the call.

He tossed his phone back on the workbench. So much for his afternoon training session.

The arrival of Irene Kennedy's friend wasn't exactly what Rapp expected. Not that he'd had anything particular in mind, but a motorcade of three SUVs so heavily armored that they blurred the lines between civilian and military wasn't it.

"I guess it could have been worse," Claudia said as they stood together on the front porch. "You could have bought me one of those."

"They were back-ordered," he joked.

"Thank goodness. The other parents at Anna's school already think I'm crazy."

"Speaking of Anna . . ." he said as the motorcade glided to a stop inside the courtyard.

"The dogs are with her in her room. I told her she had to stay there until everyone leaves."

The first men out of the vehicles were serious pros. Probably former operators from Eastern Europe, though Rapp didn't know any of them personally. He doubted any were much older than thirty. Once they'd had a chance to familiarize themselves with their environment, another man stepped out using a hand to shade his eyes against the sun. He was early sixties, with a full head of hair starting to gray and stylish glasses. Despite his age, he looked reasonably fit, with a runner's build beneath casual jeans and a white linen shirt.

Claudia let out a long breath. "I better go dig out the good china."

She disappeared inside as the world's first trillionaire started toward the house. One thing that had to be said about Irene Kennedy: she had an interesting group of friends.

"Mitch," he said, extending a hand. "Nick Ward. It's a real pleasure to meet you."

"Likewise," Rapp said, taking it. The grip wasn't as overbearing as he'd have expected from someone with Ward's bank account, and his easy smile was more sincere than the ones plastered around Washington. A man who no longer had anything to prove.

"Beautiful place you have here."

"Thanks. We're set up out back. Will that work for you? It's pretty nice in the sun."

"Sounds great. Thank you."

Rapp routed him through the house, stopping briefly for an introduction to Claudia. When they exited onto the patio, he pointed Ward to a weathered table in the grass.

"I appreciate you agreeing to see me," he said as he took a seat. "Particularly on such short notice."

"I have a hard time saying no to Irene."

Ward grinned. "She seems to have that effect on people. Including me."

"You know her?"

Claudia appeared and instead of answering, Ward chatted amiably with her as she laid out a few hors d'oeuvres and a coffee service.

"What about your men, Nick? Can I get them something?"

He shook his head. "They only eat and drink things they've packed themselves. It seems kind of paranoid to me, but I don't interfere."

She nodded, gave him a quick smile, and hurried away. It took a lot to intimidate her, but the richest man in history apparently rated. It was more than the money, though; it was the man himself. What he'd created. What he'd accomplished. What he'd dedicated the latter part of his life to. Love him or hate him, he was impressive as hell.

"So, what is it I can do for you?" Rapp asked, pouring them each a cup of coffee.

"Can I assume you're aware of what happened to David Chism and his people in Uganda?"

"Just what I've seen on the news. You had a facility there and it was attacked by Gideon Auma. If I remember right, he killed the facility's director and burned the place to the ground with your people inside."

"No bodies have been found and Auma's people are still in the area. Until a couple of days ago, they were actively calling out David's name."

"Remind me. How long ago did this happen?"

"Six days."

Rapp took a sip of his coffee and looked past Ward toward the colorful bougainvillea climbing the wall. "Take it from a guy who's done it, Nick. Surviving in the jungle with what I assume was no food or equipment isn't easy. Particularly for people who've spent their lives in labs and universities."

"Actually, David worked with Doctors Without Borders in some of the most dangerous countries in the world, and Jing Liu grew up on a farm with no electricity or running water."

"Look," Rapp said. "If we were talking about three days, I might feel different. But six? You're clinging to hope that isn't there."

"The good thing about being a man in my position is that you have the resources to cling to anything you want."

Rapp leaned back and folded his arms across his chest. "You're about to ask me to fly to Uganda and find your people, aren't you?"

"Yes."

"This seems like a job for the government, Nick. Africa Command could coordinate with the Ugandans and send enough people to clear out Auma's men. Some problems can be solved by a small group of highly trained men. With others, you're better off having five hundred and heavy equipment. This is probably in the second category."

"I don't disagree, Mitch. I talked to the president personally only a few days ago. In fact, Irene was at the meeting."

"And?"

"I left the White House without any promises, but it's my understanding that a small force was sent into the jungle two days ago. As far as I know, though, they have no support and no solid intelligence."

"Where did you get that information?"

He shrugged. "I hear things."

Rapp wondered if it was from Kennedy. The fact that she'd sent Ward to see him suggested strongly that she wanted him to get involved. And that she wanted to keep her distance.

"I'm not sure I'm the best man for the job, Nick. My record isn't great when it comes to saving medical researchers from terrorists."

"Victoria Schaefer," the man responded. "An incredible tragedy. But the way you stopped those terrorists from getting YARS across the Mexican border was incredible. And I understand you contracted it. That you almost died."

Rapp neither acknowledged nor denied what Ward had said. The entire episode was beyond top secret. The public had been fed a story about ISIS trying to smuggle radioactive materials into the United States and credit for stopping the shipment had gone to border patrol.

"You're surprised I know about that," Ward said. "You shouldn't be. Irene Kennedy is a woman who always has a backup plan. She was confident that you'd succeed, but not absolutely sure. And in the face of that kind of uncertainty, who gets a call?"

"You and David Chism," Rapp responded.

"Exactly. David was already well into putting together a team to deal with a YARS outbreak when you made it unnecessary. And I think that highlights his importance pretty well. In fact, I'd go so far as to say that he's the most important person in the world right now. Make no mistake, the number one threat to humanity is pandemic." Ward leaned forward and propped his elbows on the table. "I don't know when it's coming, but I guarantee that it is. And this time it could cost billions of lives. David is our first—maybe only—line of defense."

A skeptical frown spread across Rapp's face.

"You don't believe me?" Ward said.

"I'm sure he's smart, but he's still one man. There are hundreds of pharmaceutical companies and thousands of scientists working on this kind of thing."

"There are hundreds of intelligence agencies and thousands of operatives working across the globe. And yet you're widely regarded as being unique."

"If I was susceptible to flattery, I would have been dead a long time ago, Nick."

"It was worth a try."

"Right."

Ward leaned back in his chair again. "David found something that all coronaviruses have in common. Based on that, he might be able to create a vaccine that would protect people against all of them—right down to the common cold."

"And that's a big deal?"

"One of the biggest in history. I mean, you dealt with a bioattack but that's not the real threat. The real threat is something rising up naturally. Out of a Chinese wet market. Or from someone eating bush meat. Or humans going into a cave where humans haven't been before. You experienced this directly. If something as deadly as YARS were to get out into the population, it would be game over."

That wasn't an exaggeration, Rapp knew. He'd just lived through a blackout that had killed hundreds of thousands of Americans and that would have killed a few hundred million more if it had continued. What would happen in a serious pandemic? One that took out huge numbers of people in their prime? The machinery that kept modern civilization afloat would fail. And it would happen in the blink of an eye.

"Okay, you've convinced me that your man is important. But he's also almost sure to be dead. And, while the president might be willing to send people to wander around a jungle full of Gideon Auma's men, I'm not. I take the safety of my team seriously. To me, this sounds like all risk and no reward."

Ward nodded thoughtfully. "I concede that there's a good chance that David's dead. But Gideon Auma doesn't seem to think so or he'd have pulled out. And the idea that I want you and your men to go wander around the jungle hoping to get lucky is flat-out wrong. I don't operate that way and I wouldn't expect you to. What I'm asking you to do is devise a safe, effective plan and then execute it."

"You're talking about a lot of money to chase a ghost. Equipment and good people don't come cheap."

Ward smiled and reached for his coffee. "Everything's cheap to me, Mitch."

9

THE CIA's Gulfstream G5 wasn't a bad way to fly, but it wasn't the only way. As hard as it was to believe, it had been six months since Rapp had last been on a chopper—freezing his ass off and bleeding all over everything. This time he had no bullet wounds, temperatures were in the high seventies, and there wasn't a cloud in the sky. He was sitting on the floor of the cabin with his legs hanging out, savoring the hurricane of rotor wash.

He'd been surprised by how enthusiastic Claudia had been about him accepting Nick Ward's offer, but now he was starting to understand. He'd tackled changing his life with the same all-or-nothing, sheer-force-of-will approach that he brought to everything in life. Maybe that wasn't the answer here. Maybe trying to turn himself into a devoted family man, bike racer, and gentleman farmer overnight was overly ambitious. Normality wasn't something he'd experienced since college, and it might be better to ease in.

"We're coming up on the hospital," the pilot said over Rapp's headphones. "I'll swing around so you can get a good look."

"Roger that, Fred."

The deep green of the mountaintop they were skimming suddenly dropped away, leaving hundreds of feet of air beneath his boots. He squinted into the sun as they banked to follow a red scar of a road winding through the valley below.

The terrain wasn't that different than what surrounded his house in Virginia, though the flora seemed significantly denser. They weren't far from Bwindi Impenetrable National Park and based on what he was seeing, it was accurately named.

Even at altitude, David Chism's research campus was hard to miss—a black stain on the otherwise unbroken green of the landscape. A few charred walls were still standing but it didn't look like it would take much more than a stiff breeze to collapse them. Some of the site had been excavated in what Rapp had been told was a thorough search for bodies. Apparently, a hidden safe room had been found intact but empty.

The takeaway was that Chism and his people hadn't died in the fire. Based on a couple of eyewitnesses, he would have had to run into the flames and out the back in order to escape. It had been night and the rain was reported as heavy, making it possible for him to reach the forest without being seen. Possible. But plausible?

"You ready to move on, Mitch?"

"Yeah. Nothing much to see. Go ahead and take us into camp."

The helicopter banked north, heading for one of the tallest peaks in the area. In the distance, Rapp could just make out Lake Edward, which was split about evenly between Uganda and the Democratic Republic of the Congo.

When they reached the mountaintop, Fred Mason swung around in a wide circle. He'd been Rapp's go-to pilot for a long time and knew that his passenger would want an overview before they set down.

As expected, Scott Coleman had chosen an ideal location for their base of operations. The sides of the mountain were unusually steep and covered in the dense tangle of foliage that was so ubiquitous in the region. The peak, in contrast, was rocky, relatively flat, and contained only a few widely spaced trees. Three choppers were already on the ground and canvas tents of various sizes had been erected, as had solar panels and diesel generators.

Roughly twenty men were setting up equipment, transporting supplies, or had been strategically posted around the clearing. Coleman always ran a tight ship, and this was no exception. It looked like he was only a few hours from having the camp fully online.

Mason landed under the watchful eye of the perimeter guards and Rapp jumped out. Coleman was standing by but didn't approach, instead waiting for Rapp to emerge from the swirling dust before falling in alongside him.

"Give me a sitrep."

"We're in better shape than I would have thought at this point. Twenty-three guys on-site and another twelve en route."

"Really?" Rapp said, not bothering to hide his surprise. Mercenaries were a dime a dozen, but ones they were willing to work with were rare. Probably no more than fifty worldwide and always booked.

"Yeah. Based on what you told me, I called and asked how much it would cost for them to drop everything and get on a plane. Then I said yes to whatever number they threw at me."

"Money talks," Rapp said as they closed in on a large tent near the center of the improvised complex.

"To men, yes. But equipment's been harder. There's just not that much in the area."

"What about the Ugandan government?"

"Ward's been working on them, but they don't want military aircraft being seen this close to the DRC. So, they're happy to run on at the mouth about how supportive they are of this rescue effort but when you try to turn that talk into action you hit a brick wall. It's not the end of the world, though. We can get by with civilian aircraft. Some of it's military surplus, so retrofitting weapons and armor isn't too difficult. Particularly with Ward passing out blank checks."

"What about this place? Is it secure?"

"We're mostly counting on natural barriers, but they're pretty significant. Getting people up the side of this mountain in enough numbers to attack us would be almost impossible. And even if they did manage it, we'd see them coming in plenty of time for a leisurely evacuation. The only way you're going to hit this place is from the air, and Gideon Auma doesn't have that capability. You know, other than the fact that they say he can fly and shoot fireballs out of his ass."

They entered a tent full of communications gear and Coleman fished a couple of Cokes from a cooler before throwing one to Rapp.

"What are we hearing about the US team?"

Coleman dropped into a folding chair and put his feet on a table. "Nada. I've talked to my SEAL friends, Delta, you name it. No one knows anything about the operation. Are you sure your information's good? I'm finding it a little hard to believe a bunch of guys I've never heard of just walked into the jungle a few days ago with no support."

"I hear what you're saying but I talked to Irene and she seems to think it's real."

Coleman frowned and ran a hand through his blond hair. "Okay, then it probably is. But it'd be nice to have a few more details. If we've got friendlies wandering around in our operating theater, better to know about it now than after we accidentally shoot them."

"Have you talked to Dan Lombard about it?"

"The head of Africa Command? That's your social strata, man. I'm just a simple sailor."

Rapp pulled out his satellite phone and found the number he'd thought to program in before leaving the Cape.

"General Lombard's office," a woman on the other side announced.

"Is he in? This is Mitch Rapp."

"One moment, please."

Rapp polished off his Coke and tossed it in the direction of a trash can on the other side of the tent. It bounced off the rim and landed in the dirt.

"Mr. Rapp," the woman said when she came back on. "The general has asked if he can call you right back. Is this a good number?"

The inflection she gave to the word *good* suggested she meant secure.

"Yeah. This one's fine," he said before disconnecting the call.

"Out?" Coleman asked.

Rapp shook his head. "I don't think he wants to talk to me on an office phone."

In less than five seconds, a ringtone sounded and Rapp picked up. "Danny. What the hell's going on over there?"

"Nothing good. But there are whispers about a certain SEAL you know operating in Uganda."

"Africa's full of crazy rumors. What about you? Do you have anyone in Uganda?"

"No, I don't."

This time it was the emphasis on *I* that was telling.

"Who does?"

"I'm not sure."

"Guess."

There was a brief pause over the line. "Okay. This is what I'm hearing. Nine American soldiers went into the jungle three days ago with orders to find David Chism."

"Delta?" Rapp asked.

"I don't think so. I've made a few quiet inquiries and can't find anyone in special forces who knows anything about this. Word is that all nine men were pulled from different units, but I don't know which ones."

"Who's supporting them?"

"As near as I can tell, no one."

"Bullshit, Danny. They're not just standing around in the woods holding their dicks."

"Look, here's what I can tell you. I'm not supporting them. The Ugandans sure as hell aren't supporting them. And, according to my source in military intelligence, they aren't supporting them. Honestly, this thing stinks to high heaven of the Agency. But now you're telling me it's not."

"Who sent them, then?"

"It sounds like the orders filtered down from on high. How high I can't say."

"Shit," Rapp said quietly.

"That pretty much sums it up."

"Can you give me a way to contact them?"

"Like I told you, I can't even give you their names."

"Maybe you're not trying hard enough."

"Don't break my balls, Mitch. There are nine men who've been thrown to the wolves in my backyard. I've done everything I can to get involved and come up empty."

"Okay, then tell me why? What's the point of sending them in like this?"

"I don't know. The truth is I don't know anything anymore. It's all politics. I can't take a dump without a written decree from the Oval Office."

"That's been going on since we got into this business, Danny."

"No. It's different now, Mitch. And I don't want any part of it. At the end of the month, I'm taking my retirement and heading for the beach. If you're smart, you'll do the same."

10

"**W**OULD you care to tell me what's happening in Uganda?" The president didn't look up from the document he was reading, nor offer Irene Kennedy a chair. In light of that, she remained standing, as did a very nervous-looking Mike Nash.

"Could you be more specific, sir?"

Anthony Cook threw the document on his blotter and fixed his gaze on her. "I'm not in the mood, Irene. Trust me."

"Then let me assume you're referring to the David Chism situation. The last time we spoke, you said that you'd give it some thought and that we shouldn't get involved. We haven't."

"We haven't?" he said incredulously. "I'm being told there's a rescue operation being carried out and that Mitch Rapp is leading it. Not only did I say that I didn't want *America* involved without my direct authorization, I specifically said I didn't want *him* involved."

Cook was extraordinarily well informed, Kennedy noted. Rapp's operation was still in the early stages and was being carried out by private contractors in a remote corner of Uganda. Who had provided the president with such timely intelligence?

And then there was also the issue of the nine US soldiers who were rumored to have gone into the jungle four days ago. She had to be extremely cautious about looking into the matter and because of that wasn't well informed on the subject. Did they know something she didn't about Chism's whereabouts? How were they being supported? What was the status of their mission? For that matter, were they even still alive?

"Mitch decides himself what he does and doesn't do, sir. He hasn't been on my payroll for some time. It's my understanding that Nick hired Scott Coleman's organization to search for his people. Mitch and Scott have known each other for a long time and Mitch is currently living in South Africa. I imagine that's how he got involved."

"I don't pay you to imagine!" he shouted, slamming a hand down on the Resolute Desk.

"No," she said, keeping her voice even. "But you do pay me to follow your orders And, in this case they were clear. If your position's changed and you'd like me to dig deeper, I'd be happy to."

"So, you're going to stand there and tell me that you had nothing to do with putting Nicholas Ward and Mitch Rapp together."

Mike Nash interjected on her behalf. "Scott's outfit is well known as being the best of the best, sir, and Nicholas Ward doesn't work with second stringers. It makes perfect sense that he'd hire them, just like it makes perfect sense that Scott would call Mitch knowing that he was basically right down the street. In his position, I would have done the same thing."

Nash's words seemed to have a calming effect on Cook that Kennedy's very much didn't. The former Marine had a natural gift for handling politicians and that gift seemed especially effective on the current residents of the White House. Surprisingly effective, really.

"I want Rapp's team out of there," Cook said. "It's been a week with no word from Chism or any of his people. Rapp's too valuable to be chasing a dead man through the jungle."

The concern for Rapp's safety seemed overblown. Certainly, he'd survived much more dangerous missions than this one. Was it just ego? The fact that Cook felt as though he'd been defied? Was he concerned that the soldiers he'd sent would fail and a group of mercenaries would succeed? That seemed plausible—Anthony Cook was not a man who liked to appear weak—but still unlikely. He'd have figured out that he could plausibly blame the failure on Coleman's team's interference or just take credit for their success.

She was convinced that there was something she was missing. Something that was right in front of her that she was blind to. Maybe it would be worth pushing a little to see if Cook would provide a clue.

"Nick seems to have a lot of faith in David Chism's resourcefulness and there's no question that he's operated in difficult environments in the past. The truth is that hiding in terrain that dense wouldn't be all that difficult and there's plenty of food and wat—"

"Enough!" the president said, cutting her off. "These aren't Japanese soldiers who don't know World War II ended. They're three academics, one of whom is in his sixties. They're not living in a hole, drinking rainwater, and snaring rodents. They're dead, Irene. And Mitch and his people will be, too, if they get ambushed by Auma's psychopaths or go down in some cobbled-together Ugandan helicopter. And then America's lost the point of its spear. Pull them out. Now."

Again, Nash tried to reduce the temperature of the room. "We'll do what we can, Mr. President. But if SEAL Demolition and Salvage has signed a contract with Ward, it's unlikely Scott's going to walk away. He lives and dies by his reputation and leaving the richest man in the world hanging isn't going to do much for it. Mitch is basically the same story. If Scott's asked for his help and he's agreed, he's going to take that seriously."

"More seriously than America's national security?" Cook said, picking up the document he'd been reading earlier. "This isn't up for discussion. I'm giving you an order. Get them out of there. Now."

11

"So, there's no way we can get in touch with the US team you think is on the ground? They must have some kind of communications. Even if it's a personal satphone."

Rapp wasn't sure who had spoken but recognized the accent as Dutch. The tent was packed—not just with Scott Coleman's core team but with the other operators they'd managed to bring in. A few had been left on the perimeter but everyone else was here, heating up the confined space and permeating it with the stench of sweat.

"That operation is completely black—probably put together by the president and the head of the Joint Chiefs personally. We don't even know who they are, and no one wants to push the issue." Rapp scanned the faces around him. "And that brings me to a related subject. It's my understanding the president wants us out of here. More than that, he's pretty much ordered us out of here."

Many of the men shrugged. A few laughed. Not surprising, since the majority weren't American and had no reason to concern themselves with the wishes of Anthony Cook. Rapp turned his attention to Coleman. "Scott?"

"Are you saying he's offering to buy out my contract with Ward?"

"Nobody's told me about there being any money on the table."

"Then I don't work for him and he can kiss my ass."

Based on their expressions, everyone on his team felt the same way.

"All right. Then let's move on. If those soldiers are out there, Auma's aware of it. He'll be tracking their movements in case they know something about Chism that he doesn't."

"That puts us in a tough spot," Coleman said. "If we start up a big operation on top of them, Auma might see them as having outlived their usefulness and attack."

"I agree, but there's nothing we can do about it at this point. If Chism and his people are alive, their clock is ticking."

"So, the American force is on its own," someone said.

Rapp nodded. "Chism's our mission. If we find ourselves in a position to help the others, we'll do it. But it's a secondary consideration. Understood?"

Murmurs of assent.

"All right," Rapp said. "That brings us to the question of how we're going to do it." He tapped a black circle on a map propped on an easel. "This is the hospital Chism theoretically escaped from. Because of difficult terrain and a best-case estimate of their capabilities, we think they're inside this perimeter. If we disregard some of the steeper terrain that wouldn't be navigable by them and keep in mind that they'd need to be reasonably close to a water source, that leaves the areas shaded in red. Not an insignificant amount of territory to cover, but also not half the country."

"From a difficulty standpoint, though, you've got to multiply it by fifty," Joe Maslick said. "I mean, we could walk within five feet of them and never know it if they weren't making noise."

"Agreed. We're never going to find them. That's why we need them to find us."

"Am I wrong, or does it sound like you've got a plan?" Charlie Wicker said.

"I have a plan," Rapp confirmed. "We've got a pretty solid profile on Chism and in the last couple days we've managed to send investigators to talk to his friends and family. One of the things we learned is that he's an amateur naturalist and pretty good with a map and compass. We can use that."

"How?" somebody asked.

"We're bringing in more choppers and tonight we're going to go out and bury caches in the areas where he could be hiding. Then we're going to drop maps with instructions on how to find them."

"I don't think this plan will work," a man near the open tent flap said. The ebony skin and accent suggested he wasn't too far from home. Rapp didn't know him personally, but Coleman had used him on a number of African operations and was a fan.

"Why?"

"You are right that a lot of the men who follow Gideon Auma aren't going to speak English or know how to read. But he's much smarter than people think and uses technology very well. He will have teams, and each will have a satellite phone. Even if they can't read the maps, they will be able to take a picture and send it to someone who can. If Chism gets to one of your caches, they will be waiting for him."

"We thought exactly the same thing. So, we used what we learned about him to write out instructions only he'll understand." Rapp stepped away from the map and once again examined the men crowded in around him. "Sunset's in two hours. The choppers will start coming in an hour after that. Scott has your assignments. Any questions?"

Everyone just shook their heads.

12

CLOUDS had rolled over the stars, erasing the mountainous landscape and highlighting a few points of light emanating from distant villages. Behind the foliage screen Chism had built, the darkness was so deep as to become disorienting. Every time he tried to move around the cave, his balance failed him and an irrational fear that he'd gone blind surged.

On the somewhat brighter side, the empty void surrounding him had heightened his other senses. He could smell the direction of the wind through changes in the proportion of earth, rotting plant life, and mold. He could hear Matteo Ricci's labored breathing and the more rhythmic respiration of Jing Liu. The night's cold sank more deeply into him but not so much that he couldn't feel the bugs that he no longer bothered to brush away.

Most of all, though, he felt thirst. They'd had no rain in days and trips to the stream to fill his pathetic water bottle needed to be carefully managed. Auma's men were still out there. Silent now. Waiting for him to make a mistake.

By his count, they'd been there almost a week and a half. Pretty fucking impressive for three pampered scientists, but also concerning. If no rescue effort had been mounted by now, it seemed unlikely that one was forthcoming. Everyone would assume they were dead.

Ricci began a coughing fit and Chism felt his stomach tighten. The Italian wasn't going to last much longer. There was no way to measure his fever, but it was high enough that he was no longer lucid. The infection was too strong for his body to fight off. Without antibiotics, his life was over.

Jing Liu, though, was a whole other story. With every day, she got even stronger, shaking off her privileged adulthood and returning to the impoverished child she'd once been. Her stomach seemed impervious to both their haphazard diet and the questionable water they were surviving on. She slept like a rock. And she was tireless in doing whatever she could for Ricci. Apparently, it was a role she'd played for her dying grandfather.

The bottom line was that, of the three of them, she'd almost certainly be the one who held out the longest. And that made turning himself over to Auma's men seem smarter and smarter every day. There was no longer any question that she could make it to the road and bring back help for Ricci. All she needed was for Auma's men to clear out.

Chism sat and pulled his knees to his chest. Time to put on his big-boy pants and be the hero. When Liu woke up and he wasn't there, she'd figure out pretty quickly what he'd done. Then she'd wait another day or so to ensure that the coast was clear and make a break for civilization.

What was he so worried about? Obviously, there were the stories about Auma's sect. The cannibalism. The crucifixions. The castrations. And that was just the Cs. But Auma needed him. He wouldn't be worth much with his balls sawed off, nailed to a cross, or half-eaten.

He was lucky, right?

He let out a long breath and closed his eyes. No rush. The sun had only set an hour or so ago. He could procrastinate a little longer.

Enjoy the closeness of his friends and the illusion of safety that the cave provided.

Just a little longer . . .

Chism bolted awake, confused by what had suddenly forced him back to reality. It didn't take long for him to figure it out, though.

A helicopter.

He rolled to his knees and peered through a gap in the branches, feeling a surge of adrenaline when he saw that it wasn't *a* helicopter. It was at least five—flying low and playing their powerful lights over the canopy.

"*David Chism*," a male voice said over a megaphone. "*We're dropping supply caches and maps on how to find them. Get to one and use the phone to call us. We'll set up an extraction.*"

He felt Liu lean against him from behind, trying to see through the same hole. "They've come to save us," she said. "Mr. Ward sent them, yes? It has to be. Gideon Auma has no helicopters."

The amplified American voice started up again, repeating the same recorded message.

"David?" Liu prompted.

He found himself unable to respond. The slow loss of hope over the last few days had dulled his fear to the point that it had become nothing more than a drone in the back of his mind. Now, with the possibility of rescue flying overhead, he was terrified.

Lieutenant Jeremiah Grant was on point, giving speed and stealth roughly equal consideration as he slipped through the dense forest. All pretense at being an eco-tour group had been abandoned and it was a significant relief. No more fawning over rare plants, zooming in on colorful birds, or oohing and aahing over local mammals. But most of all, no more listening to the loud and largely inaccurate nature lectures from their scumbag guide.

And now, finally, something was happening. The question was what?

One thing he knew for certain was that he and his team were being watched and had been since the moment they'd penetrated the jungle. He was fifty-fifty that their guide was somehow communicating with the people tracking them and eighty-twenty that they would eventually be targeted. If Auma's men found David Chism—or more likely his corpse—then the American team wandering around the forest would become useless to them. And Auma's reputation was to kill anything that didn't directly benefit him. Even worse would be if Grant were the one to find Chism. At that point, they would find themselves standing between Gideon Auma and what he wanted.

Heads they win, tails we lose.

It was a sentiment he'd tried to get across a few times to a nameless, faceless man on the other end of his satellite phone. Every description of the futility of their situation, no matter how graphic, simple, or emphatic, fell on deaf ears. The response from the bored, bureaucratic-sounding son of a bitch was always the same: keep searching.

It had been the same story for thousands of years. The rich and powerful tossed poor slobs like him into the meat grinder whenever they found it convenient. Grant—and apparently his men—had thought Anthony Cook was different. But now it was clear that he was just another carefully crafted illusion.

A chopper—one of many crowding the normally empty skies—passed overhead, but Grant didn't bother to look up. With the powerful spotlight shining down on the canopy it would be impossible to see any detail. A now familiar recorded voice rose over the thump of the blades.

"*David Chism. We're dropping supply caches and maps on how to find them. Get to one and use the phone to call us. We'll set up an extraction.*"

No shooting, though. Auma's men were playing it cool. Probably calling back to their god for instructions.

Another five minutes brought Grant to what he'd been looking for. He stopped and crouched in the darkness before toggling his throat mike.

"I'm at the edge of the clearing."

His men would fan out to provide cover while he searched the open area through a night vision scope. Nothing. But it was hard to know if that conclusion was real or just the result of the limitations of his optics. Not that it mattered. He didn't have anywhere to be and eventually one of the choppers would provide an unintentional assist.

It took twenty minutes, but finally a helicopter streaked overhead, dropping four pink streamers that glimmered in the spotlight. Two disappeared into the jungle, one got hung up in a tree to the west, and the last dropped right in the center of the clearing. He focused on that one, doing his best to memorize its location as the darkness once again descended.

"I'm going in," he said, easing into the grass on his belly.

His low position would make him virtually impossible to see, but that went both ways. Every minute or so, he was forced to lift his head and make a course correction. Not ideal, but an acceptable risk. Auma's men weren't known for being particularly well equipped—machetes and AKs mostly. Night vision gear or thermal scopes were probably out of their reach.

Probably.

Grant finally reached the streamer and pulled it toward him until he came to what was attached: a single sheet of laminated paper.

"Got it," he said into his throat mike. "On my way back."

The return trip went much quicker. Locating the streamer had been a challenge but finding tree cover in this part of Uganda was like finding hay in a haystack.

He settled in a few feet from the edge of the clearing and retrieved a tiny penlight from his pocket.

"Approaching from the east."

The voice over his earpiece was recognizable as belonging to the man he'd made his second-in-command.

"Come."

By the time he appeared, Grant was scanning the sheet under the dim red glow of his flashlight.

"Looks like our friendly neighborhood guide has taken off."

"Big surprise," Grant said.

"What've you got?"

"Looks like fifteen caches in total. These are detailed instructions on how to find them."

His man let out an understandably frustrated breath. "There are only eight of us. Are you thinking you want to split up and try to cover some of them?"

Grant shook his head. "No way to find them. The directions were written in a way that only David Chism will be able to understand."

He turned off the flashlight and grabbed his satphone, dialing from memory. Despite being 6 a.m. in Washington, the call was picked up on the second ring.

"Go ahead," said the now familiar voice.

"We've got at least ten choppers overflying the area, using megaphones to try to communicate with David Chism. Do you know anything about it?"

There was a long pause. Grant pictured the man standing in the kitchen of his McMansion, foaming milk for his coffee. "It's a mercenary operation. Not military."

"Well, whoever they are, they're a hell of a lot better equipped than we are and they seem to have a hell of a lot better plan. Auma's men are still watching us and the guide you set us up with just disappeared. There's nothing more we can do here. Request permission to pull out."

Another long pause before the man spoke again. "Stand by for further instructions."

The line went dead.

"Problems?" his man said.

Grant didn't answer, contemplating his options. After a few seconds he concluded that there was only one. He wasn't leading his men to their deaths while a bunch of mercs watched from the clouds. And if that meant a court-martial, then he'd deal with it. But he doubted it'd come to that. For him to be court-martialed, someone would have to figure out who these bullshit orders were coming from. And Mr. Pumpkin Spice Latte didn't sound like the type who handed out business cards.

"We've been told to pull out," he lied. As long as his men thought they were following orders, they'd be safe from any repercussions. "Now let's move."

Chism froze as voices became audible, followed by the swish of people coming toward him through the trees. The language was recognizable, but indecipherable. Despite his time in Uganda, he learned only a few local words.

This couldn't be where his luck finally ran out. He was too close. Maybe as little as an hour from saving his friends and landing safely at Nick Ward's compound. Crouching silently, he tried to ignore the sensation of his heart trying to escape his chest.

The two men passed within a few feet but despite the sun having been up for a couple of hours they never suspected anything. It was the upside to the sea of plant life they were all trapped in. The downside was that it made finding what he was looking for damn near impossible.

He started moving again, now focusing upward instead of at the ground. The new strategy paid off. A bright pink streamer appeared, hanging about twenty feet up in a tree that looked climbable. He started up, carefully testing each branch before committing his full weight to it. Except for all the heavily armed psychotic cult members, it was just like when he was a kid.

The streamer took a few good yanks to free, but he was eventually rewarded with a single sheet of laminated paper. Despite his awkward position, he couldn't help skimming it before starting back down.

When he did, a faint smile spread across his face. Whoever had created the document was both very smart and very thorough.

Every cache had a separate set of instructions and he went through them, trying to find the closest. After a couple of minutes of reading and cross-referencing with the topo map on the back, he decided that cache 9 was the most promising.

From where you camped when you found the butterfly you think is a new species: there is an obvious square rock about two feet across embedded in the ground. With your heel in the middle of it, start walking one foot directly in front of the other in the direction you'd take the highway from your old office in Chicago to your house there. The distance in steps is the first and fourth digits of your Social Security number. . . .

13

"I JUST made another grand," Coleman said.

At some point, he'd realized that he was making a thousand dollars a minute on this job and had taken to calling out his income at regular intervals.

Rapp searched blindly for the Coke next to his lawn chair, lacking the energy to turn his head. A rare heat wave had pushed temperatures into the low nineties and caused a cloud of humidity to rise from the jungle and settle on their camp. Despite the shade from a chopper to their right and the baby pool their feet were soaking in, it was suffocating. Nothing like the dry heat of the Middle East.

His hand finally brushed the icy can and he brought it to his lips.

"While you were looking for your drink, I just made another five hundred bucks," Coleman pointed out gleefully.

Rapp didn't respond. There was no doubt that working for Nicholas Ward had its benefits. The money pretty much grew on trees, obviously. More than that, though, he was smart, reasonable, and knew when to stay out of the way.

Maybe it was the perfect job to usher in the next phase of his life. Profitable. Strategically interesting. No shooting. He had to admit it. A little dabbling in the private sector going forward wouldn't be the worst thing.

"What do you think?" Coleman asked after a long silence.

"About what?"

"Chism."

"He's dead. And even if he's not, he's in too bad a shape to follow those instructions."

"He'd be motivated, though. And he's a genius."

"Yeah," Rapp said noncommittally.

All of the caches were in place, each containing food, medical supplies, a couple of bottles of Gatorade, and water purification tablets. Most critical, though, was the satellite phone.

There were still a few choppers dropping maps at the boundary of what they'd calculated to be Chism's maximum range, but that would be done by sunset. Afterward, it would be nothing but lawn chairs, coolers full of soft drinks, and a thousand dollars a minute.

"I'm having charcoal grills flown in later," Coleman said. "And some meat. Do you have a preference?"

"Maybe a rib eye?"

"No problem. How long are you planning on staying?"

It was a good question. He'd agreed to the job for Irene's sake, so he had to make an effort. But he also had a fledgling family and a couple of ten-thousand-dollar bikes waiting for him in Cape Town. Coleman was certainly capable of handling an operation like this on his own. It's what he and his guys did.

"A couple more days. Then you can milk it for as long as Ward will keep writing checks."

"If I can drag it out another couple of weeks, I might buy a place in Greece. You know, one of those white houses that hangs off a cliff and overlooks the ocean? I've always liked Greece. Good olives."

After ten minutes of silence the phone lying in the dirt between them started to ring and they both looked down at it. The screen was flashing *Cache 9*.

"You gotta be kidding me," Coleman muttered as Rapp picked up. "Yeah?"

While it was vaguely possible that one of Auma's men had stumbled upon a cache, the idea that they could make this call was farfetched. The number included digits from Chism's mother's birthdate.

"This is David Chism. Who's this?"

He honestly didn't even sound that bad. A little breathless and hoarse, but that was about it.

"The guy who's going to pull you out. Lie down on the ground, don't move, and don't make any noise. We'll be over your position in . . ." He paused and glanced over at Coleman, who was holding up eight fingers. "Eight minutes."

"What about my people?"

"What?"

"My people. They're still alive but they're not with me. One's not going to make it much longer."

"Shut up, David. You're making too much noise. We're on our way and once you're safe, we'll go back for the others."

"No."

"What do you mean, no?"

"You're not government. I've seen your helicopters. You're mercenaries. And I'm your payday. If you want your money, you pick up all three of us at the same time."

"Don't be stupid, David. What incentive do I have to leave them out there? I get paid by the hour."

"I'll call you when I get back to them and give you instructions on how to get there."

The phone went dead.

"What?" Coleman said.

Rapp shook his head and reached for another Coke. "Nothing's ever easy."

14

"WE'RE taking fire," a voice said over Rapp's headphones. "Permission to return it."

"Only if it's focused and absolutely necessary," Rapp responded. "We have friendlies on the ground, and we don't know exactly where they are."

Their entire complement of choppers was in the air, skimming the trees over the search area and occasionally lowering lines to the ground. The idea was to make it impossible for Gideon Auma's men to discern the real rescue from the decoys. Not a perfect plan, but the best they could implement under the circumstances.

Fred Mason was keeping their aircraft well above the canopy and out of range of any potential small arms fire. They had coordinates for their target, but the chances of being able to land were low. Apparently, David Chism was hunkered down in a shallow cave halfway up one of the seemingly endless mountains in the area.

"I think I see it," Mason said over the comm. "Three prominent rocky bands, just like you said." As they passed overhead, a human form emerged from a curtain of foliage hanging from a cliff face.

Chism gazed up at them, waving his arms over his head a couple of times before disappearing again.

"How are we looking?" Rapp asked.

"I think the description was even more optimistic than we thought. Forget landing, I can't even get close enough to drop you down without putting my rotors into the rock face."

"I'm not interested in problems, Fred. Give me solutions."

"We can toss a rope out. If you rappel about forty feet down it, I can probably swing you onto the ledge. When you hit, though, you'll have to disengage fast as hell. Otherwise, you'll get dragged back off."

Rapp looked down at the loose, rocky slope that was his potential landing zone. "That's a lot of 'abouts' and 'probablys,' Fred."

"Relax. There's definitely a nonzero chance you won't die."

"Great. Okay, swing around again. Let's do this before someone starts shooting at us."

Rapp slung a tired-looking AK-47 over his shoulder before connecting a rope to the belay device on his harness. Mason's copilot came back to help him put on a ragged backpack and then used a marker to blacken a section of the rope.

"That's about forty feet," she said, slapping him encouragingly on the back before returning to the cockpit.

Rapp stared into the blinding sunlight for a few seconds, then put his boots on the edge of the open door and rappelled to the designated mark. After that, there wasn't much he could do but dangle helplessly as the chopper began a collision course with the cliff. Fred Mason was unquestionably the best in the business. Hopefully, it would be enough.

When it seemed certain they were going to crash, the chopper reared back, sending Rapp swinging out from beneath it. He hit the ground harder than anticipated, dazing him badly enough that his fingers were incapable of disengaging the rappel device connecting him to the aircraft. He finally managed to release the brake but continued to be dragged toward the drop-off by the friction of the rope passing through the mechanism. It cracked like a whip when it finally cleared, the end contacting Rapp's forearm and leaving a deep gash.

"Stop rolling!" he heard Mason shout over his earpiece. "Stop fucking rolling, Mitch!"

Free of the line, he changed his focus to trying to follow his pilot's advice. Most of the rocks he grabbed were too small or loose to have much of an effect, but he eventually managed to aim for one that looked solid. And it was. He slammed into it shoulder first, coming to an abrupt halt three feet from the drop-off.

"Mitch! You all right? Say something!"

"Son of a bitch . . ." he managed to get out, blood drooling from his mouth as he spoke.

"Oh, man!" Mason said. "I'd have bet my life savings on that not working! Am I good or what?"

Rapp just lay there as the chopper disappeared over the mountain. Nothing felt broken or torn. Nothing important, anyway.

He finally struggled to his feet and stumbled toward the tangle of foliage that Chism had built to camouflage the cave entrance. By the time he passed through, his mind was more or less clear.

"Jeez . . . That was crazy. Are you okay?"

By way of response, Rapp slapped Chism in the side of the head hard enough to almost drop him.

"Ow! That hurt!" he said, stumbling back. An Asian woman watched from the rear of the cave, where she was hovering over a man lying in a bed of fronds.

Rapp pointed. "Is he still breathing?"

"Yeah."

"You're sure?"

"I'm a fucking doctor, man."

Rapp stepped forward and slapped him in the side of the head again.

"Ow! Stop it! I couldn't risk that you'd just leave them. They wouldn't be in this mess if it weren't for me."

"And that's the only reason I didn't just collect my paycheck and go home," Rapp said, walking back toward the cave entrance. The dull hum of helicopters was audible outside, punctuated by the occasional burst of automatic fire.

"Fred," he said into his throat mike. "I'm going to need the stretcher. Can you get it in here?"

"Apparently, I can do anything!"

"Focus."

"Sorry, Mitch. Yeah. Basically, the same drill. But you're going to have to catch it."

"Understood. ETA?"

"Two minutes."

"Roger that. Two minutes out."

He turned and pointed to Matteo Ricci. "Drag him out. We don't have a lot of time."

They broke into the sunlight just as Mason came overhead. The litter was already dangling beneath the aircraft as he banked and bore down on them. When he pulled up, the fiberglass stretcher came at Rapp like a projectile. In this instance, Mason's aim was a little too good—forcing Rapp to dive to one side. It skidded past and smashed into the rock wall, resting there for a moment as Mason's copilot let the cable reel spin free. Then the weight of the line started dragging it back. Rapp grabbed hold as it slid by but didn't have enough body weight to arrest its momentum. His bike-racing diet was going to get him pulled over a cliff.

He was about to let go when David Chism dove onto the other side. The added weight was enough to stop the slide and they managed to anchor it behind a boulder. Not a long-term solution, but it didn't have to be. The Asian woman whose name Rapp couldn't remember was already dragging Ricci downslope toward them.

Dust and pebbles from the rotor wash hammered him as he put the Italian inside. The first strap was barely cinched over Ricci's chest when automatic fire erupted from the jungle below.

"Bad news," Mason said over the comm. "Those guys are shooting at *us*. They're still a little out of range but I can see them coming up the slope."

"Shit," Rapp muttered as Mason's copilot began firing controlled bursts from the chopper's open door. This was going to turn into a complete clusterfuck if he didn't get them out of there fast.

"We're inbound," he heard Bruno McGraw say. "Approximately one minute out."

"Not sure we have that long," Mason said. "We're a stationary target here."

"Everybody in," Rapp said.

"What?" Chism was a little wide-eyed.

"You heard me. Get in on top of him."

"Will this thing even hold three people's weight?"

"We're about to find out," Rapp said, shoving him down on top of Ricci. The Asian woman was both more cooperative and quite a bit smaller. She settled in with her face between Ricci's feet and her knees in Chism's side while Rapp threw the rest of the straps over them.

Another burst of automatic fire became audible, this time accompanied by the sound of rounds finding their target. As expected, Mason kept his hover steady. He didn't seem happy about it when he came back on the comm, though.

"We just took a couple, Mitch. Did you stop for a drink down there?"

Rapp finished with the last buckle and dragged the litter out from behind the boulder. "They're all in! Go!"

Mason didn't need to be told twice. The overfilled litter slid toward the cliff and then went over it, swinging wildly as its occupants screamed in terror. The chopper had gained maybe fifty feet of altitude when a contrail appeared from the jungle.

"Rocket!" Rapp shouted reflexively as Mason took evasive action. The projectile missed by a good fifty yards and the aircraft continued to climb as another helicopter—this one containing Bruno McGraw—

came into view. They'd retrofitted his rig with a minigun, and he began firing from the open door, hosing down the area where the rocket had originated. Accuracy wasn't great, but it was hard to blame the marksman. The chopper wasn't designed for the recoil and it was getting pushed all over the place.

Mason's erratic climb had set the litter to spinning out of control, but it was high enough now that Rapp had to squint to make out detail. Another contrail appeared, missing by a good five hundred yards before plummeting back into the jungle and failing to detonate. If the black-market SAMs Auma's army used had ever had guidance systems, they'd rusted away long ago.

McGraw redirected his fire on the second rocket's launch point just as a series of rounds stitched the rock wall ten feet over Rapp's head.

"It's too hot for me to go down," he said over his throat mike. "I'm gonna have to climb up and over. I'll contact you when I get to a viable extraction point."

15

THE sound of distant automatic fire became audible again, but Rapp ignored it. He suspected that he knew its origin and it had nothing to do with him. He had his own problems.

He'd made it over the mountain and managed to skid, climb, and occasionally roll down the other side. Now he was crouched in a particularly dense thicket a few hundred yards from the base.

A tactical knife had been sufficient to shave off his beard and he was in the process of further darkening his skin with dirt. A bit politically incorrect in the current world, but it would give him a brief edge in the unlikely event he was spotted. Combined with the ratty fatigues and even rattier Yosemite Sam T-shirt beneath, Auma's men would likely take him for one of their own in the visual chaos created by the forest.

While he couldn't see the sky through the canopy, the relative silence suggested it was free of choppers. Unless something had gone very wrong, Chism was safe, and Coleman was already tearing down their temporary command post. Rapp's extraction would be the last detail in a mission that despite leaving him isolated in enemy territory had gone a hell of a lot better than expected.

At first, Rapp thought the sound was some kind of jungle creature he wasn't familiar with. After a life spent fighting in the Middle East, though, his knowledge of jungle wildlife admittedly wasn't particularly reliable. Based on his calculations, he should be approaching cache 3, which was the closest viable extraction point. What he didn't need now was to run into a gorilla, a guerilla, or some sharp-toothed mammal that he'd never heard of. If things could keep going his way for a little longer, he could be back in Cape Town for a late dinner.

The noise took on a metallic ring, forcing him to discard the idea of an animal. It appeared that Auma's men had managed to find the cache he was headed for and were trying to access the heavy steel case. From the sound of it, they'd resisted the urge to try to shoot the lock off and were instead beating it with a rock.

Not just surprising, but pretty impressive. There was no way anyone could just stumble upon something buried in the middle of the jungle. More likely, Auma had managed to dig up enough background on Chism to decipher the cache's location. Uganda was right to be afraid of that freak.

Fortunately for Rapp, Auma's competence fell short of allowing him to decipher the lock's combination, forcing his men to announce their position for half a mile in every direction. Apparently, being God's representative on earth wasn't enough to get him Chism's ATM pin.

Rapp slowed to a literal crawl, being careful to remain aware of his surroundings and not to get too focused on the sound just ahead. It was possible that they'd summoned friends with better tools and there was no telling what direction they might come from. In the end, though, he made it to what he guessed was twenty feet without incident. Close enough to hear the unintelligible conversation between what he determined were two men—probably about whose turn it was to tear their arm off hammering on the lock. As the exchange got more heated, he texted Coleman that he was in position. The extraction point that corresponded with cache 3 was only about fifteen yards from the strongbox, though, suggesting it would be necessary to deal with the men before his people arrived.

Coleman responded almost immediately.

UNDERSTOOD. CACHE 3. SIX MINUTES OUT. ISSUES?

TWO TANGOS. STAY HIGH. DON'T RETURN FIRE.

Five minutes, forty-eight seconds later, the dull sound of the chopper blades became audible. Coleman would be in the Airbus H130 they'd rented from a sightseeing company. Not exactly combat capable, but the quietest thing they could find.

Predictably, the shooting started about twenty seconds later—undisciplined bursts that melded with the growing sound of the rotors. The noise level rose to the point that Rapp could abandon stealth and move as fast as the foliage would allow. Instead of the AK, he'd opted for the Glock 19 that had served him so well over the years. There was a silencer in his pack, but he'd decided not to mess with it. If all went to plan, the two men would be dead before they heard the shots that killed them.

The flashes of their weapons became visible in the dying afternoon light, allowing him to make on-the-fly adjustments to his trajectory. When he finally got eyes on the two men, both were focused entirely upward, firing wildly toward the chopper hovering well out of their reach.

The jungle was so dense that Rapp was forced to hold his fire until he was at nearly point-blank range. The first round hit the man on the left between the shoulder blades, pitching him into a tree where his body got tangled and hung like a discarded doll. The second tango didn't even notice. He just kept shooting skyward until the side of his head disintegrated.

Rapp let his momentum carry him to a clearing large enough to land the chopper. It began to descend, and he dove through the open door while the skids were still a couple of feet from the ground. A moment later, he felt the increased gravity as Fred Mason started to climb.

"You good?" Scott Coleman shouted, and Rapp gave him the thumbs-up before putting on a headset.

"Have you been able to hear the shooting?" Coleman asked over the comm.

"Yeah. Kind of intermittent and hard to pinpoint, though."

"Not anymore. It's turned into a full-blown firefight."

"You think it's the American team?"

"I don't know who else it could be. Not exactly a high-traffic area down there."

Rapp nodded, taking a moment to consider what he wanted to do. "Fred, can you fly us over their position?"

"No problem, Mitch. Give me two minutes."

The sun had just disappeared over the mountains when they arrived, putting the forest in shadow and highlighting the muzzle flashes beneath the canopy. Coleman was right. It wasn't just harassment anymore.

"Do we have external sound?"

They'd rigged some of their aircraft with megaphones to provide instructions to Chism. If this was one of them, they might be able to use it to find out what was going on down there.

"Yeah," Mason responded. "You want me to patch you in?"

Again, Rapp paused to think. He was a private contractor now. The self-inflicted problems of the US military really weren't any of his business. A cooler full of beer and a lift to the Entebbe airport were only a few minutes away.

"Shit. Yeah. Do it."

"Okay, you're live."

"American team. This is Scott Coleman of SEAL Demolition and Salvage . . ."

It seemed more practical to use that name. Rapp's own wouldn't be recognizable to anyone but top operators. Coleman, on the other hand, was a legend throughout the armed forces.

"If you can hear this, the following is my phone number. Call it." He began repeating the number over the megaphone and on the fourth time, his satphone started to ring.

He shoved it beneath one side of his headphones and shouted into it.

"Go ahead."

The response was a string of what he assumed were extremely graphic threats, but the English was too heavily accented to be sure. Apparently, Auma supplied his disciples with phones and actually paid the bill.

Coleman held out his own. "Try again."

"Okay," Rapp said over the megaphone. "New number. The first digit is . . ." He pondered for a moment. "The amendment that gives you the right to bear arms. The second is the last number in the White House address." Then he just read off the rest.

After a few repeats, the phone began ringing. This time, the accent on the other end was American.

"Who am I talking to?" Rapp said.

"Lieutenant Jeremiah Grant, US Army."

"Give me a sitrep."

"We're engaging hostiles on the south, east, and west. Moving north. Six of us left. One injured." A burst of gunfire drowned him out for a moment. "They've been watching us for days, but when you pulled Chism out, they decided there was no reason to just watch anymore."

"They're driving you into an ambush," Rapp said.

"I one hundred percent agree with you, sir, but there's not a hell of a lot I can do about it."

Coleman held out a map and aimed a penlight at it.

"Stand by, Lieutenant," Rapp said.

"We can't shoot blind down on them," the former SEAL said. "But we could bring in a couple of choppers with miniguns. Using thermal, we should be able to find the ambush and take it out. Then we create a scorched-earth path right to the clearing west of cache six."

Rapp nodded. "Lieutenant. Keep heading north. We'll deal with anybody waiting for you. I'm sending coordinates for an extraction point. You should be able to reach it in . . ."

Coleman held up two fingers and then five.

"Twenty-five minutes. Copy?"

"Continuing on our current heading, waiting for coordinates for extraction. Twenty-five-minute ETA."

"I'll see you there," Rapp said. "And good luck."

16

" **P**ASS over one more time, Fred."

"I'll do it, but I don't like those rockets, Mitch."

Three had gone up so far, one aimed at them and the others at the additional choppers they had in the air. The aim and trajectories were so erratic, though, that Rapp was starting to wonder if they were rockets at all. If he had to bet, he'd say they were some kind of glorified firework that Auma used to keep the Ugandans off balance.

Rapp leaned out the chopper's open door and sighted through a thermal scope mounted to a Sage International EBR M14. Gray splashes of human heat were visible through the canopy, but they appeared and disappeared like ghosts. The chance of getting off a kill shot from his current position was pretty much zero—too much movement from the aircraft, too much foliage, and too much erratic movement from potential targets.

He'd hoped to bring some heavier weaponry to bear, but the American team hadn't been able to outpace their pursuers enough to discern who was who. Auma's men—as undisciplined as they were—had the home field advantage and superior numbers. They also didn't seem concerned about friendly fire, which allowed them to come along either side of the Americans and put them in crossfires. In all likelihood, they were whacked out on ajali, a locally produced narcotic that acted like a ten-foot line of PCP-laced cocaine. According to Rapp's intel, it made things like death, fear, and fatigue irrelevant. Users fought like wounded civet cats until either they caught a bullet or their heart gave out.

"Mitch," Joe Maslick said over Rapp's headphones. He was in a chopper just to the north, searching for the ambush. "We've found 'em and it's not pretty. Hard to get an exact count, but I'm going to guess twenty-five guys. All dug in directly in front of our new friends. Permission to fire?"

"Fire at will."

In the distance, two helicopters that had been invisible a moment before were lit by the muzzle flashes of their door-mounted guns.

"Lieutenant," Rapp said over the satellite phone now linked through his headset. "We've located and are neutralizing the opposition ahead of you. You're clear to pick up your pace. Keep those assholes from getting alongside you for just a few minutes."

"Copy. We'll go as fast as we can."

"Understood. We're going to drop in in front of you. Two men. We should make contact in about five minutes. Copy?"

"Two friendlies dead ahead. Contact in five."

Rapp switched the comm back to Joe Maslick. "Mas, are you going to have that ambush cleaned up in time?"

"We've flushed them and they're on the move. Driving them east and west—away from your corridor. You should be good."

"Copy that." Rapp looked over at Coleman in the dim red light. "We ready?"

The former SEAL finished arranging their ropes and gave him the thumbs-up.

"All right, Fred. Take us about two hundred yards north and then put us in a hover."

The chopper sideslipped for a few seconds while Rapp gripped a handle on the fuselage to stabilize himself.

"That's about two hundred yards, Mitch. Go!"

He and Coleman threw themselves from the aircraft, sliding fast down the ropes and crashing through the jungle canopy. There was no graceful way to get to the ground and they found themselves half climbing, half rappelling the last fifty or so feet.

"We're clear, Fred!"

"Good luck," he heard over his earpiece. "I'm out of here."

They'd purposely set down in an area where the jungle was less dense, but the concept of less dense was relative in this part of the world. Both he and Coleman crouched and sighted through their thermal scopes, searching for any sign of life around them. For the moment, the only indication was the crack of intermittent gunfire.

"We've mopped up the stragglers," Maslick said over Rapp's earpiece. "Hanging thirty seconds out and waiting for your signal."

"Roger that," Rapp said, continuing to scan the empty jungle through his scope.

Another two minutes passed before he saw a glimmer of movement. "I've got one."

"I see him," Coleman confirmed.

It turned out to be not a single man, but a pair of them. One had his arm thrown over the shoulders of the other, stumbling and trying to contribute what little he could to their forward momentum.

"Lieutenant Grant. I've got eyes on your point man and the man he's assisting," Rapp said.

"That's me," came the response.

"Angle a few degrees to your right. Contact in less than one minute."

Despite having warned him, Grant seemed a little startled when Rapp and Coleman melted from the jungle. The former SEAL took hold of the injured man and started north.

"Still six of you?" Rapp said.

"Yes," the soldier responded, struggling to catch his breath. "But one more injured man near the back."

"Okay. Keep going but slow the pace a little."

"We'll get bunched up."

"It's my party now, Lieutenant."

It was hard to read his expression in what little light was able to filter to the jungle floor, but after a couple of seconds he responded. "Yes, sir. I guess it is."

Rapp found a position next to a particularly thick tree, staying invisible while he counted the passing Americans. As Grant had predicted, the intervals between them were reducing. Not normally a good idea, but Rapp knew something they didn't. Both he and Coleman had powerful infrared lights attached to their packs and aimed at the sky. The beams were invisible to the naked eye, but Joe Maslick and Bruno McGraw in the choppers weren't using their naked eyes.

The last man passed and Rapp fell in silently behind him. Now the location of the American team would be clearly delineated by the beams at the front and back of the column.

"Mas, Bruno. I'm in position at the rear."

Thirty seconds later all hell broke loose. Rapp could see the two flashing arcs of tracer rounds coming down into the forest around him. In a few seconds, there wouldn't be anything larger than a cockroach alive for twenty-five yards in any direction around the column. His main worry now was one of the miniguns cutting a tree down on top of him.

17

THE buzz of the phone on Anthony Cook's night table awoke him with a start. He reached over and picked up, trying to shake off his grogginess. "Go ahead."

"I'm sorry to disturb you at this hour, Mr. President, but Deputy Director Nash is on the line and he says it's urgent."

That was enough to wake him fully. Michael Nash wasn't a man prone to hysteria or calling in the middle of the night over trivial matters.

"Put him through."

There was a brief pause and then Nash's voice came on. "I'm sorry to—"

"It's okay. Get to the point, Mike."

"Yes, sir. We're getting reports of what appears to be a massive rescue operation in the mountains west of David Chism's research facility."

"Meaning what?"

"We don't know exactly. Somewhere around ten helicopters were involved and there was a fair amount of shooting. But we don't know at what."

"What about Chism?"

"Unknown."

"Was it Rapp and Coleman?"

An uncomfortable silence.

"Answer the fucking question, Mike!"

"Again, I can't say for certain, sir. This is brand-new information and we're working with less than reliable sources. But I don't know who else it would be."

"So, they didn't leave."

"We relayed your message, sir. But like I said, we have a limited ability to tell Mitch Rapp and Scott Coleman what they can and can't do. Particularly outside the country."

Cook sat up in bed. "I need to know what's going on over there, Mike. Now."

"Yes, sir. I'm on my way out the door and Irene's in the process of trying to contact Mitch. We'll be at the office in just over an hour and should know more by then."

The mention of Kennedy's name made Cook's teeth clench. She'd stonewall, lie, cheat, and steal to protect Mitch Rapp. Nothing she said on this subject—or any other—could be trusted.

"I expect to hear from you ninety minutes from now. And I want answers. Do you understand me?" Cook turned on a light and saw his wife standing in the doorway to his bedroom. Years ago, it would have been startling, but now it would have been more startling if she hadn't been there. Her mind no longer seemed capable of completely turning off. The best she could do was to enter something akin to a semiconscious trance for five hours a night.

"Yes, sir. I understand completely."

He disconnected the call as his wife pulled her silk robe closer around her neck.

"What happened, Tony?"

"Mitch Rapp just ran some kind of rescue operation in Uganda."

"Was it successful?"

"No one knows. No one knows shit."

She disappeared back into the adjacent room where she slept as he slipped out of bed. He tried to quell the rage and frustration that so often overwhelmed him, concentrating on the simple task of pulling on a pair of sweatpants. He'd made strides in hiding his emotions but, like everything in life, it was a delicate balance. Passion translated into charisma, and charisma was what had allowed him to fill the power vacuum created by Christine Barnett's death. It was what made leaders. And rulers.

Voters didn't care about public policy or economics or even their own well-being. What they wanted was to connect with their leadership on a gut level. To feel a part of something. To believe that they had power. And he could make that happen because to some degree he felt the same things. He understood what they wanted. What they loved. What they hated. The difference was that he had the strength and intelligence to act on it while they wallowed.

Cook slipped a T-shirt over his head and walked into his wife's bedroom. She had her back to him, tapping calmly on a laptop.

"What are you doing?"

"Looking at the investments I made when the Saudis assured us that they had the resources to get rid of David Chism."

"And?"

"In the less than two weeks since his disappearance, we're up just over twenty-three million dollars."

Cook had enjoyed a close relationship with the Saudis going back to his days as the governor of California and that bond had become even stronger since he'd taken control of the White House. The new prince had approached him through back channels to float the idea of using Gideon Auma to neutralize David Chism.

While Ward and Chism were unquestionably an existential threat to the general world order, they were a very specific threat to the Saudis. Ward's research into renewables was accelerating the collapse of the Middle Eastern energy industry just as Chism's research was undermining the royalty's heavy bets on the pharmaceutical industry. Bets that they were relying on to pay for their eventual—and almost certainly inevitable—escape from their country.

Pledging not to interfere in their assassination plot had been risky, but also potentially very rewarding. The Saudis had unlimited financial resources, penetration into terrorist groups throughout the world, and a power structure that allowed them to move decisively. Most important, though, was their refreshing lack of pretense when it came to moral norms and international law. They were simple creatures who sought power and wealth. Period.

"How hard will it be to close out our positions?"

"Hard," she responded. "I made these investments very carefully and over a fairly long period of time. If I were to suddenly reverse all of them, it'd be noticeable. The question is, does it matter? Your supporters in the general public don't seem to care what we do as long as you tell them what they want to hear. Our senators and congressmen certainly won't object as long as you help them stay in power. If the other party were to find out, though, it could cause legal problems that we're not powerful enough to just make disappear. Not yet."

"Would they get traction, though? We have majorities in both houses and complicated financial transactions don't make good TV. Too hard to understand."

"Maybe. Or maybe not. It's hard to say what the press will be interested in."

"But if we don't close out those positions, we lose the twenty-three million we've gained?"

"Plus more. I'd say we'd take a thirty-five-million-dollar hit before I can completely extricate us."

"Thirty-five million," he repeated, confident that it would be almost exactly that. The icy analysis of probabilities, alternatives, and pitfalls was very much her realm. "And the Saudis' debt to us isn't going to be as great."

"Why not? We promised them that we wouldn't make any real effort to save Chism—not that we'd actively block a private rescue effort if they screwed up. This isn't our fault."

"It doesn't matter. We were involved and there's nothing human beings are better at than sharing the blame for their failures. And Mitch Rapp's involvement makes it that much worse. We can say whatever we want about him working independently but no one's going to believe it. He has too long a history with the US government."

She sighed quietly. "It's a brave new world."

That was something they both agreed on. In fact, it was the shared belief that had brought them together. They'd come to power in an environment of massive international corporations and billionaires. Of strongmen in Asia, Eastern Europe, and Africa. Of constantly evolving technologies and a media that became more pervasive and malleable with every passing day.

An even cursory survey of history suggested that the unparalleled equality and freedom the average person had enjoyed over the last seventy-five years was an aberration. Nothing more than a bubble created by a perfect storm of the postwar economic boom, industrial revolution, and rise of workers' unions.

Now, though, that bubble was bursting. An international ruling class was forming. Borders were becoming increasingly meaningless to that privileged group, as was citizenship and the rule of law. Going forward, alliances would no longer be forged between countries so much as individuals and private entities. Those shrewd, strong, and courageous enough to rule would be given that privilege. A privilege that would quickly become an unassailable right. Nationality, patriotism, and religion would go back to what they had been in centuries past—a convenient way to control the masses.

"So, do we take our losses?" Cook said. "Both financial and with the Saudis? Or do we try to salvage this?"

"I don't know, Tony. We're in a unique position and unique means there's not a lot of data to help us. The attack on the power grid scared the hell out of people and made them more willing to cede power to a strong leader. On the other hand, we've spent the last six months digging out of it. We've been looking backward, not forward like we expected."

"Three and a half years left before the next election," he said. "We talked about controlling this office for sixteen and beyond. Now I'm starting to worry whether I can even count on a second term. At some point we're going to have to stop making excuses and start making the kind of moves that are going to get us where we want to be."

Catherine looked up at the blank white of the ceiling, collecting her thoughts. "Gideon Auma's not a man who likes being denied what he wants. And it's unlikely that Chism—or Ward for that matter—will leave Uganda. Their research is too important."

"Meaning what?"

"Meaning that they're still within Auma's reach. We know he's motivated, and we know the Saudis have access to him. Maybe he just needs a little guidance."

18

RAPP leaned a little farther through the helicopter's open door, straining against his safety harness. Below, the details of an elaborate compound built into the top of a mountain came into sharp relief. The terrain around it was the same green he'd become accustomed to over the past few days, but somewhat less dense than where he'd found Chism and the American soldiers. To the west, Lake Edward gleamed beneath a cloudless sky.

As they came overhead, he saw that the complex was surrounded by a primitive fence built from local trees. It looked like it had been designed more to keep animals out than people, but that was changing. Two bulldozers were busy building a berm that would both reinforce the barrier and provide a platform for shooters.

Buildings were largely obscured, tucked into stands of trees and connected by flagstone walkways. Various solar arrays were in evidence, as were a number of water towers that undoubtedly fed underground pipes. The eastern side of the mesa had fewer trees and was dedicated to a series of neat agricultural plots. The exception was an airy house surrounded on two sides by a swimming pool. Undoubt-edly the residence of the man himself—Nicholas Ward.

To the west, Rapp spotted some buildings that didn't seem to fit into the understated architectural theme—prefab structures that ap-peared to have been recently assembled and were fed by visible cables and hoses. Barracks for the men that SEAL Demolition and Salvage had contracted.

The chopper set down on a pad not far from the new structures and Scott Coleman jogged out to meet him.

"How are things shaping up?" Rapp shouted over the sound of the rotors winding down.

"Good," Coleman responded as they moved along a path that looked newly cleared. "We're plopped in the middle of about a hundred thousand acres that Ward bought a while back. No roads in or out and totally self-sustaining. Also, well outside of Auma's operating area."

"He has a way of deciding himself what his operating area is," Rapp said.

"Agreed. But if he still poses a threat, we're in reasonably good shape to engage him. Thank God Ward wanted lake views and put his compound on the high ground. I also convinced him to let us push some dirt up behind his fencing as long as I promised to plant local flora on it. We'll mount some guns on the top and we're installing sen-sors and cameras in the forest. Razor wire's on its way but delayed be-cause Ward insisted that it be painted to match the forest. I've also got to find a way to keep the local wildlife from getting hung up on it. Still working on that."

"So, you feel confident?"

"Yeah," Coleman said, drawing the word out a little longer than Rapp would have liked. "I mean, it's a compromise. Ward doesn't want to feel like he's living in an armed camp and he thinks we're going a little overboard with his cash, but I convinced him better safe than sorry. Particularly where Gideon Auma is concerned. Besides, it's not like he doesn't have money to burn."

Rapp nodded, turning in a slow circle to take in as much as he could of the compound.

"How are Chism and his people?"

"Not bad. Ward already had a well-equipped infirmary up here and a doc on staff. Ricci's in rough shape, but they say he's going to pull through. Chism and Liu are a little malnourished, but otherwise barely a scratch. What happened in Kampala?"

Rapp had been in Uganda's capital debriefing Jeremiah Grant and making sure his injured men got treatment. The silence from the US government had been deafening enough that Nicholas Ward was paying for their care and planning to fly them back stateside in one of his jets. Rapp had considered getting Danny Lombard at Africa Command involved, but then decided it would be better to keep his old friend as far from this train wreck as possible.

"Grant's guys are going to be fine. Full recovery. What about the bodies they had to leave behind?"

"The news isn't good. We went looking where he said they'd been killed and came up empty. Not to put too fine a point on it, but word is that Auma eats his enemies. He thinks it gives him their power."

"Shit," Rapp said.

"Yeah," Coleman agreed. "What did Grant have to say?"

"Basically, that we were right. He was sent out to wander around with no backup and pretty much no intel. Orders came through his CO and originated from somewhere higher up. He doesn't know where. His only contact was a voice on the other end of a phone. They'd been set up with a guide, but he disappeared when things started getting hot. Grant thinks they were being watched from the first day they walked into the jungle."

"Auma probably thought they knew something and was hoping they'd lead his men to Chism."

"That was Grant's take on it, too."

"Weird," Coleman said. "More like theater than an op. But theater for whose benefit?"

Rapp just shrugged and his old friend pointed to a stone path leading to the other side of the compound.

"Ward's house is up that way. He said he wanted to see you when
you got here."

Modern bungalows constructed of wood, steel, and glass began to appear, set back into the trees on either side of the path. Having built
something of a compound himself in Virginia, Rapp had to appreciate
the design. Clean, modern, and conceived from the ground up for off-
grid use. With the moderate climate, they had it easier than he did—no
cooling necessary and small woodstoves would be enough for the few
times a year that heat was necessary. On the other hand, everything that
wasn't locally sourced would have had to be flown in by cargo helicopter.
Not cheap. But then, at some point it all became play money. His own
brother had reached that level a while back. And his net worth was less
than one thousandth of Ward's. Rapp let that sink in for a moment. His
mega-millionaire brother was a literal pauper compared to the man who
owned this compound. Poor Steven. The kid was just barely getting by.

Ward's house was unlike anything Rapp had ever seen. Its two
stories cantilevered out on every side and the exterior walls consisted
of wood louvers. At this time of day, all were open, allowing a view
straight through, past a large central kitchen to the panorama beyond.
Machinery camouflaged in the corners suggested that the entire place
could be closed up at the touch of a button.

The man himself was sitting cross-legged on a terrace by the pool,
absorbed by the book he was reading. Rapp's approach went unnoticed
until he was about ten feet away.

"There you are!" Ward, said, tossing the book aside and getting to
his feet. "I saw your chopper come in. Can I get you a beer?"

Because some of the louvers had been raised instead of just being
opened, there was no obvious entrance. In this configuration, the
structure was more like a giant covered deck than a house. Rapp picked
a random spot and climbed into what seemed to be the living room.

"Sure."

He watched the richest man in history pull a couple of bottles from a stainless-steel refrigerator that was the same high-efficiency brand that Rapp had in his Virginia house. It could run off of a single solar panel and had served him well during the blackout.

"I can't tell you how grateful I am for everything you've done, Mitch."

"Nice place," Rapp said by way of a response. No gratitude was necessary. He was there because of Kennedy and Coleman.

"You like it? I have to admit that I thought it was a little weird when my architect showed me the plans. But my motto is hire the best, then get out of their way. Usually it works out." He grinned. "Though she tells me the roof's not designed to support ICBMs."

Ward handed him one of the beers and then took a seat on a sofa, indicating the one across from him. He studied Rapp carefully, absently bobbing one flip-flop on his toes as the former CIA operative sat.

"So, what's the verdict? How did you like working for me?"

"The private sector's not as relaxing as I was hoping."

"I suppose not. But it wasn't boring, right? And it was important. In my experience that motivates men like you. To the degree that there are men like you."

Rapp took a pull on his beer. A home brew judging by the lack of a label. Pretty good.

"So, what are your thoughts on my problems, Mitch?"

"What problems?"

"Gideon Auma. If I send my people back to that area, what's to stop him from attacking them again?"

"Nothing. Don't send them back."

"I don't really have a choice. We're doing vaccine trials there and the people have a unique genetic resistance to a potential serious side effect. Probably from a plague they survived at some time in prehistory."

"Move them. Buy them all houses in Beverly Hills."

"I tried. But they like it here. It's their ancestral home."

"Then I don't know what to tell you."

"We could rebuild the facility with more security features."

"You could. But Auma's a bad combination of smart and insane. And his people are happy to die for him. The problem with trying to defend yourself by living behind walls is that you have to be perfect. If you get a hundred things right and one thing wrong, you lose. And you *always* get one thing wrong."

"Then what would you recommend?"

Rapp took another drink of his beer. "The one thing you've got going for you with Auma's organization is that it's all about one man. With him gone, most of his followers would probably just go home. If I understand right, a lot of them were kidnapped when they were kids. Without him to tell them what to do and think, they'd be lost."

"I've tried everything I can to get the Ugandan government to move against him, but they see it as too risky. And the American government's even worse. The only person who cares less about Uganda than President Alexander did is President Cook."

Rapp pointed through the slats that made up the house and toward the horizon. "You've built yourself your own little principality here. And that means no government's going to have much of an incentive to interfere with you. But they're not going to have much of an incentive to help you, either. Being the master of all you survey is only half the job. The other half is defending it."

"I've never really thought of myself as a prince or the master of all I survey."

"Really? Why not?"

Ward didn't seem to have an answer. And it clearly bothered him.

"Do you think it's possible to find him, Mitch? No one else has been able to. But if we did, we could turn him over to the Ugandan government."

"Anything's possible, Nick. But I don't think turning him over to the Ugandans would be in anybody's best interest. As long as he's alive, he's going to have followers who want him back. What you don't need is some suicide squad turning up in Kampala to try to break him out of prison."

"Then what?"

"Put a bullet in the back of his head and feed him to some hyenas."

Ward gazed thoughtfully at the bottle in his hand. "Having a lot of money doesn't give me the right to sentence people to death."

"You talk like governments have legitimacy. Most leaders aren't elected—they cheat, inherit, or murder their way to the top. How does that give them any more right than you to preside over a legal system? You're a hell of a lot smarter. And a hell of a lot less crazy."

"That's a very dangerous philosophy."

"If you say so."

Ward finished his beer and put the empty bottle on the coffee table between them. "You think I'm a do-gooder walking around with stars in his eyes."

Rapp shook his head. "Do-gooders with stars in their eyes don't make a trillion dollars. But now you want to change the world in fundamental ways. And that is going to take more than a little grit and a fat wallet."

"What if I say yes?"

"To what?"

"To giving you what you need to . . ." His voice faded for a moment. "To resolve the Gideon Auma issue."

"I think you might be getting a little ahead of yourself, Nick. I'm not looking for a job. Scott's your man. He and his guys are the best shooters on the planet."

"But I don't just need a shooter, Mitch. Like you said, I want to change the world in fundamental ways. In the context of the push-back I'm going to get over the rest of my lifetime, I'm guessing that Gideon Auma's just a bump in the road. As much as I'd like to avoid straying into your world, I'm not sure it's going to be possible. I need a guide."

"You might think you know what you're asking, but I'm not sure you do."

"Show me."

A smile spread slowly across Rapp's face. "That sounds like a recipe for the worst retirement in history."

"I'm not so sure. You define the job and I pay you whatever you want. Offers like that don't come along every day."

"Look, Nick. I like you. And I respect what you're trying to do. But I'm not your man. Thanks for the beer, though."

Rapp stood and started for the nonexistent door but only made it a few feet before Ward spoke again.

"Would you at least talk to Irene about me?"

Rapp jumped to the ground but didn't look back. "Next time I see her. Sure."

19

RAPP slowed the SUV to let a young couple cross the street in front of him.

No hurry, he reminded himself as they settled into a seating area in front of a café bathed in afternoon sunlight. Other than this quick errand, he didn't have anything else that had to get done that day. Absolutely nothing. How many times had he been able to say that in his life?

Rapp yawned as he accelerated up the picturesque street, feeling a familiar sense of exhaustion settle into him. Not from the Uganda op, though. From the ninety-mile training ride he'd done that morning with a group of amateur racers about half his age.

His power output had been way below his triathlon days, he'd suffered like an animal, and he was still too heavy. Despite all that, though, they hadn't been able to shake him off until the last climb. In a few months, the roles would be reversed. He'd make them wish they'd never been born. And he'd do it without a gun, blowtorch, or set of pliers.

His phone rang over the SUV's sound system, forcing him to try to figure out how to pick up. It was Claudia's vehicle, and he didn't have much experience with the endless array of modern conveniences. Finally, he managed to connect on the fifth ring.

"Hello? You still there?"

"I'm here," Claudia said in French. "You couldn't find the button again, could you?"

"It's complicated."

"We could always get something smaller and sexier."

"Haven't we had this conversation?"

"This isn't the CIA, Mitch. I don't just salute every time to speak. Conversations can be revisited."

"There's nothing wrong with a salute every now and then. Maybe you should try it."

"I'll take it under advisement."

"What's up? I'm on time. ETA under one minute."

He was on his way to pick up Anna, a chore Claudia normally dealt with personally. She didn't have a lot of faith in his ability to carry out life's more mundane tasks and was likely checking up on him again. To her credit, though, she always made an effort to come up with some lame excuse. That they needed milk. That she was afraid she'd left the gas tank almost empty. That she wasn't sure if he'd prefer a steak for dinner or Mexican.

"I just got a call from Ahmale's mother."

He was surprised and strangely proud to realize that he knew who Ahmale was. Anna's new BFF.

"And?"

"Her toddler's come down with something and is apparently vomiting every few minutes. Would it be possible for you to pick her up and drop her off at home?"

Rapp was about to give her a simple yes but was suddenly invaded by some kind of evil domestic spirit.

"Why don't we just keep her for a day or two? Anna'd love it and it'd take the pressure off her mother."

Claudia was silent for long enough that Rapp thought he might have inadvertently disconnected her. Finally, she spoke. "Are you serious? I was thinking that but didn't want to suggest it. Two girls are four times as much work as one."

"I just crawled through the jungle being hunted by an African death cult. How bad could it be?"

"Much worse than that. But since you're in a generous mood, I'll call Ahmale's mother and make the offer. I'm certain she'll take us up on it."

"Sounds good. Got to go, I'm pulling up out front."

Anna and Ahmale were among the other children crowding the sidewalk. They spotted him, said some quick good-byes, and a moment later were climbing into the backseat.

"Hey, Mitch. Mom said you could give Ahmale a ride home. Her mom couldn't come because her brother's sick."

"Hi, Mr. Rapp!"

"Hi, Ahmale. Hey, since your brother's not feeling good, do you want to just stay with us for a couple of days?"

They froze in the rearview mirror, both looking a bit stunned at the offer but then exploding into enthusiastic squeals.

By the time he pulled away, he'd already faded into complete irrelevance. They were busy making plans for their time together and plotting aloud how they could extend it.

God help him.

"And after that would you—"

"Hang on," Rapp said, cutting Claudia off and opening the kitchen window. "Anna! Stop feeding the dogs ice cream!"

She gave him a guilty look and put the cone behind her back as Ahmale giggled uncontrollably. The dogs circled, trying another line of attack. Hopefully, an unsuccessful one. Something he didn't need in his life was two Rhodesian ridgebacks tearing around the house with diarrhea.

"Sorry," he said, closing the window again. "What were you saying?"

"I was wondering if you could go pick up a few of Ahmale's things later. Her mother's leaving them on the porch, so you don't have to go in the house."

"Sure. No problem."

Her eyes narrowed suspiciously.

"What?"

"Who are you and what have you done with Mitch Rapp?"

"Funny," he said, continuing to stack plates in the dishwasher.

"What are you thinking about? Gideon Auma?"

"Nope."

"President Cook?"

"No."

"Really," she said, unconvinced. "Just focusing on the dishes, huh?"

"And strategizing for Operation Get Ahmale's Stuff. After that, I'm going to fully devote myself to drinking a couple beers on the patio."

"Sounds like a nice afternoon. Can I join you?"

"If you play your cards right."

She turned on the oven light and peeked at the croissants inside. "You know, Nicholas Ward's hired us to design security features into the research facility he's rebuilding."

"Really?"

"Scott says he's going to suggest a moat full of hippos."

"Hippos are good," Rapp said absently. "Mean."

"You're seriously not interested?"

"You and Scott will get along fine without me."

"What about a croissant hot out of the oven? Surely, you're interested in that."

He shook his head. "It's either a croissant now or the beers later. Calories."

"I'm finding this sudden change in you a little hard to believe."

"You're complaining?"

"No. I'm just wondering how long it's going to last."

20

THERE was a quiet knock on the door and Irene Kennedy looked up to see one of her assistants poke his head in.

"Marcus Dumond would like to see you, Dr. Kennedy. He says it's urgent."

She felt her eyebrows rise involuntarily. Dumond was a young hacker whom Mitch Rapp had stumbled over a few years ago. He'd been on his way to jail when they'd provided him another option: give working for the Agency a try. The combination of gratitude and genius had turned out to be a good one and Dumond had become a critical part of her team. Having said that, he was easily intimidated and a bit of a recluse. In fact, she was having a hard time remembering an instance of him requesting a face-to-face meeting.

"How am I looking for the next fifteen minutes?"

"We can juggle."

"Then tell him to come up."

"Actually, he's standing in front of my desk."

"Really?" Kennedy said, even more surprised. "Then by all means send him in."

Dumond entered a moment later, looking a bit haggard for his thirty-four years. Other than that, he didn't seem much different than the day they'd first met—same thin frame, slightly crooked Afro, and vaguely stunned expression. He seemed perpetually unable to believe that he was working a high-level CIA job and not in a prison laundry.

"What can I do for you, Marcus?"

"There's been an incursion into our system," he said, a little breathlessly.

"From the outside?"

He shook his head. "Inside."

"How far were they able to penetrate?"

"That's what's weird. They seemed to be after one very specific thing. Information on Nicholas Ward."

"Ward?" she said, reflecting for a moment on how often the man had come up in her life over the past few weeks. "I wouldn't think we'd have much sensitive intelligence on him."

"We don't. What little's classified is classified at a low level. The truth is that you could dig most of it up from Wikipedia and old magazine articles."

"If it wasn't particularly critical information, why do you look so worried?"

"It's not what the person was after, it's how they did it. Whoever they were, they have a lot of clearance and a lot of brains."

"But not so much of either that you didn't discover them."

He didn't respond, looking even more concerned.

"Marcus?"

"The only reason I caught it is because I was running an unannounced diagnostic when the query came in," he blurted. "I'm sorry, Dr. Kennedy. But it was just dumb luck. If I hadn't been running it at that exact moment, they would have had pretty much full access to all our databases, and I would have never known anything about it. I'm really sor—"

She held up a hand, silencing him. In a way, Dumond was one of the most trustworthy people she worked with. He was brilliant, obsessive, and driven by motivations that were easy to decipher. Despite his history of draining corporate bank accounts that didn't belong to him, he genuinely wanted to please her and do the right thing.

"If you wouldn't have caught it, I'm confident no one else would have, either. Now, tell me this. Did this person get the information they were after?"

He shook his head. "All the files were off-line because of the diagnostic."

"And I assume they still are?"

"*Very* off-line. I actually disconnected some hardware. You'd have to have a wrench and physical access to the server to get to them."

"Now that we know what's happening, can we track this person if they try again?"

"I doubt it," he said uncomfortably. "The way the system's designed—"

Again, she silenced him with a wave of the hand. What she didn't need was an hours-long explanation of circuit boards and encryption algorithms.

"So, no."

"That's correct, ma'am. I can set things up so we know if there are any more attacks, but the way they're being done makes it impossible to trace back to the person behind the keyboard."

"You're saying our system is just wide open to this person for the foreseeable future? That's not acceptable."

"No, ma'am. I can reprogram the system to shut them out, but it's not going to be a smooth transition. Everyone at the Agency will get locked out and have to redo their log-ins."

"Can I assume that our perpetrator will know we're onto him or her if we do that?"

"Definitely."

She leaned back and pondered the problem for a moment. "If we bring the system back online soon, am I correct in saying that it'll just look like you're finished with the diagnostic? That our mole would have no reason to be suspicious and would feel free to try again?"

"Yes. If we just go back online without a major security update, then, frankly, we can't keep them out."

"Can I make changes to Ward's file before we go back online?"

"Absolutely," he said, clearly following her thought process. If tracing this person electronically was impossible, there was another option. She could introduce subtle errors into the CIA's information on Ward. Then, if those errors were acted upon, they might lead to the person who had so skillfully penetrated their defenses.

"Can you send me the files in question?"

He pulled a thumb drive from his pocket, having anticipated the request. "I can't send them because they're air-gapped. So, I put them on here." After placing the storage device on her desk, he immediately started retreating toward the door. "I'm really, really sorry about this, Dr. Kennedy. Don't worry, though. I'll figure out a way to fix it. When you're ready, just tell me, okay?"

She conjured up her warmest smile. Dumond didn't do well under pressure and she needed him operating at one hundred percent. "I have complete confidence in you, Marcus. If anyone else had been at the helm, I doubt we would have ever known about this. So, thank you."

His expression melted into something between a smile and a wince as he continued backing toward the door. "When you're done making the changes, save them to that thumb drive and let me know. I'll come get it and upload the files to the server. Sooner is better than later, though. The longer the system stays down—"

"You'll have it by tonight."

He turned to finish his escape but was forced to pause when she spoke again.

"Does anyone else know about this, Marcus?"

"No one."

"Let's keep it that way."

"Yes, ma'am."

After she'd finished skimming the CIA's file on Nicholas Ward, Irene Kennedy took off her reading glasses and leaned back in her chair. She'd learned a few details she hadn't known before but nothing that changed her opinion of the man.

There was no superlative that didn't trivialize what he'd managed to accomplish in a single lifetime. The wealth was what everyone saw but it made up only a small part of who he really was. His motivations at this point appeared to be entirely altruistic. Clearly, he couldn't be bought. He had no definable political or religious ideology. His only goal seemed to be to use the resources he'd accumulated to lift humanity out of the mire.

Unfortunately, it was those same resources that were making him an increasingly prominent target. For competing commercial interests. For politicians. Even for the people he wanted to help.

Ironically, it might be that latter category that would prove most dangerous in the long run. The average person had no hope of understanding the depths of someone like Nicholas Ward. His motivations. How a mind like his perceived the world. The effortlessness with which he manipulated the technologies he'd created. And what people didn't understand they distrusted—a tendency that had been amplified a thousand times over by the Internet. It was getting hard to keep up with all the conspiracy theories that swirled around him. That he was using his medical research to track patients. That he was Q of the imaginary QAnon organization. Even that he was, in fact, some kind of lizard-human hybrid. The last one in particular would have been easy to laugh off if it weren't for the startling number of people who subscribed to it. The belief in witches had been ridiculous, too, but that hadn't been much comfort to the innocent people watching the flames rise around them.

Having said that, it would be very much a mistake to paint Ward as either innocent or a victim. Like the introduction to the old *Star Trek* television program, he was attempting to go where no man had gone before. There were risks to that kind of action. To him. And, frankly, to everyone else.

If she were to make a list of the most powerful entities in the world—the ones that would shape the next one hundred years of human existence—how would it be ordered? The United States and China would be on top, she imagined. But after that, was it possible that she'd write the name Nicholas Ward?

It was incredible that she was even asking that question. The first two entries encompassed the better part of two billion people. The last was a single man. A single man who still didn't fully understand the power he had. One day he would, though, and she wasn't sure what the consequences would be.

What she was sure of was that he needed to be protected. His involvement in telecom, space exploration, energy, and artificial intelligence was critical to America's national security and economy. The rest of it—the existential danger and hope he represented—was something for another day.

21

A NOTHER perfect Ugandan day. Another helicopter ride. Another dense forest streaking by beneath Rapp's boots. Unfortunately, it had also been a perfect day in South Africa, where he had managed to spend less than two weeks before Irene Kennedy's courier had appeared at his gate.

The hand-delivered message was unusual enough to get his full attention. Modern technology provided endless options for encrypted comms and the fact that she'd chosen not to use one was notable. Instead, he'd been handed a sealed USB drive designed to fit only into a laptop he'd been provided years ago. It would be the first—and last— time it was used.

Upon reading the document it contained, the reason for avoiding normal CIA communications protocols was understandable. The threat, though, wasn't what he'd expected in such a dramatic communiqué. Not to him or Kennedy or America, but to Nicholas Ward.

And so here he was, heading back to a job he'd just quit. But less to solve Ward's problem than Kennedy's. Marcus Dumond had run into a dead end identifying the person digging around in the CIA's mainframe. That meant they were going to have to go low-tech: using disinformation she'd introduced into Ward's file to trick the perpetrator into revealing himself. An old-fashioned mole hunt.

And, if he was being completely honest, it wasn't the worst time to get out of the Cape. The day before, he'd taken Anna on a little ride outside the wall and there had been a minor incident involving a tree. And a ditch. And maybe a few spiny plants.

Despite the fact that there hadn't been all that much blood, the top of Claudia's head had nearly blown off. He was alive today only because there had been no sharp objects within reach when he and Anna had pushed their bikes back through the gate.

He smiled into the wind coming through the chopper's open door. Anna had really been drilling it when she went down. And while there had been a few tears, they hadn't been accompanied by any sniveling. His smile faded. If she ended up with her father's ruthless determination and her mother's brains, she'd become one dangerous woman. And an impossible-to-control teenager.

As they overflew Ward's compound, Rapp noted that the berms reinforcing the fence were all but done. So were various chain gun mounts and a number of other defensive measures. All reasonably subtle but, when combined with the strategic location, also deceptively formidable. Coleman had once again proved that he was the best in the business.

"Looks like the place is in pretty good shape," Rapp shouted to the former SEAL as he jumped out of the aircraft and jogged from beneath its rotors.

"Yeah. We finally took delivery of the green razor wire, but we can't set it up until we install ultrasonic bullhorns to keep animals from walking into it. That'll all be done today, though."

"And the mines?"

"Even more behind schedule. Ward's absolutely forbidden them, so we have to lay them at night when he's asleep. Complete pain in the ass. Between the foliage and the dark, mapping them is a nightmare."

"But you're almost there?"

"Two nights out," he said, frowning. "What are you doing here, Mitch? Are those kids slapping you around on the bike? Maybe you should get one of those three-wheeled ones. You're not exactly a spring chicken anymore."

"Younger than you, asshole."

"But nowhere near as beautifully preserved," Coleman said as they entered the tent that acted as a command center.

Rapp walked to a map detailing the security measures that had been put into place and those yet to come.

"Seriously, Mitch. What are you doing here? I don't need you to tell me how to do my job."

"Somebody's got to," Rapp joked, dropping into a folding chair and stretching his legs out. "So, you're comfortable with what you've been able to accomplish here?"

"Yeah," Coleman responded after a few seconds of silence. "We've talked about this. You can always do more, but we're in good shape. There are no roads in or out, so any attacking force would have a tough slog through the jungle just to get here. That also prevents them bringing in anything much heavier than a few shoulder-fired missiles. We've got sensors set up that are going to give us good lead time on any attack and drones in the sky twenty-four/seven. Ward would be long gone before anyone even got close."

"So, no weaknesses."

"A significant force coming in from the air would be a problem. We've got some SAMs but we're not really set up for that. My assumption is that I'm not going to have to deal with the 82nd Airborne."

Rapp scanned the map across from him and pointed to the eastern slope that descended from the compound. "What about that? Looks thin."

Coleman shook his head. "The terrain is working for us there. It's really steep and funnels into a gully that terminates in a twenty-foot-high cliff maybe a hundred yards from the perimeter wall. Anybody smart enough to get this far wouldn't be stupid enough to walk into that death trap. We decided it wasn't a good use of limited resources to focus on it."

"Actually, that's exactly where you need to focus your resources."

Coleman just stared at him for a moment. "Did you trip over your dogs and hit your head? No one's attacking from that direction."

Rapp stood and tapped a point on the map about halfway up the gully. "I also want you to run an underground wire here. North to south. Make it span the entire depression."

"A wire? Attached to what?"

"Nothing."

The former SEAL's eyes narrowed. "You know something I don't."

It was interesting—and a bit pathetic—that the blond man standing in front of him was one of only two people in the world Rapp completely trusted. And as such, he would join him, Kennedy, and Dumond as the last person who knew what was happening.

"What I'm about to tell you doesn't leave this tent."

The short nod from his friend was all that was necessary.

"There was a high-level computer breach at Langley. The only thing we really know beyond the fact that it happened is that whoever's responsible was interested in Ward."

Coleman smirked. "Probably some CIA exec trying to get insider stock information. Wouldn't be the first time."

"Maybe. But we need to know for sure. And until we do, we can't trust any of the Agency's technology."

"Or any of its people. But what's that got to do with the eastern slope of the compound?"

"Whoever wanted to get Ward's file failed the first time. But Irene let them in the second."

Coleman pondered that for a moment and then a light dawned. "There was information on this place. And she changed it."

"Yeah. And her revised map shows the east being the best bet for an attack."

"What's up with the wire you want buried?"

"Irene included a bogus diagram of all the compound's electronic defenses that showed one weakness. Not obvious, but a specialist would be able to find it."

"That wire."

"Exactly. She made it look like cutting it would disrupt the whole system."

Coleman scanned the map for a few seconds. "So, you think this is a credible threat?"

Rapp returned to the chair and stretched out again. "No. I think you're probably right that it's someone on the seventh floor looking to pad out their retirement portfolio. But I've learned to take Irene's hunches seriously."

"It's hard to ignore the fact that you're using Ward as bait."

Rapp didn't react.

"He's not going to like that, Mitch. And frankly I don't either. He's my client and now I have information suggesting he's in danger."

"But he's not, right? You said this place is secure."

"Don't throw my words back at me. You know as well as I do that there are no guarantees."

"What's that mean to me?"

Coleman's jaw tightened. "Nothing. You already know that. But just because I agree to do something doesn't mean I have to like it."

"I'm surprised to see you here, Mitch."

Nicholas Ward seemed to have an aversion to his expensive furniture and this time was sitting on the steps that led to the pool.

"I had a change of heart," Rapp said as he approached. "Probably a brief one."

"A change of heart . . . Can I assume Irene had something to do with that?"

"Things are looking shipshape," Rapp said, changing the subject. "Scott's gotten a lot done in a week and a half."

"If you mean he's changed my home into Fort Ward, I agree. And don't think I don't know about the mines."

Rapp smiled. "These aren't World War II surplus, Nick. They can be turned on and off remotely."

"Oh, I know all about them. In fact, I've spent a fair amount of time and money trying to get that entire class of technology wiped from the face of the earth. And now here I am surrounded by them. Ironic. And hypocritical."

"Desperate times . . ."

"Are they, though, Mitch? I admit that I underestimated Gideon Auma, but isn't it possible that you're *overestimating* him? There's a big difference between an opportunistic attack on a hospital and trying to get up here."

"Irene thinks there might be someone out there who wants to make a move against you."

"Who?"

"We don't know. It's just chatter at this point. But it makes sense to be cautious. You can afford it."

He looked skeptical but unwilling to entirely discount what Rapp was telling him. "Maybe it's time for me and my people to go stateside for a little while. I feel like my presence here is creating a lot of drama."

"I'm not sure you'd be any safer there."

"That's a specific enough statement to suggest that the threat to me is more than just chatter. Would you care to elaborate?"

"No."

Ward's smile carried a hint of frustration as he stood and walked back inside. When he reappeared, there were a couple of beers in his hand. He gave one to Rapp.

"I can't shake the feeling that you have some hidden agenda here, Mitch."

"Really?"

"Really. But what is it? Gideon Auma? Maybe he's getting a little too close to Islamic terrorist groups and you want to use me to get to him? Or maybe your operation to save David went so well that it made Anthony Cook look bad. Could you be here to stab me in the back as penance?"

"Maybe I just like you."

"I doubt it."

"Well then you just keep thinking on it. Maybe you'll come up with something."

"I always do."

Even having known the man for only a short time, Rapp didn't doubt it.

"What do you say we change the subject to something a little less depressing," Ward continued. "Matteo's back on his feet and I know that he, David, and Jing would love to thank you personally. They're in cabins just down the way. Why don't we walk over?"

"Not necessary," Rapp said before taking a pull from his beer.

Ward picked up on the finality in his statement. "You prefer anonymity to gratitude. Understood. But they'd also like to know when they can start their work again. The facility's gone, but their test subjects—and some patients who need them—are still in the surrounding villages."

"That's not something we want to rush into."

"They'd disagree. This is an ongoing study and they're losing critical data."

"Come on, Nick. You know as well as I do that the day they set foot in one of those villages, Auma's going to hear about it. And he's a persistent son of a bitch."

"You could provide security."

"It's not that easy. Those villages are wide open, they're surrounded by dense jungle, and Auma has no problem with losing as many people as he needs to to get what he wants. That's not a great combination."

"And if they're willing to take the risk?"

"That's noble and all, but it's not just their risk, is it? While they're getting lifted out in one of your luxury helicopters, my guys will be getting their asses shot off."

Ward nodded thoughtfully, but didn't respond.

"Look, Nick. I'm not as much of a Cro-Magnon as you think. I understand how important that research is. Once we're satisfied with the security here, we'll look at our options down there. Maybe some quick, random hits. In and out in an hour with air support and a reasonable ground force. That'd give Chism enough time to take a few samples and make some house calls."

Ward reached out with his beer and clinked it against Rapp's own. "Thanks, Mitch."

22

MUHAMMAD Singh had spent his adult life as a contractor
for Saudi intelligence, doing a job no one in the government
was willing to touch. After a strict Islamic education and a youthful
tryst with al-Qaeda, he'd been hired to be the Kingdom's liaison with
the complex web of Islamic terrorist groups throughout the world.
When the royals needed to secretly coordinate with al-Qaeda, ISIS,
the Taliban, and myriad others, he was their man.

In the beginning, it was work he'd been proud to perform. The
Saudi government was making fools of the Americans, using the tril-
lions of dollars they paid for oil to hire jihadists to kill them. It never
ceased to amaze Singh how willing the Americans were to look away
when their oil supply hung in the balance. Cash transfers to terrorist groups, the killing of their troops around the world, 9/11, the royalty's continued support of radical madrassas. None of it mattered. The
Americans would sell their own daughters into slavery for a few precious drops of what lay beneath the Saudi desert.

Over the past few years, though, the landscape had begun to
change. At first, it was almost imperceptible. Slight shifts in the focus

of his clandestine meetings. Additional buffers between him and real power. The work that had once been for the glory of God had been corrupted to nourish the greed of a handful of men. The young royals who had recently come into power cared nothing about what their country had once been. They knew nothing of hardship and the comfort of Allah's blessing. Instead, they took their comfort from palaces, Western whores, and bottles of forbidden liquor that cost more than many of their subjects earned in a year. Islam was just a convenience to them. Like Christianity in the West, it was something to be played at when useful. If there was anything that could surpass the Americans' thirst for oil, it was the Saudi royalty's thirst for wealth and power.

The scent of the forest around Singh began to change as he continued forward. Rotting vegetation and blooming flowers were slowly overcome by something very different. Sweat and excrement. Sex and rotting flesh.

Gideon Auma had rejected every offer of a civilized location for their meeting, insisting that Singh come to him in the jungle. It wasn't entirely unexpected, of course. Auma continued to survive the ire of the entire world based on shrewdness and caution.

The foliage began to thin, and his young guide put away his machete. The stench intensified to the point that Singh felt compelled to cover his nose and mouth with his hand. Discarded human figures appeared on either side of the poorly defined trail, strewn randomly and in various stages of decomposition. Later, they were secured to trees with barbed wire or nailed to makeshift crosses erected in the soft earth.

Singh felt a revulsion that he hadn't suffered even in the most decadent of ISIS camps. At least ISIS maintained the pretense of remaining faithful to Allah. Gideon Auma adopted any and all belief systems that suited him. Above it all, though, was the man himself. God's representative on earth.

They weaved through the looming Christian symbols, watched by the empty eye sockets of the corpses hanging from them. After a few hundred meters more, they passed from the realm of the dead to the realm of the living. Haggard girls, stolen from surrounding villages and now existing as sex slaves, scurried for cover. He imagined that their bodies, filthy, scarred, and broken, would soon end up with the others at the perimeter of the encampment.

Many of Auma's youthful army appeared to be intoxicated, though it was impossible to know with what. They watched him from the trees like the girls had. Like the corpses had. With curiosity. With indifference. With rage. But none dared approach or even meet his eye. None had the ability to act on their own or think for themselves. For some, those were skills that had been beaten out of them. For others, they were skills they'd never acquired. Only serving Gideon Auma mattered. Their god.

The clearing they finally entered wasn't really a clearing at all—just a place where the ground cover had been torn away and the canopy had been woven together in a way that would hinder a search from the air. Singh's guide signaled for him to wait and then disappeared into the trees.

He stood motionless near a stone altar dried with blood and fitted with chains that suggested the sacrifices performed there weren't limited to animals. After more than half an hour, the Great Man appeared from a cave to the north. He was wearing fatigues that were somewhat more complete and in better condition than those of his followers. His beard was patchy and his hair a bit wild where it escaped a camouflage cap. The skin around his vaguely glassy eyes was dark and surprisingly undamaged.

Weak cheers erupted from his followers as he approached and offered Singh his hand. Not to shake, though. In a way reminiscent of the pope offering his ring to be kissed. Trying to strike a balance between further insulting God and ending up on one of the crosses he'd passed, Singh took the man's hand and bowed his head over it. The gesture seemed to be sufficiently reverential because a moment later the cult leader spoke.

"What message do you bring from your masters?"

Singh was only a messenger and he would do his best to disappear into that role. An irrelevant little man unworthy of Gideon Auma's notice. And more important, unworthy of his fury.

"They are concerned with David Chism's escape."

Auma's expression remained impassive, though it was likely that there was quite a bit more lurking behind that façade. He'd made commitments that depended on Chism's ransom and now those promises of reward and victory had been dispersed to the wind. Hardly in keeping with his image.

"God didn't will it," he said finally.

"Indeed," Singh responded. "Perhaps he wants you for greater things."

That seemed to awaken some interest in the man. "What?"

"We believe there is an opportunity to kidnap Nicholas Ward himself. The ransom for Chism would have been millions. But for Ward? It would be billions."

Auma shook his head. "No one knows where his compound is and even if we did it would be difficult to access and heavily secured."

Singh retrieved a manilla envelope from his backpack and opened it. "Is this what you need?"

Auma began leafing through the laminated pages. Maps. Diagrams. Overhead photos. Even schematics and electrical diagrams of their early warning system.

"Our experts suggest that the defenses to the east are particularly weak and they've discovered a way to defeat Ward's electronics. A relatively small force—perhaps as few as fifty men—could breach his defenses and overrun the compound with minimal casualties."

Auma studied what he'd been given. "Where did you get this?"

"From the highest levels."

A very human excitement began to bleed through the African's messianic façade. "And you're confident all of this is accurate?"

"More than confident. My masters guarantee it." Singh fell silent for a moment, but then decided to press. "Imagine, your worship. Imagine what you could do with a billion dollars. What weapons you could buy. What followers you could attract. Uganda would be yours. And then Congo and beyond. You would be the most powerful man in Africa. Its savior."

His eyes turned reflective, almost mirrorlike in the fading afternoon light. "What do you want in return?"

"We want David Chism dead."

"And Ward?"

"The same if feasible."

"His people aren't stupid, and neither am I," Auma said. "They're not going to just give me a billion dollars without guarantees."

Indeed, he was not stupid. It was another thing that Singh had noted in his long career. Never mistake insanity for a lack of intelligence. More than once, his survival had turned on him being able to make that distinction.

"As long as Chism dies, we understand that it may be necessary for Ward to survive. But we trust that the man you return will no longer be the one the world knows today. And that he never will be again."

23

"FIFTEEN tons?" Irene Kennedy said, reaching for the cup of tea on her desk. "Impressive."

Mike Nash nodded. "One of the biggest drug seizures in Italy's history."

ISIS had been in decline for some time now, discovering that holding and governing territory was quite a bit harder than pillaging and murder. Now, with much of their leadership dead, they were transforming into just another bloodthirsty drug cartel.

"Our take on this is that it's business as usual and not some kind of resurgence?"

"That's the general consensus. They're still holding on to a little of their political and religious veneer in Syria, but it seems like they're more interested in using the country as a base for their drug operations than a new caliphate. So, basically, that slow train wreck is now sinking in the mud."

She glanced at a printed agenda on her desk. "Next up is the potential bioweapons factory in North Korea."

"Yeah, we just got in some new satellite photos. Definitely not operational and our people are starting to question whether it ever will be."

"Saber rattling?"

"There's a good chance. Those assholes will do anything for attention."

"Not our attention, though. China seems to be pulling back their support. They have better places to concentrate their resources."

"Agreed. More and more, China's about giving Kim just enough to keep his head above water."

It was a fair analysis in Kennedy's estimation. Chinese leadership despised instability, which prevented them from pulling out entirely. But as a rising world power, their relationship with Pyongyang was becoming an embarrassing relic.

"And that's it," her second-in-command said with the grin that had helped make him such a star inside the beltway. "Things have stayed at a slow simmer a lot longer than I thought it would."

"The calm after the storm," Kennedy agreed. The collapse of America's power grid, even though it lasted a relatively short time, had shaken the world to its core. The desire and resources to cause trouble were still in short supply. That wouldn't last forever, though. It never did.

"Even the Russian trolls have backed off. What do you think, Irene? Have we finally put the fear of god into that prick Boris Utkin?"

"I doubt it."

"No? You think he's sitting back planning something?"

"I think he's sitting back watching."

"Watching what?"

"Anthony and Catherine Cook. I've met Utkin a number of times and I can tell you that he's genuinely confused by why anyone would want to live in a democracy. He sees it as chaos for the man on the street and stifling for the born rulers like him."

Nash leaned back in his chair and stretched the familiar kink in his back. A souvenir from a bomb blast in Afghanistan. "And you think he might see the Cooks as sharing that worldview?"

"It's a possibility. What about you? What do you think?"

"Honestly? I think democracy's tricky. We've seen that over and over again when we've tried to export it. And even organic movements like the Arab Spring tend to fall flat on their faces. I thought we were particularly good at it, though. And why not? We don't just learn it from birth. In a way, it's baked into us. With obvious exceptions, our ancestors took a lot of risks for the opportunity to breathe free."

"You said *thought*. That you *thought* we were particularly good at it. Past tense."

"Democracy has always been messy, but now it seems to be going beyond that. *Chaos* is too strong a word, but we may be moving in that direction. And faster than I would have guessed." He shook his head in irritation. "I wish I could send everyone in America to live under the dictatorship in Turkmenistan. Or to spend a little time in a New Delhi slum. Maybe they'd gain a little perspective about how good they have it. But I can't. So instead, they'll listen to politicians tell them how they're getting screwed. Or the media telling them about all the things that can kill them. Or some YouTube influencer showing off their fake idyllic life. Where's it all leading?"

"I wish I knew," Kennedy said.

"Me too, but I'm starting to get glimpses of possible futures that didn't exist only a few years ago. I can see our democracy collapsing into something that more resembles what they have in Moscow. I can see states actually trying to secede again. And what's weird is that I can see those things happening in our lifetime. Think how much this country's changed in the last five years. The last ten. And it seems like it's accelerating. Where will we be at the end of the next decade?"

"But what side of all that is Anthony Cook on?"

Nash laughed. "I know you don't like him, but he's actually not that bad. He's thinking about the future in a way that maybe no president has had to. He doesn't seem particularly happy about it, though. I imagine he wants four years of smooth sailing, to get reelected, and to build a nice library. But the way I see it—and probably the way he sees it—he doesn't have that luxury. Wrong place. Wrong time."

Kennedy nodded slowly, warming her hands on the teacup. Not really an answer, but at this point maybe there wasn't one. Or maybe there was, and she just couldn't find it. She was pulling back too much. Counting on Mike Nash to run too much interference. She needed either to do this job to the best of her ability or to step aside.

"Contact the Chinese," she said finally. "I want to talk to them about the North Korean facility. Over the phone if possible, face-to-face if necessary. Even if this is just a feint by the Korean leadership, it's crossing the line. But if it's real, then we need to decide how far we're willing to go to head it off."

"Will do," Nash said, gathering his things. "And on another subject. Have you heard anything out of Mitch lately?"

"I haven't. My understanding is that Scott's still in Uganda but I'm not sure where Mitch is. I assume back home."

A lie, but she wasn't sure whether she should say more. Rapp and Nash had known each other for years. If he wanted to know where his old friend was, he could pick up a phone.

"That Chism guy seems next level. I'm glad that they got him and his people out."

"Someone had to."

"Yeah," Nash said, slipping his file portfolio under his arm. "Cook made a mess of that. Hopefully, trying to put an operation like that together himself was just a rookie mistake. I'd hate for him to turn out to be one of those politicians who thinks getting elected makes them the world expert on every subject under the sun."

Kennedy just nodded, wondering if either of those explanations fit. Cook was many things, but he wasn't stupid. Nor was he particularly tolerant of failure. Given those two observations, it was hard not to wonder if he'd really wanted Chism rescued. Certainly, there was no love lost between him and Nicholas Ward. Was it possible that he was that petty? Would he let people die just to burn someone who hadn't supported his political rise?

She watched Nash leave and then spun her chair to look out the large windows behind her desk. The sprawling campus represented an incredible amount of power. Thinking about what it could become under the wrong leadership was terrifying. It would be so easy to turn the Agency against the very American people it was meant to serve. All that would have to happen is for the definition of "enemy of the state" to drift to "enemy of the administration."

She thought about how effective East Germany's Stasi had been at controlling their citizens with capabilities that seemed so quaint now. Hardwired listening stations. Film cameras. Handwritten transcriptions and warehouses full of paper files. This, compared to high-definition video cameras, GPS tracking, and artificial intelligence capable of combing through millions of hours of cell phone conversations and terabytes of email.

The question that had consumed her predecessors—that of what was possible—had become almost irrelevant. Everything was possible now. The challenge was resisting the temptation to use the tools that were right at her fingertips.

Would the next occupant of this office be as prudent? What about the one after that? And after that? No matter how she turned the question over in her mind, she always came to the same answer.

No.

24

RAPP glanced at the glow of his watch and read the time: 8 p.m. The darkness was almost as deep as the boredom.

The airplane hangar sixty miles southeast of Nicholas Ward's compound was in danger of becoming his permanent home. One he shared with a single Learjet and twelve mercenaries drawn from all around the world. None were from Coleman's core team, but all were top operators the SEAL had worked with in the past.

The sound of the jungle that surrounded the structure was inaudible through the walls, or maybe it was just overpowered by the snoring of the men scattered along its edges. Footsteps sounded on the metal roof and he instinctively turned his attention upward. The men on it were hooking up a few additional solar panels to power exterior surveillance equipment.

The CIA database had included a description of this place and anyone with the brains to access Ward's file would also have the brains to understand the hangar's purpose. If there was a problem on the mountaintop, Ward could be evacuated by chopper, brought here, and put on a plane to Johannesburg in less than an hour.

If Rapp had been trying to get his hands on the world's first trillionaire, the hangar would figure heavily in his plan. It was too risky to send a significant force to the compound. Even if it managed to arrive unnoticed and breach the fence, the fog of war could cause accidents. Ward wasn't worth much full of bullet holes.

No, the smart money was to send a small, disciplined team to kick up just enough dust to force Ward's evacuation. Then it would be a relatively simple matter to ambush him and his minimal security team here.

Or at least that was the theory.

After spending four days shuttered up in this place, Rapp was starting to wonder. The much simpler theory of some CIA executive searching for insider investment information was looking more and more plausible.

He heard the steady gait of someone approaching. They'd cut a few ports high in the hangar's walls to provide enough starlight for night vision gear. Whoever was closing in on him would be using a monocular to avoid stepping on his sleeping comrades.

The footsteps went silent when they were still a couple feet away and Rapp heard the rustle of cloth as someone crouched.

"We're all hooked up, Mitch. Everything's operational."

The quiet voice was immediately recognizable. Levi Mizrah—a former Israeli operator whom Rapp had known for years.

"Is it going to be enough?"

"The cameras aren't too bad a draw, but when you add in the night vision gear and communications, it's tight. They're calling for overcast on Thursday, but with backups and a little prioritization, we should be all right until we get full sun again on Friday."

"What if the cloud cover lasts longer than that?"

"Unless we're willing to risk bringing in precharged batteries, we'll have to start conserving, including intermittently cutting power to the surveillance equipment. It's a tolerable risk, though. Like you've said, anyone wanting to secure this piece of ground would probably just drive up the road like we did. There's no reason for them to think anyone's here."

"And the protocols for all this are worked out?"

"Absolutely. Unless we get really heavy cloud cover for multiple days in a row, we shouldn't see a significant impact to our readiness. We should all pray for sun, though. Because one of the first things that get cut is the latrine fan."

Rapp nodded in the darkness. "What's the status of our air support? Any improvement?"

The Ugandan air force had offered to loan Ward six Mi-24 helicopters based on the lie that they'd be used to relocate Chism's research operations to the north. One small detail the government had left out, though, was that none of them actually worked.

"Believe it or not, our guys have gotten two of the choppers flying by scavenging parts from the other four. They say that's the best they can do until they get the shipment from Russia next week."

"Are they going to be able to get here from Mbarara?"

"It's about twenty minutes flying time, so yeah. But not much more than that. The mechanics say they probably only have about an hour of operating time before they start falling from the sky."

"Armament?"

"Door guns. The sexy stuff is either broken or there's no ammo. They'll put on a good show, though. No one likes to see a Russian chopper bearing down on them. I figure you probably know that better than me."

It was a true statement. Those things made even the Afghans shit themselves.

"Thanks, Levi. Why don't you go get some sleep?"

"Roger that. And don't forget that it's your turn on the surveillance monitors at noon."

Generally, Rapp would pass on staring at a bank of screens depicting empty roads and jungle. In the current environment, though, two hours of studying waving branches and blowing dust sounded downright thrilling.

"I'll be there."

Rapp woke to a shrill tone in his earpiece. Normally, it would be Irene Kennedy checking up on him, but she'd lost confidence in electronic communications since the breach at Langley. Instead, his satphone displayed an alphanumeric code that corresponded to Claudia's secure mobile.

"Yeah? What's up?" he said, connecting the call.

Instead of Claudia's elegant French accent, he was greeted with Anna's increasingly South African one.

"Mitch? Is that you?"

"What are you doing on this phone?" he said quietly.

She ignored the question. "Mom won't let me ride my bike 'cause she's sick and can't watch me. But there aren't any big trees in the yard. There's nothing I can hit. It's, like, totally safe."

Rapp stood and peered through a small peephole cut into the wall behind him. Outside, the moonlight illuminated a runway and the dark tree line exactly 133 yards beyond.

"Back up. Did you say your mom is sick?"

"Yeah. I think she got what Ahmale had. She says it's going 'roun'. But I don't have it. I could ride. And I want to be faster when you get back!"

Shit.

"Can you put her on?"

"She's asleep. Want me to wake her up?"

"No. Do *not* wake her up."

They'd been there for days and there was still no sign of anyone moving against Ward. Everything was set up and now it was just a waiting game—something the men dozing around him were happy to do for the amount of cash Nicholas Ward was shelling out. He, on the other hand, didn't need the money and had better things to do. Maybe it was time to tell Joe Maslick to get his feet out of the baby pool and come run this end of the operation. Or hell, just put Levi in charge. He'd proven himself a hundred times over during the course of his career.

"If your mom says to stay off the bike then stay off it. And you should be helping out around the house. But don't get too close to her. And wash your hands."

Was he really doing this? Was he really standing in the middle of nowhere Uganda, surrounded by mercenaries, lecturing a seven-year-old about personal hygiene? This family man crap was getting out of hand.

"I'm being careful. And I *am* helping. I made soup all by myself. And crackers. Well, I didn't make those, but I opened the box. And I took them up to her. But that doesn't mean I can't—"

"You heard what I said, Anna. The bike's off-limits. Your mother has enough on her plate without you running over one of the dogs and going over your handlebars."

"Fine."

He grimaced. She'd picked up that response—and the pissed-off tone that carried it—from him.

"Look, I've got a couple things to tie up here and then I'll get on a plane home."

"When?"

"I don't know. Probably sometime tomorrow. Just hold down the fort until then. Can you do that?"

"Sure," she said with the unshakable confidence of someone who had less than a decade under her belt. "Easy."

25

THE day that had been foretold was finally here.

After more than forty-eight hours trudging through the forest, Sanyu Nabirye was now crawling. Not because of exhaustion, though. For stealth.

He had become part of the darkness, part of the jungle around him. Like he always did. Never once had his victims seen him coming. He appeared in their villages like a ghost, moving among them as their screams filled his ears. As the heat from their burning villages warmed his skin and the smoke burned his throat.

Such was God's glory. Such was the glory of Gideon Auma.

Three days ago, Nabirye had been called into the great man's presence. He had been a disciple for years, listening to his sermons, kneeling before him, giving thanks to him for their victories. But this had been different. The great man had spoken to him directly. Called him by name. Touched his shoulder. And given him a sacred mission.

Nabirye inched forward, staying beneath bushes that were in turn hidden beneath the jungle canopy. It was a gift from God that neutralized the Whites' aircraft. And without their machines, they were nothing. Weak. Cowardly. Faithless.

Gideon Auma had told him so.

The force behind him—seventy men in all—would hold their positions, following the plan Auma had devised. He, on the other hand, would continue forward, privileged to carry out the most critical part of the mission.

He glanced at the GPS in his hand, following the course it laid out for him. Only ten more meters, but he didn't let his pace increase with his growing excitement. Auma had warned against that. Discipline. God was watching. And God could be trusted to guide the faithful.

Even without the Sacrament—what the rest of the world disparagingly called ajali—his senses heightened. The scent of the trees and mold became overwhelming. He could discern the scrape of individual rocks beneath his stomach and chest. Differentiate the buzz of the insects around him.

Two more meters.

He almost laughed when he saw the obvious line of churned earth and chopped roots. The Whites were even stupider than Auma had prophesized. Dependent on their technology, but not the masters of it. He would turn it against them. He would gouge their eyes out and leave them blind.

Nabirye fantasized about his reward as he slipped a small spade from the thigh pocket of his fatigues. It seemed almost certain that he would be brought into Auma's inner circle—the small group of disciples who had personal access to the man. Would there be more, though? Rumors were endless. Some said these men had been given the power to read minds. To conjure storms. That they could meld with the souls of animals to gain their strength. Some even said they could fly, but he wondered if Auma would gift such an ability even to his most trusted followers. It seemed something that he would reserve for himself.

Nabirye chose a place in the disturbed earth that seemed free of rocks and began to dig. The wire he was looking for was hidden only a few centimeters beneath the surface. Sheathed in black plastic, it looked like nothing. But that was deceiving. In fact, it was everything.

His fingers trembled as he typed a text into the phone he'd been given.

WIRE FOUND

The response was almost immediate and likely from Gideon Auma himself.

CUT IT

He did as ordered and then sent a confirmation. In the fortress above, the Whites would be scrambling, frantically trying to discover why their sophisticated early warning system had gone dark. According to Auma, they would initially assume it was a malfunction. That would be the time to strike—before they realized they were in danger.

There was a quiet rustling from behind and he quickly found himself surrounded by the men under his command. The Bearer of the Sacrament stopped next to him, taking off his backpack and removing various purpose-built containers. They were fashioned from local trees, intricately carved with magical symbols. Nabirye accepted one and shook it before removing a small lid. Beneath was a tiny chamber containing the proper dose. As commander, it was his honor to be the first to be blessed.

He leaned forward and breathed it in, feeling the familiar surge. The blood throbbed at the base of his skull. The strength in his limbs became infinite. Any hint of uncertainty, fear, and compassion slipped away. All that remained was a blinding, ecstatic rage.

26

SCOTT Coleman tried to ignore the voice and hang on to sleep. In his dream, he was driving a tractor through an endless field of wheat. Complex patterns came and went across it, written by an intermittent breeze that also tossed the hair of the woman riding next to him. Sonya Voronova spoke, but not in the bland midwestern accent she'd worked so hard to perfect. And not in the Rocky and Bullwinkle Russian accent that she reverted to when she was joking. Instead, the sound that came from her was the gruff southern drawl of Joe Maslick.

"Scott! Wake up!"

He finally opened his eyes to see the former Delta operator's face hovering above him.

"What?"

"We're picking up something on the cameras."

"Let me guess. Down in that death gully to the east."

"Yeah. How did you know to pump up our capability there?"

Coleman threw the blanket off and stood. "A little bird told me."

"Mitch," the big man grumbled.

Getting dressed wasn't particularly time consuming. In situations like these, Coleman tended to sleep in his fatigues. He slipped into a pair of boots carefully lined up near the bottom of the bed.

"What're we looking at?"

"At least fifty men. The one in the lead dug up and cut that wire you had us bury and now the rest are forming on him." He glanced at the real-time image on his phone. "Not sure what's going on. Visibility's shit because of all the trees. They seem like they're in a huddle or something."

Coleman reached for his own phone and scrolled through various video feeds and sensor logs. It was indeed hard to figure out what they were doing. Passing something around maybe? Assault rifles all around, but nothing heavier visible. Bunched up like amateurs.

"So, they're basically sitting on top of that wire?"

"Right. At the bottom of the gully."

The steep two-hundred-meter climb ahead of them had taken Charlie Wicker seven and a half minutes to cover, full-gas and under ideal conditions. But the assholes weren't Charlie Wicker and Coleman had the power to make conditions less than ideal. A lot less.

Maslick touched his earpiece for a moment, listening to someone talking over it.

"We have more contacts west."

"How many?"

"Looks like four. A hundred yards out. They might have handheld rockets. Hard to tell for sure."

A diversion. They'd make a lot of noise while their main force attacked up that gully. Or so they thought.

"Pull our guys off the west wall. Those berms should be enough to handle a few rockets. Tell Wick to take a few men outside the perimeter and get in position to neutralize those assholes. Not until I give the signal, though. I want them to do a little shooting first."

When Coleman reached the east fence, Maslick had already climbed to the top. Dirt had been tamped into a path behind it that allowed fast movement from sandbagged gun placements set up every twenty feet.

Not that they'd likely be necessary.

Coleman jogged to something that appeared to be a massive chain gun but was actually a water cannon. They had good flow from a well at the center of the compound and the diesel pumps they'd brought in were capable of blasting a jet seventy-five yards down the gully in question. Like the gun placements, though, that would probably be overkill. Unless things went very wrong, it would be the mines that Nicholas Ward hated so much that would do the majority of the work.

"Should I give the order to evacuate Mr. Ward and the rest of the civilians?" Maslick asked, though his tone suggested the question was just a formality. Of course he should.

Coleman didn't answer immediately, instead staring out into the moonlit trees. The air was barely moving, highlighting the rhythmic drip of a loose fitting on the water cannon. He'd always loved the calm before battle. It was a moment of serenity with an intensity that was impossible to reproduce in civilian life. These were the rare moments that he could fully clear his mind of all the garbage that had piled up over his half century of life.

"No. Not yet. We'll wait for the shooting to start."

"What?"

"You heard me."

"I'm not sure I did, Scott. You're saying you want to wait until people are shooting rockets at us before we put our client on a chopper?"

"Correct."

"Our client, who happens to be the richest man in the world, and might be able to make disease a thing of the past?"

"Yes."

Maslick let out a low breath. "You know what you're doing, right, boss?"

Coleman kept scanning the trees despite the fact that there was nothing to see. "Probably."

They didn't have to wait long. The sound of an explosion along the west wall was quickly followed by two others and a barrage of undisciplined automatic fire. As expected, the men at the bottom of the east gully started to move—climbing toward the compound at a pace that was a little shocking. He'd assumed Charlie Wicker's time was on the edge of what was humanly possible. Now he wasn't so sure.

"Can I evacuate them now?" Maslick said.

Coleman gave a short nod and toggled his throat mike. "Wick. Give me a sitrep."

"Three rockets," came the reply. "All hit the fence. The berm held in two places, but in another there's a viable incursion point. They don't seem to be interested, though. They're just shooting at nothing from the jungle. I'm saying this is just a diversion and the main force is coming in from somewhere else."

"Copy that. Unless you're in direct danger, let them run through their ammo and then take them."

"Roger. Shouldn't be a problem."

By the time Coleman toggled his mike off, all the east gun placements were manned and Maslick was dispersing the rest of their men. In less than a minute, the breach Wick had noted would be secure and evacuation protocols would be under way.

Coleman stepped behind the water cannon and pulled the trigger. The pumps came on and a moment later a thick stream of water began arcing into the forest. When the dirt got wet in this part of the world, it turned into something with a viscosity midway between motor oil and snot. In a few minutes, the attacking force would arrive at an over-hanging rock wall that was conveniently missing from the map Irene Kennedy had created. At that time, they'd have no choice but to try to go up the steep sides of the gully—now being turned into something akin to the Slip 'N Slide that Coleman had loved so much as a kid.

After that, things were going to turn ugly.

"Now!" Sanyu Nabirye shouted over the sound of distant explosions.

His feet seemed to barely skim the ground as he started upslope. The branches whipping his face caused no pain, only more rage and the warm sensation of blood running down his cheeks. His lungs heaved, but didn't burn, and his heart beat with a force that made his entire body shake in time.

It was a sensation he was familiar with from countless village raids and occasional skirmishes with Ugandan government forces. He'd come to crave it. To imagine that it was a glimpse into the afterlife that he would one day enjoy as an acolyte of Gideon Auma. The world and everything in it seemed to fall away. His body felt disconnected and remote—more like a weapon he carried than part of him. He had become a spirit guided by Auma and his warrior ancestors.

The steepness of the slope continued to increase but it didn't cause him to slow or to question the conflicting information he'd been given about the terrain. A helicopter became audible over the ecstatic shouts of the men behind him and the blood rushing in his ears. The incline became sharp enough that he had to use his hands to help propel himself, but still all he could think about was reaching the Whites cowering behind their flimsy wall. Watching them scatter in terror. Feeling the earth turn thick with the blood of Gideon Auma's enemies.

The rushing in his ears reached an intensity that he didn't remember from the times before. Less than a minute later, he felt a cold, misting rain against his back. Through the trees above, though, the sky was full of stars. A miracle? He tilted his head back and let a few drops fall into his mouth, quenching the thirst he barely registered. Rain from a clear sky. What else could it be but a gift from his master?

A few men surged past him and he began sprinting again. He'd been given the privilege of command. Not them. It was *his* honor to lead God's forces. Nabirye caught them easily, but not because of his superior speed. Because they'd arrived at a cliff blocking their path. The rain was coming harder now and the roar of it mixed with the sound of water flowing down on them.

He stopped, trying to form coherent thoughts in his clouded mind. He'd been told that the gully would take them directly to the weakest part of the compound's wall. That it would be a relatively flat approach with abundant cover. It was only then that he noted how steep the slopes had become on either side.

His men began to pile up behind him, shoving him into the rock wall. He turned, trying futilely to push back against them, watching as some tried to get around the natural barrier by climbing the sides of the gully. They would make it a few meters and then slide down again, rolling over the top of the people coming up behind. The miraculous rain hadn't just sated Nabirye's thirst, it had covered the terrain in a slick layer of mud.

A blinding flash was followed by a wave of heat and shredded foliage that assaulted the exposed skin on Nabirye's face. Bodies catapulted into the air, some getting hung up in trees and others coming back down as lifeless lumps of flesh. A detached arm bounced off the cliff and then cartwheeled across the heads of the men closest to him. They began to scatter, trampling each other as more explosions erupted.

The pressure of the bodies against Nabirye eased and he stumbled away from the cliff, tripping over a body and falling next to it in the mud. The shredded backpack identified what was left of the boy as the Bearer of the Sacrament. The holy receptacles lay next to his severed hand. Nabirye picked one up, finding that the water had turned its contents into a thick paste. It didn't matter. He shoved it in his nostrils, inhaling hard enough to make him choke and finally vomit.

A sense of euphoria more intense than any he'd experienced before took hold, relegating the odd hiss of the rain and the heat of the explosions to another realm. He climbed over his dead comrades and began flailing desperately up the north slope. He wouldn't fail. He was blessed by God and filled with the Sacrament.

He was invincible.

27

RAPP was lying on the concrete floor with a jacket piled behind his head when Levi Mizrah's voice came over his earpiece.

"Mitch. We have contacts to the west. Three vehicles coming in on the road. One SUV and two pickups, each with a full complement of men in the back. They don't look like pros, though. Just a bunch of locals."

Rapp was about to respond when the phone in his pocket began to vibrate. He activated the screen and squinted through the inky darkness at it. Scott Coleman.

"Hang on, Levi," he said before picking up. "Go ahead, Scott."

"We . . . force . . . in . . . air . . ."

"I did not copy that," Rapp said. The dull roar of what he suspected were water cannons overwhelmed Coleman's voice, hinting at what was happening at Ward's compound.

The roar faded to a hiss and the former SEAL came on again. "We're under attack from the east. Fifty-plus men are on the move after digging up your wire. Ward and his people are in the air."

"You all right? Everything under control?"

"We have one minor breach in the wall to the west, but I don't think anything is going to come of it. The main force in the gully is toast."

Rapp stood. "Let me know if anything changes."

The roar started again, and Coleman shouted over it. "Copy that! I'm out!"

"Levi," he said, switching back to his throat mike. "Give me an update."

"We have good video of these guys now—they're driving with headlights. They're definitely from around here."

"Could they be disguised?"

It seemed unlikely that someone who had the ability to dig so deep into the Agency's mainframe would send a bunch of locals to ambush Ward and Chism. They'd use the same kind of top private talent that Rapp was.

"No way. A lot of them look like they're in their teens. Some may be even younger."

"ETA?"

"About six minutes."

Rapp strode across the hangar using night vision gear that could barely collect enough light to navigate by. Various pieces of equipment had been brought in and placed strategically around the building. None of it served any purpose other than to provide cover for his men, but to the casual observer it would look like it belonged. The incursion point was easy to anticipate since the hangar only had entrances on the north side—the main bay doors and a single smaller door for pedestrian traffic.

"Levi. Get our support choppers in the air. Have them hang back, though. We don't want to spook these assholes."

"Roger that," he said as Rapp continued to make a quick circuit of the building. Everyone was in their designated position. All pros ready to rock. He patched into the main comm.

"To reiterate our mission: we are capturing these men. Not killing them. Unless your life is in imminent danger, you are not to use lethal force. If anyone isn't clear on that, speak up."

Silence from the men in the hangar with him, but then the voice of one of his scouts came on.

"This is Exterior Two. We have one truck slowing. My guess is that they'll set up along the tree line to provide cover for the incursion team."

"Can you handle them?" Rapp said.

"Shouldn't be a problem. We'll tuck in behind them and wait until the fireworks start."

"Copy that. Let me know if you run into any issues."

Rapp stopped at the front of the main hangar doors and examined their hazy green image in his monocular. It would be impossible to get through without explosives, which would create obvious damage that the force coming in couldn't tolerate. The smaller door would be the target. It wasn't as heavy, and any damage done breaching it would be easy to obscure.

Kennedy's gut had proved accurate once again. Whoever had accessed Nicholas Ward's CIA file clearly wasn't after a few stock tips. They wanted it all.

Rapp crouched to perform a final check on four small devices strategically placed near the door. They were additional prototypes of the Taser bomb that had dropped him and Coleman's team at their training session a few weeks ago.

"This is Exterior Two," came the voice over his earpiece again. "The SUV and one of the pickups have cleared the tree line and are on their way to the hangar. ETA less than one minute. The remaining truck has stopped before the clearing and the men are getting out. Looks like I was right. They're going to set up in the woods as cover. We're in good position to take them out. Permission to use deadly force if necessary to keep them from reinforcing the incursion team?"

Rapp wanted to take as many of them alive as possible, but the perimeter force wasn't of much concern. They'd just be soldiers. Whoever was directing this operation was almost certainly in the SUV. That was the person he was interested in talking to.

"If *necessary*, Exterior Two. Permission granted."

"Copy that. The truck and the SUV are pulling up to the bay doors. Stand by . . . Okay, the men in the back of the pickup have what looks like a battering ram. Actually, I think it's just a log with ropes tied around it, but it's big enough to go through that door pretty easy. The occupants of the SUV are stepping out . . . two of them. The one who came out of the back seems to be giving the orders."

"Can you give me a description?" Rapp said, crouching behind a generator that was his designated position.

"Negative. African. Fatigues. Nothing stands out."

"Roger that," Rapp said as a loud clang echoed through the hangar. The first blow against the door.

"They're pulling the vehicles back toward the trees. The men at the hangar don't have rifles. Some are carrying what could be handguns, but I'm not sure. Might just be flashlights."

"Copy," Rapp said.

Not entirely unexpected. They would have no reason to believe the hangar was anything but empty. The goal would be for Ward to arrive not realizing anything was amiss. He would be rushed inside, where he and his people would be immediately overwhelmed. Providing the men trying to get through the door with weapons would endanger Ward. When guns were involved, accidents had a way of happening.

The door held longer than expected, finally bursting open on the fifth strike. Men began flowing through the opening with what indeed turned out to be flashlights. One on the left located a switch box on the wall and attempted to turn on the lights, but Rapp's people had rerouted the circuit. The Africans didn't seem overly bothered, continuing to flow through the door and fan out, playing their flashlights over the building's interior and the private jet it contained. If any of them noticed the four small cylinders on the floor, none gave any indication.

It took about twenty seconds before the men had dispersed into what Rapp calculated to be an optimal spread. It was possible that a few were out of range, but if he waited much longer, a number of the men would penetrate the building far enough to flank some of his people. He ran a thumb over the detonator, but hesitated. These were worker bees. Where was the queen?

He was rewarded a moment later when a man strode regally through the doorway, barking orders in Swahili. Rapp waited until he approached the first Taser unit and then depressed the button. Showers of sparks were accompanied by a sound reminiscent of spattering grease, and a moment later most of the incursion team was down. The unit closest to him misfired, leaving a few more men standing than he'd hoped, but the fact that they weren't armed made them a minimal threat.

"Lights!" Rapp said into his throat mike and then replaced his night vision monocular with a pair of dark sunglasses. After the agreed-upon two-second delay, powerful overhead lights bathed the space in a fluorescent glare.

One African came even with Rapp's position, squinting and raising an arm to shade his eyes. He was close enough that Rapp could have extended a leg to trip him, but it wouldn't have been wise to expose any flesh with the quiet puffs of tranquilizer darts sounding throughout the hangar. Instead, he waited for the man—boy really—to go by and used his own dart gun to shoot him in the ass. He made it about another ten steps before stumbling and going down on his face.

"Clear!" someone shouted. That was followed by similar shouts around the hangar. Rapp loaded another dart and came out from behind the generator, swinging the unfamiliar weapon smoothly in front of him, looking for any movement that his men might have missed. Snipers were covering from the rafters, but it didn't look like they'd be necessary. What little movement existed was just the weak flailing of the electrocuted or drugged.

"Exterior teams," Rapp said into his comm. "Give me a sitrep."

"This is Exterior One," came the immediate reply. "We're secure with no injuries to our team. On the other side, we have two fatal gunshot wounds and one man who got hit with multiple darts and is having some kind of seizure. Two escaped into the woods. We have people in pursuit."

"Copy that. Keep me apprised of any problems."

Rapp pulled off his sunglasses, wiping the sweat from his eyes and looking at the men littered across the floor. He'd lost track of the man who had been giving orders, but he turned out to be easy to find. Gray hair at the temples and fatigues that were free of holes and bloodstains.

Rapp crouched, grabbing the man by the hair and lifting his head enough to examine his face. There was a string of spit connecting the side of his mouth to the concrete and his eyes fluttered sightlessly, but he was immediately recognizable.

Gideon Auma. God's representative on earth.

28

WHEN Mike Nash entered the Oval Office, the president was sitting behind his desk, poring over a document in front of him. Not the Resolute Desk, which had been there during their last meeting, but a new one constructed from steel, glass, and polished wood. Catherine, who was reading over his shoulder, straightened and unleashed a smile that seemed to get warmer every time they met.

"It's good to see you, Mike."

"Thanks for fitting us in," Nash responded as she indicated the seating area at the center of the office.

Us wasn't entirely accurate as he seemed to be the Agency's only representative in the room. "Is Irene stuck in traffic?"

"No," the president responded, walking to his customary chair in the conversation area. "There wasn't any reason to tie you both up."

Nash nodded and lowered himself onto a sofa across from Washington's new power couple. More and more he was flying solo at these kinds of meetings and he wasn't exactly sure why. It was almost as if Kennedy was knowingly allowing herself to be pushed out of the government's inner circle. She'd always been one step ahead of everyone else in this town, but now the combined brainpower of Anthony and Catherine Cook was providing serious competition. Was she struggling with the reality that she might no longer always be the smartest person in the room? Or was it more than that? Was it possible that she was reaching her expiration date? It happened to everyone eventually. At some point, the changes just came too fast and hard to keep up with.

Whatever it was, she seemed to be purposely inching her way toward irrelevance. While everyone else inside the beltway would kill their own children for two minutes of face time with the Cooks, she was retreating from them. And the more she worked herself out of her job, the more he appeared to be working himself into it. Or better said, sucked into it. Like some black hole. Dark. Irresistible. Inescapable. What was the term he'd learned helping Rory with his astronomy homework? *Event horizon.* Once crossed, there was no coming back.

"I'm sorry to rush you, Mike, but there's only so far I could rearrange my schedule," the president said. "I understand this has something to do with Nicholas Ward again?"

There was a coldness in his voice that said volumes about his feelings regarding the tech mogul. It had been bad enough before, but then the press had gotten hold of the fact that Chism had been rescued by a team of mercenaries and not US spec ops. It made his administration look a little impotent—which infuriated him—but it could have been much worse. The existence of the Cooks' spectacularly botched rescue effort was still under wraps and neither Coleman nor Ward was the type to run his mouth unnecessarily. That went double for Mitch Rapp. His ambition was to go through life as a ghost.

"Mike?" the First Lady prompted.

He realized he'd been silent too long but, still, he didn't speak. The truth was that he didn't want to be there. In fact, his reaction to the photos that had landed on his desk that morning was to think he should get out. And not the playful threats of becoming a Hawaiian fishing guide he muttered ten times a day. Serious thoughts about running screaming from Langley and rethinking his life. His wife wouldn't give a shit. She made five times what he did.

But what about his kids? What about the grandkids that would eventually come? Could he just turn his back on the world they'd inherit and tell them to figure things out on their own?

Nash pulled a series of eight-by-tens from his portfolio and laid them on the coffee table.

"What are we looking at?" the president asked.

"What's left of Nicholas Ward's compound in Uganda."

Cook reached for the top photo and examined it while his wife picked up the one beneath. Nash had learned early on to bring two of everything.

"Those are satellite photos. Not great, but the best thing we have at this point."

"I can make out the burned areas and buildings," Catherine said, oddly expressionless. "But what are all the dots?"

"Bodies, ma'am. You can see where they breached the east and west walls. The pattern of casualties suggests a running fight with Ward's security forces."

"Who won?"

"It appears the attackers did. The fact that Ward's chopper is gone suggests he made it out, though."

"To where?"

"He had a hangar to the southeast that he was to be evacuated to if something like this happened. There was a jet there that would then take him to Johannesburg."

"And is that what happened?"

"No, sir."

Cook's eyebrows rose and he leaned back in the sofa. "Then what?"

"We haven't been able to get anyone to the compound, but the hangar isn't far from Mbarara and we had someone there we could use.

According to him, both Ward's chopper and the jet are still there. And there's evidence of a firefight."

"Can I assume that no one's heard from Ward since?"

"That's correct, sir."

"So, they flushed him out of his compound and then took him at his hangar where the situation would be more controllable," the First Lady said. She seemed almost purposefully monotone. No concern. No surprise. All the gains she'd made in feigning humanity suddenly melted away. To the point that it seemed almost intentional. A subtle message so that she could measure his reaction?

"That's our take on it as well, ma'am."

"What about David Chism?" the president asked.

"Our assumption is that he was on the chopper with Ward."

Nash looked on numbly as the Cooks pondered what they'd heard. Finally, the president spoke. "Then it sounds like we're playing a waiting game. I assume the FBI will be contacting Ward's people to handle any potential ransom negotiations?"

"Yes, sir."

"And we're coordinating with the Ugandans to see if there's any way of finding him."

Nash nodded.

"We appreciate the briefing," the president said, standing. He took Nash's hand and held it in a crushing grip, looking straight at him with an intensity he normally softened. "And we appreciate everything you've done for us since I took office. I know it's been a difficult transition. Now, what about your friends? Mitch, Scott Coleman, and the others. Were they at that camp?"

Nash's mouth suddenly went dry enough that it was hard to get the words out. "We believe so, sir."

"I'm sorry, Mike," Catherine interjected. "But we need to stay positive. They probably escaped into the jungle, right? They're the best in the world and no one's been able to kill them yet. We'll set up a conference call between you, the secretary of state, and the Ugandan president for later this morning. He should be able to help us determine what happened and coordinate a search if necessary."

"Thank you, ma'am, but I think it would be more appropriate if you had the secretary of state coordinate with Irene. Not me."

The First Lady shrugged noncommittally. "Whatever you prefer."

29

Rapp toweled off and walked from the bathroom to the cabin's living area. It encompassed about five hundred square feet, with a rattan ceiling, hanging woodstove, and stylish African furniture. Through the open windows, he could see the ubiquitous emerald mountains stretching to the horizon. It was hard to ignore the peaceful beauty of the place. Having said that, it was also hard to ignore that it was an illusion. The calm before the storm. Or, more accurately, the calm between the endless series of storms that had been battering him for the last twenty years.

Overall, though, not a bad place to ride things out for a while. He imagined that a stay at this particular Ugandan eco-lodge would cost a significant chunk of the CIA paycheck he no longer officially received. At the moment, though, everything was on the house. Scott Coleman had rented the entire mountaintop facility and replaced most of the staff with loyalists. All at Nicholas Ward's expense, of course.

Someone had left a duffle on the bed while he was in the shower and he dug through it. Most of his stuff was still at what remained of

Ward's compound and Claudia had sent replacements. Because he was a captive audience, she'd limited herself to all the things she'd bought for him that lurked unworn in the back of his closet. Linen slacks, leather sandals, Italian silk shirts. All meticulously pressed, folded, and separated by sheets of tissue paper.

Once dressed, he crossed his polished wood porch to a boardwalk that undulated through a series of similar cabanas. The main lodge was to the east and he assumed it contained the kitchen, which was all he was interested in at this point. What he needed right now was a few hours kicking back in the sun eating everything he could get his hands on. Achieving his ideal bike-racing weight would have to be put on the back burner for a while.

"Mitch!"

Scott Coleman appeared in the doorway of a cabin similar to the one he'd been put up in. Choppers had been arriving on a regular basis since early that morning, bringing in people and supplies. He'd likely come in on the last of them. Still clad in sweat-stained bloody fatigues, he let out a low whistle as Rapp approached.

"You look amazing! Like a movie star or something. Next time I want the hangar gig."

"I'm not in the mood, Scott."

"You're never in the mood," his friend responded dismissively.

"Where are we at?"

"Thanks to all the hard work I did while you were here having the wrinkles steamed from your ascot, we're in good shape. Though I have to admit that the water cannons turned out to be not as good an idea as I thought."

"How so?" Rapp said, putting on a pair of expensive sunglasses to cut the glare. He'd thought the cannons were one of Coleman's customary strokes of genius.

"That slope turned so slick we had to set up a winch to get the bodies out."

"But everything looks convincing?"

"Yeah. The mines made a little bit of a mess, but we managed to piece together enough bodies to make it work. And I mean that literally. We had to use duct tape to put some of them back together. Then we blew a hole in the east wall and laid them out around the compound."

"And you got it all done before the spy satellites came overhead?"

"Two hours to spare. Anyone looking at those photos will figure that we held our own for a while, but then were overwhelmed by the superior numbers."

"Has anyone showed up to take a closer look?"

"Not yet, but when they do, I've got guys on the ground that'll turn them back. Some bargain-basement rockets, AKs, and the like. What we've done out there won't bear close scrutiny, but I'm guessing no one's going to want to die trying to confirm what they already think is obvious."

"Communications?"

"We set up in a storage shed with satphones and Internet access but have it completely locked down. No one gets anything in or out except you and me. Ward isn't happy about it and he's asked for a word. It's hard to tell with him, but he seems pretty hot. I get the feeling that he knows more about what's going on than he lets on."

"And your men?"

"No one got so much as a scratch. Wick took out the diversion team in less than sixty seconds and the people in that gully . . ." His voice faded for a moment. "Well, let's just say that once we activated the minefield, they didn't have much of a chance. You should check out the video, though. That drug they take is no joke. There were guys that didn't slow down even after they'd lost limbs. Watching a guy with no legs trying to drag his way up that slope to get to us was kind of disturbing. Like a bad zombie movie or something."

"Maybe later. I need to find something to eat first."

"Roger that. Ward's cooks are hard at it. Springbok steaks with a rosemary reduction and roasted, locally grown vegetables."

"Working for the richest man in the world has its perks," Rapp observed.

"If you ignore all the death and destruction."

"Yeah. Anyway, nice work, Scott. And relay that to the guys."

"More than nice. You snatched Gideon Auma and I took out at least fifty of his guys. I know you're here to figure out who's digging around in the CIA's mainframe, but in the process, we may have just dismantled a terrorist group that makes ISIS look like a bunch of nuns. Seriously, man. You know what Auma's been doing around here for the last decade. When we get to the pearly gates, this might be the one that gets us through."

Rapp laughed. "Maybe you. But I'm pretty sure I'm screwed."

"Yeah. Probably. But until then, at least you've got the springbok steaks and rosemary reduction."

There was a long line leading into the lodge's kitchen facility. Joe Maslick was near the front, holding a plate that suggested he was going in for seconds. The dirty faces of the men Coleman contracted with were familiar but not so much so that he could put a name to most of them. Then there were Ward's people—softer, cleaner, and more nervous looking.

He took a place at the back of the line but stood there for only about fifteen seconds before a young man in khakis approached hesitantly. "Mr. Rapp?"

"Yeah."

"Mr. Ward would like to invite you to dine with him." He pointed toward a plank walkway that led to a set of stairs. "He's up there. In the main cabin."

Rapp nodded and climbed the steps that seemed to lead straight into the deepening blue sky. He found Ward on a massive deck that cantilevered over the side of the mountain. Despite the fact that temperatures were still in the high sixties, he was standing in front of a fire built in a stone enclosure that matched the scale of the deck. Near the north railing, a table had been set up with place settings for two.

Upon hearing Rapp's footsteps, Ward glanced over his shoulder and then returned his gaze to the flames. The glass in his hand looked like it contained a couple of fingers of whiskey, but his expression suggested the alcohol hadn't kicked in yet. Coleman was right. The man didn't look as happy as he should have been to be alive, richer than anyone in history, and no longer in danger from Gideon Auma.

It was likely that his dark mood had something to do with the program playing on a television inside the cabin. It was a newscast relaying unconfirmed reports that Ward's compound in Uganda had been attacked and that he and his people were missing. Possibly even dead.

"Do you know how much money I've lost today, Mitch?"

"Is it more than a hundred bucks?"

"It's more than a hundred billion bucks."

Rapp wasn't surprised by the number. It hadn't been at the forefront of his mind, but there was never any question that his plan was going to tank the stocks of any company that Ward or Chism were involved in.

"You're still not exactly short rent money."

"My wealth—and my ability to generate it for others—is like Samson's hair. The source of all my power—"

"To save the world."

A bitter smile spread across Ward's face. "I'm being prevented from sending or receiving messages. Can I assume you have something to do with that?"

"Yes."

"I didn't hire you to imprison me, Mitch." He took a sip of his drink. "Or to bankrupt me."

"What if I convince Scott to give you a discount?"

"Funny."

"Are you going to offer me a drink?"

Ward indicated a sideboard next to the door leading into his cabin. A stellar bottle of bourbon was sitting next to a bucket of ice. Rapp took advantage of both.

"You have problems and I'm trying to solve them," he said, taking a position close enough to the fire to feel its heat. The sun was starting to sink in the west, throwing the landscape into shadow.

"How so?"

"Someone powerful wants you and Chism in Gideon Auma's hands. It's plausible that Auma orchestrated the attack at the research facility by himself, but he needed sophisticated intel to get to you at your compound."

Ward nodded slowly, considering his situation. "It's my understanding that you have him?"

"Correct."

"May I speculate?"

"Go ahead."

"It's clear that you didn't set all this up on the fly. You knew the attack was coming and you were ready for it. You had my pilot divert from the hangar he was supposed to take me to, suggesting the intelligence you're referring to included its existence and my escape plan."

"I'm impressed. Go on."

"The fact that the world seems to think I'm either dead or in the hands of a terrorist suggests that you created a little theater at my compound. Maybe made it look like you lost the battle."

"Yes."

"It occurs to me that you could have just told me I was in danger and moved me to a location well out of Auma's reach. But you didn't. Why?"

"You tell me."

"Because you're not working to solve my problems. You're working to solve your own. And putting me out as bait was convenient."

Rapp took a sip of his drink. Ward continually proved he wasn't a stupid man. In a way, it was like dealing with Irene Kennedy's private-sector mirror image.

"What problem do you figure I'm trying to solve, Nick?"

"Clearly not the question of my safety or the economic ramifications of my American-based companies taking a hit."

"Your point?"

"A minute ago, you mentioned sophisticated intelligence on me. If I had to bet, I'd say that's the problem."

"Why would I care who has what information on you?"

"I don't know. Maybe it's a foreign enemy who's playing out a strategy you don't understand. Or maybe you think the information came from the US government. Maybe even the CIA itself. In that case . . ." He waved a hand around him. "All this could be nothing more than an attempt to find a spy in your organization. What do you people call it? A mole hunt?"

"There's such a thing as being too smart for your own good, Nick."

"Not in my experience," he said. This time his smile wasn't as bitter. "Besides, Irene won't let you kill me—she sees me as a useful idiot. And you still listen to her, right? She's the only one now that Stan Hurley and Thomas Stansfield are gone."

"You're heading out onto some pretty thin ice now, Nick."

"I live my life on thin ice. There's no way for someone like me not to."

Two men with trays appeared on the steps and Ward pointed to the table by the railing. Rapp took a seat, and they were served the springbok that Coleman had promised.

"Can I assume you're going to question Auma, Mitch? Find out where he got his information and put an end to all this?"

Rapp didn't answer immediately, calculating how much to say. "Yes. But it probably won't be that simple. People with the kind of information he was fed don't deal directly with men like him. They work through intermediaries. Finding the original source will take a little effort."

"Everything worthwhile does," Ward said, popping a bite of meat in his mouth and chewing thoughtfully. "So, we'll be kept here incommunicado until you've tied everything up? With me watching everything I've built collapse? With my people's families thinking they're dead?"

"Look, Nick. I know this isn't ideal, but if you want to help the world, here's a good opportunity. We've got Auma and we've killed a lot of his followers. But there are a lot left and most of them are probably beyond redemption at this point. Without central leadership, they'll break up into small terrorist cells and still have the capacity to bring down a lot of misery on the people around here. One of the things I can find out is the location of their camp. The Ugandan government doesn't want to operate on the border, but Scott can. And with an exact location, he can turn that camp into a burning hole in the ground."

They ate in silence for a few minutes before Ward broke it. "I suspect that there are a lot of children in that camp who *aren't* beyond redemption. And a lot of slaves—largely young girls. They'd all die."

"Happens every day, Nick. You're a big-picture person. You know as well as I do that all those pictures aren't pretty."

Ward shook his head. "I can't order people dead and then pay mercenaries to make it happen."

"Why not?"

"We've talked about this before, Mitch. I'm wealthy. Or at least I was until I met you. But that doesn't give me the right to do whatever I want."

"Are you sure? I see that as a lack of imagination. You have more money than a lot of countries. You are the undisputed master of technology. And you have Scott Coleman, the most talented private contractor in the world, on your payroll. The reality is there's *nothing* you can't do. And that scares the shit out of you."

Ward went back to his food, falling silent for almost a minute before speaking again. "It does scare the shit out of me."

"Don't live your life in fear, Nick. You've got an opportunity to dip

your toe in the water here. I find my mole. You get miraculously rescued. And Gideon Auma's entire organization goes up in a fireball."

Ward looked a bit dejected as he stabbed at the vegetables on his
plate. "Can I think about it?"

Normally, Rapp would have said no, but he still hadn't questioned
Auma. Until then, he really didn't even know what he needed from
Ward.

"Sure. Sleep on it. We'll talk in the morning."

30

THE game trail turned steep enough that Rapp had to grab at trees to slow his descent. The backpack he wore contained an assortment of implements that wouldn't normally be carried by the ecotourists who eagerly flocked to this region. Nor the former CIA operative who'd come so reluctantly.

Thanks to a combination of exhaustion, luxurious bed linens, and the hum of jungle insects, he'd slept like a rock the night before. By the time he'd staggered to the shower, though, his mind was already consumed. Not by Gideon Auma, though. By Nicholas Ward.

Of course, he'd read what the Agency had on the man, but it was mostly just mundane factoids and columns of shockingly large numbers. In truth, his background was largely what would be expected. Top of his class at MIT until he dropped out. Various tech start-ups, a number of which had shot straight into the stratosphere. Finally, investments in cutting-edge technology and controlling interests in companies that largely enjoyed similar trajectories. He seemed to be a man who could see the future and take advantage of that vision on pretty much every level.

But now he'd backed away from his empire to focus on saving the world. Rapp could understand the instinct—it wasn't that different from his own motivation. What *was* different, though, was the scale. There was no question that he'd put out a lot of raging fires during his career, but Ward wanted to take away the fuel that allowed them to burn.

Rapp had seen him on news programs over the years but hadn't paid much attention. Another do-gooder. More impressive than the rest, but not fundamentally different. A lot of pie-in-the-sky ideas that sounded great in a conference room full of geniuses but that would crash and burn the moment they were released into the wild. Now that he'd met the man, though, he wasn't so sure. Maybe Ward really could get some of his grand plans off the ground. The odds were still low, but possibly not the zero percent that Rapp would have bet on a few weeks ago.

The path cut right, and he followed two separate sets of footprints, one booted and spread out in long, confident strides; the other shuffling along in bare feet. Finally, he came upon Bruno McGraw leaning against a tree whittling the pieces of a chess set. He glanced up from a half-finished rook to acknowledge Rapp's arrival and then went back to work.

The other man occupying the small clearing was positioned somewhat differently. Gideon Auma was naked, with hands flex-cuffed to a thick branch over his head. He'd been standing there all night, unable to rest without the plastic bands cutting into his wrists. He still had the energy to shoot Rapp the wild, messianic glare that he was so famous for, though. People like him found it hard to comprehend when they'd lost control. Rapp would have to spell it out for him.

"I've heard a lot about you, Gideon," he said, emptying the contents of his pack onto the ground and looking down at it disappointedly. "I know what you're thinking, and I agree. You're a connoisseur. Crucifixions, drawing and quartering people with motorbikes. I heard you actually have an iron maiden. Where do you even buy something like that? A museum?"

Auma stared silently at the household tools and kitchen implements at Rapp's feet.

"A man like you deserves one of those big metal cows they used to roast people in. Or a proper rack. But I'm staying in a thousand-dollar-a-night tourist lodge, so I have to make do. Don't worry, though. What I lack in equipment, I make up for with imagination."

The messianic fervor in Auma's eyes had been replaced by fear. Not surprising. People who derived pleasure from torturing others tended to be the easiest to break. For reasons a psychologist once tried to explain to him, the role reversal amplified the pain and anticipation.

"God . . ." the African managed to get out through his dry, disused throat. "God will strike you down." The effort caused him to start coughing violently, putting pressure on his bound wrists. The agony was immediately visible in his face and Rapp turned his attention to the clear sky.

"Doesn't look like lightning weather. But maybe you can conjure up a few clouds."

"You'll die screaming!" Auma said, his voice gaining strength and desperation. "If you touch me, your flesh will rot from your bones and your soul will burn forever."

"I appreciate the Shakespearean flair, Gideon, but I'm not some illiterate eight-year-old whose parents you just murdered. On the list of pieces of shit I've skinned alive, you barely rank in the bottom third."

Rapp picked up a garlic press, thought better of it, and instead selected a meat tenderizer.

"Who gave you the information on Nicholas Ward's compound?"

"What?"

Rapp walked up and rammed a knee up between the man's legs. Auma let out a low moan, gagged a few times, and then vomited what little his stomach still contained.

"That was not an acceptable answer. So, let's try again. Who told you how to attack Nicholas Ward's compound?"

"A Saudi," the man choked out, spit and vomit drooling from his mouth as he tried to keep his feet under him.

Rapp frowned. Saudi Arabia was a convenient ally for America's politicians, but also a major thorn in the side of the intelligence community. It made good TV to say Iran was the world's number one sponsor of terror but, in truth, it was the Saudis by a country mile.

"Name?"

"Muhammad."

"Yeah, I figured. Last name?"

"I don't know."

All probably true, so Rapp took a half step back. The secret to interrogations was restraint. It couldn't be all stick. There had to be some carrot, too.

"Tell me about him."

When Auma didn't respond, Rapp cycled the meat tenderizer in his hand. The subtle swish of stainless-steel blades brought the terrorist back into the present.

"I first met him perhaps five years ago. He's given me money. Some weapons. Information on the Ugandan army. That's all."

Also likely true. The Saudis maintained a quiet relationship with pretty much every terrorist organization on the planet. Auma had started hitting the radar about six years ago, so the time frame seemed right. As did his description of what they'd provided. Just enough to keep a channel open in case he could be useful, but not enough to draw attention.

"Description?"

"There's nothing to say. Not tall or short. Not dark or light. Not fat or thin. His beard is neither long nor short . . ."

His tone suggested that he was leading to something. "And?"

"I have pictures. At my camp. I had my people take pictures of him. Many pictures."

Again, everything he was saying rang true. If you worked as a liaison between the Saudi royalty and scumbag terrorist groups spread throughout the world, best not to have a lot of distinguishing features. And if you're a terrorist who might one day want something from the Saudi royalty, not a bad idea to collect information that could be used for blackmail.

"Tell me about the information he gave you."

"It was on paper. Not electronic. Overhead photos of the compound and hangar. Topographical maps. Details on the electronic security—"

"Your people attacked from the east. Why?"

"Based on the information we were provided, it was the easiest approach. And there was a wire that could be cut that would disable all of Ward's early warning systems."

That confirmed what Rapp already suspected. The information came directly from the CIA file that Irene Kennedy had modified. The question now was how the Saudis had obtained it.

"What were your orders?"

"I don't take orders! I am God's repre—"

"What did the Saudi *suggest* you do with the information he gave you?" Rapp rephrased. What he didn't need right now was to get dragged into a semantic argument with this piece of shit. He just wanted to slit the man's throat and get some lunch before the buffet was completely picked over.

"Kill the scientist. Ransom Ward."

"What if it worked and you got the ransom?"

"Kill him if it was feasible. But if not, I was to return a man who was no longer the one I took. And never would be again."

Interesting. Why would the Saudis want to walk out on this particular limb? The obvious answer was Ward's advances in renewable energy, but still. It was a pretty bold move.

"Very good, Gideon. Just one last question. How do I find him?"

"I don't know."

Rapp considered slamming the meat tenderizer into the man's thigh, but then thought better of it. He had a hunch that he was going to need Gideon Auma in one piece.

Fortunately, a perfect tool was close at hand. Normally, he would have gone for a torch used for sweating pipes—nice weight, felt good in the hand, intimidating hiss. But you went to war with the army you had, not the army you wanted.

Bruno McGraw shook his head in abject disappointment when Rapp picked up the crème brûlée torch. It fired right up, though, and despite its humbleness, Auma locked on the pinpoint flame.

"No! Stop! I—"

Rapp passed it over the man's stomach slowly enough to catch the scent of burning hair but not so long as to kick up the stench of crisping skin.

Auma jerked away and Rapp prepared to clamp a hand over his mouth. They'd set up pretty far from the eco-lodge, but a scream might still reach it and Rapp wanted to insulate Ward to the greatest degree possible. For now, at least.

It turned out to be unnecessary. Instead of screaming, Auma started to blubber. It made Rapp want to cut his throat even more. How many lengthy, savage torture sessions had this man presided over in his lifetime? How many women and children had he put to death over the course of days—maybe even weeks—while he fed off their pain? And all it took to get him to sobbing like a lost toddler was a dessert torch?

"How do you set up meetings with this Saudi, Gideon? How do you coordinate bank transfers and the delivery of the weapons they give you?" Rapp moved the torch toward the man's stomach again.

"I have a phone!"

"Tell me more," Rapp said, pulling back but leaving the torch lit. How long would the tiny canister last? Claudia made crème brûlée but he'd always been more interested in eating it than the vagaries of how it was made. Having it sputter out during an interrogation would be a little like losing your hard-on during sex. Not good for the mood.

"It's a burner phone. He gave it to me. It's my only way of contacting him."

"Where is it?"

"At my camp."

Sadly, that was probably true, too. They'd searched him, his car, and all his men before burying the whole lot of them in a mass grave behind the hangar. There would be no reason for Auma to carry a phone like that on an operation.

Rapp found himself left with few options. In fact, only one.

Go to Auma's camp and get it.

31

GIDEON Auma looked more dead-eyed than normal, but other than that not too bad. He'd been hosed off and put back in his fatigues. The flex-cuff wounds on his wrists had been tended to and the cuffs of his shirt had been glued down to hide the bandages. He seemed reasonably steady on his feet as he stood in a clearing bathed in natural light. If this took longer than expected and his knees started to buckle, they could probably find a way to prop him up. It was amazing what camera angles could hide.

It appeared that Auma's time dangling from a tree branch and the subsequent swipes with the crème brûlée torch had completely broken him. Stripped of his minions and surrounded with people unimpressed by his carefully crafted image as the instrument of God's wrath, he was surprisingly pathetic. No attempts at escape, no more dramatic calls for divine retribution. Just quiet obedience. Exactly the way Rapp liked it.

Scott Coleman had found a folding cloth chair somewhere and someone had scrawled "DIRECTOR" on the back in marker. He was settled into it, holding his hands out in front of him, thumbs together, framing the shot. Joe Maslick stood obediently at his side trying to figure out the video app on his iPhone.

Behind Auma, a young woman wearing a khaki vest was putting the finishing touches on Nicholas Ward's makeup. They'd flown her in from one of his movie studios under the auspices of doing some pro bono work for an African charity. Now she found herself trapped in an unimaginable nightmare, kept going only by Ward's promise of obscene financial rewards.

Despite being on the verge of a nervous breakdown, she'd done an amazing job. Ward's clothes were tattered, filthy, and smeared with blood left over from last night's zebra roulade. His greasy hair was appropriately tangled, and a couple of twigs hung in front of a forehead smeared with sweat and caked dust.

She stepped back to examine her handiwork for a moment and then glanced over at David Chism, who had been given a similar makeover. Finally, she turned to Rapp and gave a short nod.

"You're sure?" he asked. "Every news and intelligence agency in the world is going to go over this video with a microscope."

"They won't find anything."

He had no reason not to take her word for it. Everyone looked incredible. He was standing right in front of them and couldn't find the slightest crack in the façade she'd built.

"Fantastic work, Lisa," Coleman said, giving voice to Rapp's thoughts. "We might have to call you to do a little consulting work now and then."

"Please don't," she said and then started up the trail to the lodge.

He shrugged and returned his attention to the actors in his little drama. "Okay. Everyone's read the script and found their marks?"

Auma, Ward, and Chism all nodded.

"Gideon. All you've got to do is insane anger. Not exactly a stretch, right? Mr. Ward. Your job is easy. Catatonic. Just kind of stare off into space like you don't really know where you are. David. Remember what we practiced. It's not like in the movies where people get shot and fly backward twenty feet. Just completely relax and crumple, okay? The dirt under you is soft and we've cleared out any rocks or roots. Your mind's going to tell you to put your hands out or not land on your face or whatever. Fight it."

"Don't worry," Chism said. "I'm about to be up for an Oscar."

"Dr. One-Take. I like your confidence. Stay on the ground but don't worry too much about having to stay completely still. Once you hit, we'll take you out of frame." The former SEAL craned his head around toward Maslick. "Got it, Mas?"

The big man, who had apparently figured out his phone, nodded.

"Okay. Let's do this. And, Gideon, every time you flub a take, Mitch here is going to cut off one of your toes. Understood?"

"I told you I would do what you ask!" he said as Rapp brandished a pair of kitchen shears.

"All right then. Make me feel it, baby! Action!"

"As near as I can tell, it's as Auma described," Coleman said.

Rapp had his eye to a small magnifying glass designed to be slid along photographs. The eight-by-ten lying on the table depicted an image taken from a commercial chopper they'd rented. The resolution wasn't bad, but it was not exactly the military quality he was accustomed to.

"You see the edge of the altar?"

"Could just be a rock," Rapp said.

"It's pretty rectangular. What about the guy in position A-six?"

Rapp moved the lens to that coordinate. "You mean the indistinct shadow?"

"You say tomato . . ."

Finally, Rapp leaned back in his chair and rubbed his tired eyes. Coleman's core team was gathered around the table. Among them sat Nicholas Ward, freshly showered, and wearing a polo shirt emblazoned with the name of one of his companies.

"What do you think?" he asked.

"I agree with Scott. This is the place Auma described. The altar seems to exist and the hill where he says there's a cave is in the right place. But the canopy is dense as hell and if he's good at anything, it's keeping his followers hidden. Without a high-altitude surveillance plane, ultra-high-res video, and a bunch of professional analysts to go over it, we can't be sure if the rest of his people are really there."

"You think he might have pointed you to an old encampment he's abandoned? Why?"

"It could be a decoy site," Coleman said. "A place that any of his people who get captured would be trained to give up. Or worse, an ambush site. Auma might have people waiting there. They'd know to kill anyone who shows up."

"Do you think he's that smart?"

"Yes," Rapp answered. "The question is whether he's that cautious. It's a lot of complexity, particularly with the illiterate child army he's got backing him up."

"Okay," Wicker said. "Then this is easy. We took delivery of the armament for those Russian choppers the Ugandans lent us. Let's go in there with guns and rockets blazing. Kill everything in a thousand-yard radius. Auma says the stuff you're after is in the cave, right? That'll protect them."

Despite having all the hallmarks of an excellent plan, Ward started shaking his head. "I see two problems. The first is that those are government choppers and the Ugandans have been clear about not wanting to be seen performing military operations that close to DRC territory. It could provoke a war."

"Surmountable," Rapp said. "We go in fast and low using night vision gear and then we spread a little money around to politicians on both sides of the border. No one's going to get too twisted up about a few fireworks. Particularly if Auma's cult is under them."

"The second problem is one we've already talked about," Ward said. "Auma keeps slaves. Mostly young girls he's stolen from local villages. They'd be killed along with his people."

"That's sad," Rapp admitted. "But collateral damage is a fact of life. How many of those girls could there be? Twenty? Thirty tops? And they're not exactly living large. They're going to die soon whether we go in or not. We can save the next round of girls that Auma's people are going to go after, though. And the next. And the next."

"No," Ward said firmly. "I'm not some CIA assassin or African dictator. And I paid for the choppers. If that's your plan, leave me out of it."

Rapp examined the man silently. This wasn't just about Gideon Auma or the CIA's mole problem. Rapp was interested in figuring out what lines the richest man in the world would and would not cross.

"Okay," he said finally. "What about a plan B?"

Virtually everyone at the table groaned before Coleman spoke up. "Your plan Bs always suck. Remember that time in Libya? The one where that whole building fell on us?"

"This one's better than that," Rapp said.

"Like the one where the train crashed?" Bruno McGraw said.

"When are you going to let that go?"

"I almost lost my arms, man."

Rapp frowned. "Fine. This one involves no risk to anyone but me."

"In that case, I'm in," Coleman said.

"What's that drug Auma's men like so much?"

"Ajali," Ward said.

"Ajali. Do we know anything about it?"

The man nodded. "David was interested and got a hold of a sample a while back. Basically, it's the worst thing you could possibly imagine. An engineered narcotic that has effects similar to what most people would attribute to PCP, but much more powerful and much more destructive. Over time it causes significant damage to the lungs and cardiovascular system, leaving regular users slowly drowning in their own bodily fluids. And the psychotic state it creates seems to persist in a way that makes people increasingly violent and paranoid. We don't—"

"Since you know what it is, could one of your pharmaceutical companies manufacture it?" Rapp said.

"Sure. Hypothetically."

"Not hypothetically. In reality."

The man's eyes narrowed. "Okay. Yes. The manufacturing process isn't that complicated."

"Could they poison it?"

Ward stood. "Could I have a word with you outside, Mitch?"

Rapp shrugged. "Sure."

They stepped out onto a broad deck and crossed to the far railing. Beyond, the mountains were a black outline against the stars.

"What are you doing?"

"Is it not clear? I'm trying to figure out who's after you and how they got the information for that attack on your compound."

"No. You're testing me. Trying to see how far I'll go to get rid of Auma's people. If I'm willing to risk starting a war. Or murder a bunch of children."

"What do you want from me, Nick? You said no to the gunships and I'm trying to work with that."

"By turning me not just into a narcotics manufacturer, but a poison narcotics manufacturer."

"More surgical, though, isn't it? I doubt they'd share their ajali with their sex slaves."

"If it's such a great idea, then why wasn't it plan A?"

"Because it forces me to fly Gideon Auma to a camp full of his armed worshippers with nothing but a Glock and a lucky rabbit's foot in my pocket."

"So, you were going to kill all those girls because you were concerned with your own personal safety."

"No. I was going to kill all those girls because I was concerned with *our* personal safety. I think it would be more realistic if you came along, don't you? I mean, you being the hostage and all."

Ward's face froze somewhere between fear and confusion. Not surprising, but a little disappointing.

"Feels kind of different when it's *your* rich ass on the line, doesn't it, Nick? And it's not just a bullet in the head, either. You know as well as I do the kinds of things Auma does to people. My best guess would be crucifixion. But when he's nailing me to that cross, at least I'll have the comfort of knowing you're right there with me."

Ward didn't seem to have a response, instead just swallowing some excess spit as Rapp broke into a grin. "Relax, Nick. I'm just fucking with you. I'll go myself. But I would appreciate your people whipping up a batch of ajali for me."

"It . . . It seems risky," Ward stammered. "I'd have to contact someone outside of this compound and then they'd know I hadn't been kidnapped."

"But you're the smartest guy in the world, right? I'm sure you can figure out a way to do it without tipping our hand."

"But wouldn't it be safer for you to manufacture it? Not a very big ask for Irene."

"No. Not a very big ask," Rapp said noncommittally.

"What reason is there to involve me, then? So you can see me get my hands bloody? Is it just cruelty?"

Again, Rapp smiled. "I've spent the last twenty years of my life drowning in cruelty, Nick. It doesn't hold all that much fascination for me."

"Then why?"

"Honestly? Because the more I'm around you the more I think you might actually be able to accomplish something. But people don't accept salvation easily. You have to ram it down their throats. And if you're not willing to do that—if you're not willing to help me poison people who go into villages and make kids watch them burn their parents alive—then you're wasting your time. And worse, you're wasting mine."

Ward turned his attention back to the dark horizon. "You win, Mitch. I'll do it."

"Okay. Then we're done. Why don't you go have a drink and get some sleep. We'll handle the rest."

When Rapp reentered the lodge, Coleman and his men were leaned over the table talking in hushed tones.

"You guys got plan B figured out yet?"

Coleman looked sideways at him. "Pretty much. You fly in there with Auma, get him to tell his people you're some kind of Arab ally, and pass out a bunch of poisoned ajali. He'll call it a victory celebration for getting his hands on Ward."

"Sounds perfect," Rapp said, settling back in his seat. "What could possibly go wrong?"

"You want the list alphabetically or by order of probability?" Joe Maslick said. "Auma could have some way to signal he's in trouble that we don't know about. Or he could just tell his people to kill you in Swahili and you'd never know. Or he could have booby traps and hidden weapons in that cave . . ."

Coleman nodded in agreement. "Or, hell, those people could just go nuts on the ajali and tear you apart before the poison kicks in."

"I don't want to hear about problems," Rapp said. "I want to hear about solutions."

"Let's just blow it like we talked about," Charlie Wicker said. "Nice and clean. I mean, I feel bad about the girls, but if this turns into a shit show and you get killed, how has that helped anyone? Those assholes will have their messiah back and they'll scatter into the jungle. How many more kids will end up soldiers or slaves? A hundred? A thousand?"

"He's right," Coleman said. "You're taking a lot of risks just so some rich guy can sleep a little better at night."

32

THE monitor next to the president's desk was playing the same video that had been looping at Langley since it appeared on the Internet a few hours ago. Still, Irene Kennedy and Mike Nash feigned concentration as a slightly out-of-focus Gideon Auma demanded ten billion dollars in ransom.

A filthy and haggard Nicholas Ward was standing near him, his expression almost catatonic as he stared blankly into the camera. David Chism, partially obscured behind the African, appeared to be in a similar state.

"And to be certain that everyone understands I'm serious . . ." Auma continued in his oddly elegant accent. Kennedy knew what was coming but still tensed when he turned and fired a round into Chism's chest. The young man collapsed out of frame as his killer turned his attention back to the camera.

"When I have received payment, I will provide instructions on where you can collect Nicholas Ward."

Anthony Cook used a remote to pause the video and then swiveled his chair toward his two guests.

"What do we know?" he asked, meeting Nash's eye and then letting his gaze wander to Kennedy. "Has he provided instructions yet?"

"No, sir," Kennedy responded. "Under the direction of the FBI, Nick's assistant has tried to contact his satellite phone, but it appears to be turned off and isn't currently trackable."

"So, we have no idea where Auma is or where Ward is being held?"

"Based on the foliage visible in the background, we're reasonably sure he's still in Ugand—"

"You're telling me you managed to narrow it down to the country where he was kidnapped?" Cook said sarcastically.

"The framing is pretty tight," Nash interjected. "Auma's psychotic, but he's smart and well educated. He hasn't kept himself and his army hidden for this long by making careless mistakes."

"Have you gotten people into Ward's camp to see if there's anything we can learn?"

"No, sir," Kennedy said. "We're working on it, but every time we get someone close, they're fired on. We have managed to go through the hangar where we believe Ward was taken but didn't find anything that could lead us to him."

Cook didn't seem any happier than she was, but likely for different reasons. She was sitting in the Oval Office spinning a web of lies that she wasn't sure she could control. Without fully understanding what kind of access their mole had, contacting Rapp was too dangerous. And now he seemed to have gone off script. The plan was for this operation to have been carried out in a much quieter manner. The story fed to the news agencies was to have been that Auma was killed in an attempt to kidnap Nicholas Ward. Rapp would question him, get whatever information he had, and the African would disappear forever. Clean, undisruptive, and completely plausible. A far cry from the story being plastered over every news site in the world and putting Ward's stock prices into free fall.

It was hard not to consider the possibility that this was real. It was improbable but still feasible that the mole they were chasing had discovered the changes Kennedy made to Ward's file. If that was the case, it was also feasible that Coleman and his people really had been overrun at the compound and Rapp had been ambushed at the hangar. And that Nicholas Ward was in the hands of a madman.

Fortunately, the deeper she looked, the less likely that scenario seemed. While her analysts hadn't been able to find anything in the video that seemed outright fake, there were curiosities. The first and most obvious was that it was too succinct. Whenever a camera was pointed at Gideon Auma, he never failed to ramble endlessly about his power, God's love for him, and whatever other delusions he was having on that particular day. The second—noticed by a young analyst with a particularly sharp eye—was that his sleeves didn't seem to behave naturally. She'd made a show of laughing off the observation but once pointed out, it became impossible to ignore. No matter how much Auma moved his arms, the cuffs stayed in place. Almost as though they'd been glued there. The obvious hypothesis was that this had been done to hide something. And the only thing she could think of was marks from being bound.

In light of that, the most likely scenario was that Rapp hadn't been able to get everything he wanted from the terrorist. He needed to extend this drama, probably to use Auma to lead him up the chain somehow.

"Today, Irene. I want people at that compound *today*."

"Yes, sir," she said, knowing full well it would be impossible. She needed to find a team she could trust to report only to her, and they had to be made up of people from outside the CIA. Not just because of the mole, but because what they found there would likely have to be kept from the president. It wasn't a political risk she wanted to expose any of her people to. If someone was going to be fired and prosecuted for this, it would be her and her alone.

"Can I assume that there's still no sign of Mitch Rapp and his team?" Cook said.

"That's correct, sir."

He nodded, but his face was an empty mask. "Do you think there's any chance he's in the jungle? Hiding out like David Chism did?"

"I doubt it, sir. He and his people have satellite phones. They would have contacted me."

Another nod, another blank expression at what he likely would take as news of Mitch Rapp's death. "So where do we stand? If Auma hasn't contacted Ward's people yet, he will soon. Can I assume that we'll be ready for that call when it comes?"

Kennedy glanced at Mike Nash, who had been working directly with the Bureau on this.

"This is a complicated situation for Auma," he said, taking over the briefing. "Obviously, it can't be done in cash. It'd be multiple transport planes full of it. That means wire transfers. And since Auma isn't stupid, he's going to want them laundered through banks we have no penetration into. Places like Syria, Iran, North Kor—"

"All of whom will take a cut," Cook pointed out.

"Yes, sir."

"So not only will Ward's organization be funding one of the most brutal terrorists in Africa, but they'll also be funneling money into virtually every one of our worst enemies. It seems to me that we need to come up with some way to get him back without actually paying the ransom."

"Agreed. But that's easier said than done."

Cook took a deep breath and let it out slowly. "David Chism is dead, which is probably going to set back the development of his vaccines twenty-five years. And Ward . . ." His voice faded for a moment. "I consider Nicholas Ward critical to America's future and the health of our economy. It's strange to say that about a single man, but he's probably responsible for sixty percent of the advances going on in tech right now. And those are the industries that are going to keep us on top for the next century."

"Yes, sir," Kennedy and Nash said, almost in unison.

"Find something. Find a way to get him back."

"And if there's no way to do that without paying?" Kennedy asked.

"Unacceptable."

"But also potentially unavoidable."

"I'm confident that you can do better," Cook said.

They both mumbled their understanding and stood, knowing that the meeting was over. Kennedy nodded respectfully in the man's direction and started for the door with Nash close behind. The president didn't bother to stand.

"I guess that fortune really does favor the bold," Catherine Cook said, appearing from the door leading to a private space connected to the Oval Office.

"You heard?"

She took the seat Irene Kennedy had abandoned moments ago. "Chism's dead and one way or another, Nicholas Ward's done."

"Not just Ward and Chism, Catherine. Mitch Rapp. That could make us a lot of friends in the Arab world. Friends that no American president has ever had before."

She nodded. "I have to admit that I'm not unhappy to see him go. I think he could have been a useful tool, but maybe a harder one to control than I initially thought. He wasn't as blunt an instrument as he appeared."

"What he *was*, though, was a big part of Kennedy's power base. Not only is this going to be a major emotional blow for her—to the degree that bitch has emotions—but it's going to significantly weaken her political position. Her ability to virtually guarantee the success of her operations is right now lying dead somewhere in the Ugandan jungle."

33

THEY were only a few klicks to the north of the supposed landing site, but all Rapp could see was unbroken jungle in the moonlight. He manipulated the chopper's collective and felt the aircraft obey his command. It wasn't always the case. On a scale of one to ten, he'd put his piloting abilities somewhere in the four range. Fred Mason had suggested on more than a few occasions that it might be an optimistic estimate.

"There," Gideon Auma said, pointing through the windscreen to a flicker of firelight ahead. He sounded unusually subdued for God's representative on earth, but it was understandable. Joe Maslick had spent hours designing, building, and attaching a radio-controlled explosive to the African's scrotum. Not powerful enough to kill him, but enough to launch his balls a good twenty feet.

The hope was that it would keep him obediently following the plan Rapp had devised. And in return, he would be delivered—alive and well—to The Hague. There, he would be put in a nice clean cell, fed three times a day, and tried for crimes against humanity. All in all, a more attractive fate than watching his testicles careening into the forest or what the Ugandan government would do to him if they got the opportunity.

But would he see it that way? Once surrounded by his adoring disciples, would Auma start to feel invincible again? Would he lose his fear and go on the attack? If so, it was going to be an exciting—and likely short—evening.

Rapp circled the clearing, looking down at the tiny campfires that defined its edges. Mason could have easily landed a chopper twice this size in the available space but Rapp preferred LZs that could be measured in acres, not yards.

The winds remained calm as he eased the aircraft downward, watching to make sure he stayed dead center and that his rotors were nowhere near the surrounding trees. In the end, it was a pretty decent landing. A better start than most of his plan Bs enjoyed. No derailed train cars, collapsing buildings, or avalanches.

He began shutting the bird down, keeping an eye on the vague human forms already busy putting out the fires that had acted as primitive runway lights.

"Are you still clear on your role?" he asked.

"Yes," Auma responded in a lifeless voice. Not really the right tone for what they were about to embark on, but it was unlikely anyone would notice.

"Tell me."

"The remote control for the explosive is in your pocket and you will have your hand on it at all times. The earpiece in your ear is connected to an open satellite link. There is a Ugandan native on the other side. If I say anything that is not in English, he will translate."

"And if you say something I don't like?"

"You will detonate the explosive."

"Sounds about right," Rapp said, grabbing a knapsack from behind his seat and stepping out. "Hold it together for a few more hours,

Gideon. And then you can live out the rest of your life enjoying a little Dutch hospitality."

Auma exited the other side and they came together at the front of the helicopter. A fatigue-clad man whose age was difficult to determine in the poor light ran up to them and bowed reverently. As expected, Rapp's presence was completely ignored. He was nothing. Just another servant to their prophet.

The conversation was carried out in Swahili but, as promised, Rapp got a real-time translation in his right ear. Mostly pleas to be commanded, assurances that it would be an honor to die for his lord and master. Yada, yada, yada.

Auma, for his part, didn't respond—the man in front of them apparently wasn't worthy of that. Instead, they followed in silence as they were led along a randomly winding trail that had been cleared of rocks but was still tangled with foliage. Likely designed to not create a pattern that could be seen from above and bring an attack down on them. Their survival depended entirely on the jungle's ability to hide them and their proximity to the DRC border.

What the jungle couldn't hide, though, was the smell. The unmistakable stench of human decay hit first, eventually combining with the duller odor of open latrines. Rapp couldn't see much through the darkness, but human figures occasionally separated from the gloom on either side of the rudimentary path. Some were completely still— likely the source of the rot that hung in the air. Others moved silently, almost drunkenly, to watch them pass. Probably the girls they'd enslaved. Or what was left of them.

The hard angles of the crosses were easier to make out, as were the bodies nailed to them. One man—boy, really—was still alive. He choked out a few entreaties as they passed, all dutifully converted to English by the translator in Rapp's ear. There was nothing he could do for the kid and he couldn't allow himself to be distracted from studying his operating environment. If he had to run, shit was going to get ugly. Auma's followers would know the terrain like the back of their hands and their lack of discipline would work in their favor. All they had to do was fill the air in his general direction with lead. He was fast, but not fast enough to outpace a bullet.

Rapp kept Auma in front of him, glancing back when a number of men fell in behind. He hated having people flanking him but there wasn't much he could do. If Auma had managed to transmit some kind of signal that he'd missed, he was likely going to get shot in the back. It was Coleman's greatest concern—that Auma had some kind of "all clear" sign and that, in its absence, his disciples would tear whoever he was with apart.

They crashed through a particularly dense section of jungle and then exited into a clearing that Rapp recognized from the overhead shots he'd studied. The rectangular object at the center was indeed an altar—complete with chains and streaked dark with what he assumed was dried blood. Behind was the muddy cliff and cave entrance that Auma had described. Next to that was something he'd thought was just a legend meant to scare the locals. A fucking iron maiden. Nothing fancy—little more than a simple coffin with a hinged lid and nails driven through it—but functional. The unit was open and leaned against the dirt wall with a body inside. Kind of like an Old West display but with a corpse covered in rotting perforations.

Auma climbed the mound that contained the altar as the clearing filled with his followers. Rapp, not sure what his role in this twisted ceremony should be, took a position on the other side of the stone structure.

The African raised his arms, feeding off the glassy eyes staring up at him. "We have him!"

The cheers were deafening, and Rapp didn't need the earpiece to get the gist of what was being said.

Praise be unto Gideon Auma.

The cult leader opened his hands, silencing them. "Soon we will have the tools to take Uganda. And then Africa. And then the world. In the name of God and his one true prophet."

The cheers erupted again as he slowly turned full circle and gazed out over his disciples. Rapp tightened his grip on the remote in his pocket. Better to err on the side of caution and blow this guy's nuts sky high at anything that even hinted at betrayal. He might be able to disappear in the confusion that would ensue. If Auma called him out first, though, there was a good chance he'd be joining that poor asshole in the iron maiden.

When the clearing descended back into silence, Auma spoke again. "In celebration, we will all take the Sacrament."

That brought a second round of cheers that went beyond enthusiastic and crossed into ecstatic. Rapp pulled the pack off his shoulder and was about to toss it on the altar, but then caught himself. Instead, he bowed his head and placed it there with exaggerated reverence.

The innocuous canvas knapsack was filled with a special batch of ajali produced by one of Ward's pharmaceutical companies. Good stuff, they had assured him—better than anything cooked up in the region's hidden jungle labs. It wasn't the quality of the high he was interested in, though. It was the secret ingredient. Ricin.

The lab was experimenting with using the toxin to kill cancer cells, but it had another property that made it ideal for this operation: a delayed effect. Once inhaled, initial symptoms wouldn't present themselves until well after everyone had partaken. Difficulty breathing. Fever. Nausea. Fluid would start to build up in the lungs and the victim's skin would take on a bluish hue. Finally, the outcome he was interested in. Death.

"Take it!" Auma shouted. "All of you. And enter the presence of God!"

Rapp followed him toward the cave as his men rushed the altar. Their shouts became almost desperate as a few designated specialists began loading the ajali into devices designed to measure the dose.

A leafy barrier constructed in the cave entrance swung open when he and Auma got close. They passed into the darkness and it was closed firmly behind them before a single lightbulb flared to life.

A girl of around fourteen with close-cropped hair and elegant features secured the barrier in a way that wouldn't allow light to bleed through and then dropped to her knees before Auma. She touched her head to the ground and then looked up at her master with a smile that revealed a stunning set of teeth.

She said something, but interference from the cave prevented Rapp from getting a translation. It was a situation that he'd discussed specifically with Auma. One word in anything but English while they were in the cave and he'd be chasing his balls around the floor like a couple of dropped marbles.

The self-proclaimed prophet had apparently gotten the message because he ignored her, instead continuing deeper into the cavern. It seemed to be as described—living quarters first, followed by something that passed for a war room. After that, just darkness. According to Auma, it went back a ways and then dead-ended. Rapp assumed that was a lie. Someone as smart as Auma wouldn't pick a lair that lacked a back door. Probably more than one.

The African used one of the keys hanging around his neck to open a filing cabinet and dug around inside. Rapp tensed, but the man didn't pull out anything more dangerous than a flip phone and an iPad.

"This is the phone I use to contact the Saudis," he said, handing it to Rapp. "The tablet has pictures of him."

They weren't particularly good as it turned out—taken surreptitiously by his followers in bad light and from less-than-ideal angles. What they lacked in quality, though, they made up for in number. Enough that a good composite could be stitched together, he guessed.

"Where's the information you were given on Ward's compound?"

Auma retrieved a large envelope as the shouts of the people outside intensified. It sounded like Ward's scientists weren't bullshitting—they really did know how to turn out some high-grade product. Rapp ignored the din as he shuffled through the photos of Ward's compound, schematics on his defenses, and detailed attack strategies written in English but sprinkled with grammatical errors common to native Arabic speakers. There was no question that these had been downloaded directly from the CIA's secure database. By whom, though, was still a mystery.

Rapp had insisted that the light remain on and was sitting with his back against one of the cave walls. Gideon Auma was lying on a bed fifteen feet to his left, fully clothed, motionless, eyes closed. Given his dire situation and the party exploding outside, though, it was unlikely he was asleep. Screams, singing, and the shouts of people goading on hand-to-hand combatants bounced around the confined space with no sign of abating.

Gunshots, though, were conspicuously absent. Rapp had peeked outside earlier and discovered that all weapons had been caged up and were being guarded by two men who didn't appear to have joined the festivities. Of course, the drug-frenzied mob could have easily overwhelmed them, but so far there had been no attempts to do so. Their prophet had undoubtedly laid out the safety protocols for these events long ago and the penalty for not following them would be sufficiently biblical as to discourage noncompliance. A rare stroke of luck in Rapp's favor.

He lifted his head and looked into the confused eyes of the girl sitting in a similar position across from him. Auma had refused her desperate attempts to provide him sexual favors and she now looked even more terrified than when they'd arrived. It seemed likely that she was thinking that he'd become bored with her. That after barely making it into her teens, she was going to end up nailed to a cross or tossed to his men.

Rapp let his eyes go out of focus but remained alert. He hated everything about caves. The darkness, the smell, the thick, still air. While he had learned to control his claustrophobia, it was still there, scratching at the back of his mind like a cornered rat. If he had any aspiration for his death, it was to go down in an open desert beneath a blanket of stars. He had the next billion years to lie in a hole.

A sliver of light flashed in Rapp's peripheral vision, suggesting that the sun had risen sufficiently to beam directly on the makeshift blackout shade covering the cave entrance. The girl had fallen asleep a while back and was slumped in the dirt, moaning quietly as she navigated a dream that didn't sound much better than her reality.

Now just over twelve hours since Rapp's arrival, the party outside had gone more or less silent. The few cries that occasionally rose up sounded as though they were motivated more by terror and suffering than bloodlust or ecstatic vision. All were weak and most ended in uncontrolled coughing fits. Still, no one had ventured to the cave entrance to seek help from their messiah. Incredible. They were still more afraid of Gideon Auma than they were of what was happening to them. Maybe they thought it was a punishment he had brought down on them for some unknown transgression? Or that they were on their last, painful journey to paradise?

"Get up," Rapp said as he pushed himself to his feet. Auma did as he was told, face blank, eyes wandering around his familiar surroundings. By the look of him, he'd spent the night trying to make sense of what was happening. He'd almost certainly thought that the purpose of the ajali was just to create confusion—to provide cover for their departure after Rapp got what he wanted.

And that would have been the smart move. In fact, it was the move that Rapp would have made only a few years ago. The mole was the mission, and the job was to complete the mission in the most efficient way possible. All other considerations were irrelevant.

The more gray hair he got, though, the more relevant those other considerations became. While he hadn't had the power to completely shut down ISIS, the Taliban, or al-Qaeda, that possibility existed here. He'd seen what Auma and his followers were capable of. What they'd done. And that made it hard to ignore that he had a shot at stopping them. Not winning a skirmish. Not taking out a few high-level leaders who would be immediately replaced. Not stemming the flow of blood but shutting it off forever. A first in what had been a sometimes frustrating career.

"What's happened?" Auma mumbled as he moved to the middle of the cave and awaited further instructions. There had likely been similar ceremonies in the past and this wouldn't be what they sounded like when they finally died down. He knew something was wrong.

"A deal's a deal," Rapp said, ignoring the man's question. "Let's go."

He kept Auma in front of him as they exited into the sunny clearing. The girl leapt to her feet and followed, eager to prove her continued value. Not ideal, but it was easier to let her do what she wanted than to convince her otherwise.

In daylight, the place had an even stronger resemblance to hell. The shadowy figures he'd seen the night before were now in stark focus and full color. Worse, the climbing temperature was raising a translucent mist that seemed to magnify the stench of excrement and death, now joined by an acidic hint of vomit.

Most of Auma's followers were down. Some already dead from the ricin, the others were on their way. Girls—badly broken versions of the one trailing Auma—surveyed the scene from the trees. A few that had started to venture out retreated at the sight of the cult leader.

Rapp turned his attention to the two armed men guarding a wooden cage full of weapons. They glanced at Rapp but were much more interested in Auma. Despite everything they'd just witnessed, their eyes still brimmed with an odd mix of terror, adoration, and gratitude. Did they think he had saved them? That God had deemed them his only worthy followers?

An interesting question, but not one Rapp really needed answered. He pulled his Glock from a holster in the small of his back and fired a single round into the forehead of each man. Both collapsed unceremoniously to the ground.

Auma apparently saw that as his moment. He grabbed the girl, pulling her to him in a way that would both shield him from Rapp's bullets and cause the explosives glued to his genitals to kill her if detonated.

The African backed toward the cave as Rapp tracked him lazily with his Glock. In truth, he was more concerned with the surviving men strewn around him and even the girls in the trees. In a situation like this, it was hard to know how people would react and who might attack.

In the end, the answer was no one. While some of the boys on the ground still had the energy to writhe around a bit, they no longer seemed to have any idea what was going on around them. And the girls just inside the tree line seemed content to stay there.

"Tell them I'm dead!" Auma said as he continued to pick his way through what was left of his disciples. "You got what you came for."

Rapp didn't react, even when Auma dragged the stunned girl back into the cave. There was no reason to. The cult leader was playing checkers while Joe Maslick was playing chess. While there was indeed a detonator button in Rapp's pocket, it didn't send a signal as Auma assumed. In fact, the opposite was true. The remote was in constant communication with the bomb placed on the man and the button shut down that connection. More simply put, the explosive wasn't designed to go off when signaled. The signal was what kept it dormant. Once Auma moved out of range, he was going to get a very unfortunate surprise.

It didn't take long. There was a dull bang—not much louder than a couple of firecrackers—followed by inevitable screams. The girl's were like breaking glass and Auma's, if anything, were even more piercing.

She appeared first, splattered with blood, but sprinting with an athletic grace that suggested it wasn't hers. Auma staggered from the cave a few seconds later, crimson from mid-thigh to mid-belly. No weapons were visible on him and there were none accessible beyond the two AKs tangled up in his fallen guards. Gideon Auma—the terror of Africa—now posed so little threat that Rapp turned away and started toward the chopper.

He paused just inside the trees when he heard the quiet voices of young girls. They were starting to inch into the clearing and he couldn't help but watch.

He missed his guess as to who the instigator would be. She was smaller than most of the others, wearing a tattered dress that had probably once been a floral print. Rapp saw her pick up a hefty rock, stare at it for a moment, and then bring it down on the skull of one of the boys who was still breathing.

And that broke the dam.

There were more of them than he'd first estimated. A good twenty came flooding out of the trees, picking up rocks and going to work on the survivors. When no live victims were at hand, they went after the corpses. Auma tried to make it to cover but was slowed by blood loss and what looked like a badly damaged pelvis. Four girls tracked him like lions trying to decide whether a wounded buffalo was still capable of defending itself. When the man stumbled and dropped to his knees, they swarmed him.

It was only then that Rapp continued toward the chopper. Hopefully, they wouldn't let that iron maiden go to waste.

34

THE dirt track turned steep enough that even the Land Cruiser was struggling to hold traction. There was a landing zone near the camp they'd stashed Nicholas Ward in, but it was a little tight for Rapp's piloting skills. Coleman had suggested that he put down in a clearing near the base of a mountain and had left the vehicle there for him.

Rapp knew he was being watched from the trees on either side of the road, but never saw any evidence of it. Any unwanted guests trying to take this path to the lodge would find themselves caught in a withering crossfire. Anyone coming through the jungle would be picked up by sensors and die never even having laid eyes on Charlie Wicker's team. And, finally, anyone coming in from the air would face a state-of-the-art SAM battery purchased with Ward's inexhaustible checkbook.

When Rapp came around the last turn, he saw Coleman waiting at the open gate. Surprisingly, Nicholas Ward was standing next to him, hands shoved in his pockets and a deep frown on his face. Or maybe it wasn't so surprising. He was probably getting pretty bored at this point. Going from running the largest private empire in history to wandering around looking at the bird life was a pretty stark transition.

"I can't believe that worked!" Coleman said as Rapp stepped from the vehicle. "I bet Mas ten bucks you'd be hanging from a cross by now."

"Sorry to disappoint you," Rapp said.

He shrugged. "I'll win it back."

"Is he dead?" Ward interjected.

"Auma? Yeah."

"What about his people?"

"Same. And by now the girls will be on their way back to their villages. Congratulations, Nick. Your first field operation was a spectacular success."

"My first field operation . . ." he repeated, suddenly losing himself in thought.

"Are we still good here, Scott?"

"One hundred percent. The only people in the outside world who know we're alive are Claudia, Marcus, Irene, and the woman Nick contacted to get your drugs made. And let me tell you that people seem really broken up about my death. You, not so much. In fact, I'm hearing rumors about parties breaking out all over the Middle East."

Rapp ignored the jab. "What about the woman Nick called. She's solid?"

The trillionaire responded immediately, clearly concerned for his employee's safety. "Erica's been with me for twenty years and she's never been anything but completely reliable. You don't need to worry."

"I assume we're worrying?" Rapp said and Coleman nodded.

"We've got a seven-man team on her. Electronic surveillance on her house, office, and car, plus all her communications. So far, she seems to know how to keep her mouth shut. If that changes, we'll snatch her."

A flash of anger crossed Ward's face, but he managed to remain silent. Clearly, he cared about his people but knew better than to waste his breath on something that was beyond his control. Both rare traits in powerful people.

"Irene sent an encrypted email to one of our dummy Gmail accounts this morning. Nothing but a number. Sixteen hundred and nine. Mean anything to you?"

It did. Sixteen hundred was a time—4 p.m. his time. The nine was code for a pay phone that still existed outside of Baltimore. He'd memorized the number years ago.

"What time is it?"

Coleman glanced at his watch. "A little after noon."

"I need to make a phone call at four."

"Secure?"

"No. To a US pay phone."

"No problem. We have a box of brand-new satphones registered to a front company in Indonesia. I'm on it. Anything else?"

Rapp shook his head and the former SEAL started jogging up the walkway toward the comms area they'd set up.

Ward watched him go, not speaking again until he was out of sight. "Does this mean we'll all be coming back to life soon? Do you have what you need to identify your mole?"

"The mole you don't know anything about?"

"Right. That one."

"Let's just say I'm closer than I was yesterday."

Ward's expression suggested that it wasn't the answer he'd been looking for.

Rapp closed himself up in the metal shed and settled onto a rickety stool. The structure was located at the end of a dirt path, hidden from the well-heeled guests who would normally be staying at the lodge. Cleaning products and landscaping equipment had been shoved to one side and a small satellite dish was now perched on the roof. The box of phones Coleman had mentioned was lying on a desk built from fuel cans and an old door. Rapp selected a handset at random, double-checked the time, and started dialing.

He'd never seen the phone booth he was calling, but imagined Kennedy closed up in the glass enclosure wearing dark sunglasses and turned away from anyone who might be passing by.

It rang only once before she picked up. The first thing he heard was a quiet hum that, hilariously, was likely generated by a battery-operated sex toy. Some enterprising tech in the Agency's Office of Technical Services had noticed that the vibrating suction cup was capable of shaking glass at a frequency ideal for defeating passive listening devices. And, as a bonus, getting caught with it would be embarrassing but not at all suggestive of espionage. Apparently, there were other benefits, too, but he couldn't speak to those directly.

"It's good to connect," she said, her voice low and slightly distorted by the fact that she would have a hand cupped around her mouth. "Your show was so convincing you actually had me worried."

"No need," he responded. Despite all the precautions, they'd be as vague as possible. Further, he was speaking through a mike attached to his phone via a box that changed his voice. And not one of the old distortion boxes that people equated with testimony from old mobsters and DEA agents. This one generated the perfectly natural voice of a young woman.

"Did you like the stuff I sent?"

He was referring to the numbers that had been dialed on the phone Auma used to call the Saudi liaison, as well as the photos taken of him.

"Not so much the numbers."

No big surprise there. Auma's contact would use a burner.

"But the pictures were lovely."

What followed would sound to anyone listening like a discussion of a foreign vacation and a bit of reminiscing on Kennedy's part. In truth, though, she was referring to people and situations that would lead him to a name.

It took a while, but he finally got it. Muhammad Singh.

"Understood. Does he work for our friends in that country?"

She would know that he was referring to Saudi Arabia's General Intelligence Directorate.

"Oh, probably. But also for the oil company."

ARAMCO. A convenient cover for a GID agent or, more likely, a contractor used to put as much distance between the royal family and people like Gideon Auma as possible.

"Did we know him?"

"Not at all. He's a very private fellow."

"Not anymore. Seems like someone should go talk to him."

"My thought exactly. But our travel agents are unreliable right now. Can you handle it yourself?"

"No problem. For the time being at least, I'm flush."

35

"DOCUMENTS?"

Rapp handed his Iraqi passport to the control officer while myriad cameras—on the walls, in the ceiling, behind the glass in front of him—studied his features.

The king, whom he knew well, had stepped back and turned the country over to his extraordinarily ruthless son. The prince had immediately consolidated his power, imprisoning critics and rival family members, murdering journalists and bloggers, and inserting people loyal to him in every level of government. Phase two of his takeover had been to spend billions creating an elaborate surveillance system designed to spy on every corner of Saudi society. With virtually unlimited funds he'd already surpassed the Chinese in both the number of cameras per capita and the sophistication of the artificial intelligence running it. The technology wasn't perfect yet, but gaming it was becoming increasingly difficult.

Rapp was wearing glasses that looked clear to the human eye but caused distortion when filmed. He'd also taken advantage of having Ward's movie makeup artist at the lodge, but with full acknowledgment of the risks. If he got flagged, there was a good chance they'd uncover the artificial bump in his nose and the surprisingly painful wires flaring out his nostrils.

And then Mitch Rapp, the man everyone thought was dead, really would be.

The control officer flipped through the well-worn pages, occasionally glancing up to examine Rapp's face. With the alterations, it didn't exactly match the photo, but the changes would be less obvious to a human than to a computer algorithm. Or at least that was the theory.

The passport was a gift from an Iraqi official whose life Rapp had saved a few years back. He'd kept it in reserve for a situation just like this one. The CIA had no knowledge of it and thus it wouldn't appear in the database that Kennedy now believed to be compromised.

After less than a minute, the official gave him the stamp he needed and slid the document back across the counter. Rapp nodded respectfully and shoved it in his pocket before joining the crowd flowing toward baggage claim.

If anything, there were even more cameras watching the conveyors than there had been in passport control. Fortunately, he had carried on his luggage and was able to pass through quickly with his head down. Not that it mattered at this point, but old habits died hard.

The rental of his car went smoothly, and he slid behind the wheel of what passed for a low-profile vehicle in the Kingdom—a new Porsche Cayenne. He pulled out of the parking garage and used the built-in GPS to navigate to an apartment he'd rented on Airbnb. The Saudi computers would already know where he was staying and what car Enterprise had assigned him, so no point in trying to hide. With precisely zero help from the Agency, his best bet was to just act in as predictable a manner as possible. Of course, the General Intelligence Directorate would figure out who he was eventually. The trick would be to make sure he was long gone before that particular light dawned.

Rapp turned on the radio and listened to a man sing in Arabic about unrequited love. He knew both the artist and the song well. Perfect language skills weren't enough—he spent an enormous amount of time keeping up with the Middle East's popular culture. Music, television, politics. It was a mash-up of a hundred different things that made passing as a native possible.

He rolled down the window and let the warm night air flow through his car. The GPS continued to call out turns, allowing him to focus on his rearview mirror and the light traffic surrounding him. Again, though, it was mostly just habit. With the cameras set up along the highway and modern drones, old-school tails were becoming a thing of the past. Roughly the equivalent of exchanging a suitcase full of cash for a suitcase full of documents on a lonely Siberian bridge.

He finally arrived in a neighborhood lined with low-rise apartment buildings—utilitarian white squares with tiny balconies and decent-sized windows. The passcode the landlord had given him worked and he descended into an underground parking area. Cameras were once again ubiquitous, likely installed by the property owner but undoubtedly also uploading to the government.

Rapp passed the numbered space he'd been assigned, driving hesitantly and leaning into the windshield. Airbnb guests getting confused about where to park wouldn't be all that uncommon and he used that fact to take a full tour of the parking area. The car owned by Muhammad Singh was near the southeast corner and he made note of the location before circling back to his space. One small duffle was all he had with him and he pulled it from the backseat before locking the car and taking an elevator to his apartment.

It wasn't bad. Faux hardwood floors, heavy curtains, and Oriental rugs lent a stylish utilitarianism that avoided the Saudi tendency toward garishness. He'd chosen it for tactical reasons, but no point in complaining about a decent kitchen and comfortable mattress. Particularly after so many years sleeping in bombed-out buildings and caves.

It was 11 p.m. by the time he unpacked but still he changed into running clothes and headed for the door. It wouldn't raise any major alarms—the Arabs tended to be night owls in general and avoided exercising in daytime temperatures that were currently exceeding 105 degrees Fahrenheit. He hit the elevator button that corresponded to the parking garage and after a few moments stepped back out into it.

Empty.

Preferable, but not really critical to what he was there to do. Walking by Singh's parked car, he knelt and made a show of tying his shoe. Nothing he was doing was particularly creative or high tech, but with no Agency support, it was the best he could come up with.

As he stood, he stuck a cell phone to the inside of the vehicle's fender with the aid of some epoxy putty. It would provide a way to track the man's movements and hopefully lead to something interesting. But the clock was ticking. Saudi Arabia's facial recognition software would eventually kick the airport photos of him out for further analysis. And then there was the phone he was using as a tracer. It was in a battery case and the app was designed to maximize battery life, but he wouldn't get more than a couple of days out of it.

With Gideon Auma's ransom video out in the wild, though, Rapp had a hunch that two days would be enough. The moment it hit the Internet, Singh would go from critical operative to untidy loose end. And in Rapp's experience, the Saudis didn't much care for untidy loose ends. They'd move against the man. Soon.

36

RAPP adjusted himself into a more comfortable position on the sofa and dug some noodles from the takeout carton balanced on his chest. Not the best he'd ever eaten, but not the worst, either. After a quick shake to dislodge the last few vegetables from the bottom, he set the box on the coffee table and returned to his phone.

Despite the fact that he was using a sophisticated VPN to hide his tracks on the Internet, he kept his surfing generic. Mostly Al Jazeera's Arabic site with a quick detour to scroll through the headlines on Google News.

Not surprisingly, the cycle was consumed with the kidnapping of Nicholas Ward and the death of David Chism. There wasn't a whole lot to say, though—mostly general background on them and Gideon Auma, as well as speculation as to what this would mean for Ward's business empire. So far, "sources" said that no demands had been made to secure his release and "experts" assumed this was Auma's ploy to soften up his opponents in the upcoming negotiation.

Rapp found a headline different from the rest and couldn't resist clicking on it. The article contained a sketchy description of the attack on Ward's compound and actually went so far as to acknowledge other people—ones without a trillion dollars—had died in it. Scott Coleman and his organization were mentioned by name.

Of course, there was nothing at all on Rapp. He'd set up his life to be as anonymous as possible and it seemed to have worked. Having said that, it was kind of strange to find that his passing was a blank page. After saving the president of the United States from an attack on the White House, stopping a nuclear bomb from exploding in DC, and preventing a bioterror attack that could have wiped out half the world's population, his legacy would be . . . nothing.

Not that it bothered him. It just felt odd. At home in Virginia, he imagined that Maggie Nash would be taking charge like she always did. Decorating the barn, lining up speakers and mourners, ordering food and flowers. He had nothing but confidence that the wake for him, Coleman, and the guys was going to be an eminently tasteful affair.

Claudia would play along from Africa, isolating Anna and telling everyone that she hadn't yet had the heart to break the news. If things dragged on long enough, she'd be forced to fly back, turn on the water-works, and thank everyone for what they'd done. It wouldn't be a problem. She was a former professional liar.

And then everyone would just move on, doing everything they could to forget. To not think about the fact that next time it could be them being eulogized. It could be their spouses standing in stunned silence as people offered meaningless condolences. Their kids trying to understand why their mother or father was never coming home.

Man, he could use a beer. But that wouldn't be particularly good for his cover. An Iraqi seeking booze in a Muslim country was just another way to push himself onto the GID's radar. Instead, he shut down the news app and launched one connected to the tracker on Muhammad Singh's car. Despite having been in place for more than twenty-four hours, it still had a seventy percent charge. Not that there was much reason for it to be drained. It only ran when in motion and

Singh led what appeared to be a pretty quiet life. Other than going to his cover job at ARAMCO, and a quick trip to the grocery store, he spent his time holed up in his apartment two floors above. Had the GID gotten soft on loose ends? Was Singh a more critical player than they thought and thus immune to being disappeared? At some point, Rapp was just going to have to jump in the elevator and pay his target a visit.

But that came with significant risks. While everyone in Saudi Arabia was being watched to some extent, a man like Singh would be absolutely lousy with surveillance. Rapp doubted it would be possible to swing a dead cat around the man's apartment without hitting a hidden listening device or camera. And the tracker he'd put on Singh's car was probably only one of many much more sophisticated ones put in place by his handlers. And then there was the fact that he almost certainly had significant training in resisting interrogation.

At half past midnight, Rapp finally rolled off the sofa, tossed the remnants of his dinner in the garbage, and headed for bed.

Rapp's eyes opened to a rendition of Creedence Clearwater Revival's "Fortunate Son" emanating from his phone. That particular song meant only one thing: Singh's car was on the move.

He glanced at the alarm clock on the bedside table, squinting at the reddish glow of the numbers. Just after two thirty in the morning.

Was Singh making a quick run to his favorite twenty-four-hour falafel shop? Based on his habits so far, probably not. It would take something more pressing to pry him out of his apartment at this hour.

Rapp flipped on the light and grabbed his jeans off the floor. Maybe the GID wasn't getting soft after all.

37

RAPP was already hanging back far enough that he couldn't see Singh's vehicle. Still, he exited the highway when the navigation program on his phone made the suggestion.

It was a slick CIA app overlaying Google Maps. The purpose was to allow a single operator to perform a pretty functional tail of someone with an enabled tracker on their car. Not only could Rapp stay well behind, but the program suggested opportunities to disengage and then re-intercept later. Admittedly risky, but the traffic was light at this time of night and Singh was a pro. At the first sign of a tail, he'd either bolt or head back home.

Rapp accelerated until his cell's screen flashed green—a confirmation that he'd achieved the speed necessary to rejoin the highway in the same relative position to his target. Now all he had to do was hope that there were no overzealous cops around looking to pass out tickets to speeding Porsches.

Another half an hour and a couple more complicated detours led him to an industrial area at the edge of town. The dot on his phone stopped and almost immediately went dark as the unit attached to

Singh's bumper switched into battery saver mode. Rapp turned up a side street three blocks to the north and parked out of range of security lights bolted to the buildings around him.

The absence of the Glock 19 under his arm made him feel a little naked as he stepped out of the car. Getting a weapon into Saudi Arabia without CIA support was virtually impossible and acquiring one in-country was overly risky. He actually had a safe house in Riyadh that no one knew about, but once he retrieved the gun hidden beneath the floorboards, it would be blown forever. Better to save that for a rainy day even if it would likely lead to a little more improvisation than he'd normally tolerate. For the time being, anonymity was more valuable than firepower.

He pulled up the collar on his light jacket and walked up the middle of the street where the darkness was the deepest. A half-moon hung to the east, but barely provided enough illumination to keep him from tripping over the cracks in the asphalt. After a few minutes at a casual pace, he spotted Singh's car parked inside a chain-link fence that surrounded a partially built warehouse. Maybe he wasn't such a pro after all. Rule number one when contracting for an intelligence agency: don't agree to predawn meetings at construction sites.

The cameras mounted to the fence all appeared to have been deactivated—something that didn't happen in Saudi Arabia without the government's blessing. Whatever was going to happen there, someone powerful didn't want any record of it.

The sound of an engine reached him from the west. He climbed the fence and dropped to the ground before headlights became visible. Once inside the perimeter, he ran to the building, slipping through the deep shadows that clung to the walls. With the cameras off, he was probably safe, but it didn't pay to take those kinds of things for granted. When he reached the front, he peered past Singh's car at two approaching vehicles. They stopped at the gate and a man stepped out to open it. He moved like a professional—graceful, silent, and paying as much attention to his environment as he could while also getting a key into the padlock. A bulge in his silhouette suggested that he was armed with something more formidable than the paring knife Rapp had brought from his rental.

The bulky SUVs pulled in and the man closed but didn't lock the gate. Clearly, preparing for an efficient departure when their meeting was over. Probably not good news for Singh.

There was no way for Rapp to get in through the front—the men staying with the SUVs would have that covered. But the back of the building looked like it had sections that weren't finished and had been covered with tarps to keep the sand out. If there was a gap in one, he could probably slip through. Tarps were tricky, though. While not particularly solid, they were shockingly loud if you had to move them.

Rapp found a potential ingress point beneath a sheet of plastic that didn't quite reach the ground. He was on his belly with his head already partly beneath it when the darkness was interrupted by two flashes accompanied by what sounded like a silenced .22 pistol.

Shit.

There were a few indistinct Arabic voices and then someone announced he was leaving. Rapp extricated himself from the plastic and started back around the building, moving as quickly as possible while still remaining silent.

An engine started but he managed to reach the front before it pulled away. Three men were standing outside the idling SUV talking quietly among themselves. The darkness hid their features while the glare of headlights illuminated the twenty yards separating Rapp from them. If there had been one man behind the wheel and only two absorbed in conversation, he might have had a chance. Cover the distance at full speed. Take down the two talking men. Get hold of a weapon. Kill the driver before he could get a shot off. Deal with the people still inside the building.

Maybe a sixty percent chance of survival.

With three men outside the SUV, though, that probability dropped into the single digits. Particularly because one didn't seem all that interested in what was being said. Instead, he was searching the darkness around him, keeping one hand inside his jacket and moving his head randomly so Rapp couldn't take advantage of a pattern. Definitely not some run-of-the-mill Arab dipshit. If Scott Coleman had been there, he'd be looking to make this asshole a job offer.

Rapp was trying to come up with some kind of diversion when one of the men lit a cigarette. The flare briefly revealed his features as he and one of his companions got back into the SUV. They pulled away while the third man got into Singh's car and left via the same route, undoubtedly on his way to a junkyard where the vehicle would be crushed and shipped off for scrap.

Rapp stayed put, waiting for almost a half hour before the other two men reappeared from the building. They climbed into their SUV, pulled through the gate, and then headed out after locking it behind them. Rapp waited until their taillights were no longer visible before entering. The gloom was even deeper and he relied on his nose to guide him as his eyes struggled to adjust. There was no mistaking the smell of fresh concrete.

The wet slab he found was about ten feet by ten feet—filling a mold next to a completed section of floor. Time was of the essence, so he just waded in, scooping his hands through the thick concrete until he found Singh's ankle. There was no point in dragging the body out, so he just searched it there. A wallet. A cell phone with the back missing that looked to be in pretty bad shape. A flip phone that was a little better protected. And, finally, a soggy Browning Hi-Power. That was it.

Rapp used a foot to sink him again and then the tools that had been left behind to smooth the slab. His work wouldn't win any prizes, but he needed to be the hell out of there before those cameras came back on.

He went back out front, climbing the fence and running toward his vehicle. A quick glance over his shoulder confirmed that the surveillance systems were still shut down. The GID probably figured that there was no hurry. Singh wasn't going anywhere and work on the building wouldn't start again for at least another few hours.

Rapp finally allowed himself to relax a bit when he turned onto the freeway. He kept the Porsche steady, splitting his attention between searching for tails and making sure the concrete he was dripping stayed on the floor mat.

Bashir Isa.

The GID man had lost some hair and gained a good twenty-five pounds but he was still unmistakable. They'd actually done a few operations together back when Rapp was still in his early thirties. He remembered the man as reasonably solid, a bit cynical, and not particularly religious by Saudi standards. Last Rapp had heard, he'd moved into middle management and become another anonymous cog in the Saudi intelligence machine. Probably the best a man with lukewarm feelings toward Allah and no relation to the royal family could do.

Or was it? Would someone like Isa be tapped as the handler of a CIA mole with the kind of access that Kennedy had described? Rapp doubted it. More likely the Saudi was just another buffer designed to separate the mole, the GID leadership, and the prince from Gideon Auma. And now that the Saudis thought that Auma had performed his function, the continued existence of those buffers had become an inconvenience.

The question was how high would the purge go. Based on the fact that even Marcus Dumond couldn't figure out how the Agency had been hacked, probably pretty high. And that meant that Isa would likely be the next man on the ladder to find himself holding up the edge of a building.

38

EVERYTHING was unknown now. And if there was anything Rapp despised, it was unknowns.

He piloted his rented SUV through the empty streets, using an address for Bashir Isa that he'd gotten from a private intelligence company's database. Was it current? Accurate? Those were a few more unknowns. Being cut off from both the CIA and Claudia wasn't particularly convenient. Digging up and filtering information wasn't really his end of the business.

Did Isa have a family? Probably. And if that was the case, it would be tricky to take him at home. The safer bet would be to head out into the open desert where the royal family had been hiding its skeletons for centuries.

On the other hand, someone like Isa would probably have a home office, a laptop, and maybe even some inconvenient information he was keeping as an insurance policy for just this kind of eventuality. Rapp sure as hell did. Loyalties in this business could turn on a dime and it paid to have an exit strategy.

Or maybe Isa had moved up in the hierarchy enough to rise

above loose-end status. Rapp continued to doubt it, though. Giving high-level CIA records to one of the world's most brutal terrorists in order to help him attack the richest man in history was a path that led over some pretty thin ice. The prince would want the number of people who knew about a bullshit move like that to be pretty low. Best guess, two: the prince himself and his handpicked intelligence director.

The neighborhood Rapp ended up in was one of the many planned communities going up at the edges of Riyadh. Modern white stucco units sat on lots crammed with palm trees and other plant life that signaled status to desert-dwelling people. Walls were about seven feet high but broken by sections of horizontal wooden slats designed more for architectural interest than security. Gates were metal, each with unique artistic embellishments and widely spaced bars.

His phone informed him that his destination was on the right and he maintained his speed as he passed. The gate was closed, but the SUV that had been at the construction site was visible just inside it. The fact that it was still in Isa's driveway didn't bode well for his old acquaintance. It was a potential stroke of luck for Rapp, though.

He parked next to the curb and stepped out, noting that the neighborhood's cameras appeared to be shut down like they had been at the construction site. Another thing in his favor. But, again, not so much Isa's.

When he reached the gate, the two men who had left with Isa were nowhere to be seen. Rapp took advantage of their absence to climb a slatted section of wall and drop onto the lawn on the other side.

He weaved through the trees, noting the light bleeding around drapes and shades that had been carefully closed. There was no practical way to get around to the back and based on his continued ignorance of his tactical situation, one method of entry was as good as another. No reason not to just climb the steps leading to the front door and get this thing moving. If Isa wasn't already dead, he would be soon.

The door was unlocked, so Rapp turned the knob and gave it

a nudge. His left hand was wrapped around Muhammad Singh's Browning Hi-Power, which he'd cleaned with a bottle of water on his drive over. Would it shoot? Who knew? What he was absolutely sure of, though, was that he wasn't getting his deposit back on the Porsche.

The door swung partially open with no reaction from inside, so he peeked around the jamb. A tasteful entry with a living area on the right and a hallway to the left. The dim light that had been visible around the drapes was coming from an open door near the back. So were human voices, too low to be intelligible or even to differentiate. Were all three men in there or was one of them ensconced somewhere else in the house, searching for signs of trouble?

Only one way to find out.

The floor was stone, so Rapp opted to take off his shoes before easing across it. He approached the door cautiously, holding the potentially useless weapon in both hands. All the lights were on inside the room, but the hallway was in shadow, giving him an advantage. He managed to stay invisible while putting himself in a position to see about a third of the room. Bashir Isa was in nearly full view, sitting in a chair with his ankles secured to the legs and his hands bound behind it. His expression was a mix of anger and resignation—tight jaw, nostrils slightly flared, staring straight ahead at nothing.

"There's another password. What is it?"

The man speaking was sitting behind Isa's desk, a position that left him mostly obscured.

Isa gave it up, his tone suggesting that he knew exactly how this was going to end and just wanted to get it over with. It was a shitty way to go out after years of loyal service, but not one that would surprise him. Betrayal was the number one killer of intelligence operatives.

"I'm in," the man said.

"What about hard copies?"

The sound of the second man's voice allowed Rapp to relax a bit. Both shooters were now accounted for. One partially visible behind the desk, another invisible somewhere near the northwest corner of the room.

"I don't know what you mean," Isa responded.

"Bashir. Please. We've known each other for a long time. Don't make this harder than it has to be and don't force me to involve your family. It would break my heart."

Isa's eyes shifted to the unseen man who had just spoken. Undoubtedly someone he'd once considered a friend. And, in fact, probably really was. But business was business and personal was personal.

"In the garage," Isa said finally. "There's a series of drawers to the left of the door. If you remove the bottom one, there's a lockbox at the back."

By the time he'd finished his sentence, Rapp was already on the move. He retraced his steps and turned right, slipping through a door that led to a spacious one-car garage. Navigating by the red glow of his penlight, he grabbed a screwdriver before lying down in front of Isa's Range Rover.

The door opened and the lights came on a few seconds later. He could see the man's black running shoes below the cuffs of dark blue slacks. Not a brand that Rapp favored, but they were light, had good traction, and were designed to hold up to fast changes in direction.

He opened the drawer, swearing in Arabic as he tried to find the hidden latches that would allow him to free it. Finally, Rapp heard it drop to the concrete and he waited as the man worked the surprisingly loud combination lock. When the creak of the top opening became audible, Rapp slipped from behind the car, staying low so as to throw a minimal shadow. The man's back was to him and Rapp's socks made no sound at all against the garage slab. Unfortunately, his target had the sixth sense that many top operators possessed and began to spin, reaching for his gun when Rapp was still a couple of feet away.

It was too late, though. Rapp clamped a hand over his mouth and nose from behind before slamming the point of the screwdriver into the back of his head. The man's body convulsed briefly and then went still. Rapp eased him to the ground and looked in the box he'd opened. The contents were basically what he expected—cash from various countries, passports, a few burner phones.

He took everything and then retrieved the SIG P226 holstered under the man's arm. Well maintained, fully loaded, and completely free of wet concrete. Definitely an upgrade and the silencer in the pocket of his jacket was a flat-out godsend. Rapp screwed it on and started back toward Isa's office. No need to be quiet. The man behind the desk would expect his compatriot to be returning right about now.

He didn't even look up, never knowing anything about the bullet that hit him square in the forehead. Isa, however, did. He stared wide-eyed at Rapp as his freshly deceased captor slumped forward and began leaking blood onto the keyboard in front of him.

"And I thought my night couldn't get worse," he said in Arabic. "The years have been kind, Mitch. You look fit."

"Really? Because you look like you've put on a few pounds."

"Too much of the good life. Two wonderful children. A wife. By the looks of you, not something you have experience with."

Rapp ignored the dig. "Are they in the house?"

Isa shook his head. "My son is at university and my wife's visiting our daughter in Lebanon. I was to be a grandfather soon."

"Then it's your lucky day."

"I don't think being tied to a chair in front of Mitch Rapp has ever been a Muslim's lucky day."

"There's a first time for everything," Rapp said, cutting Isa's hands free and then handing the penknife to him so he could do his legs.

"Did Irene Kennedy send you?" he asked while he used the blade.

"No. I work for Nicholas Ward."

Isa, the consummate professional, kept his face a mask as he handed the knife back to Rapp.

"What would someone like you or Nicholas Ward want with a meaningless bureaucrat like me?"

"Don't ask questions that you already know the answer to, Bashir. I've got your passports, your money, and your phones. Anything else you need before we get out of here? We can use the SUV. If they've turned the cameras back on, all they'll see is two men shoving a body in the back and driving away. Just what they expect."

Isa examined Rapp's face for a moment, undoubtedly reevaluating his loyalties in light of the night's events. Were they to the government that had been about to kill him? Or to the American assassin standing in front of him? Neither would be the answer he'd come up with, but there weren't a lot of options at this point.

"Not the SUV. I have a better way out."

"Then lead on, Bash."

Isa pulled a courier bag from the hall closet and then exited through the sliding back door. They stayed beneath the trees as they crossed his backyard and scaled the fence separating him from his neighbor to the east. The process was repeated four more times, the last of which Rapp had to give the exhausted man a push to get him over. That landed them in the backyard of a corner unit with a two-car garage. Isa entered through the side door and closed it before turning on the lights. He grabbed a set of keys off a hook on the wall and slipped behind the wheel of a Lincoln Navigator. Rapp got in the passenger side, closing his door a little more gingerly than Isa had.

"Won't the owner hear us?" he said when Isa started the engine and used a button to open the garage.

"A few years ago, I smoothed over an incident involving his youngest daughter," he said, starting to back out. "It's made him a very sound sleeper."

Rapp kept his eye on their surroundings as they cleared the gate and started up the road. The red dots on the neighborhood's strategically placed cameras were still dark, but that wouldn't last more than a few blocks. Still, Isa's exit strategy would be enough to buy them some time. The government would have to review all the footage in the area, make note of all pedestrian and auto traffic, and finally track down Isa's neighbor, who would probably already have reported the car stolen.

It wasn't quite like disappearing into thin air, but maybe the next best thing in the current technological era.

"Okay," Isa said, adjusting the seat into a more comfortable position. "Where to?"

39

THE palm trees and stylish fences of Bashir Isa's neighborhood were gone, replaced with utilitarian four-story concrete buildings on both sides of the street. They'd been constructed on a site that had once been a chaotic slum—one of the government's many halting efforts to provide affordable housing for immigrant labor.

His old mentor Stan Hurley had purchased a top-floor unit shortly after completion and it had become one of many similar dwellings that he and Rapp shared around the world. Only the two of them knew these safe houses existed and now Hurley was gone. He'd undoubtedly appreciate the operational compartmentalization his demise had created. One of his favorite quotes had been from Ben Franklin: *Three can keep a secret if two of them are dead.*

Rapp pointed through the windshield at one of the anonymous buildings and Isa eased the massive SUV into the parking garage beneath it. There were a few people inside, but none paid any attention to the unusually opulent vehicle. People in this strata of Saudi society tended to mind their own business. The government wasn't particularly bashful about how it treated foreign workers, and the local criminal gangs were even less so.

"So, this is it?" Isa said, pulling into an empty parking space. He sounded as resigned as he had when he'd been tied to the chair.

"Fourth floor," Rapp said, stepping out and pointing to a metal door about twenty feet away. He stayed behind the Saudi as they crossed the garage and entered a dimly lit stairwell. Isa's labored breathing echoed around them as they climbed and finally exited into a narrow hallway. The numbering system on the individual apartments wasn't terribly straightforward, forcing Rapp to abandon his normally purposeful stride.

"Is something wrong?" Isa said quietly.

"Never been here."

Rapp finally found the door he was looking for and used the key Hurley had given him so many years ago. The lock was predictably stiff, but finally surrendered with a sickly click and the loud creak of hinges. Once they were inside, Rapp closed the door and felt along the wall for a light switch. Miraculously, it worked. Hurley didn't like utility bills, so he relied on electrical modifications that siphoned power from the neighbors. A little risky, but not excessively so. This was probably only the second time the lights had been on in the tiny flat, and it would definitely be the last.

"Nice," Isa said, looking around at the space.

The main room had a minuscule kitchenette with a few drawers, a toaster oven, and an empty space where the refrigerator should have been. The indoor-outdoor carpeting would have been a bit gaudy if it hadn't been covered in a thick layer of dust. Walls were bare concrete and there was no furniture. Rapp peeked through an open door into the only bedroom—about the size of a modest walk-in closet. The bathroom was similarly utilitarian and tight.

Isa took a position on the floor and dropped his courier bag next to him. His eyes seemed to fix on nothing. Or perhaps that wasn't entirely true. Maybe he was staring at the future he now didn't have. The grandchild he'd never see. The endless possibilities of what could have been.

Rapp grabbed a few tools from a drawer and pulled up the carpet near the entrance to the bedroom. A rubber mallet was enough to break through the thin concrete veneer and wouldn't make enough noise to disturb the neighbors.

With a little work he was able to get the lid off the metal box hidden beneath and peer inside. A piece of notebook paper had been laid over the contents and he pulled it out, scanning Stan Hurley's familiar scrawl.

I told you the shit would eventually hit the fan, pencil dick.

The next thing that came out was a bottle of scotch that even Nick Ward would approve of. Below that was a Glock, a suppressor, a few mags, and a number of passports. He opened an Irish one and double-checked its expiration date. The meticulous notes he kept on a spreadsheet back home had been right—still two years to go.

The remaining documents belonged to Hurley, tucked in among a few wrapped bundles of cash and a laptop. Rapp pulled out the computer and turned it on. Windows had been replaced by a now eight-year-old operating system that was designed entirely for security. He typed in the password, connected to a hot spot created by his anonymous phone, and started an update. A timer appeared on the screen, estimating an hour for the download. Plenty of time to sample the scotch.

He found a couple of glasses in a drawer and filled each with a generous pour before handing one to Isa.

"Who are you going to contact?" the Saudi asked, accepting the drink and nodding toward the laptop. "Kennedy? I thought you said you don't work for her anymore. Do you think she'll help?"

Rapp didn't answer. In fact, he wasn't going to contact Kennedy. Better to reach out to Claudia. She could use her criminal contacts to bypass the intelligence community. Less skilled than the operators he typically worked with but generally reliable. They were motivated entirely by money and fear—two things he could generate a lot of.

"Let's talk, Bashir."

"About what?"

"Muhammad Singh. Where did he get the information he passed to Gideon Auma?"

"I don't know what you're talking about. And speaking of Gideon Auma, shouldn't you be in Uganda trying to save your employer? I can't imagine it's going to do much for your reputation to let a maniac steal the richest man in the world right from under your nose."

"I do need to get back. But I still have time."

"For what?"

"To torture you to death."

Isa let out a short laugh and finished his drink in one gulp. Rapp handed him the bottle and he gave himself an even more generous refill.

"Do you ever get tired of the games, Mitch?"

"More tired every day."

"I used to believe in God. And even the royalty. Now I see the first as delusional and the second as naïve. All that pomp and circumstance is just a weapon the strong use against the weak. And a strangely effective one. Have you ever thought about how these men gain power? We give it willingly to precisely the ones who shouldn't have it. There's something that attracts us to their insatiable hunger. Their ruthless, single-minded drive. We toil and die for them expecting nothing in return. Dreaming that one day they'll bless us with a word or a casual wave of the hand. Knowing that eventually we'll be discarded without a thought."

"I'm not here for a philosophical discussion, Bashir. You know what I want."

"For me to betray the country I've spent my life serving and tell you where I got my information on Ward."

"To betray the men who are discarding you without a thought. The ones you've given power to but who shouldn't have it."

The Saudi just smiled and took a sip of his drink.

"This can go easy or hard, Bashir. I'm not the kid you worked with all those years ago. You know what I've become. And what I'm capable of."

"A fitting end for a professional liar and backstabber like myself. I just escape being murdered by my friends and am now in danger of being murdered by one of my old allies. What a business we've chosen for ourselves, eh, Mitch? There must be something very wrong with us."

"Who gave you the information?" Rapp prompted with uncharacteristic patience. Like the men at Isa's house, he had no desire for this to turn ugly.

"The director."

"And where did he get it?"

"I don't know for certain, but I suspect directly from the prince."

Rapp let out a long breath. Not an easy man to get to. And not a man who would divulge the identity of his CIA contact to anyone who didn't need to know—including the GID director. Rapp altered his line of questioning.

"Then tell me why. Why risk so much to go after Ward?"

The Saudi freshened his drink for a second time. "This wasn't initially about Ward. It was about David Chism."

"I assume you were behind that, too?"

Isa nodded. "It wasn't hard to goad Gideon Auma into going after him. A little outside his normal operating area, but the potential rewards were astronomical."

"But it didn't work. So instead of backing off, the prince decided to double down."

Again, the Saudi nodded.

"Then I'm asking you again, Bashir. Why?"

"About that I can only guess."

"Then guess."

"The royal family sees the writing on the wall, Mitch. In the coming decades, their oil will become worthless and Ward's technologies are leading that change. In an effort to get their money out, they're betting heavily on health care and pharmaceuticals."

"So, Ward's not just destroying their business model—"

"He's deflating the parachute that they were counting on to give them a soft landing. When my country descends into chaos and bloodshed, its rulers—my masters—want to be comfortably installed in London, New York, and Paris. Nicholas Ward and David Chism are complicating that plan."

Rapp considered what he'd heard for a moment. "But the kind of penetration I'm talking about . . . I'm having a hard time believing Saudi Arabia could pull it off."

In truth, he was having a hard time believing anyone could. There were only a handful of people with that kind of access and they were watched constantly. Things like payments deposited in anonymous bank accounts, communications with foreign agents, and the introduction of malware onto Agency systems were extremely hard to get by Irene Kennedy.

"The Saudi royalty aren't the only people threatened by Ward, Mitch. The wealthy and powerful all over the world have one thing in common. They're very good at negotiating the existing playing field. And just as it was tilting more and more in their favor, Ward wants to reverse that trend."

"So, you don't think the move against Ward originated here?"

Isa shook his head. "I think my government was just an efficient and willing intermediary. We had the contacts in Uganda and someone else had the information. A match made in heaven, no?"

"But who?"

"I have no idea. Ward has a lot of very powerful and very capable enemies."

Rapp took a pull on his drink and then set it back down on the filthy carpet. This wasn't what he wanted to hear. Investigations weren't his thing and even if they were, performing one at this level would take a lot more than one man with a Glock, a few wads of cash, and an out-of-date laptop.

"Do you know your weakness, Mitch?"

"No. Why don't you tell me?"

"It's your unwavering belief in America. In the glory of it. In its uniqueness. I realized it was all lies a long time ago and now I fear it's your turn. Soon the curtain will be pulled back and you'll see that your country is no different than any other. Democracy is an interesting idea but if you look at history, it's an idea that burns bright but short. With the widening divisions in your country and the man you just elected to lead you, that flame is beginning to flicker. And soon you will find yourself in the dark."

The computer update had finally finished, and Isa was huddled in a corner sleeping off Hurley's scotch. Understandable. In his position, who wouldn't have crawled into that bottle?

Rapp launched an encrypted texting program and sent a brief message to an account that had never been used before. In South Africa, Claudia would get a notification and immediately understand that Hurley's prediction had come true. The shit had hit the fan.

He adjusted the laptop's screen so he could keep an eye on it and leaned back against the kitchen cabinets. Blackout shades were closed, along with a second layer of heavy curtains just to be sure. All his and Hurley's safe houses were set up exactly the same way. It made sense to stick with what worked and to keep protocols consistent.

He'd expected a quick response to his text but after ten minutes, Claudia was still a no-show. The tension in his back and shoulders was getting worse with every tick of the second hand. She was never without her phone. Even when she took a shower, it sat on the counter close enough that she could hear notifications. Had someone gotten to her?

He shook his head violently, trying to clear it. Caution was good, but there was a fine line between it and paranoia. While he, Kennedy, and Coleman were staying off comms to the greatest degree possible, they knew how to contact him. If something had happened to her or Anna, he'd have heard about it.

Ten more minutes passed, and he started to feel the apartment's darkness sinking into him. Maybe no one needed to get to her. Maybe she'd decided on her own that it was time to bail.

Claudia's genius for logistics hadn't been honed at FedEx or General Motors. She'd been the organizational force behind one of the most successful private assassins in modern history. She hadn't stayed alive this long by being stupid. And she had a daughter to think about. It didn't take someone with her mental horsepower to figure out that people who got close to him tended to end up dead.

At the thirty-minute mark, Rapp was forced to start reassessing his situation. He had a little cash, a couple of pistols, a stolen SUV, a few fake passports, and a drunk Saudi bureaucrat. Also, the apartment. Hurley had selected it because it allowed access to the roof where it was possible to jump from building to building and eventually disappear down between them. But that plan had been formulated years ago. With modern surveillance cameras and drones, the advantage pretty much disappeared. If the Saudis found out who he was and where he was, things weren't going to go well.

He was about to stand when the light in the room wavered subtly. Glancing over at the laptop, he saw hesitant writing appearing on-screen.

SORRY FOR DELAY. KID CAUGHT WHAT'S GOING AROUND. SOOOOOO SICK. WHAT DO YOU NEED?

The relief he felt was mixed with a touch of shame. Why had his mind gone so quickly to betrayal? Claudia was the woman he slept next to. The woman he finally might have a future with. It was still hazy, but he could almost make out the day he walked Anna down the aisle. Him limping through the rows of guests, gray haired, beat to hell, and clad in an overpriced tuxedo. Claudia nearby, rounded out with another twenty pounds, laugh lines marking her once flawless skin.

Was that the source of his suspicion? Was that fuzzy image more terrifying to him than dragging Bashir Isa across the roof with a Saudi spec ops team a few steps behind?

AN EXIT, he typed.

INJURIES?

NONE.

FROM WHERE?

CAN YOU FIND ME FROM THIS CONNECTION?

IMPOSSIBLE.

He hated the idea of sending his location over the Internet, but with no other choice, he typed it in.

GOT IT. SAFE PLACE?

FOR NOW. BUT A LOT OF CAMERAS AND THE CLOCK IS TICKING.

40

I T had been seven hours since Rapp's last contact with Claudia but that wasn't unexpected. Arranging an exit from Saudi Arabia without the help or knowledge of the Agency was no small task. In fact, the more he thought about it, the more it seemed like too much to expect.

On the positive side, the sun was overhead and from his position at the window he couldn't see any activity that might hint at an operation mounting against him. Not exactly conclusive, but better than watching a bunch of black-clad men swarming the building.

Isa was still lying on the floor with his eyes closed, but Rapp doubted he was sleeping. More likely waiting. For what, neither of them yet knew.

The laptop finally pinged, and he knelt in front of it.

A GREEN RANGE ROVER WILL BE OUT FRONT AT 17:43. DRIVER SAYS THAT TIME JUST AFTER SUNSET IS WORST FOR THE CAMERAS.

TRUSTWORTHY?

THE FIRST MAN YOU MEET HAS ALWAYS BEEN RELIABLE BUT IS DANGEROUS. IF YOU GET A BAD FEELING FROM HIM, KILL HIM IMMEDIATELY. I DON'T THINK YOU WILL, THOUGH. I'M PAYING TEN TIMES THE GOING RATE AND TOLD

HIM THE MAN HE'S TRANSPORTING MAKES MY LATE HUSBAND SEEM EASY-
GOING. HE UNDERSTANDS HIS POSITION. THE SECOND MAN IS EQUALLY COMPE-
TENT AND VERY TRUSTWORTHY. PLEASE DO NOT KILL HIM UNLESS ABSOLUTELY
NECESSARY.

NO LINKS TO LOCAL INTELLIGENCE?

NONE. DRUGS. SMUGGLING, EXTORTION, KIDNAPPING, MURDER FOR HIRE,
ETC. NO FRIEND OF THE GOVERNMENT.

THANK YOU.

BE CAREFUL.

Rapp gave Isa a kick and he opened his eyes.

"Forty-three minutes after five. There'll be a car out front."

"Then what?"

"And then we get out of the country."

The Saudi's eyes wandered around the dim room. "Your new president isn't going to help me or my family. America has always sided
with the royalty no matter what they do."

"But I don't work for him, remember? I work for Nick Ward."

"You mean the man who is in the possession of Gideon Auma because of me?"

"If we get him back, I'll put in a good word."

Isa laughed. "One last adventure. Why not? I deserve at least that."

The Range Rover was exactly on time. Rapp let Isa lead, watching the
man feign interest in his phone to keep his face obscured from surveillance cameras. The street was quiet, still waiting for the working-class
locals to begin arriving home.

They slipped in the back and the driver pulled away at an unhur-
ried pace. Only one man, but unquestionably a rough customer. He
likely slotted into the kidnapping or murder-for-hire part of Claudia's
list. She was a woman with friends in low places, thank God.

"We will drive through the city and then into the desert," he said,
keeping his eyes on the road. "The police have cameras on poles along
the route, but there is a place where the topography has created a weak-

ness in their coverage. We can block their field of view and make a transfer. But they will only be blind for a few seconds." He thumbed toward the floorboard behind his seat. "Everything you need is in the bag."

Rapp watched from the backseat as the driver made another call, speaking clearly and simply on speakerphone. Apparently, Claudia had indeed imparted how Rapp felt about betrayal and the man wanted to make sure he didn't come under suspicion. There didn't seem to be any reason to question his motivations. So far, all communications had been with spotters stationed along the sparsely traveled two-lane highway they were on.

There was still a dim glow on the western horizon, occasionally overpowered by oncoming headlights on the other side of a broad median. The moon was growing increasingly brilliant, revealing the flat desert around them in greater and greater detail. A light breeze was kicking some dust in the air, adding to the visual distortion of that time of evening. Overall, conditions for what they had to do were about as good as could be hoped for. Whether it would be enough, though, remained to be seen.

"Five minutes," their driver said after disconnecting the call. "Our people will be in position as I described earlier. The cameras will only be blind for twenty seconds and if you exceed that I will drive away and leave you lying on the highway. Understood?"

"We'll make it work," Rapp said, winding a piece of tape around Isa's right shirt cuff to secure the loose fabric. He pulled back and checked his handiwork before reexamining similarly taped areas on his own body. Everything looked smooth. Nothing to get hung up.

"You ready, Bashir?"

The man smiled in what little light could make its way to the vehicle's backseat. "It's been a long time since I've done anything like this. These days, I mostly golf. Good for the career and much safer."

"All evidence to the contrary."

"You make a valid point."

"Our man is coming up from behind," the driver announced.

Rapp twisted around and spotted a set of headlights approaching fast. Ahead, he could see a low hill where the road split into three lanes and the semi that was there to block the cameras. Their driver was on the phone again, speaking to both vehicles and watching a timer on his phone. They would all come together at the beginning of the surveillance blind spot.

"One minute," the driver announced. "Forty-five seconds . . . Thirty seconds."

Rapp rolled down the window. He'd go first and then help Isa, who was hopefully a little more nimble than he looked. At least his waistline hadn't swelled to the point that he'd be in danger of getting stuck.

The dusty desert air began swirling through the vehicle as they eased into the middle lane and came up on the semi. In the left lane, the headlights continued to approach at a speed favored by the Saudi privileged class.

"Ten seconds," the driver said, shouting over the wind. "Nine . . . Eight . . ."

Rapp grabbed his duffle and waited at the open window. They came alongside the semi just as the trailing vehicle pulled even with them and slowed to match their speed. The driver was clearly experienced, bringing his SUV to within a foot of them and holding steady. Still, one mistake—or perhaps an intentional tap on the brake pedal—would leave Rapp's broken body cartwheeling across the asphalt at sixty miles an hour. Claudia seemed to think it wouldn't happen and that had to be good enough.

The duffle went first—through the SUV's open window and into the back of the adjacent Rolls-Royce Cullinan. He went next, slipping across the gap and into the soft leather seat before immediately turning back toward the window. Isa was looking directly at him from the other vehicle, an expression of sadness etched across his soft features.

Only eight seconds until they came back into view of the cameras.

Rapp stuck an arm through the window and tried to grab him by the shirt. Isa retreated out of reach and held up a hand in salute. A moment later, Rapp's driver rolled up the window and jammed the accelerator to the floor. By the time they reentered the surveillance area, the Rolls had regained its speed.

Rapp let out a long breath and settled back into the extraordinarily comfortable seat.

"Well done!" the driver said in heavily accented English. His tone suggested he was prouder of his language skills than he should have been. "But what of your friend? He decides not to come? This is very bad decision. My colleague is a man of no humor."

Rapp didn't respond. The truth was it had to happen this way. If it had just been Isa, they could have worked something out. But it wasn't just him. By now, the Saudis had almost certainly found the dead men at his house and would already be watching his wife and children. If he didn't turn up quickly, they'd be arrested and used against him. He'd always been smart. And in this case that meant being capable of understanding that his luck had run out. That everyone would be better off if he were dead.

"What you need is in the bag on the floor. The one on the right. That one on the left has no meaning. Not now. It was for your friend."

He dug in, finding a Ziploc bag containing a set of hair clippers, shaving implements, and a pair of tweezers.

"The tweezers are to make your eyebrows much more beautiful," the driver explained. Based on his jovial tone, it was likely that he was from the smuggling part of Claudia's list. High-end smugglers were generally the smartest and most cheerful of the criminal class. Creatives, she would call them.

"Look at the passport, my good friend."

He found it in the top zipper pocket and used his penlight to examine an old, beardless photo of him that had been put through some kind of filter to turn him into a woman. His eyebrows really did look much more beautiful.

The main part of the bag contained a padded body suit to round out his hips and add an ample set of breasts. The final insult, though, was at the bottom. A pair of tennis shoes covered in gold glitter and topped with pink laces. He held them up and the driver glanced in the rearview mirror.

"They will help you move quickly, though I think it will not be required. And my wife tells me they are the very latest fashion!"

41

RAPP'S driver bypassed the private airport's small but opulent terminal, piloting the Rolls through seemingly endless rows of private jets. The sleek white shapes of Cessnas, Gulfstreams, and Bombardiers glowed dimly in the light from the main building, descending into shadow as they drove deeper into them. Through the windshield, the glare from the open door of a Global 7500 became visible. A Saudi official stood by the steps and Rapp was relieved to see that it was a man.

There had been a time when Saudi women could leave the country with their faces covered. Those days were gone, but still they were only obligated to reveal themselves to female officials. Normally, one would be on hand to check facial features against passport photos. Apparently, the rules were a bit more relaxed for people who drove Rolls-Royces and flew in the top of Bombardier's range.

"Because of air traffic control, we have no choice but to make a true flight plan to take you out of our country. You need an exit stamp in your passport. I don't think we will have problems."

"And if we do?"

"I am told that you know how to solve these kinds of problems. The plane is parked so cameras cannot see us. I can take the body and hide what has happened for the hour it will take for you to leave our airspace. After this I do not know what happens to you. I have not been told."

"Understood."

His driver slowed, focusing for a moment on the rearview mirror. "You look good, yes?"

"Yeah. Good enough to sell it, I think."

The fat suit fit perfectly and was doing a good job obscuring his V-shaped torso. The fact that he'd dropped some muscle weight in order to return to endurance racing didn't hurt, either. His face and hair were completely hidden by the burqa, leaving only his made-up eyes and neatly groomed eyebrows visible behind a light mesh. Overall, the effect was solid—right down to eyelashes a little heavy on the mascara.

His driver seemed to agree, nodding approvingly before gliding to a stop near the jet. Stepping out, he moved to the rear door to open it. His garb was just as traditional—red checkered headgear and a spotless white thobe that stretched over his stomach in a way that made him look vaguely pregnant.

Rapp had transferred his belongings from his duffle to a couple of Gucci shopping bags that were more in keeping with his disguise. Combined with the fat suit, though, they made it a little difficult to get out of the car. The fact that his driver felt compelled to guide him onto the tarmac by the elbow would serve to make the whole thing look even more authentic. Just a couple of wealthy Saudis doing the things that wealthy Saudis did.

No neck snapping or jugular slicing turned out to be necessary. The official barely even looked at him, flipping the passport to an empty page and stamping it before wandering back toward the terminal.

Rapp didn't wait for the inevitable good-bye hug from his driver, instead ending their brief relationship with a nod and heading for the jet. His glittery shoes squeaked relentlessly as he climbed the steps and walked along the rows of plush leather seats. Once through a divider at the back, he dropped his bags and closed the door behind him.

The engines started to spool up and he reveled in the dull whine as it increased in volume. Over the years, that sound had come to elicit a powerful psychological response in him. It meant safety. Survival. Escape. When the plane started to move, he dropped onto the couch and closed his eyes.

What the hum of private jets didn't always mean, though, was success.

He was leaving behind two dead men—one who'd had too much concrete in his mouth to talk and the other who hadn't been able to provide much more than the obvious observation that this thing went pretty far up the chain. Singh's burner would likely prove useless and his cell was probably unsalvageable. Possibly the most useful thing he'd learned by risking his ass in Saudi Arabia was that Fendi made a pretty comfortable pair of sneakers.

The plane lifted off and Rapp realized he didn't have any idea where it was going. Trying to find out would be risky with comms potentially compromised and there wasn't much he could do about it anyway. Best to just peel off his fat suit and see where Claudia took him.

42

ONCE through the White House gate, Mike Nash was almost immediately waved down by a Secret Service agent. He eased his SUV to a stop and rolled down the passenger window.

"'Morning, Mike," the man said, leaning his forearms on the sill.

In fact, it was more like the middle of the night—not a great time to be suddenly called into a meeting with the president. Particularly when the call came from an anonymous secure phone that Cook wasn't supposed to have and that virtually no one knew about. A device he used to coordinate things that he never wanted to appear in the papers.

"Oval Office?" Nash responded by way of greeting.

Predictably, he shook his head. "The residence. There's an escort waiting for you."

He was tempted to ask whether Kennedy was on the list, but it was just a nervous tic. If she were going to sit in, the call would have come through official channels.

The man stepped back, and Nash accelerated again. He could feel the event horizon of that black hole hovering right in front of him. The compulsion to turn back was incredibly strong, but not strong enough. Now that he was this close, the pull of the Cooks' gravity had become inescapable.

As promised, an escort met him out front and, after a perfunctory greeting, led him to the second floor. There she pointed to a closed door before disappearing without another word.

The Treaty Room, Nash knew from being a bit of a history buff. It had been used for various purposes over the years, but most notably by William McKinley to sign the treaty ending the Spanish-American War in 1898. Or was it 1899? Shit. He was just stalling now.

A timid knock was answered by a muffled voice that he took as an invitation. After entering, he closed the door behind him and examined his environment. Like the other areas of the White House regularly used by the Cooks, it had been significantly modernized. The structural elements—molding, fireplace, and wood floor—remained, but most of the furniture and artwork had been replaced. The exception was the treaty table itself. Originally used by Ulysses S. Grant for cabinet meetings, if he recalled correctly.

Both of them were there but not sitting together. The president was on a sofa that dominated the central conversation area, while his wife sat at a writing desk near the far wall. She turned when Nash entered, her movement highlighting the stillness and silence that dominated the room.

"You wanted to see me?" he said when that silence stretched to the breaking point.

The president just pointed to a stack of eight-by-ten photos on the coffee table in front of him. Not sure what else to do, Nash advanced and picked them up. He hadn't been invited to sit, so he retreated to a more comfortable distance and examined them standing.

At first, there wasn't much to see. The shadowy silhouettes of two men partially obscured by palm trees. He paused when he came upon a depiction of one of them climbing a fence that separated two residential properties. Based on the quality of the images, all were likely taken by private security cameras.

"Who are they?" Nash said, glancing up at the president.

"The fat one is Bashir Isa."

Nash shook his head to indicate that the name didn't register.

"Keep going," the president said. "There's a better picture of the second man near the end."

Nash leafed through the rest of the photos, finally stopping on one near the end of the stack. It looked like it had been captured at an airport's passport control area and this time the man couldn't keep his face out of the camera.

"When was this taken?" he asked.

"Four days ago."

Nash suddenly didn't care if he'd been invited or not. He took a seat in a chair that maintained some distance between him and the Cooks, continuing to stare down at the image.

Mitch Rapp. Alive.

Emotions crashed over him with an intensity and speed that made it impossible to distinguish between them. Fear. Relief. Shame. The sensation of gravity being replaced with the sensation of drowning.

"He's not dead," Catherine said. "He—"

The president held up a hand, silencing her. Nash felt a glimmer of gratitude at Cook's intervention. He needed to think. About the history of this thing and his role in it. About where it was going and whether it could be stopped.

After Rapp rescued Chism from the mountains near his research facility, Nash had received a personal call from the president asking for a copy of whatever information the Agency had on Nicholas Ward. It hadn't been a particularly suspicious request. Ward was unquestionably the most influential private citizen in the world and one of his most critical people had nearly been lost to terrorists. What *was* unusual, though, was that Cook didn't want Irene Kennedy to know.

It hadn't been easy, but with the help of a team of the president's loyalists at the NSA, he'd managed to download the files anonymously and hand them over. At the time, he'd told himself that the secrecy was just politics. The Cooks neither liked nor trusted Kennedy and didn't want her to get the wrong idea that they were trying to use her organization to dig up dirt on Ward. Or, hell, maybe they *were* trying to get something on the man and knew she'd see through them. It was impossible to say. And, frankly, who cared? Anthony Cook was the president of the United States and he could have whatever fucking file he wanted delivered to him in any fucking way he wanted.

After Ward's kidnapping, though, it had become ever more difficult for Nash to keep his head buried in the sand. The file he'd delivered contained detailed information on the compound, its security, and the hangar that was to be used in case of trouble. Still, he'd managed to keep looking away. It was one thing to get caught up in the Cooks' orbit, but it was another to face head-on that you may have played a role in the deaths of the best friends you'd ever had.

"Mike?" Cook prompted. Apparently, his reprieve was over.

Nash raised his head and looked directly at the man. The time for games was over. "Tell me what the hell's going on."

Cook let out a long breath and sank a bit deeper into the sofa. "Why don't *you* tell *me*?"

"The file I gave you. You somehow got it to Gideon Auma. So he could get rid of Ward and Chism for you."

"Not exactly. I gave it to the Saudis. And it appears that *they* gave it to Auma."

Nash shook his head incredulously. Did Cook really think he'd believe the Saudis would make a move like this without his blessing? Or was he just hedging? Not wanting to say anything out loud until he understood Nash's loyalties?

"Why?"

"That's a big question but let me give you my best guess. The Saudis want Ward and Chism gone and a lot of people agree with them. He's moving too fast and on too many fronts, Mike. Health care, energy, communications, artificial intelligence, robotics . . ." The president's voice faded for a moment. "The human race can't absorb that many fundamental changes all at once. But this isn't news to you. You've spent your life protecting the world order that Ward's taking a sledge-hammer to."

There was some truth to the man's words. The idea that Ward might be paving the road to hell with his good intentions was a topic of discussion in elite circles throughout the world. His brilliance had put him completely out of touch with common people and their ability— even willingness—to constantly reevaluate their place in society. While people like Ward were able to take advantage of constant cultural and technological upheaval, there weren't all that many people like him. None, in fact.

"And the Saudis are good people to have in your debt," Nash said, unwilling to let Cook get away with pretending to be a passive observer.

The president didn't respond, instead shrugging in a way that was an unequivocal confession. And why not? He was the most powerful man in the world and Nash worked for him—not Irene Kennedy or Mitch Rapp. And certainly not Nicholas Ward. Cook was well within his rights to give the Saudis whatever intelligence he saw fit and could deny any knowledge of what they would do with it.

It likely wouldn't be necessary, though. In the America of today, values and principles had been replaced by partisanship. The Cooks owned the White House, both chambers of Congress, and more than half the voting public. They could molest children in the Rose Garden if they wanted to. Their followers would not only accept it, they'd fig-ure out a way to make it the other party's fault. The Cooks were all but untouchable and it was now crystal clear that it wasn't enough. They'd continue to consolidate their power by any means possible. And, as near as Nash could tell, there was nothing to stop them.

"David Chism should have died in the jungle," the president said finally. "But Rapp interfered. Not ideal, but the Saudis recalibrated.

After that, everything seemed to be going to plan. Until now. I'm told that Bashir Isa is one of the buffers between the Saudi government and Gideon Auma. The man who worked directly with Auma—Muhammad Singh—is already dead. Saudi intelligence was in the process of dealing with Isa to clean up their loose ends when Rapp intervened. He killed two Saudi agents at Isa's house and then helped him escape. The GID is tracking them, but so far they've come up empty."

Nash barely heard. He hadn't slept more than a couple of hours a night since Rapp, Coleman, and his men disappeared. Not only had they been friends and comrades in arms, but many had been his neighbors. Their houses now stood like mausoleums in the remote subdivision. Accusing him every time he passed.

Maggie took his insomnia and creeping depression for grief. But that's because she didn't know what he'd allowed himself to be dragged into. And she never would despite the fact that, in many ways, he'd done it for her. For their children. With or without Nicholas Ward, the world was changing. The wealthy and powerful were rising and leaving everyone else behind. When the gate finally slammed shut, it needed to be behind them, not in their faces.

"Mike?" Catherine said. "Where do we stand."

He looked up at her, not bothering to hide his horror at the situation. It was a little late for that now.

"How did Mitch find out about Bashir Isa?" he asked.

"We don't know," Cook said. "The Saudis' facial recognition system only ID'd Rapp a few hours ago. They're working on it."

Again, Nash paused to think. Almost a minute passed in silence before he spoke again. "Best-case scenario, Mitch somehow identified the Saudi's direct contact with Auma—Muhammad Singh, right? And that led to Isa, who he went after to see if he had information that might help him get Ward back. I assume he came up short, though. Isa would have no need to know. And if that's the case, he's at a dead end unless he wants to go after the head of Saudi intelligence or the prince. Possible, but a big ask even for Mitch Rapp."

"If that's the best-case scenario, what's the worst case?" Catherine Cook asked.

Nash rubbed his hands together. "Worst case? That Irene and Mitch know the information on Ward came from the CIA and everything we're seeing—the video, the ransom negotiations—is theater. Scott has Ward and Chism on ice somewhere and Mitch is on a mole hunt."

A mole hunt, he reminded himself, that would eventually lead directly to his door.

"How likely do you think that is?" Catherine asked.

"I don't know. But it could explain why we still haven't gotten any specific ransom demands from Auma yet."

"Do you think you could have made a mistake accessing Ward's files?" Cook said. "That you could have revealed yourself?"

Nash glared at the man. "Maybe you should ask your people at the NSA. I just answered their questions about our system and did what they told me."

"If that came off as an accusation, it wasn't intentional," Cook said. "Look, I think it's time for everyone to put their cards on the table. As far as we're concerned, the rarest commodity in this world is smart, loyal people. And you've proved to be both. We don't leave our allies twisting in the wind. Ever. So, if you want, I'll have my people write up a press release saying that Irene Kennedy is out. That'd make you acting director and then we'll do what's necessary to make the position permanent."

Nash stood and began pacing. "It may not be enough."

"Why not? Kennedy trusts you as much as anyone to protect her from the baggage she's carrying from her time running the Agency. For my part, I'll send her off to a seven-figure think tank job with glowing speeches and a Medal of Freedom. If your worst-case scenario is the one that's playing out, she'll have to tell you everything about Ward and her mole hunt on the way out. Then all you have to do is find a satisfactory scapegoat."

Nash shook his head. "It won't be that easy. If Nicholas Ward's alive, she won't take a seven-figure think tank job. She'll take an eight-figure job as his head of security. And the first thing she's going to want to know is who's after him. Some anonymous fall guy from the tech department isn't going to fool her. And it sure as hell isn't going to fool Mitch."

"Maybe," Catherine said. "But as destructive as a war with them could be, we have the resources to fight it. In fact, you could go so far as to say we have *all* the resources to fight it."

Nash continued wandering at random through the room, trying to wrap his mind around the sea change in his reality. He'd spent the last week being eaten alive by the deaths of his friends and the realization that he'd had a hand in it. Second chances were a rare thing in his business and they never came without a cost. In this case, likely a heavy one.

"Right now, what we need is information. We need to know what Irene knows."

"How can we accomplish that?" the president said.

"I have some ideas."

"And if your worst-case scenario turns out to be the reality?"

He began to feel the same sense of disassociation that he experienced in combat. The creeping numbness that kept him from thinking about death or family or future. That had allowed him to go to a country where he'd never been and kill people he'd never met at the behest of a politician he didn't vote for.

"Then we deal with it."

43

"**M**Y jailer returns. Successful trip?"

Ward was in his usual spot, rocked back in a chair with his feet on the unlit outdoor fireplace. Temperatures had risen into the eighties, forcing him to set up in a sliver of shade cast by the chimney. He was reading a dog-eared paperback from the lodge's used book exchange since any devices with an ability to connect outside were being carefully controlled. He tossed it on the hearth as Rapp settled into a chair.

"You have enemies in high places, Nick."

"I could have told you that and saved you the trip. Did you get the information you needed to plug the CIA's leak? If so, I think I'd like to end our relationship. Obviously, David and I owe you our lives and I plan to make a wire transfer to your friend Claudia that will demonstrate that gratitude. Then we can shake hands and go our separate ways."

"What about Scott?" Rapp said, evading the question.

"I've been impressed by him and his men. They're all very professional and once they're away from your influence, probably pretty easy to work with. I'm hoping to put together some kind of retainer deal with them."

Rapp smiled. "I know you don't like me much, Nick, but the feeling's not mutual. You think I'm working just for my own account here, but that's not true. I've done everything I can to keep you out of harm's way."

"You've done everything you can to keep me out of harm's way as long as it doesn't interfere with your mole hunt," Ward corrected. "And the truth is that I don't dislike you, Mitch. I just don't trust you."

Rapp put his feet on the hearth and gazed out over the landscape. "*Trust* is a hard word to define. At this level, it gets mixed up with motivation. I trust that you want to save the world and that you don't want to get nailed to one of Gideon Auma's crosses. You can trust that I want that mole's head on my front gate and to protect my country. And we can both trust that the other is going to chase those interests hard. In the world we live in, those are the building blocks of a productive relationship."

"In the world *you* live in."

"Quit busting my balls, Nick. You and David are alive. Your research team will have a safe working environment going forward and you've eliminated one of the most brutal terrorists on the planet. When the president of Uganda finds out what you've done, you won't be able to get arrested in this country. Take the win."

"Mitch Rapp. Employee of the Month," Ward said.

"Tell me about someone who's done more for you in less time. Hell, maybe you should cut me in for ten percent of your stock price increases when you miraculously come back from the dead."

"That'd make you richer than your brother."

Rapp grinned, savoring the thought for a moment. "You can't imagine how bad that would chap his ass."

"So, we can make it public that David and I are safe?"

"Give me a few more days."

Ward sighed quietly. "It's always a few more days, isn't it, Mitch?

You can't keep me here forever. You have armed men, but eventually you're going to have to use them. If you expect me to just sit here for the next year watching everything I've built collapse, you might want to shoot me now."

He fell silent and stared Rapp directly in the eye, proving to be one of the few people on the planet who was able to.

"Fuck it," Rapp sighed, scooting his chair closer to Ward and leaning into the man. "The Saudi government was behind the first attack on Chism. When it didn't work, they decided to take it to the next level. They got information on you from a CIA mole with a very high level of access and used it to plan the attack on your compound. Gideon Auma's orders were that Chism was to be killed."

"And me?"

"They left it up to him. But if you did survive, they made it clear that there shouldn't be enough of you left to be of much good to anyone."

"Why?"

"Do you really need to ask?"

"I'm a threat to the oil industry, which is the source of their wealth, and the medical industry, which they see as their escape hatch. But the truth is that it's not just them, Mitch. I'm looking to disrupt industries that a lot of powerful people rely on to stay powerful. This may be what my future looks like, unfortunately."

"If that's the case, then it seems like you'd want to know who this mole is just as much as I do."

Ward nodded, taking in what he'd heard with an expression that was almost completely opaque.

"I appreciate the honesty, Mitch. But I'm going to ask you for a little more. Do you have anything solid to pursue? Because if not, it's going to be time for David and me to take our chances. I understand that it's a dangerous world, but we'll have to figure out how to mitigate those dangers as best we can and move forward. It's true that I'll eventually make my money back, but David's research is in real jeopardy.

If he can't get to his test subjects soon, his timeline could be set back years."

"I don't have as much as I hoped I would at this point," Rapp admitted. "Basically, the written plan Auma was given for the attack, his phone, and two more phones from the man the Saudis used as a liaison. Another from that liaison's boss. I need to figure out a way to get them to Irene and see if she can do anything with them."

Ward's dead expression suddenly came to life. "Phones?"

"Don't get too excited. One's a personal phone so I doubt there's going to be anything interesting on it. Plus, it's full of concrete."

Ward opened his mouth to speak, but Rapp held up a hand, silencing him. "Don't ask."

"What about the others?"

"Three burner phones. One has a little cement on it, but the design kept it protected enough that it probably still works."

"Tell me how people in your business use burners."

Rapp shrugged. "Not much to tell. They're phones without GPS capability bought with cash so they don't have a name attached to them. We try to keep things compartmentalized, so we generally have a separate one for every operation. And we only call other burners—so anonymous phones calling anonymous phones from ambiguous locations. That means there's really no practical way to trace them to the owner."

"Marcus Dumond told you that?"

"You know Marcus?"

"I know of him."

"Are you saying he's wrong?"

"Not entirely."

"What do you mean by *entirely*?"

"Governments have a lot of restrictions—both legal and with penetration into foreign countries or private companies that aren't inclined to cooperate. My situation's more . . . flexible."

"Meaning what?"

"That I might be able to put a name to those burners."

Rapp's initial reaction was to call bullshit on the man. But the fact that he'd literally made a trillion dollars in technology suggested it might be worth hearing him out.

"How?"

"I'm not a rival government or intelligence agency. And I own interests in telecom and Internet companies all over the world. There's a pretty robust system for cooperation in place. If not, your cell wouldn't work when you cross borders."

"So, you think you can do better than the Agency on this?"

"Absolutely. Plus, it solves some other problems. You're concerned about communicating with Irene because those lines of communication could be compromised, right? Now, not only do you have to communicate with her, you have to physically deliver phones to her that she'll then have to hand over to your technology people. Keeping all that compartmentalized will be impossible. Particularly when she has to get warrants and ask for the cooperation of the Saudi government."

"What are you proposing?"

"We send them to my assistant with instructions. She already knows I'm alive and she can get the phones in the hands of people your mole wouldn't have access to."

44

"IRENE?" Mike Nash stuck his head into her office. "You wanted to see me?"

She waved him inside and he dropped into one of the chairs in front of her desk.

"You look terrible," she said.

He let out a slightly bitter laugh. "Thanks a lot. You do, too."

"I guess neither of us has slept much since Mitch and the others went missing."

He just looked down at the floor.

"Well, you'll be happy to hear I have some good news, Mike."

He kept his eyes locked on the carpet. Of course, he already knew what her news was. He'd told the Saudi government to send Kennedy the photos of Rapp that had been taken in Saudi Arabia. She would have received them about an hour ago.

Kennedy slid an eight-by-ten across her blotter and he picked it up, furrowing his brow as he looked down at the now-familiar image. He had to play this extremely cool. Irene Kennedy was the queen of the lying game. One nervous foot tap, out-of-character comment, or errant bead of sweat and all their history together wouldn't mean shit. The alarms in the back of her mind would explode.

"What is this?"

"That was taken five days ago at Riyadh airport."

Nash furrowed his brow a little deeper. He'd spent a fair amount of time considering how to react when this moment came. "That's impossible!" was the obvious go-to. But would he really say that? Where Mitch Rapp was concerned, everything was possible.

"*Son of a bitch*," he decided on, letting a fair amount of anger slip into his voice. "He's been alive all this time? He just left us twisting in the wind?"

"So it would seem." He could feel her eyes on him but didn't look up.

"What about the guys?"

"Unknown."

Finally, he met her gaze. "He hasn't been in contact with you?"

"No."

Truth? A lie? He was here to find out what she knew, but that was never easy. The likelihood that Mitch hadn't found some way to let her know he was alive seemed far-fetched. The main question remained, though. Had Rapp stumbled onto Isa's involvement and gone after him in an attempt to figure out where Nicholas Ward was being held? Or was this another one of Kennedy's elaborate games? If she discovered someone mucking around in her mainframe, she'd be laser focused on finding out who and how. But faking the kidnapping of one of the most important men in the world? That was a pretty bold move for a woman who had lost her power base in the White House. Unfortunately, bold moves were something she and Mitch were known for.

"The Saudis suspect him of killing a mid-level operative named Bashir Isa and two of his associates," she continued. "They found his body in the desert and the other two in his house."

"Do we have any idea where Mitch is now?"

"My counterpart at the GID believes he got on a private jet outside of Riyadh two days ago and headed toward Africa."

"Not home, I assume."

She shook her head.

"Can we trace the jet?"

"No. It seems to have been conjured from thin air and then disappeared back into it."

He chewed his lower lip and looked down at the photograph again. Best to meet Kennedy's eye as little as possible.

"Thoughts?" she said.

"You don't need my help on this one, Irene. Appearing and disappearing jets without any Agency involvement? That has Claudia's name written all over it. Have you talked to her?"

"Only to offer my condolences about Mitch's disappearance."

Finally, he tossed the photo back on her desk. Now was the appropriate time to run his fingers through his hair. Two-handed felt right, given the circumstances.

"My wife's talked to her probably every day since then. But not to Anna. Claudia said she hadn't broken it to her yet. Now we know why." He paused for a moment, creating the illusion of building anger. "That *prick*! We already ordered the food for his wake and we're past the time we can get a refund. When he gets back, I'm billing his ass. And you know what else this means? Mitch wouldn't leave Scott and the guys hanging. They're out there somewhere, too."

"I don't know if we can be sure of that," Kennedy cautioned.

"Yeah, but you've got to admit there's a good chance," he said, transforming his rage into hope accompanied by just a dash of joy. "A hell of a lot better chance than there was yesterday."

He let a slow smile spread across his face. "And to think. I was gonna go over and mow his stupid lawn. You know what I'm going to do instead? Let the goats loose in there."

She just sat there, undoubtedly wanting to give him time to assimilate what he'd heard, but also to examine his reaction. This was the most dangerous part of their conversation because he was feeling pretty much the opposite of what he was trying to portray. But he still didn't have the information he'd come here for. How would he approach this if he really were just now finding out about Rapp being alive? The answer was simple. Directly. He wouldn't believe that Kennedy was in the dark and he wouldn't get sucked into a verbal sparring match. That was her wheelhouse, and she was the queen of it.

"The one thing you've never been good at, Irene, is playing dumb. So, what's it going to be? Are you going to tell me what's going on or are you just going to keep stringing me along?"

She remained silent, but with the question out there, she couldn't stay mute forever. The CIA directorship could be a pretty lonely place and it was getting lonelier for her every day. Would she allow herself an ally?

Kennedy reached for her tea and it was in that simple action that he knew he'd passed the test.

"Oh shit," he said slowly. "You knew. You knew the whole time."

She took a sip and then put the mug back down. "Yes."

"Then I'm going to ask you again. Straight up, now. Scott and the guys?"

"They're fine. As are Ward and David Chism."

He leaned forward and put his elbows on his knees, letting his bodyweight sag onto them. Fortunately, relief and resignation read about the same from a body language standpoint. He really was deeply grateful that Coleman and his boys were okay. They could still be saved. But the Cooks were going to explode when they got confirmation that Ward's and Chism's deaths were all just an elaborate illusion. As usual in this shit business he'd gotten dragged into, the worst-case scenario was the one playing out.

"What the hell's going on, Irene?"

"We had an incursion into our computer system. Marcus found it entirely by chance. Whoever's responsible has extremely high-level access and the ability to cover their tracks to the point that even Marcus ran into a blank wall."

"What did they get?"

"Information on Nicholas Ward."

"That's it? They were deep in our system and *that's* what they went after?"

She nodded. "It seems that the information made its way to the Saudis and then to Gideon Auma so that he could attack Ward's compound."

Nash's jaw tightened. "The Saudis. Remind me again why we don't bulldoze that entire country into the Red Sea?"

Her only reaction to his question was a barely perceptible smile.

"Can I assume that Mitch was in Saudi Arabia trying to figure out the identity of our mole?"

"Yes."

"Did he?"

"I doubt it, or he would have contacted me. With the mole still out there, we're only communicating when it's absolutely necessary. It's impossible to be one hundred percent certain of any of our technology at this point."

"Does the president know about any of this?"

"No. The possibility of a leak was too high."

"Shit. He's going to blow a *gasket*. Your chances of keeping your job just dropped to somewhere around zero."

"My job security is my business. Besides, I don't see me getting fired as being all that bad for you."

"I don't want your chair, Irene."

Strangely, that was the truth. He didn't want it. But with the storm he saw brewing, it looked more and more like he needed it.

"Maybe we can spin this in your favor. The Saudis have a lot of money and are about as morally flexible as anyone on the planet. If there's anything the Cooks love, it's someone powerful they can control. If we can prove the Saudis went after an American citizen who also happens to be the richest man in history, then they'd have something to hold over the royalty. It might be a shiny enough gift to make them overlook the rest."

"But the Cooks wouldn't use that to push back against the Saudis," Kennedy said. "They'd just want to blackmail them in an effort to further consolidate their power."

"You really can't stand them, can you, Irene?"

"My feelings about them are irrelevant."

"Okay. Maybe I'm getting ahead of myself. What I think we can both agree on is that it'd be helpful to find out what Mitch knows. Until then we have no idea where we stand, let alone where we're going."

"Agreed."

"If you're worried about comms, then why don't I get on a plane and go see Claudia. No phones, no email, and it's thousands of miles away from Langley. We can have a quiet conversation and I'll see if I can get a face-to-face with Mitch."

She considered the idea for a few seconds before nodding. "When can you leave?"

45

RAPP unlocked the communications shed door and went inside. He sat on a five-gallon bucket, turned on the computer, and used his fingerprint to gain access. The laptop screen offered to connect him to a satellite, but he hesitated. Claudia had pinged him last night to set up a chat, but the only truly secure comm was one you didn't use. The problem was that she knew that better than anyone. She wouldn't have contacted him if it wasn't important.

With ten seconds to go, he logged into the encrypted chat room that she'd given him the link for.

SORRY I MISSED YOU LAST NIGHT.

He waited for a response, feeling increasingly nervous. Could the signal be traced to this dish? Could a name and location be attached to it? One way or another, they'd soon have to move off that mountaintop. This was dragging out a lot longer than he'd expected.

NO PROBLEM.

Claudia's response made him feel a little better. It was code for "everything's all right." If she'd responded with "it's okay," that would mean someone was looking over her shoulder.

He wanted off this connection as soon as possible, but for some reason couldn't help typing IS THE KID FEELING BETTER?

Claudia, however, was having none of it. YOUR MARINE FRIEND IS COMING FOR A VISIT. WANTS TO TALK ABOUT THE PROBLEMS YOU HAD ON YOUR RECENT TRIP.

Rapp nodded in the gloom around him. The Saudis' facial recognition had finally tagged him. He imagined that they were kicking up a lot of political dust over their two dead GID operatives and maybe even Bashir Isa, who he assumed was in the same condition.

Kennedy would be between a rock and a hard place, but still reluctant to have detailed discussions over potentially compromised electronics. What better solution than to send his Marine friend—Mike Nash—in person.

Dangerous, but worth the risk. He needed an update on Kennedy's situation and to let her know that Ward was attempting to track their mole through Muhammad Singh's phones. If there was a better way to accomplish that update, he couldn't think of it. Nash was a very old and competent friend, and Uganda was still a country where you could get lost.

WHY DON'T WE SET UP A GET-TOGETHER HERE?

HAPPY TO. HOW ABOUT YOUR FAVORITE DAY TO EAT OUT?

He had to think about that for a second before connecting the reference to a café in Franschhoek that made an amazing chicken dish every Thursday.

FINE.

WILL SEND DETAILS IN THE MORNING. GOOD LUCK.

The chat room disappeared and all records of it would be deleted. The entire exchange had lasted less than a minute.

Rapp shut down the computer and exited the shack, finding Nicholas Ward leaning against a railing out front.

"Interested in what's going on with your phones?" he asked. "My assistant, Sara, will have had them for at least twenty-four hours now."

One of Coleman's men had couriered them to the United States and delivered them to her house disguised as a FedEx contractor.

"You can get to her without anyone knowing?"

"Technology's kind of my thing, Mitch. And your mole wouldn't have any reason to know about the back channels I keep with her."

Giving Ward access to a computer was like giving Osama bin Laden a bomb-making kit, but there wasn't much choice at this point. Rapp needed whatever information the man's assistant had been able to come up with in order to pass it on to Nash and, ultimately, Kennedy.

He motioned to the still-open door behind him. "Go ahead."

"Can I come up?"

Rapp didn't respond to Ward's shout, focusing on getting his teeth through the piece of meat in his mouth. They were limiting the movement of people—and thus supplies—in and out of the camp. That meant living off the land to the greatest degree possible. He could identify very few components of the salad in front of him and suspected that the protein was something recently shot by Charlie Wicker.

"Yeah! Come on!" he said when he finally managed to swallow.

Ward had gotten it into his head that coming up the stairs without any warning would get him shot. He seemed to have decided that the men in Rapp's business spent their off hours dozing in the sun and when startled awake sprayed everything with whatever firearm was at hand.

He appeared a moment later and took a seat on the other side of the rattan table.

"Sara received the phones no problem. The personal one is probably too full of concrete to salvage, but she has some of our hardware people doing what they can. The burners started right up."

"Has she gotten anything off them yet?"

"Nothing interesting. She's still working on a cover story for the international data collection protocol we need to run."

"What kind of cover story?"

"I don't know exactly, but it'll work. She's smart as hell and this kind of request isn't all that unusual."

Ward couldn't help but notice Rapp's skeptical expression. "Do you know what captcha is, Mitch?"

"Like when you get into a website and it asks you to identify some distorted numbers to prove you're not a bot?"

"They're not all like that, though. Have you ever seen one that shows you a bunch of pictures and asks you, say, which one has a streetlight in it?"

Rapp sawed off another piece of mystery meat and put it in his mouth. "Yeah. Streetlights, intersections, ladders. Stuff like that."

"Exactly. Those pictures were likely images that Google's artificial intelligence couldn't identify. So, while it worked well as captcha, the real purpose was to make millions of people teach their AI to identify a streetlight, a ladder, or whatever. Sara will come up with something similar—a reason to mine anonymous data for a purpose that appears to have nothing to do with actually identifying or locating individual phones."

Rapp chewed thoughtfully. If he lived for a million years, he'd have never thought of any of that. Yet another reason to stay away from electronics to the maximum degree possible. Cameras, artificial intelligence, phones, the Internet. He didn't envy the next generation of operatives. They'd have no way to escape it.

"But you said you could give me a name. If your data is anonymous, I don't see how you accomplish that."

Ward chewed his lower lip for a moment, then pulled out a marker and began drawing on the place mat in front of him.

"This is a hypothetical chain of communication from your . . . Tangos, right? Scott's been tutoring me."

"Sure."

"Okay. Let's say the head of Saudi Intelligence calls Bashir Isa to give him instructions," Ward said, writing HSI on one side of the mat and then drawing a line to a point where he wrote BI. "Then Bashir Isa calls Muhammad Singh." He drew another line, this time from the BI to a point where he wrote MS. "Then Singh calls Auma. Then Auma fails to kill David and he calls back to Singh, who then reports that to Isa. Who, in turn, reports back to the head of Saudi intelligence." With each thread, he drew another connecting line. "Then the head of Saudi intelligence uses the same burner phone to call your mole for information on me." He drew a line to a point where he wrote *mole*. "Obviously, this chain is hypothetical. There might be more actors, but you get the idea."

"Not really," Rapp said, looking down at the spiderweb of connections. "All you have there is a bunch of anonymous phones calling other anonymous phones. No names."

"Correct. All we know is what phone called what phone at what time and what cell tower they were connected to at the time of that call."

"So, we're a little better off. We have a general location of the phones at the times the calls were made because of the tower connection. But that's still a long way from putting owners to them."

"Not as far as you might think, Mitch. Let me ask you a question: When you use a burner, is your regular cell phone in your pocket?"

"Usually."

"And is it turned on?"

"Probably," he said, starting to get a glimmer of where Ward was going with this.

"Okay. Let's say your mole made or received five calls to our nefarious little group here. And—using a best-case scenario—he's done so from five different places. Like I said before, we know the time of those calls and the cell tower he was connected to when they were made. Do you see his problem?"

Shit. Rapp actually could see the problem. And now it made him think back on every burner call he'd made since the invention of the smartphone.

"All you have to do is figure out what cell phones were communicating with those towers at the same time."

"See! You're more tech savvy than you thought. For the sake of argument, let's say a million people were connected to each of those five individual towers at the times in question. We would end up with a list of five million phones. We then just search to see which of those numbers connected to all five towers at the same time as the burner. That's probably not going to be very many. Let's pick a number out of the air and say it's ten. At that point it's just a matter of using billing records to put names to them and see of any of those names set off alarms."

"You said that was the best-case scenario. What's worst case?"

"That your mole always makes and receives calls from the same place. Say, his office at Langley. That would only narrow it down to someone who works at the Agency. Not all that helpful."

"How long?"

"Sara says she'll start getting raw data in the next twenty-four hours. It'll be spotty at first, though. Some companies respond faster to these kinds of queries than others. Probably a couple weeks before we receive all the data and analyze it."

"Get me what you can by the day after tomorrow."

"Why? What's important about that?"

"I'm setting up a meeting with a friend of mine from the Agency. I'd like to give him as much as I can and tell him when to expect something more definitive."

"Irene?"

"No, not Irene."

"But someone you trust?"

Rapp started in on his mystery salad. "I don't trust anyone. But he and I have fought together, and I've known him for a long time. In fact, he lives right down the street from me. Nothing's ever perfect, but he's about as good as it gets."

46

M IKE Nash's surroundings should have brought some sem-
blance of calm, but they were having precisely the opposite
effect. The late morning sun was crystal clear, illuminating the mountains and vineyards around him. Temperatures were a little cold for an
open car window, but he had it down anyway, searching for the scent of
the ocean some twenty miles away.

It almost didn't feel real. The cool wind. The stunning scenery. The
empty road. Rapp could have gotten out. Raced his way back to the top
of the endurance athletics circuit. Raised Anna. Loved Claudia. Fuck,
he *had* been out. All he'd had to do was not let himself get dragged
back in.

Nash turned off the paved rural highway and headed down a road
that devolved into dirt as it passed neat rows of vines. The stark white
wall that surrounded Rapp's South African home was somewhat reminiscent of the one protecting his property in Virginia. That's where the
similarities ended, though. In the States, he lived in an ultramodern

bunker packed with state-of-the-art technology. This felt like something out of a history book. A sprawling wine estate deposited there last night by a time machine.

Nash and his family had been invited to come and stay many times. Claudia personally guaranteed them a vacation to remember—shark cage diving, amazing restaurants and beaches, a plush safari up north. The kids would go nuts, she'd assured them. Maggie was fully up for it and already trying to coordinate everyone's schedules. No small task with work, school, sports, and everything else.

Now it would never happen. He'd never be back. Of that he was certain. He wanted to put this all behind him forever. Impossible, but that was the goal. This time next month he'd be the acting director of the CIA, working fifteen-hour days, seven days a week. Looking back would no longer be an option. He'd have to focus fully on moving forward in the world that the Cooks and others like them were building.

The gate began to slide open and he eased through, careful not to run over the two dogs trying to figure out how to tear the vehicle apart. Anna shouted at them from the front porch and finally managed to get control. In what seemed like a reasonable precaution, he stayed in the car until she dragged them inside and closed the door.

It reopened a moment later and Claudia fought her way past the swirling, barking mass. When she waved, he decided it was a signal that it was safe to emerge.

"Beautiful spot," he called as he started toward the house.

She gave him a warm hug that he managed to return without gritting his teeth.

"I can't believe you finally made it to Africa and you're alone!"

"Me neither. Maggie would kill me if she knew. But don't worry. We'll get the whole crew out here soon. That is, if you're still up for it."

"Of course we are. You're always welcome."

He made sure his smile was enthusiastic as she led him around the side of the house to a table on the back lawn. It was set with a freshly opened bottle of local wine and a light lunch that looked typically delicious. He refused the alcohol, instead accepting a bottle of sparkling water. Claudia took the chair next to him and scooted it close enough that their arms touched. The walls and house behind them would thwart prying eyes and the clear sky would make drones obvious. She'd have swept for active listening devices and passive wouldn't be workable in this environment. Despite that, she remained cautious. Her appearance and the way she got on with Anna and his own kids made it easy to forget that Claudia Gould was a consummate pro.

"I take it you're still up for a face-to-face meeting?" she said at a level that was barely above a whisper. An olive, held between her thumb and forefinger, hovered in front of her mouth as she spoke.

"That's why I'm here."

It was impossible not to wonder how much she knew. Had Rapp told her about the mole hunt? The involvement of Saudi intelligence? Did she know his current location? Would she even be aware that Ward and his people were alive? Rapp would only feed her what she needed to know to play her role. For his protection and for her own.

"Uncle Mike!"

Anna ran out of the back door and he abandoned his chair, crouching to pick her up. "You've got those dogs chained tight, right?"

"They're in the kitchen. They like it there best because sometimes they can steal food. Sausage mostly. It's called *boerewors* here. Did you know that?"

"I didn't," he said, setting her down again.

"How are the animals back home? Are you taking care of them? Snowball gets lonely when Mitch is gone, you know."

"Snowball's fine. And so are all the others. I have all the retired people taking care of them. It's probably a good thing. Some of them are getting a little fat." He blew out his cheeks and pulled out the front of his shirt to demonstrate the former operators' increasing girth.

Anna slapped him on the leg. "You're mean!"

"Sweetheart," Claudia said, "Uncle Mike and I have a few things to talk about and then he's going to want to see your new bike. Why don't you get it out of the shed so you can show him how good you are at riding now?"

She ran off.

"And don't forget to oil the chain!" her mother called after her. "Just like Mitch showed you. One link at a time."

Nash watched her disappear around the side of the house before sitting back down. He needed to get this over with before his brain— and his heart—exploded.

"So, everything's okay with Mitch and the guys?"

Again, she nodded.

He let out a long breath calculated to look like relief. "He has a way of causing problems, doesn't he? The president is going to think Irene's been holding out on him. The Saudis think he's responsible for the deaths of three of their people. And I can't get a refund on the caterer for his wake."

"I'm sorry, Mike. I know how hard this has been on everyone. If there had been another way, Mitch would have done it."

He didn't respond, suddenly realizing he was blithering like an amateur. The tendency to run on at the mouth when you were under stress was something he normally wasn't prone to. The problem was that he'd never been under this much stress. Not in combat. Not during the births of his children. Not when he'd woken up in the hospital after getting blown to kingdom come in Afghanistan. Never.

"I'm sure that everything will be clear once you've had a chance to talk to him," she continued.

"When?" Nash said.

"Tomorrow."

"Uganda?"

She nodded and slipped him a piece of paper. "You'll need to drive north to this address. It's a private airstrip. Be there at nine a.m. A pilot will meet you and take you where you need to go."

———

Nash looked in the rearview mirror and waved through his window as the gate slid open. Anna was on her bicycle, steering confidently with one hand and returning his wave with the other. Claudia was at the front door watching the dogs bolt after him.

He thought that some of the weight pressing down on him would disappear when he cleared the fence line, but it didn't happen. If anything, it got worse. He was already starting to see the world in terms of BR and AR—Before Rapp and After Rapp. His life would be changed forever. Who he was would be changed forever.

He glanced over at the phone lying on the passenger seat but didn't reach for it. The update he'd promised to provide could wait. Instead, he just stared out at the road and forced his mind to go gloriously blank.

After an hour, he couldn't put it off any longer. Reaching for the phone, he connected a wired headset and dialed a number that precious few people had.

"Hold on," a familiar voice said when the call was picked up.

He waited, listening to muffled voices as a meeting was hastily adjourned and its attendees ushered out.

"Go ahead," President Cook said finally.

"I'm on for tomorrow in Uganda."

"Is there anything more you need from me?"

"No. I have people on the ground already. After this call, I'm going to have to go dark. Claudia will move me around until she's satisfied I'm not being tracked. If anything looks even slightly suspicious, she'll pull the plug."

"Then you're on your own."

"Yeah."

"We understand how difficult this situation is for you. It's not something we take lightly. Or forget easily."

"Thank you."

"I'll look forward to you getting back and starting the next phase of your career. And your life."

"Yes, sir."

"Try to relax, Mike. You have the most powerful weapon ever devised by nature on your side."

"What's that?"

"Your opponent's trust."

The line went dead, and Nash looked over at the phone before ripping the headphones out and throwing them against the passenger-side window.

47

A S African buses went, this one wasn't so bad. Nash had a double seat to himself with only ten or so other passengers on board. No children, no farm animals. Just darkness and silence so thick it made it hard to breathe. In truth, he'd have welcomed a few crying kids and pissed-off chickens.

The Cessna turboprop that he'd boarded outside of Clanwilliam, South Africa, had dropped him at a dirt landing strip in a mountainous area of what he assumed was Uganda. There he'd been picked up in a Toyota sedan that had been on the road since he was in grade school and shuttled to the nearest town. After spending an afternoon being led through crowded markets and random buildings, he'd been ushered onto this bus. That had been two hours ago.

The dusty headlights caused the forest on either side to glow a deep green and he watched the trees pass from his position next to the window. Claudia had accomplished her goal with the expected efficiency. He was completely alone and off the radar now. His only possessions were contained in the small backpack in the seat next to him:

two liters of water, a few energy bars, a tablet, a satphone, and a Colt M45 pistol.

Beyond that, he had the clothes on his back and a small tin of Excedrin in his shirt pocket. Nash availed himself of the latter, popping two in his mouth and swallowing without the aid of a drink. Whether they'd do anything about his cracking skull remained to be seen. Likely not.

He closed his eyes and tried to empty his mind. It didn't work, though. Instead, he drifted back to his time in the Marine Corps. Fighting an enemy that could be seen and defined. The clearly delineated battle between good and evil. The strange comfort of being a piece on the chessboard and not the player hovering over it.

He should have never left. He'd been well respected and well liked. His combat record had been impeccable. He could have risen to the rank of colonel and spent his career commanding loyal operators without hidden agendas or grand plans. Just a desire to protect their countrymen and defend their comrades.

But he *had* left. He wasn't a simple soldier anymore. He was a spy. A politician even. He was one of the elite class of people who ruled the world. Someone who couldn't be trusted any more than he could trust. Nothing was simple for him and it never would be again.

Nash didn't realize that he'd fallen asleep until he felt the bus lurch to a stop. The driver stood and started back, undoubtedly to help someone with their bags as they got out. Where they'd be going, though, was a mystery. The bus was surrounded by dense forest and submerged in the same darkness that it had been before he'd closed his eyes.

He wasn't particularly surprised when the man halted in front of him and pointed through the window at a narrow dirt track leading north. Nash grabbed his pack and walked past the curious passengers before stepping out into the cool night air. The path he was apparently supposed to take was visible in the glow of the headlights, but not for long. The bus pulled away and he found himself left with nothing but a little starlight shimmering through a cloud of diesel exhaust.

This just kept getting better and better.

After a couple of hours of walking, the jeep track narrowed to something more like a trail. He hadn't seen or heard anything, but it was possible that he was being watched. Maybe even scanned for transmissions from a phone or other communications device. He doubted it—this was likely more about making sure he wasn't being followed than testing him. Still, he'd removed the battery from his satphone before leaving South Africa. Mitch Rapp and Claudia Gould were a suspicious pair.

Another fifteen minutes took him to a clearing with a much better road coming in from the east. It was undoubtedly the route Rapp had taken to get his SUV up there.

"Asshole," Nash said, striding across the clearing and enveloping Rapp's hand in his own.

"I thought you were lost. Too much time behind a desk."

"I refuse to be lectured by a talking corpse."

"You drive," Rapp said, walking around the front of the vehicle.

They climbed in and Nash bounced the SUV down the road toward what he assumed would be the rural highway he'd come from.

"Congratulations, Mitch. You're the first person in history to add explosions to what should have been another boring mole hunt."

"Where does Irene stand?" Rapp said. He wouldn't give anything away until he knew what Nash had been told.

"Basically, nowhere. We know it was some kind of worm, but Marcus can't figure out how it was introduced or under whose credentials. What we do know, though, is that the mole's interests were pretty specific. They wanted to know about Nicholas Ward and not much else. Can I assume that the fact that you were in Saudi Arabia suggests you're further along than we are?"

He nodded.

"Did you kill Bashir Isa?"

"No."

"What about the other two?"

"Yeah. Those are mine."

Nash let out a long breath. "That's not exactly what I wanted to hear."

"Why not?"

"Because the top of the president's head is blowing off, Mitch. What I needed was to go back and tell him you didn't have anything to do with this. And the truth is, that ain't nothin'. Irene still hasn't told him about the mole or the fact that Ward and Chism are alive. When he finds out she's been holding out on him, it's not going to just be his head that's exploding, it's going to be everything inside the beltway."

"It looks like the Saudis wanted David Chism dead and they put Gideon Auma up to that first attack. When it didn't work, they accessed our mainframe to get information on Ward and passed it on to Auma with a detailed plan on how to get to him."

"Can you prove any of that?"

"I'm working on it."

"Working on it? Are you fucking kidding me? Irene's going to be lucky to still have a job by the end of the week. We need to do more than work on it. We need the Saudis dead to rights. The only thing that's going to appease the Cooks at this point is if you give them the Kingdom on a silver platter."

"It all comes down to finding the mole."

"And where are you with that?" Nash said, feeling the sweat break under his hairline. He'd taken every precaution to remain hidden, but no cover was perfect.

"I managed to get a hold of Isa's burner phone and the one used by the man the Saudis had dealing directly with Auma."

Nash glanced over at Rapp's silhouette in the dashboard light. "How does that help us? I assume they were using strict protocols and only communicating with other burners?"

"Yeah, but that might not be as secure as we thought. I handed the phone off to Ward's people. They think they might be able to put names to the people called from it."

"Bullshit."

"That's what I said. But I have to admit he talks a pretty good game."

Nash rolled his window the rest of the way down when the sweat that had been limited to his hairline began to ooze from every pore. The names of the director of the GID. Of the Saudi prince. Of the president of the United States. But most important, his fucking name.

"If Ward can pull it off, he's going to be Irene's favorite person in the world. I honestly don't know if it'll be enough for her to keep her job but having something to show for all this won't hurt her on her way out. How soon will you know?"

"He says we're still a couple weeks out. If it works at all."

Nash relaxed a bit and began slowly shaking his head. "So now we can't even trust burners? Shit."

Rapp ignored the observation. "Tell Irene to back off the mole hunt. If she's not getting anywhere, she's just risking spooking them. Let them think we've hit a dead end. With a little luck, Ward will be able to deliver."

"And then miraculously come back to life."

"That's the plan."

"So, we've got to keep all this from the president for another two weeks?"

"Somewhere around there. If his office gets hold of the fact that Ward's alive, it's going to leak. And then our mole is going to disappear."

Nash chewed his lip for a moment. "It's a big ask, Mitch. Irene's under a huge amount of pressure. For the first time, the cracks are starting to show in her."

"You don't think she'll be on board?"

"I have no idea," Nash said, thumbing toward the backseat. "But she gave me a tablet with a message for you on it. It's in my pack."

"Do you know what it says?"

Nash shook his head. "She said you should use the password from Belarus. I assume that means something to you?"

Rapp didn't immediately react, but his hesitation was to be expected. It would be unusual for Kennedy to ask him to reuse an old password, but Nash wasn't privy to their current protocols. The Belarus one was the most obscure thing he'd been able to access. Suspicious, but in the current context probably not fatal.

Rapp retrieved the tablet, started it, and put on a wired headset. Out of the corner of his eye, Nash saw him enter the indicated password and click a video file in the center of the screen.

When Irene Kennedy's image came on, Nash returned his attention to the rutted dirt road ahead. He'd already seen the video more than thirty times. Generated by one of Cook's people, the computer-generated masterpiece was indistinguishable from the real thing. Nash had known Kennedy for years and even after repeated, detailed viewings couldn't find a single flaw. If he hadn't been involved in its creation, he would have never even thought to question its authenticity. Deep fake videos were an incredible, terrifying technology that would soon change the world.

On-screen, Kennedy's doppelgänger was telling Rapp that she had flown to Uganda to meet with him personally. That she suspected betrayal at the highest levels of government and needed to talk to him face-to-face about what she'd discovered. In closing, the counterfeit image told him that Nash wasn't aware of the meeting, but that he should attend and could be trusted. The video then faded into a map showing her supposed location. Rapp studied it for a moment before turning to him.

"When we get to pavement, turn right."

48

"IT'S going to be a pretty serious party," Mike Nash said. "The barn'll be decorated. Top-notch caterer. Kegs. Wine brought in from a boutique producer in Napa. You and the guys should fly back for it. Not every day you get to attend your own wake."

Rapp managed a vague smile. "Since it sounds like I'm paying for it, maybe we will."

They fell silent again and Nash returned his attention to the moon-lit farmland beyond their headlights. They were an hour and a half into what would be a fairly long drive. While Claudia had run him around quite a bit, he was pretty sure the mountains where he'd met Rapp were part of the Rwenzori range in the southwestern part of Uganda. Their fictitious rendezvous with Kennedy was located more in the middle of the country. Based on the map he'd committed to memory, Nash guessed they had another six hours in the car.

And then that was it. In less time than it took him to drive to his place in Hilton Head, all this would be over.

A quiet ping sounded, and Rapp dug a phone from his pocket. At first it seemed surprising that it would be powered up, but upon further consideration it was to be expected. Rapp believed he was soon to be face-to-face with Irene Kennedy and he'd want to have the latest information for that meeting. Nash concentrated on his peripheral vision, but Rapp held the phone in a way that he couldn't see the screen.

"Anything interesting?" he finally felt compelled to ask as Rapp returned the text.

"No," was the simple answer.

Undoubtedly one of the many lies people in their business told every day. This wasn't a situation where you sent texts back and forth about the weather. And this particular exchange went on for almost five minutes before Rapp tossed the phone on the floorboard and demolished it with the heel of his boot.

Less than six hours, Nash reminded himself as his old friend went back to staring blankly through the windshield. Less than six more hours and this would all be behind him.

A brightly painted railway container with windows cut in it appeared at the edge of the road. When Rapp saw the gas pump out front, he broke from his trance.

"Why don't we stop and fill up. I need to take a piss anyway."

Nash pulled over and Rapp got out, disappearing into the shadows at the edge of the dirt parking area for a moment before entering the improvised building. When he reappeared, he was holding a couple of cans of Coke and a bag of chips. Nash finished filling the tank and slid back into the driver's seat. "Mine?" he said, pointing to the can on his side of the console.

Rapp nodded and then spoke through a mouthful of chips. "We're going to have to take a right up here in about a mile."

"A right?" Nash made sure his voice didn't betray his confusion. The map that had been included with Kennedy's deep fake didn't say anything about getting off the main road yet.

"The guy at the gas station says a bridge got washed out up ahead. We have to go around. Should only be a couple hours out of our way."

"Out of our way to where?"

Rapp didn't answer, instead holding out the bag so Nash could dig in. He did so, keeping his body language relaxed. Inside, though, he was feeling very differently. The six hours he'd steeled himself for had just become eight. Not that it mattered to the operation—he'd given his ETA as a forty-eight-hour window rather than a precise time. He just wanted this done.

The turn appeared in the headlights and Nash exited the tarmac in favor of a dirt road not quite wide enough for two cars to comfortably pass. Based on the emptiness of the landscape at that time of morning, though, it likely wouldn't be an issue.

Two hours turned into five—including three river crossings and a couple of opportunities to test the SUV's winch. Finally, they dead-ended into a paved two-lane road.

"Which way?" Nash said.

"Right. We're back on track. This is the same road we turned off of after the gas station."

By the time they passed through a small village that was their last landmark, it was late morning. Rapp reached over and reset the vehicle's odometer. "In twenty-seven point three kilometers there'll be a dirt road on the right. Easy to miss in the dark, but we should be okay now that the sun's up."

Nash nodded, feeling a surge of adrenaline drive back his exhaustion. That dirt track would take them to a forested area that was too steep and rocky to be useful to the surrounding farms. A clearing near the middle was where Rapp believed he would be meeting Irene Kennedy.

Nash rolled down his window, breathing in the morning air. Hopefully, it would be enough to quiet the nausea building in his gut. But probably not.

As predicted, the turn was easy to spot and they began climbing a rough track that headed into the trees. After another few miles, Rapp pointed to a small break in the foliage. "There."

Nash pulled in and stopped. "This is it?"

Rapp responded by throwing his door open and stepping from the vehicle. Nash did the same, using a hand to shield his eyes from the sun's glare. The clearing was roughly a hundred yards in diameter and ringed by densely packed trees. The ground rolled a bit, broken by a few rocky outcroppings but otherwise empty.

Rapp stayed near the vehicle, but Nash walked away from it, wanting to put some distance between them. Finally, when he was about twenty yards out, he turned.

"Care to tell me what we're doing here, Mitch?"

"We're supposed to meet Irene."

"Irene? What the hell are you talking about?"

Rapp broke free from the cover of the vehicle, starting to move in Nash's direction. "The message on that tablet was to meet her here."

Nash conjured a skeptical expression with just a hint of caution. Ironic in an agonizing kind of way. "I left her looking pretty comfortable in her office, Mitch. And why would she send me if she was planning on coming herself? Is there something you're not telling me?"

Rapp didn't look suspicious yet and hadn't made a move for the weapon that would be hanging beneath his right arm. His good humor wouldn't last, though.

The men appeared from the forest before Rapp had even made it fifteen feet from the vehicle. Three of them, covered head to toe in camo, eyes invisible behind goggles, and assault weapons in hand. Their positions were perfect, allowing them to keep their weapons trained on Rapp while avoiding any potential for crossfire.

Not surprisingly, Rapp didn't even bother reaching for his gun. He would have registered how these men moved, read his tactical position, and concluded that any action on his part would be suicide. Still, Nash felt the need to drive the point home.

"There are four more in the trees, Mitch—all aiming at your head. Every one of them is a top operator and they know who you are. Even with superior numbers and position, I guarantee they're scared. One twitch from you and everybody's going to start shooting."

Rapp nodded with the dead expression that Nash had seen before during combat. This time, though, it wasn't aimed at a bunch of terrorists. It was aimed at him.

"Just keep your hands at your sides and everything will be okay."

"Why do I doubt that, Mike?"

Nash pulled his Colt and backed away, putting another ten or so feet between them. Not doing so would be arrogance. There was a long list of people who at one time or another thought they held all the cards against Mitch Rapp. Talented people. Dead people.

"This isn't personal, Mitch."

"How the fuck is this not personal? We've been friends for years. We've fought together. We've bled together. And now I'm standing here in the woods waiting for you and your friends to execute me. For what? A bunch of Saudi money? Your wife makes more than you can spend."

"Not money, Mitch. And not the Saudis. The president of the United States. It's probably hard for you to wrap your mind around this, but I don't work for you. I don't really even work for Irene. I work for the man elected to the White House."

"So, you sided with a politician? That doesn't make me feel any better."

Nash stiffened. "You think this is what I wanted? Are you fucking kidding me? You can't imagine what I've gone through to try to keep us from ending up here. David Chism should have died in that first attack. Then it would have been over."

"What's he to you?"

"To me? Nothing. But to the Saudis a lot. After you saved Chism, Cook asked me to get him information on Nicholas Ward. He said he didn't want Irene to know but I didn't think that much of it. I just figured he was fishing for dirt on Ward so he could blackmail him into supporting him or something. But then Ward's compound gets taken out and he gets snatched at his hangar. It didn't take long for me to figure out what I'd gotten myself into."

"But you didn't go to Irene."

"For what? To tell her that I'd just gotten my best friends killed? That with my help, the president of the United States had colluded with a foreign government to get rid of the richest man in the world? What would be the point? Chism was dead. Ward was in the hands of Gideon Auma. And you and the guys were gone." He started pacing. "The world we've been fighting for is gone, Mitch. We collapsed the Soviet Union and killed damn near every Islamic terrorist who's ever even looked at us sideways. The era of wars between superpowers is over—it has to be or none of us survive. Your friend Nicholas Ward thinks that's going to bring in a golden age. But you know that's bullshit even better than I do. People need hardship. They need something to struggle against. Someone to hate and feel superior to. Without those things they lose their identity and sense of purpose. And they can't handle it. Without a real enemy, they start turning on each other. That video of Irene you just watched? One of the president's people made it in less than a day with software you can get for free online. In another few years, half the videos people see on the Internet will be fake. Served up by right-wing nuts, left-wing nuts, foreign powers, and anyone else with a laptop and a sixth-grade education. If we don't take control of that, we'll end up in a civil war. But instead of the North against the South, it'll be four hundred different factions all swinging in the dark. Flat-earthers. Anti-vaxxers. Nazis. Communists. Antifa. The gluten intolerant—"

"And the Cooks are going to fix all that."

"I think they have a better shot than most," Nash responded. "They don't have any illusions about humanity. They know that ninety-five percent of people are going to fight tooth and nail against the utopia that Nicholas Ward wants to force on them. And more important, they understand that they'll drag the other five percent down with them. The Cooks just want to give people the leadership they need. They want to make their lives simple. Focus their energy. Give them something to belong to."

"And that other five percent? I assume they get what they want too, too?"

"Yeah. Wealth, power, and a nice tall wall between us and them."

"What a beautiful vision."

Nash let out a bitter laugh. "My entire career has been about fighting for America and the American dream, Mitch. But at some point, it's time to wake up. At some point, you've got to admit that the monkeys are going to figure out a reason to throw feces at each other. The question is how much of it are you willing to let stick to you. I've spent my entire life trying save people who don't want to be saved. Now it's time for me to save myself and my family. Twenty years from now, I want my kids to be kicking back in penthouses, not scrounging for scraps and killing each other over every conspiracy theory that comes across Facebook. The job's not stopping al-Qaeda from taking out a few people here and there. Not anymore. Now it's about stopping the mob from destroying themselves and everything people like us have built."

Rapp nodded and looked around at the men holding their weapons on him. "So, what's the plan, Mike? I don't have all day."

"The plan . . ." Nash looked down at the pistol in his hand. "The plan is to clean up as much of your mess as I can."

"My mess?"

"Yeah. Your mess. You made Ward and Chism dead and they need to stay that way. If they get resurrected, it's going to be inconvenient to a lot of people who don't like being inconvenienced. I assume you've got them stashed somewhere around here with Scott? Tell me where. I'll drive over, have a couple of beers with the guys, and then tonight I'll kill both of them and drive out before anyone knows what happened. After that, if everyone agrees to keep their mouths shut, they can just walk away."

"And Irene?"

"I can protect her. Cook will make me the new director and he doesn't have any reason to pick a fight. All she has to do is fade into retirement." He paused for a moment, finally pointing an accusatory finger at Rapp. "Like always, the problem is you. You're the part of this shit sandwich everyone's going to choke on."

"And that's why I'll never leave here."

"I don't know. Maybe you do. How about I offer you the deal of the fucking century? You give me your word right now that you'll just let this go. That you'll forget about me, the Cooks, the Saudis, Ward, and all the rest. That you'll go back to the Cape, race your bike, spend time with your new family, and never set foot back in the States. Do that and I'll give you a ride to the airport."

Rapp remained silent.

"Yeah. That's what I thought," Nash said, shaking his head slowly. "But I want to tell you something. I'm going to make you a hero. All the shit you've done that no one knows about? I'm going to tell them. You deserve that."

Rapp walked to a rock outcropping, tracked by the men covering him. He sat and rested his elbows on his knees. "I got an interesting text on the way here."

"I meant to ask you about that."

"Like I said, Ward's people are still a few weeks out from putting names to the network of burners you were using. But he has put together some of the towers they connected to."

"So?" Nash said, starting to feel his anxiety notch upward despite the men covering his old friend.

"So, he noticed something interesting. That one of those phones connected twice to the same tower I do when I'm at home in Virginia."

Nash's brow furrowed as he tried to understand the ramifications of what he'd just heard. Rapp helped him out.

"Apparently, Nick Ward's memory is better than mine. I don't recall telling him that the man I was meeting today lived in my neighborhood. But he did."

"I don't understand," Nash said, backing away a few more steps and making sure his people were still alert and in position.

"I didn't, either. The video from Irene telling me to meet her in the middle of nowhere. The old password from Belarus that anyone high up enough in the Agency could get hold of. The mole who was too smart for anyone to identify. But then the cell tower put it all together for me."

This time when Nash looked at the men covering Rapp, he took the time to scrutinize every detail—their physiques, the way they stood, how they held their rifles. And then he knew. He knew before Rapp could give the subtle nod that prompted them to remove their goggles and face coverings.

Nash looked away before he could meet Scott Coleman's eye, returning his attention to Rapp. As terrifying as his dead stare was, it was better than the pain that would be etched so deeply in the former SEAL's face. He assumed that the other two men were Joe Maslick and Bruno McGraw, but he refused to confirm it.

"What did you find in the forest?" Rapp asked Coleman.

"Seven mercs."

"All dead?"

"All but the one we left alive to interrogate. They were solid operators. Too dangerous to play around with."

Rapp nodded and the silence in the clearing began to stretch out. Nash focused on the warmth of the sun on his face. On the happy memories he had of his wife and children. Other than that, his mind was strangely blank. The things he'd done—both good and bad—didn't come flooding back. On the contrary, they no longer seemed to matter. Just the sun and his family. Two things he'd never see again.

"I'm giving you a five-minute head start," Rapp said finally. "For old times' sake."

49

RAPP took not so careful aim and fired a single round into the trees. The sound of the shot was deafening and the snap of the bullet as it cut through the foliage would be terrifying. Which was the goal.

Thirty minutes into the chase, the grade of the forested slope had increased to probably five percent. Barely noticeable to him, but a significant obstacle for Nash. Things would have been different during his time as a Marine, but those days were long past. He'd largely abandoned his cardio workouts for weight lifting and ballooned to a solid 210 pounds. Good for stabilizing the damage done to his spine back when he'd still been a man of honor, but not so great for uphill running.

Rapp adjusted his aim a few degrees to the left and fired another round. He'd keep herding Nash up the incline as long as possible. Even after years of kissing political ass and polishing desk chairs, Michael Nash wasn't a man to be underestimated.

Rapp started forward again, making some effort to be quiet but not going overboard. The same explosion that had damaged Nash's back had also damaged his hearing. It was unlikely that he'd be able to separate the rhythm of human movement from the sound created by the intermittent breeze.

A historically satisfying end for the son of a bitch. Humans had evolved not that far from where they were now with very few physical advantages. They weren't fast. Or strong. They lacked sharp claws or big teeth. Their only talent was an ability to keep going, wearing down prey until they finally stopped, stunned and unable to defend themselves.

Rapp wasn't going to involve himself in hand-to-hand combat with a desperate former Marine who outweighed him by almost forty pounds. No, Nash would end up on his fucking knees—gasping for air and waiting for the bullet that would kill him. Or maybe that wasn't entirely accurate. The truth was that the loyal soldier Rapp had known for so long was already dead. He had been for some time. The bullet would just make it official.

As he weaved through the trees, Rapp couldn't help thinking about how it had happened. He remembered the battles they'd fought together, some against America's enemies and others between them. He remembered shouting matches about strategy, tactics, and personnel. He remembered drinking on Nash's deck with Maggie and the kids and teaching their oldest son lacrosse.

Rapp slowed as his white-hot rage faded to a dull red.

A few years back, he'd forced Nash to take credit for something Rapp himself had done, turning him into a hero. He'd received the Distinguished Intelligence Cross, the fawning attention of Washington's elites, and an enormous amount of media coverage. The unexpected celebrity had made it impossible for him to continue as a clandestine operative. Through no fault of his own, he suddenly found himself shut out of the career he'd built.

He'd been pissed as hell and, in retrospect, probably had a right to be. At the time, Rapp had told himself he'd done it for the man's own good. That he was losing his edge and had a family that needed him. He'd convinced himself that he was protecting his old friend. But was that really his decision to make? And had his motivations really been so pure? It had been clear that someone was going to have to take credit for what had been done and Rapp didn't want it to be him. The problem was that he hadn't just fled the spotlight like he'd been doing his entire life; he'd shoved his friend into it in his place.

Rapp came to a stop, listening to the forest around him for any indication of his target. But there wasn't anything. When properly motivated, Nash could apparently still move his fat ass up a hill.

He started forward again but found that his pace had slowed even more. He thought back to a particularly ugly fight he and Nash had gotten into years ago. It had ended up with Rapp leaving the man lying on the shoulder of the road.

Now he couldn't even remember what they were arguing about.

He tried to refocus on the task at hand, reminding himself that the penalty of taking Mike Nash for just another manicured bureaucrat could very well be death. But the focus wouldn't come. Only the memories.

The hard-to-face truth was that he'd made Nash the man he was today. He'd sent the Marine to the executive floor kicking and screaming. Once there, what had he expected him to do? Nash always excelled. In school. In sports. In combat. Why wouldn't he examine his new battlefield and calculate how to win on it? Why wouldn't he recognize that Washington was an operating environment that didn't reward loyalty and courage? It rewarded treachery and self-interest.

Adapt or die.

As Rapp slipped through the trees, he reflected on the things Nash had said to him back in that clearing. Was it possible there was a kernel of truth in it? Over the course of their relationship, they'd probably disagreed more than they agreed, but Rapp had always taken the man seriously. Sometimes more seriously than he was willing to admit.

Son of a bitch.

Above all things, Rapp hated doubt. It was almost as bad as regret on his scale of bullshit wastes of time. But there he was. Walking through the jungle wallowing in it. Setting a pace designed to ensure that he never caught his target.

By God, he'd make Nash suffer, though. He'd keep running him up this hill until the forest opened onto farmland and forced the man to double back. He'd keep shooting at random, suspending the man at the edge of panic. Then, eventually, he'd collect Coleman and the guys and just slink away. Nash would stay hidden in the woods—probably for days—starving his ass off, getting eaten by bugs, and hopefully ingesting some amoeba that would cause truly catastrophic diarrhea. Eventually he'd emerge, filthy, unshaven, and dehydrated. Separated from his Agency support and his family. Not knowing whom he could trust.

When he finally slipped back to the United States, he'd be Kennedy's problem. Maybe she'd ship him off to surveil a Siberian weather station for the rest of his career. Or shove him in a forgotten warehouse full of Cold War intelligence reports in need of filing.

The sunlight intensified just ahead, indicating a break in the trees. Rapp turned to skirt its edges before spotting a figure near the middle.

Nash.

He hesitated for a moment, but then moved into a position where he'd be visible but still have reasonable cover. Nash had taken no such precautions. He was out in the open with his gun hanging loosely from his hand.

"You're even slower than I thought," Rapp said.

"I didn't figure there was any hurry. Just putting off the inevitable, right? I'm not going to let you push me up this hill until I drop. I'd like to die with a little more dignity than that. If I'm going down, I'll damn well do it with a shirt free of puke and the crease in my pants still holding."

"Whatever works for you."

"It's been a wild ride, huh, Mitch? The things we've done? The things we've seen? Even if we could talk about it, no one would ever believe it."

Rapp just shrugged.

"I stopped to tell you something, man. And there's no reason for me to lie anymore, right? So, you should take this seriously. None of this shit matters. Just Claudia, Anna, Irene, and Scott and the guys. That's it. Everyone else is just waiting to stab you in the back. That's what I've learned traveling the world's conference rooms. We all die and, in a few years, no one will remember we even existed. Nothing we do means anything."

"Do you have a point?"

"Yeah. I do. Make peace with the president, Mitch. Even you and Irene can't stand against the storm that's coming. I know you don't want to join him, but at least be smart enough to back away. And while I know you haven't listened to me much over the years, you should think about what I'm telling you. It's good advice."

He raised his sidearm until the barrel was tucked under his chin.

"Mike! No!"

But it was too late. The gun sounded and he collapsed to the jungle floor.

EPILOGUE

RAPP increased the speed of the rental car's windshield wipers and then notched up the air-conditioning. Through the mist, the road outside felt strangely foreign. He'd driven it a thousand times before but now he was a trespasser in his own home. In his own country.

He'd flown into a private airport in Maryland a few hours ago, using a private jet Claudia had rented through a web of offshore corporations. The passport was one of the fakes from the safe house in Riyadh and the credit card number he'd used for the car belonged to a Slovenian export business.

He was starting to wonder if he really existed. Was he the patriotic Agency man? The Iraqi national renting a nondescript Airbnb in Riyadh? The South African living with his brand-new family among the vineyards of Franschhoek?

Maybe none of them. Maybe one day all the fronts, aliases, and lies would collapse and he'd find out there was nothing behind them.

His quest for anonymity would prove so successful that he'd become a ghost before his time.

When he pressed the button on his remote, the gate leading into his neighborhood didn't respond. He had to get out and open it manually, unable to shake the idea that it was sending him a message.

The rain was already starting to soak through his suit as he slid back behind the wheel and pulled through. A few blocks later, he passed a parked GMC Yukon that immediately pulled out to follow him. Deeper into the subdivision, he could see the glow of the spotlights illuminating the walls of his house, but that wasn't his objective.

He pulled into what had once been Mike Nash's driveway and threw open the door again. This time he put on a fedora and raincoat before walking hunched toward the house's front door. It would be hard for anyone else in the neighborhood to make out much more than his outline, but even if they did, the coat and hunched shoulders would keep him from being recognized. As would the fact that, as far as the world was concerned, he was dead.

They would, however, recognize Irene Kennedy, whose boots he could hear overtaking him from behind. No one would ask questions, though. Every one of them had spent enough years in the business to know better.

Kennedy caught him on the porch but neither looked at the other nor spoke. He knocked on the door and a few shouts from inside preceded the beat of someone coming down the hallway. Shoes on the wood floor he himself had walked across so many times before. The entry light that he and Rory had been forced to repair after an overly spirited lacrosse session came on a moment later.

Maggie opened the door, holding her two-year-old son in one arm. She took a hesitant step backward when the light caught Rapp's face.

"Oh my God! You're alive!"

She threw her arms around him, crushing a writhing Chuck between them for a moment before pulling back. "What happened? What are you doing here? Mike's—"

She suddenly fell silent, taking in his expression and then looking at Kennedy standing silently next to him.

Maggie Nash was not a stupid woman. Very much the opposite. And she'd lived with a former Marine and CIA operative long enough for her razor-sharp mind to absorb a great deal about the business. More than was necessary to determine the purpose of their visit.

For a moment, she looked like she was going to collapse. Her arms lost their strength and Rapp took Chuck while Kennedy reached out to steady her.

"Let's go inside," she said gently.

By the time Rapp had closed the door, Maggie was standing under her own power again. She turned and walked stiffly down the hall to a cluttered home office she used when she didn't want to make the trek downtown.

He and Kennedy stood by motionless as Mike Nash's widow cleared files and children's toys from two chairs. She was a take-charge woman and this was her way of preparing for what she knew was coming.

They sat and she positioned herself behind her desk, back straight and chin thrust slightly forward.

"He's dead, isn't he?"

Chuck squirmed a bit when he heard the unfamiliar tone of his mother's voice. It was as though he understood that his life—his future—had just been transformed.

"I'm sorry," Kennedy said.

Maggie stared straight forward for a few seconds, fixated on the door behind them. "What happened?"

"He came to meet me in Uganda," Rapp said. "I can't talk about why, but we couldn't trust comms. We were ambushed by a group splintered off from Gideon Auma's militia. It turned into a running fight through the jungle. We were badly outnumbered and had to split up. Mike went with Bruno and Mas—"

"Bruno and Mas," she interrupted. "Scott and his people are alive, too?"

Rapp nodded and continued. "The people chasing us didn't see us split up and they all came after me, Wick, and Scott. We took out a lot of them, but they were loaded up on drugs and no matter how many we killed, they just kept coming. We were conserving ammo with nowhere to go when Mike and the guys came in behind them and saved our asses." He fell silent for a moment. They'd worked out the entire battle in gory detail in case she or any of the kids should ask at some future date, but now wasn't the time.

"The bottom line is that I'd be dead if it hadn't been for him, Maggie. So would Scott and Wick. We owe him our lives."

"I'll call you tomorrow, Maggie," Irene Kennedy said over the sound of the rain pounding the porch's eave. "We can talk about arrangements. If you need anything between now and then, you have my personal number. It doesn't matter what time it is. Use it."

"Thank you," Maggie responded, in a voice that sounded completely empty. She'd run out of tears a while ago, but her eyes were still red when they turned toward Rapp. He nodded in her direction, but she didn't react at all. Undoubtedly, she was thinking that it should be him dead out there. That her husband had no business skulking around the Ugandan jungle. That like so many deaths over the years, this was the fault of Mitch Rapp.

And she was probably right.

When the door closed, he and Kennedy stepped back into the rain and started down the driveway.

"I don't want to be on the ground here any longer than I have to be," Rapp said. "But I told Claudia I'd get a few things for her at the house. Can I offer you a drink?"

Kennedy wiped at her face, but it was hard to know if it was rain or tears.

"You can offer me a few."

ABOUT THE AUTHOR

Number one *New York Times* bestselling author Vince Flynn (1966–2013) created one of contemporary fiction's most popular heroes: CIA counterterrorist agent Mitch Rapp. All of his novels are *New York Times* bestsellers, including his stand-alone debut novel, *Term Limits*. *American Assassin* was released as a major film in 2017.

Kyle Mills is the number one *New York Times* bestselling author of twenty-one political thrillers, including *The Survivor* for Vince Flynn and *The Patriot Act* for Robert Ludlum. He initially found inspiration from his father, the former director of Interpol, and still draws on his contacts in the intelligence community to give his books such realism. Visit his website at kylemills.com.

HAVE YOU READ ALL THE MITCH RAPP NOVELS?

From gifted college athlete to CIA superagent, discover the full Mitch Rapp story.

American Assassin
A college athlete is recruited by a group of clandestine anti-terrorism operatives working outside the usual chain of command. His name is Mitch Rapp.

Kill Shot
When a hit on a Libyan diplomat goes wrong, a wounded Rapp finds himself the object of a man-hunt.

Transfer of Power
The White House is under attack and CIA counterterrorism operative Mitch Rapp struggles to save lives.

The Third Option
Dr Irene Kennedy is named the successor to dying CIA Director Thomas Stansfield, and many insiders are not happy. Mitch Rapp is under threat and will stop at nothing to discover who set him up.

Separation of Power
The American President's position is under threat and Saddam Hussein is close to entering the nuclear arms race. With World War III looming, Mitch Rapp has two weeks to take out the nukes.

Executive Power
A leak in the US State Department and an assassin out for his life. Can Rapp prevent the outbreak of war?

Memorial Day
A nuclear strike on Washington planned for Memorial Day is defused, but Mitch Rapp knows that, in the face of a new kind of enemy, nothing is as it seems . . .

Consent to Kill
The father of a terrorist is out for retribution and Rapp becomes the centre of an international conspiracy.

Act of Treason
After an explosion in Washington, Mitch Rapp is called upon to unravel a global network of contract killers, which leads back to the inner sanctum of the Oval Office.

Protect and Defend
With tensions building between Iran and Israel, Mitch Rapp has twenty-four hours to do whatever it takes to stop terrorist Imad Muktar from doing the Iranian President's dirty work . . .

Extreme Measures
Mitch Rapp and his protégé Mike Nash need to bring down an al-Qaeda cell, but certain leaders on Capitol Hill think that men like Rapp and Nash need to be put on a short leash.

Pursuit of Honour
In order to find al-Qaeda operatives responsible for a series of explosions in Washington, Mitch Rapp needs to stop partner Mike Nash from cracking . . .

The Last Man
Mitch Rapp must do all he can to find the man he is supposed to be protecting: Joe Rickman, head of the CIA's clandestine operations in Afghanistan. Can he navigate the ever-changing political landscape in order to complete his mission?

DC SUPER HEROES

WOMAN

★ THE AMAZING AMAZON ★

GIGANTA'S
COLOSSAL
DOUBLE-CROSS

WRITTEN BY
LOUISE SIMONSON

ILLUSTRATED BY
LUCIANO VECCHIO

WONDER WOMAN CREATED BY
WILLIAM MOULTON MARSTON

raintree 🍃

a Capstone company — publishers for children

RAINTREE IS AN IMPRINT OF CAPSTONE GLOBAL LIBRARY LIMITED,
A COMPANY INCORPORATED IN ENGLAND AND WALES HAVING ITS
REGISTERED OFFICE AT 264 BANBURY ROAD, OXFORD, OX2 7DY –
REGISTERED COMPANY NUMBER: 6695582

WWW.RAINTREE.CO.UK
MYORDERS@RAINTREE.CO.UK

EDITED BY CHRISTOPHER HARBO
DESIGNED BY HILARY WACHOLZ
ORIGINATED BY CAPSTONE GLOBAL LIBRARY LTD
PRINTED AND BOUND IN INDIA

ISBN 978 1 4747 6294 6
22 21 20 19 18
10 9 8 7 6 5 4 3 2 1

BRITISH LIBRARY CATALOGUING IN PUBLICATION DATA
A FULL CATALOGUE RECORD FOR THIS BOOK IS AVAILABLE FROM THE
BRITISH LIBRARY.

CONTENTS

With countries in chaos and the world at war, Earth faced its darkest hour. To answer its cry for help, the Amazons on the secret island of Themyscira held a contest to find their strongest and bravest champion. From that contest one warrior – Princess Diana – triumphed over all and boldly entered the world of mortals. Now her mission is to conquer villainy, defend justice and restore peace across the globe.